I could not have written this book forty – or thirty, twenty or even ten – years ago. That is because, piece by piece, over the years, I have been working back to Foundation's source: Hari Seldon. Today I enjoy the gift given to me by time: Experience (some might call it wisdom, but I will refrain from such bald self-aggrandizement). For it is only now that I am able to give my readers Hari Seldon during the most crucial, creative years of his life. You see, over time, Hari Seldon has evolved into my alter ego. In my earlier books Hari Seldon was the stuff of legend – with Forward the Foundation I have made him real.

ISAAC ASIMOV

FICTION BY ISAAC ASIMOV

Murder at the ABA (*1976*)
The Heavenly Host (*1975*)
Buy Jupiter and Other Stories (*1975*)
Tales of the Black Widowers (*1974*)
Have You Seen These? (*1974*)
The Best of Isaac Asimov (*1973*)
The Early Asimov (*1972*)
The Gods Themselves (*1972*)
The Best New Thing (*1971*)
Nightfall and Other Stories (*1969*)
Asimov's Mysteries (*1968*)
Through a Glass, Clearly (*1967*)
Fantastic Voyage (*1966*)
The Rest of the Robots (*1964*)
Nine Tomorrows (*1959*)
The Death Dealers (A Whiff of Death) (*1958*)
Lucky Starr and the Rings of Saturn (*1958*)
Earth Is Room Enough (*1957*)
Lucky Starr and the Moons of Jupiter (*1957*)
The Naked Sun (*1957*)
Lucky Starr and the Big Sun of Mercury (*1956*)
The End of Eternity (*1955*)
The Martian Way and Other Stories (*1955*)
Lucky Starr and the Oceans of Venus (*1954*)
The Caves of Steel (*1954*)
Lucky Starr and the Pirates of the Asteroids (*1953*)
Second Foundation (*1953*)
The Currents of Space (*1952*)
Foundation and Empire (*1952*)
David Starr: Space Ranger (*1952*)
Foundation (*1951*)
The Stars, Like Dust — (*1951*)
I, Robot (*1950*)
Pebble in the Sky (*1950*)

FORWARD
THE
FOUNDATION

Isaac Asimov

BANTAM BOOKS
TORONTO · NEW YORK · LONDON · SYDNEY · AUCKLAND

FORWARD THE FOUNDATION
A BANTAM BOOK 0 553 40488 1

Originally published in Great Britain by Doubleday,
a division of Transworld Publishers Ltd

PRINTING HISTORY
Doubleday edition published 1993
Bantam Books edition published 1994
Bantam edition reprinted 1994

Set in 10/11pt Compugraphic California
by Colset Private Limited, Singapore

Bantam Books are published by Transworld Publishers Ltd,
61–63 Uxbridge Road, Ealing, London W5 5SA,
in Australia by Transworld Publishers (Australia) Pty Ltd,
15–25 Helles Avenue, Moorebank, NSW 2170,
and in New Zealand by Transworld Publishers (NZ) Ltd,
3 William Pickering Drive, Albany, Auckland.

Printed and bound in Great Britain by
Cox & Wyman Ltd, Reading, Berkshire

For all my loyal readers

Contents

Part I

ETO DEMERZEL

DEMERZEL, ETO – . . . While there is no question that Eto Demerzel was the real power in the government during much of the reign of Emperor Cleon I, historians are divided as to the nature of his rule. The classic interpretation is that he was another in the long line of strong and ruthless oppressors in the last century of the undivided Galactic Empire, but there are revisionist views that have surfaced and that insist his was, if a despotism, a benevolent one. Much is made, in this view, of his relationship with Hari Seldon, though that remains forever uncertain, particularly during the unusual episode of Laskin Joranum, whose meteoric rise—

ENCYCLOPEDIA GALACTICA*

1

'I tell you again, Hari,' said Yugo Amaryl, 'that your friend Demerzel is in deep trouble.' He emphasized the word 'friend' very lightly and with an unmistakable air of distaste.

Hari Seldon detected the sour note and ignored it. He looked up from his tricomputer and said, 'I tell you again, Yugo, that that's nonsense.' And then – with a trace of annoyance, just a trace – he added, 'Why are you taking up my time by insisting?'

'Because I think it's important.' Amaryl sat down defiantly. It was a gesture that indicated he was not going to be moved easily. Here he was and here he would stay.

Eight years before, he had been a heatsinker in the Dahl Sector – as low on the social scale as it was possible to be. He had been lifted out of that position by Seldon, made into a mathematician and an intellectual – more than that, into a psychohistorian.

Never for one minute did he forget what he had been and who he was now and to whom he owed the change. That meant that if he had to speak harshly to Hari Seldon – for Seldon's own good – no consideration of respect and love for the older man and no regard for his own career would stop him. He owed such harshness – and much more – to Seldon.

'Look, Hari,' he said, chopping at the air with his left hand, 'for some reason that is beyond my understanding, you think highly of this Demerzel, but I don't. No one whose opinion I respect – except you – thinks well of him. I don't care what happens to him personally, Hari, but as long as I think *you* do, I have no choice but to bring this to your attention.'

Seldon smiled, as much at the other's earnestness as at what he considered to be the uselessness of his concern. He was fond of Yugo Amaryl – more than fond. Yugo was one of the four people he had encountered during that short period of his life when he was in flight across the face of the planet Trantor – Eto Demerzel, Dors Venabili, Yugo Amaryl, and Raych – four, the likes of which he had not found since.

In a particular and, in each case, different way, these four were indispensable to him – Yugo Amaryl, because of his quick understanding of the principles of psychohistory and of his imaginative probings into new areas. It was comforting to know that if anything happened to Seldon himself before the mathematics of the field could be completely worked out – and how slowly it proceeded, and how mountainous the obstacles – there would at least remain one good mind that would continue the research.

He said, 'I'm sorry, Yugo. I don't mean to be impatient with you or to reject out of hand whatever it is you are so anxious to make me understand. It's just this job of mine; it's this business of being a department head—'

Amaryl found it his turn to smile and he repressed a slight chuckle. 'I'm sorry, Hari, and I shouldn't laugh, but you have no natural aptitude for the position.'

'As well I know, but I'll have to learn. I have to seem to be doing something harmless and there is nothing – *nothing* – more harmless than being the head of the Mathematics Department at Streeling University. I can fill my day with unimportant tasks, so that no one need know or ask about the course of our psychohistorical research, but the trouble is, I *do* fill my day with unimportant tasks and I have insufficient time to—' His eyes glanced around his office at the material stored in computers to which only he and Amaryl had the key and which, even if anyone else stumbled upon them, had been carefully phrased in an invented symbology that no one else would understand.

16

Amaryl said, 'Once you work your way further into your duties, you'll begin to delegate and then you'll have more time.'

'I hope so,' said Seldon dubiously. 'But tell me, what is it about Eto Demerzel that is so important?'

'Simply that Eto Demerzel, our great Emperor's First Minister, is busily creating an insurrection.'

Seldon frowned. 'Why would he want to do that?'

'I didn't say he wants to. He's simply doing it – whether he knows it or not – and with considerable help from some of his political enemies. That's all right with me, you understand. I think that, under ideal conditions, it would be a good thing to have him out of the Palace, off Trantor . . . beyond the Empire, for that matter. But you think highly of him, as I've said, and so I'm warning you, because I suspect that you are not following the recent political course of events as closely as you should.'

'There are more important things to do,' said Seldon mildly.

'Like psychohistory. I agree. But how are we going to develop psychohistory with any hope of success if we remain ignorant of politics? I mean, present-day politics. Now – *now* – is the time when the present is turning into the future. We can't just study the past. We know what happened in the past. It's against the present and the near future that we can check our results.'

'It seems to me,' said Seldon, 'that I have heard this argument before.'

'And you'll hear it again. It doesn't seem to do me any good to explain this to you.'

Seldon sighed, sat back in his chair, and regarded Amaryl with a smile. The younger man could be abrasive, but he took psychohistory seriously – and that repaid all.

Amaryl still had the mark of his early years as a heatsinker. He had the broad shoulders and the muscular build of one who had been used to hard physical labor. He had not allowed his body to turn flabby and that was

17

a good thing, for it inspired Seldon to resist the impulse to spend all of his time at the desk as well. He did not have Amaryl's sheer physical strength, but he still had his own talents as a Twister – for all that he had just turned forty and could not keep it up forever. But for now, he would continue. Thanks to his daily workouts, his waist was still trim, his legs and arms firm.

He said, 'This concern for Demerzel cannot be purely a matter of his being a friend of mine. You must have some other motive.'

'There's no puzzle to that. As long as you're a friend of Demerzel, your position here at the University is secure and you can continue to work on psychohistorical research.'

'There you are. So I *do* have a reason to be friends with him. It isn't beyond your understanding at all.'

'You have an interest in *cultivating* him. That, I understand. But as for friendship – that, I don't understand. However – if Demerzel lost power, quite apart from the effect it might have on your position, then Cleon himself would be running the Empire and the rate of its decline would increase. Anarchy might then be upon us before we have worked out all the implications of psychohistory and made it possible for the science to save all humanity.'

'I see. – But, you know, I honestly don't think that we're going to work out psychohistory in time to prevent the Fall of the Empire.'

'Even if we could not prevent the Fall, we could cushion the effects, couldn't we?'

'Perhaps.'

'There you are, then. The longer we have to work in peace, the greater the chance we will have to prevent the Fall or, at least, ameliorate the effects. Since that is the case, working backward, it may be necessary to save Demerzel, whether we – or, at least, *I* – like it or not.'

'Yet you just said that you would like to see him out of

18

the Palace and away from Trantor and beyond the Empire.'

'Yes, under ideal conditions, I said. But we are not living under ideal conditions and we need our First Minister, even if he is an instrument of repression and despotism.'

'I see. But why do you think the Empire is so close to dissolution that the loss of a First Minister will bring it about?'

'Psychohistory.'

'Are you using it for predictions? We haven't even gotten the framework in place. What predictions can you make?'

'There's intuition, Hari.'

'There's *always* been intuition. We want something more, don't we? We want a mathematical treatment that will give us probabilities of specific future developments under this condition or that. If intuition suffices to guide us, we don't need psychohistory at all.'

'It's not necessarily a matter of one or the other, Hari. I'm talking about both: the combination, which may be better than either – at least until psychohistory is perfected.'

'If ever,' said Seldon. 'But tell me, where does this danger to Demerzel arise? What is it that is likely to harm him or overthrow him? Are we talking about Demerzel's overthrow?'

'Yes,' said Amaryl and a grim look settled on his face.

'Then tell me. Have pity on my ignorance.'

Amaryl flushed. 'You're being condescending, Hari. Surely you've heard of Jo-Jo Joranum.'

'Certainly. He's a demagogue—Wait, where's he from? Nishaya, right? A very unimportant world. Goat herding, I think. High-quality cheeses.'

'That's it. Not just a demagogue, however. He commands a strong following and it's getting stronger. He aims, he says, for social justice and greater political involvement by the people.'

19

'Yes,' said Seldon. 'I've heard that much. His slogan is: "Government belongs to the people."'

'Not quite, Hari. He says: "Government *is* the people."'

Seldon nodded. 'Well, you know, I rather sympathize with the thought.'

'So do I. I'm all for it – if Joranum meant it. But he doesn't, except as a stepping-stone. It's a path, not a goal. He wants to get rid of Demerzel. After that it will be easy to manipulate Cleon. Then Joranum will take the throne himself and *he* will be the people. You've told me yourself that there have been a number of episodes of this sort in Imperial history – and these days the Empire is weaker and less stable than it used to be. A blow which, in earlier centuries, merely staggered it might now shatter it. The Empire will welter in civil war and never recover and we won't have psychohistory in place to teach us what must be done.'

'Yes, I see your point, but surely it's not going to be that easy to get rid of Demerzel.'

'You don't know how strong Joranum is growing.'

'It doesn't matter how strong he's growing.' A shadow of thought seemed to pass over Seldon's brow. 'I wonder that his parents came to name him Jo-Jo. There's something juvenile about that name.'

'His parents had nothing to do with it. His real name is Laskin, a very common name on Nishaya. He chose Jo-Jo himself, presumably from the first syllable of his last name.'

'The more fool he, wouldn't you say?'

'No, I wouldn't. His followers shout it – "Jo . . . Jo . . . Jo . . . Jo" – over and over. It's hypnotic.'

'Well,' said Seldon, making a move to return to his tricomputer and adjust the multidimensional simulation it had created, 'we'll see what happens.'

'Can you be that casual about it? I'm telling you the danger is imminent.'

'No, it isn't,' said Seldon, eyes steely, his voice suddenly hardening. 'You don't have all the facts.'

'What facts don't I have?'

'We'll discuss that another time, Yugo. For now, continue with your work and let me worry about Demerzel and the state of the Empire.'

Amaryl's lips tightened, but the habit of obedience to Seldon was strong. 'Yes, Hari.'

But not overwhelmingly strong. He turned at the door and said, 'You're making a mistake, Hari.'

Seldon smiled slightly. 'I don't think so, but I have heard your warning and I will not forget. Still, all will be well.'

And as Amaryl left, Seldon's smile faded. – Would, indeed, all be well?

2

But Seldon, while he did not forget Amaryl's warning, did not think of it with any great degree of concentration. His fortieth birthday came and went – with the usual psychological blow.

Forty! He was not young any longer. Life no longer stretched before him as a vast unchartered field, its horizon lost in the distance. He had been on Trantor for eight years and the time had passed quickly. Another eight years and he would be nearly fifty. Old age would be looming.

And he had not even made a decent beginning in psychohistory! Yugo Amaryl spoke brightly of laws and worked out his equations by making daring assumptions based on intuition. But how could one possibly test those assumptions? Psychohistory was not yet an experimental science. The complete study of psychohistory would require experiments that would involve worlds of people, centuries of time – and a total lack of ethical responsibility.

It posed an impossible problem and he resented having to spend any time whatever on departmental tasks, so he walked home at the end of the day in a morose mood.

Ordinarily he could always count on a walk through the campus to rouse his spirits. Streeling University was high-domed and the campus gave the feeling of being out in the open without the necessity of enduring the kind of weather he had experienced on his one (and only) visit to the Imperial Palace. There were trees, lawns, walks, almost as though he were on the campus of his old college on his home world of Helicon.

The illusion of cloudiness had been arranged for the day with the sunlight (no sun, of course, just sunlight) appearing and disappearing at odd intervals. And it was a little cool, just a little.

It seemed to Seldon that the cool days came a little more frequently than they used to. Was Trantor saving energy? Was it increasing inefficiency? Or (and he scowled inwardly as he thought it) was he getting old and was his blood getting thin? He placed his hands in his jacket pockets and hunched up his shoulders.

Usually he did not bother guiding himself consciously. His body knew the way perfectly from his offices to his computer room and from there to his apartment and back. Generally he negotiated the path with his thoughts elsewhere, but today a sound penetrated his consciousness. A sound without meaning.

'Jo . . . Jo . . . Jo . . . Jo . . .'

It was rather soft and distant, but it brought back a memory. Yes, Amaryl's warning. The demagogue. Was he here on campus?

His legs swerved without Seldon's making a conscious decision and brought him over the low rise to the University Field, which was used for calisthenics, sports, and student oratory.

In the middle of the Field was a moderate-sized crowd of students who were chanting enthusiastically. On a platform was someone he didn't recognize, someone with a loud voice and a swaying rhythm.

It wasn't this man, Joranum, however. He had seen Joranum on holovision a number of times. Since Amaryl's warning, Seldon had paid close attention. Joranum was large and smiled with a kind of vicious camaraderie. He had thick sandy hair and light blue eyes.

This speaker was small, if anything – thin, wide-mouthed, dark-haired, and loud. Seldon wasn't listening to the words, though he did hear the phrase 'power from the one to the many' and the many-voiced shout in response.

Fine, thought Seldon, but just how does he intend to bring this about – and is he serious?

23

He was at the outskirts of the crowd now and looked around for someone he knew. He spotted Finangelos, a pret-math undergraduate. Not a bad young man, dark and woolly-haired.

'Finangelos,' he called out.

'Professor Seldon,' said Finangelos after a moment of staring as though unable to recognize Seldon without a keyboard at his fingertips. He trotted over. 'Did you come to listen to this guy?'

'I didn't come for any purpose but to find out what the noise was. Who is he?'

'His name is Namarti, Professor. He's speaking for Jo-Jo.'

'I hear *that*,' said Seldon as he listened to the chant again. It began each time the speaker made a telling point, apparently. 'But who is this Namarti? I don't recognize the name. What department is he in?'

'He's not a member of the University, Professor. He's one of Jo-Jo's men.'

'If he's not a member of the University, he has no right to speak here without a permit. Does he have one, do you suppose?'

'I wouldn't know, Professor.'

'Well then, let's find out.'

Seldon started into the crowd, but Finangelos caught his sleeve. 'Don't start anything, Professor. He's got goons with him.'

There were six young men behind the speaker, spaced rather widely, legs apart, arms folded, scowling.

'Goons?'

'For rough stuff, in case anyone tries anything funny.'

'Then he's certainly not a member of the University and even a permit wouldn't cover what you call his "goons". – Finangelos, signal through to the University security officers. They should have been here by now without a signal.'

'I guess they don't want trouble,' muttered Finangelos. 'Please, Professor, don't try anything. If you want me to

24

get the security officers, I will, but you just wait till they come.'

'Maybe I can break this up before they come.'

He began pushing his way through. It wasn't difficult. Some of those present recognized him and all could see the professorial shoulder patch. He reached the platform, placed his hands on it, and vaulted up the three feet with a small grunt. He thought, with chagrin, that he could have done it with one hand ten years before and without the grunt.

He straightened up. The speaker had stopped talking and was looking at him with wary and ice-hard eyes.

Seldon said calmly, 'Your permit to address the students, sir.'

'Who are you?' said the speaker. He said it loudly, his voice carrying.

'I'm a member of the faculty of this University,' said Seldon, equally loudly. 'Your permit, sir?'

'I deny your right to question me on the matter.' The young men behind the speaker had gathered closer.

'If you have none, I would advise you to leave the University grounds immediately.'

'And if I don't?'

'Well, for one thing, the University security officers are on their way.' He turned to the crowd. 'Students,' he called out, 'we have the right of free speech and freedom of assembly on this campus, but it can be taken away from us if we allow outsiders, without permits, to make unauthorized—'

A heavy hand fell on his shoulder and he winced. He turned around and found it was one of the men Finangelos had referred to as 'goons.'

The man said, with a heavy accent whose provenance Seldon could not immediately identify, 'Get out of here – *fast*.'

'What good will that do?' said Seldon. 'The security officers will be here any minute.'

'In that case,' said Namarti with a feral grin, 'there'll be a riot. That doesn't scare us.'

'Of course it wouldn't,' said Seldon. 'You'd like it, but there won't be a riot. You'll all go quietly.' He turned again to the students and shrugged off the hand on his shoulder. 'We'll see to that, won't we?'

Someone in the crowd shouted, 'That's Professor Seldon! He's all right! Don't pound him!'

Seldon sensed ambivalence in the crowd. There would be some, he knew, who would welcome a dust-up with the University security officers, just on general principles. On the other hand, there had to be some who liked him personally and still others who did not know him but who would not want to see violence against a member of the faculty.

A woman's voice rang out. 'Watch out, Professor!'

Seldon sighed and regarded the large young men he faced. He didn't know if he could do it, if his reflexes were quick enough, his muscles sturdy enough, even given his prowess at Twisting.

One goon was approaching him, overconfidently of course. Not quickly, which gave Seldon a little of the time his aging body would need. The goon held out his arm confrontationally, which made it easier.

Seldon seized the arm, whirled, and bent, arm up, and then down (with a grunt – why did he have to grunt?), and the goon went flying through the air, propelled partly by his own momentum. He landed with a *thump* on the outer edge of the platform, his right shoulder dislocated.

There was a wild cry from the audience at this totally unexpected development. Instantly an institutional pride erupted.

'Take them, Prof!' a lone voice shouted. Others took up the cry.

Seldon smoothed back his hair, trying not to puff. With his foot he shoved the groaning fallen goon off the platform.

'Anyone else?' he asked pleasantly. 'Or will you leave quietly?'

He faced Namarti and his five henchmen and as they paused irresolutely, Seldon said, 'I warn you. The crowd is on my side now. If you try to rush me, they'll take you apart. – Okay, who's next? Let's go. One at a time.'

He had raised his voice with the last sentence and made small come-hither motions with his fingers. The crowd yelled its pleasure.

Namarti stood there stolidly. Seldon leaped past him and caught his neck in the crook of his arm. Students were climbing onto the platform now, shouting 'One at a time! One at a time!' and getting between the body-guards and Seldon.

Seldon increased the pressure on the other's windpipe and whispered in his ear, 'There's a way to do this, Namarti, and I know how. I've practiced it for years. If you make a move and try to break away, I'll ruin your larynx so that you'll never talk above a whisper again. If you value your voice, do as I say. When I let up, you tell your bunch of bullies to leave. If you say anything else, they'll be the last words you'll say normally. And if you ever come back to this campus again, no more Mr Nice Guy. I'll finish the job.'

He released the pressure momentarily. Namarti said huskily, 'All of you. Get out.' They retreated rapidly, helping their stricken comrade.

When the University security officers arrived a few moments later, Seldon said, 'Sorry, gentlemen. False alarm.'

He left the Field and resumed his walk home with more than a little chagrin. He had revealed a side of himself he did not want to reveal. He was Hari Seldon, mathematician, not Hari Seldon, sadistic Twister.

Besides, he thought gloomily, Dors would hear of this. In fact, he'd better tell her himself, lest she hear a version that made the incident seem worse than it really was.

She would not be pleased.

3

She wasn't.

Dors was waiting for him at the door of their apartment in an easy stance, hand on one hip, looking very much as she had when he had first met her at this very University eight years before: slim, shapely, with curly reddish-gold hair – very beautiful in his eyes but not very beautiful in any objective sense, though he had never been able to assess her objectively after the first few days of their friendship.

Dors Venabili! That's what he thought when he saw her calm face. There were many worlds, even many sectors on Trantor where it would have been common to call her Dors Seldon, but that, he always thought, would put the mark of ownership on her and he did not wish it, even though the custom was sanctioned by existence back into the vague mists of the pre-Imperial past.

Dors said, softly and with a sad shake of her head that barely disturbed her loose curls, 'I've heard, Hari. Just *what* am I going to do with you?'

'A kiss would not be amiss.'

'Well, perhaps, but only after we probe this a little. Come in.' The door closed behind them. 'You know, dear, I have my course and my research. I'm still doing that dreadful history of the Kingdom of Trantor, which you tell me is essential to your own work. Shall I drop it all and take to wandering around with you, protecting you? It's still my job, you know. It's more than ever my job, now that you're making progress with psychohistory.'

'Making progress? I wish I were. But you needn't protect me.'

'Needn't I? I sent Raych out looking for you. After all,

you were late and I was concerned. You usually tell me when you're going to be late. I'm sorry if that makes me sound as though I'm your keeper, Hari, but I *am* your keeper.'

'Does it occur to you, Keeper Dors, that every once in a while I like to slip my leash?'

'And if something happens to you, what do I tell Demerzel?'

'Am I too late for dinner? Have we clicked for kitchen service?'

'No. I was waiting for you. And as long as you're here, you click it. You're a great deal pickier than I am when it comes to food. And don't change the subject.'

'Didn't Raych tell you that I was all right? So what's there to talk about?'

'When he found you, you were in control of the situation and he got back here first, but not by much. I didn't hear any details. Tell me— What – were – you – doing?'

Seldon shrugged. 'There was an illegal gathering, Dors, and I broke it up. The University could have gotten a good deal of trouble it didn't need if I hadn't.'

'And it was up to you to prevent it? Hari, you're not a Twister anymore. You're an—'

He put in hastily, 'An old man?'

'For a Twister, yes. You're forty. How do you feel?'

'Well— A little stiff.'

'I can well imagine. And one of these days, when you try to pretend you're a young Heliconian athlete, you'll break a rib. – Now tell me about it.'

'Well, I told you how Amaryl warned me that Demerzel was in trouble because of the demagoguery of Jo-Jo Joranum.'

'Jo-Jo. Yes, I know that much. What *don't* I know? What happened today?'

'There was a rally at the Field. A Jo-Jo partisan named Namarti was addressing the crowd—'

'Namarti is Gambol Deen Namarti, Joranum's right-hand man.'

'Well, you know more about it than I do. In any case, he was addressing a large crowd and he had no permit and I think he was hoping there would be some sort of riot. They feed on these disorders and if he could close down the University even temporarily, he would charge Demerzel with the destruction of academic freedom. I gather they blame him for everything. So I stopped them. – Sent them off without a riot.'

'You sound proud.'

'Why not? Not bad for a man of forty.'

'Is that why you did it? To test your status at forty?'

Seldon thoughtfully clicked the dinner menu. Then he said, 'No. I really was concerned that the University would get into needless trouble. And I was concerned about Demerzel. I'm afraid that Yugo's tales of danger had impressed me more than I realized. That was stupid, Dors, because I know that Demerzel can take care of himself. I couldn't explain that to Yugo or to anyone but you.'

He drew in a deep breath. 'It's amazing what a pleasure it is that I can at least talk to you about it. You know and I know and Demerzel knows and no one else knows – at least, that I know of – that Demerzel is untouchable.'

Dors touched a contact on a recessed wall panel and the dining section of their living quarters lit up with a soft peach-colored glow. Together, she and Hari walked to the table, which was already set with linen, crystal, and utensils. As they sat, the dinner began to arrive – there was never any long delay at this time of evening – and Seldon accepted it quite casually. He had long since grown accustomed to the social position that made it unnecessary for them to patronize the faculty dinners.

Seldon savored the seasonings they had learned to enjoy during their stay at Mycogen – the *only* thing about that strange, male-dominated, religion-permeated, living-in-the-past sector they had not detested.

Dors said softly, 'How do you mean, "untouchable"?'

'Come, dear, he can alter emotions. You haven't forgotten that. If Joranum really became dangerous, he could be' – he made a vague gesture with his hands – 'altered; made to change his mind.'

Dors looked uncomfortable and the meal proceeded in an unusual silence. It wasn't until it was over and the remains – dishes, cutlery, and all – swirled down the disposal chute in the center of the table (which then smoothly covered itself over) that she said, 'I'm not sure I want to talk about this, Hari, but I can't let you be fooled by your own innocence.'

'Innocence?' He frowned.

'Yes. We've never talked about this. I never thought it would come up, but Demerzel has shortcomings. He is not untouchable, he may be harmed, and Joranum is indeed a danger to him.'

'Are you serious?'

'Of course I am. You don't understand robots – certainly not one as complex as Demerzel. And I do.'

4

There was a short silence again, but only because thoughts are silent. Seldon's were tumultuous enough.

Yes, it was true. His wife did seem to have an uncanny knowledge of robots. Hari had wondered about this so often over the years that he had finally given up, tucked it away in the back of his mind. If it hadn't been for Eto Demerzel – a robot – Hari would never have met Dors. For Dors *worked* for Demerzel; it was Demerzel who 'assigned' Dors to Hari's case eight years ago to protect him during his flight throughout the various sectors of Trantor. Even though now she was his wife, his help-meet, his 'better half,' Hari still occasionally wondered about Dors's strange connection with the robot Demerzel. It was the only area of Dors's life where Hari truly felt he did not belong – nor welcome. And that brought to mind the most painful question of all: Was it out of obedience to Demerzel that Dors stayed with Hari or was it out of *love* for him? He wanted to believe the latter – and yet . . .

His life with Dors Venabili was a happy one, but it was so at a cost, at a condition. The condition was all the more stringent, in that it had been settled not through discussion or agreement but by a mutual unspoken understanding.

Seldon understood that he found in Dors everything he would have wanted in a wife. True, he had no children, but he had neither expected any, nor, to tell the truth, had greatly wanted any. He had Raych, who was as much a son of his emotionally as if he had inherited the entire Seldonian genome – perhaps more so.

The mere fact that Dors was causing him to think about the matter was breaking the agreement that had kept them in peace and comfort all these years and he felt a faint but growing resentment at that.

But he pushed those thoughts, the questions, away again. He had learned to accept her role as his protector and would continue to do so. After all, it was he with whom she shared a home, a table, and a bed – not Eto Demerzel.

Dors's voice brought him out of his reverie.

'I said – Are you sulking, Hari?'

He started slightly, for there was the sound of repetition in her voice, and he realized he had been shrinking steadily deeper into his mind and away from her.

'I'm sorry, dear. I'm not sulking. – Not deliberately sulking. I'm just wondering how I ought to respond to your statement.'

'About robots?' She seemed quite calm as she said the word.

'You said I don't know as much about them as you do. How do I respond to that?' He paused, then added quietly (knowing he was taking a chance), 'That is, without offense.'

'I didn't say you didn't *know* about robots. If you're going to quote me, do so with precision. I said you didn't *understand* about robots. I'm sure that you know a great deal, perhaps more than I do, but to know is not necessarily to understand.'

'Now, Dors, you're deliberately speaking in paradoxes to be annoying. A paradox arises only out of an ambiguity that deceives either unwittingly or by design. I don't like that in science and I don't like it in casual conversation, either, unless it is meant humorously, which I think is not the case now.'

Dors laughed in her particular way, softly, almost as though amusement were too precious to be shared in an overliberal manner. 'Apparently the paradox has annoyed you into pomposity and you are always humorous when you are pompous. However, I'll explain. It's not my intention to annoy you.' She reached over to pat his hand and it was to Seldon's surprise (and slight embarrassment) that he found that he had clenched his hand into a fist.

Dors said, 'You talk about psychohistory a great deal. To me, at any rate. You know that?'

Seldon cleared his throat. 'I throw myself on your mercy as far as that's concerned. The project is secret – by its very nature. Psychohistory won't work unless the people it affects know nothing about it, so I can talk about it only to Yugo and to you. To Yugo, it is all intuition. He's brilliant, but he is so apt to leap wildly into darkness that I must play the role of caution, of forever pulling him back. But I have my wild thoughts, too, and it helps me to be able to hear them aloud, even'— and he smiled— 'when I have a pretty good notion that you don't understand a word I'm saying.'

'I know I'm your sounding board and I don't mind. – I *really* don't mind, Hari, so don't begin making inner resolutions to change your behavior. Naturally I don't understand your mathematics. I'm just a historian – and not even a historian of science. The influence of economic change on political development is what is taking up my time now—'

'Yes, and I'm *your* sounding board on that or hadn't you noticed? I'll need it for psychohistory when the time comes, so I suspect you'll be an indispensable help to me.'

'Good! Now that we've settled why you stay with me – I knew it couldn't be for my ethereal beauty – let me go on to explain that occasionally, when your discussion veers away from the strictly mathematical aspects, it seems to me that I get your drift. You have, on a number of occasions, explained what you call the necessity of minimalism. I think I understand that. By it, you mean—'

'I know what I mean.'

Dors looked hurt. 'Less lofty, please, Hari. I'm not trying to explain it to you. I want to explain it to myself. You say you're my sounding board, so act like one. Turnabout is fair play, isn't it?'

'Turnabout is fine, but if you're going to accuse me of loftiness when I say one little—'

'Enough! Shut up! – You have told me that minimalism is of the highest importance in applied psychohistory; in the art of attempting to change an undesired development into a desired one or, at any rate, a less undesired one. You have said that a change must be applied that is as minute, as minimal, as possible—'

'Yes,' said Seldon eagerly, 'that is because—'

'*No*, Hari. *I'm* trying to explain. We both know that *you* understand it. You must have minimalism because every change, any change, has a myriad of side effects that can't always be allowed for. If the change is too great and the side effects too many, then it becomes certain that the outcome will be far removed from anything you've planned and that it would be entirely unpredictable.'

'Right,' said Seldon. 'That's the essence of a chaotic effect. The problem is whether any change is small enough to make the consequence reasonably predictable or whether human history is inevitably and unalterably chaotic in every respect. It was that which, at the start, made me think that psychohistory was not—'

'I know, but you're not letting me make my point. Whether any change would be small enough is not the issue. The point is that any change greater than the minimal *is* chaotic. The required minimum may be zero, but if it is not zero, then it is still very small – and it would be a major problem to find some change that is small enough and yet is significantly greater than zero. Now, that, I gather, is what you mean by the necessity of minimalism.'

'More or less,' said Seldon. 'Of course, as always, the matter is expressed more compactly and more rigorously in the language of mathematics. See here—'

'Save me,' said Dors. 'Since you know this about

psychohistory, Hari, you ought to know it about Demerzel, too. You have the knowledge but not the understanding, because it apparently doesn't occur to you to apply the rules of psychohistory to the Laws of Robotics.'

To which Seldon replied faintly, 'Now I *don't* see what you're getting at.'

'He requires minimality, too, doesn't he, Hari? By the First Law of Robotics, a robot can't harm a human being. That is the prime rule for the usual robot, but Demerzel is something quite unusual and for him, the Zeroth Law is a reality and it takes precedence even over the First Law. The Zeroth Law states that a robot can't harm humanity as a whole. But that puts Demerzel into the same bind in which you exist when you labor at psychohistory. Do you see?'

'I'm beginning to.'

'I hope so. If Demerzel has the ability to change minds, he has to do so without bringing about side effects he does not wish – and since he is the Emperor's First Minister, the side effects he must worry about are numerous, indeed.'

'And the application to the present case?'

'Think about it! You can't tell anyone – except me, of course – that Demerzel is a robot, because he has adjusted you so that you can't. But how much adjustment did that take? Do you want to tell people that he is a robot? Do you want to ruin his effectiveness when you depend on him for protection, for support of your grants, for influence quietly exerted on your behalf? Of course not. The change he had to make then was a very tiny one, just enough to keep you from blurting it out in a moment of excitement or carelessness. It is so small a change that there are no particular side effects. That is how Demerzel tries to run the Empire generally.'

'And the case of Joranum?'

'Is obviously completely different from yours. He is, for whatever motives, unalterably opposed to Demerzel.

Undoubtedly, Demerzel could change that, but it would be at the price of introducing a considerable wrench in Joranum's makeup that would bring about results Demerzel could not predict. Rather than take the chance of harming Joranum, of producing side effects that would harm others and, possibly, all of humanity, he must leave Joranum alone until he can find some small change – some *small* change – that will save the situation without harm. That is why Yugo is right and why Demerzel is vulnerable.'

Seldon had listened but did not respond. He seemed lost in thought. Minutes passed before he said, 'If Demerzel can do nothing in this matter, then I must.'

'If he can do nothing, what can you do?'

'The case is different. I am not bound by the Laws of Robotics. I need not concern myself obsessively with minimalism. – And to begin with, I must see Demerzel.'

Dors looked faintly anxious. 'Must you? Surely it wouldn't be wise to advertise a connection between the two of you.'

'We have reached a time where we can't make a fetish of pretending there is no connection. Naturally I won't go to see him behind a flourish of trumpets and an announcement on holovision, but I must see him.'

37

5

Seldon found himself raging at the passage of time. Eight years ago, when he had first arrived on Trantor, he could take instant action. He had only a hotel room and its contents to forsake and he could range through the sectors of Trantor at will.

Now he found himself with department meetings, with decisions to make, with work to do. It was not so easy to dash off at will to see Demerzel – and if he could, Demerzel also had a full schedule of his own. To find a time when they both could meet would not be easy.

Nor was it easy to have Dors shake her head at him. 'I don't know what you intend to do, Hari.'

And he answered impatiently, 'I don't know what I intend to do, either, Dors. I hope to find out when I see Demerzel.'

'Your first duty is to psychohistory. He'll tell you so.'

'Perhaps. I'll find out.'

And then, just as he had arranged a time for the meeting with the First Minister, eight days hence, he received a message on his department office wall screen in slightly archaic lettering. And to match that was the more than slightly archaic message: I CRAVE AN AUDIENCE WITH PROFESSOR HARI SELDON.

Seldon stared at it with astonishment. Even the Emperor was not addressed in quite that centuries-old turn of phrase.

Nor was the signature printed as it usually was for clarity. It was scripted with a flourish that left it perfectly legible and yet gave it the aura of a careless work of art dashed off by a master. The signature was: LASKIN JORANUM. – It was Jo-Jo himself, craving an audience.

Seldon found himself chuckling. It was clear why the

choice of words – and why the script. It made what was a simple request a device for stimulating curiosity. Seldon had no great desire to meet the man – or would have had none ordinarily. But what was worth the archaism and the artistry? He wanted to find out.

He had his secretary set the time and the place of the appointment. It would be in his office, certainly not in his apartment. A business conversation, nothing social.

And it would come before the projected meeting with Demerzel.

Dors said, 'It's no surprise to me, Hari. You hurt two of his people, one of them his chief aide; you spoiled a little rally he was holding; and you made him, in the person of his representatives, seem foolish. He wants to take a look at you and I think I had better be with you.'

Seldon shook his head. 'I'll take Raych. He knows all the tricks I know and he's a strong and active twenty-year-old. Although I'm sure there'll be no need for protection.'

'How can you be sure?'

'Joranum is coming to see me on the University grounds. There will be any number of youngsters in the vicinity. I'm not exactly an unpopular figure with the student body and I suspect that Joranum is the kind of man who does his homework and knows that I'll be safe on home territory. I'm sure that he will be perfectly polite – completely friendly.'

'Hmph,' said Dors with a light twist of one corner of her lip.

'And quite deadly,' Seldon finished.

6

Hari Seldon kept his face expressionless and bent his head just sufficiently to allow a sense of reasonable courtesy. He had taken the trouble to look up a variety of holographs of Joranum, but, as is often the case, the real thing, unguarded, shifting constantly in response to changing conditions, is never quite the same as a holograph – however carefully prepared. Perhaps, thought Seldon, it is the response of the viewer to the 'real thing' that makes it different.

Joranum was a tall man – as tall as Seldon, at any rate – but larger in other directions. It was not due to a muscular physique, for he gave the impression of softness, without quite being fat. A rounded face, a thick head of hair that was sandy rather than yellow, light blue eyes. He wore a subdued coverall and his face bore a half-smile that gave the illusion of friendliness, while making it clear, somehow, that it was only an illusion.

'Professor Seldon' – his voice was deep and under strict control, an orator's voice – 'I am delighted to meet you. It is kind of you to permit this meeting. I trust you are not offended that I have brought a companion, my right-hand man, with me, although I have not cleared that with you in advance. He is Gambol Deen Namarti – three names, you notice. I believe you have met him.'

'Yes, I have. I remember the incident well.' Seldon looked at Namarti with a touch of the sardonic. At the previous encounter, Namarti had been speaking at the University Field. Seldon viewed him carefully now – under relaxed conditions. Namarti was of moderate height, with a thin face, sallow complexion, dark hair, and a wide mouth. He did not have Joranum's half-smile or any noticeable expression – except for a sense of cautious wariness.

'My friend Dr Namarti – his degree is in ancient literature – has come at his own request,' said Joranum, his smile intensifying a bit, 'to apologize.'

Joranum glanced quickly at Namarti – and Namarti, his lips tightening just at first, said in a colorless voice, 'I am sorry, Professor, for what happened at the Field. I was not quite aware of the strict rules governing University rallies and I was a little carried away by my own enthusiasm.'

'Understandably so,' said Joranum. 'Nor was he entirely aware of your identity. I think we may all now forget the matter.'

'I assure you, gentlemen,' said Seldon, 'that I have no great desire to remember it. This is my son, Raych Seldon, so you see I have a companion, too.'

Raych had grown a mustache, black and abundant – the masculine mark of the Dahlite. He had had none when he first met Seldon eight years before, when he was a street boy, ragged and hungry. He was short but lithe and sinewy and his expression was the haughty one he had adopted in order to add a few spiritual inches to his physical height.

'Good morning, young man,' said Joranum.

'Good morning, sir,' said Raych.

'Please sit down, gentlemen,' said Seldon. 'May I offer you something to eat or drink ?'

Joranum held up his hands in polite refusal. 'No, sir. This is not a social call.' He seated himself in the place indicated. 'Though I hope there will be many such calls in the future.'

'If this is to be about business, then let's begin.'

'The news reached me, Professor Seldon, of the little incident that you have so kindly agreed to forget and I wondered why you took the chance of doing what you did. It was a risk, you must admit.'

'I didn't think so, actually.'

'But I did. So I took the liberty of finding out everything I could about you, Professor Seldon. You're an interesting man. From Helicon, I discovered.'

'Yes, that's where I was born. The records are clear.'

'And you've been here on Trantor for eight years.'

'That is also a matter of public record.'

'And you made yourself quite famous at the start by delivering a mathematical paper on – what do you call it? – psychohistory?'

Seldon shook his head very slightly. How often he had regretted that indiscretion. Of course, he had had no idea at the time that it was an indiscretion. He said, 'A youthful enthusiasm. It came to nothing.'

'Is that so?' Joranum looked around him with an air of pleased surprise. 'Yet here you are, the head of the Mathematics Department at one of Trantor's greatest Universities, and only forty years old, I believe. – I'm forty-two, by the way, so I don't look upon you as very old at all. You must be a very competent mathematician to be in this position.'

Seldon shrugged. 'I wouldn't care to make a judgment in that matter.'

'Or you must have powerful friends.'

'We would all like to have powerful friends, Mr Joranum, but I think you will find none here. University professors rarely have powerful friends or, I sometimes think, friends of any kind.' He smiled.

And so did Joranum. 'Wouldn't you consider the Emperor a powerful friend, Professor Seldon?'

'I certainly would, but what has that to do with me?'

'I am under the impression that the Emperor is a friend of yours.'

'I'm sure the records will show, Mr Joranum, that I had an audience with His Imperial Majesty eight years ago. It lasted perhaps an hour or less and I saw no signs of any great friendliness in him at the time. Nor have I spoken to him since – or even seen him – except on holovision, of course.'

'But, Professor, it is not necessary to see or speak to the Emperor to have him as a powerful friend. It is sufficient to see or speak to Eto Demerzel, the Emperor's First Minister. Demerzel is your protector and, since he is, we may as well say the Emperor is.'

'Do you find First Minister Demerzel's supposed protection of me anywhere in the records ? Or anything at all in the records from which you can deduce that protection?'

'Why search the records when it is well known that there is a connection between the two of you. You know it and I know it. Let us take it then as given and continue. And please' – he raised his hands – 'do not take the trouble to give me any heartfelt denials. It's a waste of time.'

'Actually,' said Seldon, 'I was going to ask why you should think that he would want to protect me. To what end?'

'Professor! Are you trying to hurt me by pretending to think I am a monster of naïveté? I mentioned your psychohistory, which Demerzel wants.'

'And I told you that it was a youthful indiscretion that came to nothing.'

'You may tell me a great many things, Professor. I am not compelled to accept what you tell me. Come, let me speak frankly. I have read your original paper and have tried to understand it with the help of some mathematicians on my staff. They tell me it is a wild dream and quite impossible—'

'I quite agree with them,' said Seldon.

'But I have the feeling that Demerzel is waiting for it to be developed and put to use. And if he can wait, so can I. It would be more useful to you, Professor Seldon, to have me wait.'

'Why so?'

'Because Demerzel will not endure in his position for much longer. Public opinion is turning against him steadily. It may be that when the Emperor wearies of

43

an unpopular First Minister who threatens to drag the throne down with him, he will find a replacement. It may even be my poor self whom the Emperor's fancy will seize upon. And you will still need a protector, someone who can see to it that you can work in peace and with ample funds for whatever you need in the way of equipment and assistants.'

'And would you be that protector?'

'Of course – and for the same reason that Demerzel is. I want a successful psychohistoric technique so that I can rule the Empire more efficiently.'

Seldon nodded thoughtfully, waited a moment, then said, 'But in that case, Mr Joranum, why must I concern myself in this? I am a poor scholar, living a quiet life, engaged in out-of-the-way mathematical and pedagogical activities. You say that Demerzel is my present protector and that you will be my future protector. I can go quietly about my business, then. You and the First Minister may fight it out. Whoever prevails, I have a protector still – or, at least, so you tell me.'

Joranum's fixed smile seemed to fade a bit. Namarti, at his side, turned his dour face toward Joranum and made as though to say something, but Joranum's hand moved slightly and Namarti coughed and did not speak.

Joranum said, 'Dr Seldon. Are you a patriot?'

'Why, of course. The Empire has given humanity millennia of peace – mostly peace, at any rate – and fostered steady advancement.'

'So it has – but at a slower pace in the last century or two.'

Seldon shrugged. 'I have not studied such matters.'

'You don't have to. You know that, politically, the last century or two has been a time of turmoil. Imperial reigns have been short and sometimes have been shortened further by assassination—'

'Even mentioning that,' put in Seldon, 'is close to treason. I'd rather you didn't—'

'Well, there.' Joranum threw himself back in his seat.

44

'See how insecure you are. The Empire is decaying. I'm willing to say so openly. Those who follow me do so because they know only too well it is. We need someone at the Emperor's right hand who can control the Empire, subdue the rebellious impulses that seem to be arising everywhere, give the armed forces the natural leadership they should have, lead the economy—'

Seldon made an impatient stopping motion with his arm. 'And you're the one to do it, are you?'

'I intend to be the one. It won't be an easy job and I doubt there would be many volunteers – for good reason. Certainly Demerzel can't do it. Under him, the decline of the Empire is accelerating to a total breakdown.'

'But you can stop it?'

'Yes, Dr Seldon. With your help. With psychohistory.'

'Perhaps Demerzel could stop the breakdown with psychohistory – if psychohistory existed.'

Joranum said calmly, 'It exists. Let us not pretend it does not. But its existence does not help Demerzel. Psychohistory is only a tool. It needs a brain to understand it and an arm to wield it.'

'And you have those, I take it?'

'Yes. I know my own virtues. I want psychohistory.'

Seldon shook his head. 'You may want it all you please. I don't have it.'

'You *do* have it. I will not argue the point.' Joranum leaned closer as though wishing to insinuate his voice into Seldon's ear, rather than allowing the sound waves to carry it there. 'You say you are a patriot. I must replace Demerzel to avoid Imperial destruction. However, the manner of replacement might itself weaken the Empire desperately. I do not wish that. *You* can advise me how to achieve the end smoothly, subtly, without harm or damage – for the sake of the Empire.'

Seldon said, 'I cannot. You accuse me of knowledge I do not possess. I would like to be of assistance, but I cannot.'

Joranum stood up suddenly. 'Well, you know my mind

and what it is I want of you. Think about it. And I ask you to think about the Empire. You may feel you owe Demerzel – this despoiler of all the millions of planets of humanity – your friendship. Be careful. What you do may shake the very foundation of the Empire. I ask you to help me in the name of the quadrillions of human beings who fill the Galaxy. Think of the Empire.'

His voice had dropped to a thrilling and powerful half-whisper. Seldon felt himself almost trembling. 'I will always think of the Empire,' he said.

Joranum said, 'Then that is all I ask right now. Thank you for consenting to see me.'

Seldon watched Joranum and his companion leave as the office doors slid open noiselessly and the men strode out.

He frowned. Something was bothering him – and he was not sure what it was.

7

Namarti's dark eyes remained fixed on Joranum as they sat in their carefully shielded office in the Streeling Sector. It was not an elaborate headquarters; they were as yet weak in Streeling, but they would grow stronger.

It was amazing how the movement was growing. It had started from nothing three years back and now its tentacles stretched – in some places more thickly than others, of course – throughout Trantor. The Outer Worlds were as yet largely untouched. Demerzel had labored mightily to keep them content, but that was *his* mistake. It was here on Trantor that rebellions were dangerous. Elsewhere, they could be controlled. Here, Demerzel could be toppled. Odd that he should not realize that, but Joranum had always held to the theory that Demerzel's reputation was overblown, that he would prove an empty shell if anyone dared oppose him, and that the Emperor would destroy him quickly if his own security seemed at stake.

So far, at least, all of Joranum's predictions had come to pass. He had never once lost his way except in minor matters, such as that recent rally at Streeling University in which this Seldon fellow had interfered.

That might be why Joranum had insisted on the interview with him. Even a minor toe stub must be taken care of. Joranum enjoyed the feeling of infallibility and Namarti had to admit that the vision of a constant string of successes was the surest way of ensuring the continuation of success. People tended to avoid the humiliation of failure by joining the obviously winning side even against their own opinions.

But had the interview with this Seldon been a success or was it a second stub of the toe to be added to the first?

Namarti had not enjoyed having been brought along in order to be made to humbly apologize and he didn't see that it had done any good.

Now Joranum sat there, silent, obviously lost in thought, gnawing at the edge of one thumb as though trying to draw some sort of mental nourishment from it.

'Jo-Jo,' said Namarti softly. He was one of the very few people who could address Joranum by the diminutive that the crowds shouted out endlessly in public. Joranum solicited the love of the mob in this way, among others, but he demanded respect from individuals in private, except for those special friends who had been with him from the start.

'Jo-Jo,' he said again.

Joranum looked up. 'Yes, GD, what is it?' He sounded a little testy.

'What are we going to do about this Seldon fellow, Jo-Jo?'

'Do? Nothing right now. He may join us.'

'Why wait? We can put pressure on him. We can pull a few strings at the University and make life miserable for him.'

'No no. So far, Demerzel has been letting us go our way. The fool is overconfident. The last thing we want to do, though, is to push him into action before we are quite ready. And a heavy-handed move against Seldon may do it. I suspect Demerzel places enormous importance on Seldon.'

'Because of this psychohistory you two talked about?'

'Indeed.'

'What is it? I have never heard of it.'

'Few people have. It's a mathematical way of analyzing human society that ends by predicting the future.'

Namarti frowned and felt his body move slightly away from Joranum. Was this a joke of Joranum's? Was this intended to make him laugh? Namarti had never been able to work out when or why people expected him to laugh. He had never had an urge to.

48

He said, 'Predict the future? How?'

'Ah! If I knew that, what need would I have of Seldon?'

'Frankly I don't believe it, Jo-Jo. How can you foretell the future? It's fortune-telling.'

'I know, but after this Seldon broke up your little rally, I had him looked into. All the way. Eight years ago, he came to Trantor and presented a paper on psychohistory at a convention of mathematicians and then the whole thing died. It was never referred to again by anyone. Not even by Seldon.'

'It sounds as though there were nothing to it, then.'

'Oh no, just the reverse. If it had faded slowly, if it had been subjected to ridicule, I would have said there was nothing to it. But to be cut off suddenly and completely means that the whole thing has been placed in the deepest of freezes. That is why Demerzel may have been doing nothing to stop us. Perhaps he is not being guided by a foolish overconfidence; perhaps he is being guided by psychohistory, which must be predicting something that Demerzel plans to take advantage of at the right time. If so, we might fail unless we can make use of psychohistory ourselves.'

'Seldon claims it doesn't exist.'

'Wouldn't you if you were he?'

'I still say we ought to put pressure on him.'

'It would be useless, G.D. Didn't you ever hear the story of the Ax of Venn?'

'No.'

'You would if you were from Nishaya. It's a famous folktale back home. In brief, Venn was a woodcutter who had a magic ax that, with a single light blow, could chop down any tree. It was enormously valuable, but he never made any effort to hide it or preserve it – and yet it was never stolen, because no one could lift or swing the ax but Venn himself.

'Well, at the present moment, no one can handle psychohistory, but Seldon himself. If he were on our side only because we had forced him, we could never be certain of his loyalty. Might he not urge a course of action that would seem to work in our favor but would be so subtly drawn that, after a while, we found ourselves quite suddenly destroyed. No, he must come to our side voluntarily and labor for us because he wishes us to win.'

'But how can we bring him around?'

'There's Seldon's son. Raych, I think he's called. Did you observe him?'

'Not particularly.'

'G.D, G.D, you miss points if you don't observe everything. That young man listened to me with his heart in his eyes. He was impressed. I could tell. If there's one thing I can tell, it is just how I impress others. I know when I have shaken a mind, when I have edged someone toward conversion.'

Joranum smiled. It was not the pseudowarm ingratiating smile of his public demeanor. It was a genuine smile this time – cold, somehow, and menacing.

'We'll see what we can do with Raych,' he said, 'and if, through him, we can reach Seldon.'

8

Raych looked at Hari Seldon after the two politicians had
gone and fingered his mustache. It gave him satisfaction
to stroke it. Here in the Streeling Sector, some men wore
mustaches, but they were usually thin despicable things
of uncertain color – thin despicable things, even if dark.
Most men did not wear them at all and suffered with
naked upper lips. Seldon didn't, for instance, and that
was just as well. With his color of hair, a mustache would
have been a travesty.

He watched Seldon closely, waiting for him to cease
being lost in thought, and then found he could wait no
longer.

'Dad!' he said.

Seldon looked up and said, 'What?' He sounded a little
annoyed at having his thoughts interrupted, Raych
decided.

Raych said, 'I don't think it was right for you to see
those two guys.'

'Oh? Why not?'

'Well, the thin guy, whatever his name is, was the guy
you made trouble for at the Field. He can't have liked it.'

'But he apologized.'

'He didn't mean it. But the other guy, Joranum – he
can be dangerous. What if they had had weapons?'

'What? Here in the University? In my office? Of
course not. This isn't Billibotton. Besides, if they had
tried anything, I could have handled both of them
together. Easily.'

'I don't know, Dad,' said Raych dubiously. 'You're
getting—'

'Don't say it, you ungrateful monster,' said Seldon, lifting an admonishing finger. 'You'll sound just like your

mother and I have enough of that from her. I am *not* getting old – or, at least, not *that* old. Besides, you were with me and you're almost as skilled a Twister as I am.'

Raych's nose wrinkled. 'Twisting ain't much good.' (It was no use. Raych heard himself speak and knew that, even eight years out of the morass of Dahl, he still slipped into using the Dahlite accent that marked him firmly as a member of the lower class. And he was short, too, to the point where he sometimes felt stunted. – But he had his mustache and no one ever patronized him twice.)

He said, 'What are you going to do about Joranum?'

'For now, nothing.'

'Well, look, Dad, I saw Joranum on TrantorVision a couple of times. I even made some holotapes of his speeches. – Everyone is talking about him, so I thought I would see what he has to say. And, you know, he makes some kind of sense. I don't like him and I don't trust him, but he *does* make some kind of sense. He wants all sectors to have equal rights and equal opportunities – and there ain't nothing wrong with that, is there?'

'Certainly not. All civilized people feel that way.'

'So why don't we *have* that sort of stuff? Does the Emperor feel that way? Does Demerzel?'

'The Emperor and the First Minister have an entire Empire to worry about. They can't concentrate all their efforts on Trantor itself. It's easy for Joranum to talk about equality. He has no responsibilities. If he were in the position to rule, he would find that his efforts would be greatly diluted by an Empire of twenty-five million planets. Not only that, but he would find himself stopped at every point by the sectors themselves. Each one wants a great deal of equality for itself – but not much equality for others. Tell me, Raych, are you of the opinion that Joranum ought to have a chance to rule, just to show what he can do?'

Raych shrugged. 'I don't know. I wonder. – But if he had tried anything on you, I would have been at his throat before he could move two centimeters.'

'Your loyalty to me, then, exceeds your concern for the Empire.'

'Sure. You're my dad.'

Seldon looked at Rach fondly, but behind that look he felt a trace of uncertainty. How far could Joranum's nearly hypnotic influence go?

9

Hari Seldon sat back in his chair, the vertical back giving as he did so and allowing him to assume a half-reclining position. His hands were behind his head and his eyes were unfocused. His breathing was very soft, indeed.

Dors Venabili was at the other end of the room, with her viewer turned off and the microfilms back in place. She had been through a rather concentrated period of revision of her opinions on the Florina Incident in early Trantorian history and she found it rather restful to withdraw for a few moments and to speculate on what it was that Seldon was considering.

It had to be psychohistory. It would probably take him the rest of his life, tracking down the byways of this semichaotic technique, and he would end with it incomplete, leaving the task to others (to Amaryl, if that young man had not also worn himself out on the matter) and breaking his heart at the need to do that.

Yet it gave him a reason for living. He would live longer with the problem filling him from end to end – and that pleased her. Someday she would lose him, she knew, and she found that the thought afflicted her. It had not seemed it would at the start, when her task had been the simple one of protecting him for the sake of what he knew.

When had it become a matter of personal need? How could there be so personal a need? What was there about the man that caused her to feel uneasy when he was not in her sight, even when she knew he was safe so that the deeply ingrained orders within her were not called into action? His safety was all that she had been ordered to be concerned with. How did the rest intrude itself?

She had spoken of it to Demerzel long before, when

the feeling had made itself unmistakable.

He had regarded her gravely and said, 'You are complex, Dors, and there are no simple answers. In my life there have been several individuals whose presence made it easier for me to think, pleasanter to make my responses. I have tried to judge the ease of my responses in their presence and the unease of my responses in their final absence to see whether I was the net gainer or loser. In the process, one thing became plain. The pleasantness of their company outweighed the regret of their passing. On the whole, then, it is better to experience what you experience now than not to.'

She thought: Hari will someday leave a void, and each day that someday is closer, and I must not think of it.

It was to rid herself of the thought that she finally interrupted him. 'What are you thinking of, Hari?'

'What?' Seldon focused his eyes with an apparent effort.

'Psychohistory, I assume. I imagine you've traced another blind pathway.'

'Well now. That's not on my mind at all.' He laughed suddenly.

'Do you want to know what I'm thinking of? — Hair!'

'Hair? Whose?'

'Right now, yours.' He was looking at her fondly.

'Is there something wrong with it? Should I dye it another color? Or perhaps, after all these years, it should go gray.'

'Come! Who needs or wants gray in *your* hair. — But it's led me to other things. Nishaya, for instance.'

'Nishaya? What's that?'

'It was never part of the pre-Imperial Kingdom of Trantor, so I'm not surprised you haven't heard of it. It's a world, a small one. Isolated. Unimportant. Overlooked. I only know anything at all about it because I've taken the trouble to look it up. Very few worlds out of twenty-five million can really make much of a sustained splash, but I doubt that there's another one as insignificant as Nishaya. Which is very significant, you see.'

Dors shoved her reference material to one side and said, 'What is this new penchant you have for paradox, which you always tell me you detest? What is this significance of insignificance?'

'Oh, I don't mind paradoxes when *I* perpetrate them. You see, Joranum comes from Nishaya.'

'Ah, it's Joranum you're concerned with.'

'Yes. I've been viewing some of his speeches – at Raych's insistence. They don't make very much sense, but the total effect can be almost hypnotic. Raych is very impressed by him.'

'I imagine that anyone of Dahlite origins would be, Hari. Joranum's constant call for sector equality would naturally appeal to the downtrodden heatsinkers. You remember when we were in Dahl?'

'I remember it very well and of course I don't blame the lad. It just bothers me that Joranum comes from Nishaya.'

Dors shrugged. 'Well, Joranum has to come from somewhere and, conversely, Nishaya, like any other world, must send its people out at times, even to Trantor.'

'Yes, but, as I've said, I've taken the trouble to investigate Nishaya. I've even managed to make hyperspatial contact with some minor official – which cost a considerable quantity of credits that I cannot, in good conscience, charge to the department.'

'And did you find anything that was worth the credits?'

'I rather think so. You know, Joranum is always telling little stories to make his points, stories that are legends on his home planet of Nishaya. That serves a good purpose for him here on Trantor, since it makes him appear to be a man of the people, full of homespun philosophy. Those tales litter his speeches. They make him appear to be from a small world, to have been brought up on an

56

isolated farm surrounded by an untamed ecology. People like it, especially Trantorians, who would rather die than be trapped somewhere in an untamed ecology but who love to dream about one just the same.'

'But what of it all?'

'The odd point is that not one of the stories was familiar to the person I spoke to on Nishaya.'

'That's not significant, Hari. It may be a small world, but it's a world. What is current in Joranum's birth section of the world may not be current in whatever place your official came from.'

'No no. Folktales, in one form or another, are usually worldwide. But aside from that, I had considerable trouble in understanding the fellow. He spoke Galactic Standard with a thick accent. I spoke to a few others on the world, just to check, and they all had the same accent.'

'And what of that?'

'Joranum doesn't have it. He speaks a fairly good Trantorian. It's a lot better than mine, actually. I have the Heliconian stress on the letter "r." He doesn't. According to the records, he arrived on Trantor when he was nineteen. It is just impossible, in my opinion, to spend the first nineteen years of your life speaking that barbarous Nishayan version of Galactic Standard and then come to Trantor and lose it. However long he's been here, some trace of the accent would have remained – Look at Raych and the way he lapses into his Dahlite way of speaking on occasion.'

'What do you deduce from all this?'

'What I deduce – what I've been sitting here all evening, deducing like a deduction machine – is that Joranum didn't come from Nishaya at all. In fact, I think he picked Nishaya as the place to pretend to come from, simply because it is so backwoodsy, so out-of-the-way, that no one would think of checking it. He must have made a thorough computer search to find the one world least likely to allow him to be caught in a lie.'

'But that's ridiculous, Hari. Why should he want to pretend to be from a world he did not come from? It would mean a great deal of falsification of records.'

'And that's precisely what he has probably done. He probably has enough followers in the civil service to make that possible. Probably no one person has done as much in the way of revision and all of his followers are too fanatical to talk about it.'

'But still – Why?'

'Because I suspect Joranum doesn't want people to know where he really comes from.'

'Why not? All worlds in the Empire are equal, both by laws and by custom.'

'I don't know about that. These high-ideal theories are somehow never borne out in real life.'

'Then where does he come from? Do you have any idea at all?'

'Yes. Which brings us back to this matter of hair.'

'What about hair?'

'I sat there with Joranum, staring at him and feeling uneasy, without knowing why I was feeling uneasy. Then finally I realized that it was his hair that made me uneasy. There was something about it, a life, a gloss . . . a *perfection* to it that I've never seen before. And then I knew. His hair is artificial and carefully grown on a scalp that ought to be innocent of such things.'

'*Ought* to be?' Dors's eyes narrowed. It was clear that she suddenly understood. 'Do you mean—'

'Yes, I *do* mean. He's from the past-centered, mythology-ridden Mycogen Sector of Trantor. That's what he's been laboring to hide.'

10

Dors Venabili thought coolly about the matter. It was her only mode of thought – cool. Not for her the hot flashes of emotion.

She closed her eyes to concentrate. It had been eight years since she and Hari had visited Mycogen and they hadn't been there long. There had been little to admire there except the food.

The pictures arose. The harsh, puritanical, male-centered society; the emphasis on the past; the removal of all body hair, a painful process deliberately self-imposed to make themselves different so that they would 'know who they were'; their legends; their memories (or fancies) of a time when they ruled the Galaxy, when their lives were prolonged, when robots existed.

Dors opened her eyes and said, 'Why, Hari?'

'Why what, dear?'

'Why should he pretend not to be from Mycogen?'

She didn't think he would remember Mycogen in greater detail than she; in fact, she knew he wouldn't, but his mind was better than hers – different, certainly. Hers was a mind that only remembered and drew the obvious inferences in the fashion of a mathematic line of deduction. He had a mind that leaped unexpectedly. Seldon liked to pretend that intuition was solely the province of his assistant, Yugo Amaryl, but Dors was not fooled by that. Seldon liked to pose as the unworldly mathematician who stared at the world out of perpetually wondering eyes, but she was not fooled by that, either.

'Why should he pretend not to be from Mycogen?' she repeated as he sat there, his eyes lost in an inward look that Dors always associated with his attempt to squeeze one more tiny drop of usefulness and validity out of the concepts of psychohistory.

Seldon said finally, 'It's a harsh society, a limiting society. There are always those who chafe over its manner of dictating every action and every thought. There are always those who find they cannot entirely be broken to the harness, who want the greater liberties available in the more secular world outside. It's understandable.'

'So they force the growth of artificial hair?'

'No, not generally. The average Breakaway – that's what the Mycogenians call the deserters and they despise them, of course – wears a wig. It's much simpler but much less effective. Really serious Breakaways grow false hair, I'm told. The process is difficult and expensive but is almost unnoticeable. I've never come across it before, though I've heard of it. I've spent years studying, all eight hundred sectors of Trantor, trying to work out the basic rules and mathematics of psychohistory. I have little enough to show for it, unfortunately, but I have learned a few things.'

'But why, then, do the Breakaways, have to hide the fact that they're from Mycogen? They're not persecuted that I know of.'

'No, they're not. In fact, there's no general impression that Mycogenians are inferior. It's worse than that. The Mycogenians aren't taken seriously. They're intelligent – everyone admits that – highly educated, dignified, cultured, wizards with food, almost frightening in their capacity to keep their sector prosperous – but no one takes them seriously. Their beliefs strike people outside Mycogen as ridiculous, humorous, unbelievably foolish. And that view clings even to Mycogenians who are Breakaways. A Mycogenian attempt to seize power in the government would be crushed by laughter. Being feared is nothing. Being despised, even, can be lived with. But being laughed at – that's fatal. Joranum wants to be First Minister, so he must have hair, and, to be comfortable, he must represent himself as having been brought up on some obscure world as far from Mycogen as he can possibly manage.'

'Surely there are some people who are naturally bald.'

'Never as completely depilated as Mycogenians force themselves to be. On the Outer Worlds, it wouldn't matter much. But Mycogen is a distant whisper to the Outer Worlds. The Mycogenians keep themselves so much to themselves that it is a rare one, indeed, who has ever left Trantor. Here on Trantor, though, it's different. People might be bald, but they usually have a fringe of hair that advertises them as non-Mycogenian – or they grow facial hair. Those very few who are completely hairless – usually a pathological condition – are out of luck. I imagine they have to go around with a doctor's certificate to prove they are not Mycogenians.'

Dors, frowning slightly, said, 'Does this help us any?'

'I'm not sure.'

'Couldn't you let it be known that he is a Mycogenian?'

'I'm not sure that could be done easily. He must have covered his tracks well and even if it could be done—'

'Yes?'

Seldon shrugged. 'I don't want to invite an appeal to bigotry. The social situation on Trantor is bad enough without running the risk of loosing passions that neither I nor anyone else could then control. If I do have to resort to the matter of Mycogen, it will only be as a last resort.'

'Then you want minimalism, too.'

'Of course.'

'Then what *will* you do?'

'I made an appointment with Demerzel. He may know what to do.'

Dors looked at him sharply. 'Hari, are you falling into the trap of expecting Demerzel to solve every problem for you?'

'No, but perhaps he'll solve this one.'

'And if he doesn't?'

'Then I'll have to think of something else, won't I?'

'Like what?'

A look of pain crossed Seldon's face. 'Dors, I don't know. Don't expect *me* to solve every problem, either.'

11

Eto Demerzel was not frequently seen, except by the Emperor Cleon. It was his policy to remain in the background for a variety of reasons, one of which was that his appearance changed so little with time.

Hari Seldon had not seen him over a period of some years and had not spoken to him truly in private since the days of his early time on Trantor.

In light of Seldon's recent unsettling meeting with Laskin Joranum, both Seldon and Demerzel felt it would be best not to advertise their relationship. A visit by Hari Seldon to the First Minister's office at the Imperial Palace would not go unnoticed, and so for reasons of security they had decided to meet in a small yet luxuriously appointed suite at the Dome's Edge Hotel, just outside the Palace grounds.

Seeing Demerzel now brought back the old days achingly. The mere fact that Demerzel still looked exactly as he always had made the ache sharper. His face still had its strong regular features. He was still tall and sturdy-looking, with the same dark hair with the hint of blond. He was not handsome, but was gravely distinguished. He looked like someone's ideal picture of what an Imperial First Minister ought to look like, not at all like any such official in history before his time ever had. It was his appearance, Seldon thought, that gave him half his power over the Emperor, and therefore over the Imperial Court, and therefore over the Empire.

Demerzel advanced toward him, a gentle smile curving his lips without altering in any way the gravity of his countenance.

'Hari,' he said. 'It is pleasant to see you. I was half-afraid you would change your mind and cancel.'

'I was more than half-afraid *you* would, First Minister.'

'Eto – if you fear using my real name.'

'I couldn't. It won't come out of me. You know that.'

'It will to me. Say it. I would rather like to hear it.'

Seldon hesitated, as though he couldn't believe his lips could frame the words or his vocal cords sound them. 'Daneel,' he said at length.

'R. Daneel Olivaw,' said Demerzel. 'Yes. You will dine with me, Hari. If I dine with you, I won't have to eat, which will be a relief.'

'Gladly, though one-way eating is not my idea of a convivial time. Surely a bite or two—'

'To please you—'

'Just the same,' said Seldon, 'I can't help but wonder if it is wise to spend too much time together.'

'It is. Imperial orders. His Imperial Majesty wants me to.'

'Why, Daneel?'

'In two more years the Decennial Convention will be meeting again. – You look surprised. Have you forgotten?'

'Not really. I just haven't thought about it.'

'Were you not going to attend? You were a hit at the last one.'

'Yes. With my psychohistory. Some hit.'

'You attracted the attention of the Emperor. No other mathematician did.'

'It was you who were initially attracted, not the Emperor. Then I had to flee and stay out of the Imperial notice until such time as I could assure you that I had made a start on my psychohistorical research, after which you allowed me to remain in safe obscurity.'

'Being the head of a prestigious Mathematics Department is scarcely obscurity.'

'Yes, it is, since it hides my psychohistory.'

'Ah, the food is arriving. For a while, let's talk about other things as befits friends. How is Dors?'

'Wonderful. A true wife. Hounds me to death

with her worries over my safety.'

'That is her job.'

'So she reminds me – frequently. Seriously, Daneel, I can never be sufficiently grateful to you for bringing us together.'

'Thank you, Hari, but, to be truthful, I did not foresee married happiness for either of you, especially not Dors—'

'Thank you for the gift just the same, however short of the actual consequences your expectations were.'

'I'm delighted, but it is a gift, you will find, that may be of dubious further consequence – as is my friendship.'

To this, Seldon could make no reply and so, at a gesture from Demerzel, he turned to his meal.

After a while, he nodded at the morsel of fish on his fork and said, 'I don't actually recognize the organism, but this is Mycogenian cooking.'

'Yes, it is. I know you are fond of it.'

'It's the Mycogenians' excuse for existence. Their only excuse. But they have special meaning to you. I mustn't forget that.'

'The special meaning has come to an end. – Their ancestors, long, long ago, inhabited the planet of Aurora. They lived three hundred years and more and were the lords of the Fifty Worlds of the Galaxy. It was an Auroran who first designed and produced me. I don't forget that; I remember it far more accurately – and with less distortion – than their Mycogenian descendants do. But then, long, long ago, I left them. I made my choice as to what the good of humanity must be and I have followed it, as best I could, all this time.'

Seldon said with sudden alarm, 'Can we be overheard?'

Demerzel seemed amused. 'If you have only thought of that now, it is far too late. But fear not, I have taken the necessary precautions. Nor have you been seen by too many eyes when you came. Nor will you be seen by too many when you leave. And those who do see you will not be surprised. I am well known to be an amateur mathematician of great pretensions but of little ability. That is a source of amusement to those at the court who are not entirely my friends and it would not surprise anyone here that I should be concerned about laying the groundwork for the forthcoming Decennial Convention. It is about the convention that I wish to consult you.'

'I don't know that I can help. There is only one thing I could possibly talk about at the convention – and I *can't* talk about it. If I attend at all, it will only be as part of the audience. I do not intend to present any papers.'

'I understand. Still, if you would like to hear something curious, His Imperial Majesty remembers you.'

'Because you have kept me in his mind, I suppose.'

'No. I have not labored to do so. However, His Imperial Majesty occasionally surprises me. He is aware of the forthcoming convention and he apparently remembers your talk at the earlier one. He remains interested in the matter of psychohistory and more may come of it, I must warn you. It is not beyond the bounds of possibility that he may ask to see you. The court will surely consider it a great honor – to receive the Imperial call twice in a single lifetime.'

'You're joking. What could be served by my seeing him?'

'In any case, if you are called to an audience, you can scarcely refuse. – How are your young protegés, Yugo and Raych?'

'Surely you know. I imagine you keep a close eye on me.'

'Yes, I do. On your safety but not on every aspect of your life. I am afraid my duties fill much of my time and I am not all-seeing.'

'Doesn't Dors report?'

'She would in a crisis. Not otherwise. She is reluctant to play the role of spy in nonessentials.' Again the small smile.

Seldon grunted. 'My boys are doing well. Yugo is increasingly difficult to handle. He's more of a psychohistorian than I am and I think he feels I hold him back.

As for Raych, he's a lovable rascal – always was. He won me over when he was a dreadful street urchin and what's more surprising is that he won over Dors. I honestly believe, Daneel, that if Dors grew sick of me and wanted to leave me, she would stay on anyway for her love of Raych.'

Demerzel nodded and Seldon continued somberly. 'If Rashelle of Wye hadn't found him lovable, I would not be here today. I would have been shot down—' He stirred uneasily. 'I hate to think of that, Daneel. It was such an entirely accidental and unpredictable event. How could psychohistory have helped in any way?'

'Have you not told me that, at best, psychohistory can deal only in probabilities and with vast numbers, not with individuals?'

'But if the individual happens to be crucial—'

'I suspect you will find that no individual is ever truly crucial. Not even I – or you.'

'Perhaps you're right. I find that, no matter how I work away under these assumptions, I nevertheless think of myself as crucial, in a kind of supernormal egotism that transcends all sense. – And you are crucial, too, which is something I have come here to discuss with you – as frankly as possible. I must know.'

'Know what?' The remains of the meal had been cleared away by a porter and the room's lighting dimmed somewhat so that the walls seemed to close in and give a feeling of great privacy.

Seldon said, 'Joranum.' He bit off the word, as though feeling the mention of the name alone should be sufficient.

'Ah yes.'

'You know about him?'

'Of course. How could I *not* know?'

'Well, I want to know about him, too.'

'What do you want to know?'

'Come, Daneel, don't play with me. Is he dangerous?'

'Of course he is dangerous. Do you have any doubt of that?'

'I mean, to you? To your position as First Minister?'

'That is exactly what I mean. That is how he is dangerous.'

'And you allow it?'

Demerzel leaned forward, placing his left elbow on the table between them. 'There are things that don't wait for my permission, Hari. Let us be philosophical about it. His Imperial Majesty, Cleon, First of that Name, has now been on the throne for eighteen years and for all that time I have been his Chief of Staff and then his First Minister, having served in scarcely lesser capacities during the last years of the reign of his father. It is a long time and First Ministers rarely remain that long in power.'

'You are not the ordinary First Minister, Daneel, and you know it. You *must* remain in power while psycho-history is being developed. Don't smile at me. It's true. When we first met, eight years ago, you told me the Empire was in a state of decay and decline. Have you changed your mind about that?'

'No, of course not.'

'In fact, the decline is more marked now, isn't it?'

'Yes, it is, though I labor to prevent that.'

'And without you, what would happen? Joranum is raising the Empire against you.'

'Trantor, Hari. Trantor. The Outer Worlds are solid and reasonably contented with my deeds so far, even in the midst of a declining economy and lessening trade.'

'But Trantor is where it counts. Trantor – the Imperial world we're living on, the capital of the Empire, the core, the administrative center – is what can overthrow you. You cannot keep your post if Trantor says no.'

'I agree.'

'And if you go, who will then take care of the Outer Worlds and what will keep the decline from being precipitate and the Empire from degenerating rapidly into anarchy?'

'That is a possibility, certainly.'

'So you must be doing something about it. Yugo is

convinced that you are in deadly danger and can't maintain your position. His intuition tells him so. Dors says the same thing and explains it in terms of the Three Laws or Four of – of–'

'Robotics,' put in Demerzel.

'Young Raych seems attracted to Joranum's doctrines – being of Dahlite origin, you see. And I – I am uncertain, so I come to you for comfort, I suppose. Tell me that you have the situation well in hand.'

'I would do so if I could. However, I have no comfort to offer. I *am* in danger.'

'Are you doing nothing?'

'No. I'm doing a great deal to contain discontent and blunt Joranum's message. If I had not done so, then perhaps I would be out of office already. But what I'm doing is not enough.'

Seldon hesitated. Finally he said, 'I believe that Joranum is actually a Mycogenian.'

'Is that so?'

'It is my *opinion*. I had thought we might use that against him, but I hesitate to unleash the forces of bigotry.'

'You are wise to hesitate. There are many things that might be done that have side effects we do not want. You see, Hari, I don't fear leaving my post – if some successor could be found who would continue those principles that I have been using to keep the decline as slow as possible. On the other hand, if Joranum himself were to succeed me, then that, in my opinion, would be fatal.'

'Then anything we can do to stop him would be suitable.'

'Not entirely. The Empire can grow anarchic, even if Joranum is destroyed and I stay. I must not, then, do something that will destroy Joranum and allow me to stay – if that very deed promotes the Fall of the Empire. I have not yet been able to think of anything I might do that would surely destroy Joranum and just as surely avoid anarchy.'

'Minimalism,' whispered Seldon.

'Pardon me?'

'Dors explained that you would be bound by minimalism.'

'And so I am.'

'Then my visit with you is a failure, Daneel.'

'You mean that you came for comfort and didn't get it.'

'I'm afraid so.'

'But I saw you because I sought comfort as well.'

'From me?'

'From psychohistory, which should envision the route to safety that I cannot.'

Seldon sighed heavily. 'Daneel, psychohistory has not yet been developed to that point.'

The First Minister looked at him gravely. 'You've had eight years, Hari.'

'It might be eight or eight hundred and it might not be developed to that point. It is an intractable problem.'

Demerzel said, 'I do not expect the technique to have been perfected, but you may have some sketch, some skeleton, some principle that you can use as guidance. Imperfectly, perhaps, but better than mere guesswork.'

'No more than I had eight years ago,' said Seldon mournfully. 'Here's what it amounts to, then. You must remain in power and Joranum must be destroyed in such a way that Imperial stability is maintained as long as possible so that I may have a reasonable chance to work out psychohistory. This cannot be done, however, unless I work out psychohistory first. Is that it?'

'It would seem so, Hari.'

'Then we argue in a useless circle and the Empire is destroyed.'

'Unless something unforeseen happens. Unless you make something unforeseen happen.'

'I? Daneel, how can I do it without psychohistory?'

'I don't know, Hari.'

And Seldon rose to go – in despair.

12

For days thereafter Hari Seldon neglected his departmental duties to use his computer in its news-gathering mode.

There were not many computers capable of handling the daily news from twenty-five million worlds. There were a number of them at Imperial headquarters, where they were absolutely necessary. Some of the larger Outer World capitals had them as well, though most were satisfied with hyperconnection to the Central Newspost on Trantor.

A computer at an important Mathematics Department could, if it were sufficiently advanced, be modified as an independent news source and Seldon had been careful to do that with his computer. It was, after all, necessary for his work on psychohistory, though the computer's capabilities were carefully ascribed to other, exceedingly plausible reasons.

Ideally the computer would report anything that was out of the ordinary on any world of the Empire. A coded and unobtrusive warning light would make itself evident and Seldon could track it down easily. Such a light rarely showed, for the definition of 'out of the ordinary' was tight and intense and dealt with large-scale and rare upheavals.

What one did in its absence was to ring in various worlds at random – not all twenty-five million, of course, but some dozens. It was a depressing and even debilitating task, for there were no worlds that didn't have their daily relatively minor catastrophes. A volcanic eruption here, a flood there, an economic collapse of one sort or another yonder, and, of course, riots. There had not been a day in the last thousand years that there had not been riots over something or other on each of a hundred or more different worlds.

Naturally such things had to be discounted. One could scarcely worry about riots any more than one could about volcanic eruptions when both were constants on inhabited worlds. Rather, if a day should come in which not one riot was reported anywhere, *that* might be a sign of something so unusual as to warrant the gravest concern.

Concern was what Seldon could not make himself feel. The Outer Worlds, with all their disorders and misfortunes, were like a great ocean on a peaceful day, with a gentle swell and minor heavings – but no more. He found no evidence of any overall situation that clearly showed a decline in the last eight years or even in the last eighty. Yet Demerzel (in Demerzel's absence, Seldon could no longer think of him as Daneel) said the decline was continuing and he had his finger on the Empire's pulse from day to day in ways that Seldon could not duplicate – until such time as he would have the guiding power of psychohistory at his disposal.

It could be that the decline was so small that it was unnoticeable till some crucial point was reached – like a domicile that slowly wears out and deteriorates, showing no signs of that deterioration until one night when the roof collapses.

When would the roof collapse? That was the problem and Seldon had no answer.

And on occasion, Seldon would check on Trantor itself. There, the news was always considerably more substantial. For one thing, Trantor was the most highly populated of all the worlds, with its forty billion people. For another, its eight hundred sectors formed a mini-Empire all its own. For a third, there were the tedious rounds of governmental functions and the doings of the Imperial family to follow.

What struck Seldon's eyes, however, was in the Dahl Sector. The elections for the Dahl Sector Council had placed five Joranumites into office. This was the first time, according to the commentary, that Joranumites had achieved sector office.

It was not surprising. Dahl was a Joranumite stronghold if any sector was, but Seldon found it a disturbing indication of the progress being made by the demagogue. He ordered a microchip of the item and took it home with him that evening.

Raych looked up from his computer as Seldon entered and apparently felt the need to explain himself. 'I'm helping Mom on some reference material she needs,' he said.

'What about your own work?'

'Done, Dad. All done.'

'Good. – Look at this.' He showed Raych the chip in his hand before slipping it into the microprojector.

Raych glanced at the news item hanging in the air before his eyes and said, 'Yes, I know.'

'You do?'

'Sure. I usually keep track of Dahl. You know, home sector and all.'

'And what do you think about it?'

'I'm not surprised. Are you? The rest of Trantor treats Dahl like dirt. Why shouldn't they go for Joranum's views?'

'Do you go for them also?'

'Well—' Raych twisted his face thoughtfully. 'I got to admit some things he says appeal to me. He says he wants equality for all people. What's wrong with that?'

'Nothing at all – if he means it. If he's sincere. If he isn't just using it as a ploy to get votes.'

'True enough, Dad, but most Dahlites probably figure: What's there to lose? We don't have equality now, though the laws say we do.'

'It's a hard thing to legislate.'

'That's not something to cool you off when you're sweating to death.'

Seldon was thinking rapidly. He had been thinking since he had come across this item. He said, 'Raych, you haven't been in Dahl since your mother and I took you out of the sector, have you?'

'Sure I was, when I went with you to Dahl five years ago on your visit there.'

'Yes yes' – Seldon waved a hand in dismissal – 'but that doesn't count. We stayed at an intersector hotel, which was not Dahlite in the least, and, as I recall, Dors never once let you out on the streets alone. After all, you were only fifteen. How would you like to visit Dahl now, alone, in charge of yourself – now that you're fully twenty?'

Raych chuckled. 'Mom would never allow that.'

'I don't say that I enjoy the prospect of facing her with it, but I don't intend to ask her permission. The question is: Would you be willing to do this for me?'

'Out of curiosity? Sure. I'd like to see what's happened to the old place.'

'Can you spare the time from your studies?'

'Sure. I'll never miss a week or so. Besides, you can tape the lectures and I'll catch up when I get back. I can get permission. After all, my old man's on the faculty – unless you've been fired, Dad.'

'Not yet. But I'm not thinking of this as a fun vacation.'

'I'd be surprised if you did. I don't think you know what a fun vacation is, Dad. I'm surprised you know the phrase.'

'Don't be impertinent. When you go there, I want you to meet with Laskin Joranum.'

Raych looked startled. 'How do I do that? I don't know where he's gonna be.'

'He's going to be in Dahl. He's been asked to speak to the Dahl Sector Council with its new Joranumite members. We'll find out the exact day and you can go a few days earlier.'

'And how do I get to see him, Dad? I don't figure he keeps open house.'

'I don't, either, but I'll leave that up to you. You would have known how to do it when you were twelve. I hope your keen edge hasn't blunted too badly in the intervening years.'

Raych smiled. 'I hope not. But suppose I do see him. What then?'

'Well, find out what you can. What he's really planning. What he's really thinking.'

'Do you really think he's gonna tell me?'

'I wouldn't be surprised if he does. You have the trick of inspiring confidence, you miserable youngster. Let's talk about it.'

And so they did. Several times.

Seldon's thoughts were painful. He was not sure where all this was leading to, but he dared not consult Yugo Amaryl or Demerzel or (most of all) Dors. They might stop him. They might prove to him that his idea was a poor one and he didn't want that proof. What he planned seemed the only gateway to salvation and he didn't want it blocked.

But did the gateway exist at all? Raych was the only one, it seemed to Seldon, who could possibly manage to worm himself into Joranum's confidence, but was Raych the proper tool for the purpose? He was a Dahlite and sympathetic to Joranum. How far could Seldon trust him?

Horrible! Raych was his *son* – and Seldon had never had occasion to mistrust Raych before.

13

If Seldon doubted the efficacy of his notion, if he feared that it might explode matters prematurely or move them desperately in the wrong direction, if he was filled with an agonizing doubt as to whether Raych could be entirely trusted to fulfill his part suitably, he nevertheless had no doubt – no doubt whatever – as to what Dors's reaction would be when presented with the *fait accompli*.

And he was not disappointed – if that was quite the word to express his emotion.

Yet, in a manner, he *was* disappointed, for Dors did not raise her voice in horror as he had somehow thought she would, as he had prepared himself to withstand.

But how was he to know? She was not as other women were and he had never seen her truly angry. Perhaps it was not in her to be truly angry – or what he would consider to be *truly* angry.

She was merely cold-eyed and spoke with low-voiced bitter disapproval. 'You sent him to Dahl? Alone?' Very softly. Questioningly.

For a moment Seldon quailed at the quiet voice. Then he said firmly, 'I had to. It was necessary.'

'Let me understand. You sent him to that den of thieves, that haunt of assassins, that conglomeration of all that is criminal?'

'Dors! You anger me when you speak like that. I would expect only a bigot to use those stereotypes.'

'You deny that Dahl is as I have described?'

'Of course. There are criminals and slums in Dahl. I know that very well. We both know that. But not all of Dahl is like that. And there are criminals and slums in every sector, even in the Imperial Sector and in Streeling.'

75

'There are degrees, are there not? One is not ten. If all the worlds are crime-ridden, if all the sectors are crime-ridden, Dahl is among the worst, is it not? You have the computer. Check the statistics.'

'I don't have to. Dahl is the poorest sector on Trantor and there is a positive correlation between poverty, misery, and crime. I grant you that.'

'You *grant* me that! And you sent him alone? You might have gone with him, or asked me to go with him, or sent half a dozen of his schoolmates with him. They would have welcomed a respite from their work, I'm sure.'

'What I need him for requires that he be alone.'

'And what do you need him for?'

But Seldon was stubbornly silent about that.

Dors said, 'Has it come to this? You don't trust me?'

'It's a gamble. I alone dare take the risk. I can't involve you or anyone else.'

'But it's not you taking the risk. It's poor Raych.'

'He's not taking any risk,' said Seldon impatiently. 'He's twenty years old, young and vigorous and as sturdy as a tree – and I don't mean the saplings we have here under glass on Trantor. I'm talking about a good solid tree in the Heliconian forests. And he's a Twister, which the Dahlites aren't.'

'You and your Twisting,' said Dors, her coldness not thawing one whit. 'You think that's the answer to everything. The Dahlites carry knives. Every one of them. Blasters, too, I'm sure.'

'I don't know about blasters. The laws are pretty strict when it comes to blasters. As for knives, I'm positive Raych carries one. He even carries a knife on campus here, where it's strictly against the law. Do you think he won't have one in Dahl?'

Dors remained silent.

Seldon was also silent for a few minutes, then decided it might be time to placate her. He said, 'Look, I'll tell

76

you this much. I'm hoping he'll see Joranum, who will be visiting Dahl.'

'Oh? And what do you expect Raych to do? Fill him with bitter regrets over his wicked politics and send him back to Mycogen?'

'Come. Really. If you're going to take this sardonic attitude, there's no use discussing it.' He looked away from her, out the window at the blue-gray sky under the dome. 'What I expect him to do' – and his voice faltered for a moment – 'is save the Empire.'

'To be sure. That would be much easier.'

Seldon's voice firmed. 'It's what I *expect*. You have no solution. Demerzel himself has no solution. He as much as said that the solution rests with me. That's what I'm striving for and that's what I need Raych for in Dahl. After all, you know that ability of his to inspire affection. It worked with us and I'm convinced it will work with Joranum. If I am right, all may be well.'

Dors's eyes widened a trifle. 'Are you now going to tell me that you are being guided by psychohistory?'

'No. I'm not going to lie to you. I have not reached the point where I can be guided in any way by psychohistory, but Yugo is constantly talking about intuition – and I have mine.'

'Intuition! What's that? Define it!'

'Easily. Intuition is the art, peculiar to the human mind, of working out the correct answer from data that is, in itself, incomplete or even, perhaps, misleading.'

'And you've done it.'

And Seldon said with firm conviction, 'Yes, I have.'

But to himself, he thought what he dared not share with Dors. What if Raych's charm were gone? Or, worse, what if the consciousness of being a Dahlite became too strong for him?

14

Billibotton was Billibotton – dirty, sprawling, dark, sinuous Billibotton – exuding decay and yet full of a vitality that Raych was convinced was to be found nowhere else on Trantor. Perhaps it was to be found nowhere else in the Empire, though Raych knew nothing, firsthand, of any world but Trantor.

He had last seen Billibotton when he was not much more than twelve, but even the people seemed to be the same; still a mixture of the hangdog and the irreverent; filled with a synthetic pride and a grumbling resentment; the men marked by their dark rich mustaches and the women by their sacklike dresses that now looked tremendously slatternly to Raych's older and more worldly wise eyes.

How could women with dresses like that attract men? – But it was a foolish question. Even when he was twelve, he had had a pretty clear idea of how easily and quickly they could be removed.

So he stood there, lost in thought and memory, passing along a street of store windows and trying to convince himself that he remembered this particular place or that and wondering if, among them all, there were people he did remember who were now eight years older. Those, perhaps, who had been his boyhood friends – and he thought uneasily of the fact that, while he remembered some of the nicknames they had pinned on each other, he could not remember any real names.

In fact, the gaps in his memory were enormous. It was not that eight years was such a long time, but it was two fifths of the lifetime of a twenty-year-old and his life since leaving Billibotton had been so different that all before it had faded like a misty dream.

But the smells were there. He stopped outside a bakery, low and dingy, and smelled the coconut icing that reeked through the air – that he had never quite smelled elsewhere. Even when he had stopped to buy tarts with coconut icing, even when they were advertised as 'Dahl-style,' they had been faint imitations – no more.

He felt strongly tempted. Well, why not? He had the credits and Dors was not there to wrinkle her nose and wonder aloud how clean – or, more likely, not clean – the place might be. Who worried about *clean* in the old days?

The shop was dim and it took a while for Raych's eyes to acclimate. There were a few low tables in the place, with a couple of rather insubstantial chairs at each, undoubtedly where people might have a light repast, the equivalent of moka and tarts. A young man sat at one of the tables, an empty cup before him, wearing a once-white T-shirt that probably would have looked even dirtier in a better light.

The baker or, in any case, a server stepped out from a room in the rear and said in a rather surly fashion, 'What'll ya have?'

'A coke-icer,' said Raych in just as surly a fashion (he would not be a Billibottoner if he displayed courtesy), using the slang term he remembered well from the old days.

The term was still current, for the server handed him the correct item, using his bare fingers. The boy, Raych, would have taken that for granted, but now the man, Raych, felt taken slightly aback.

'You want a bag?'

'No,' said Raych, 'I'll eat it here.' He paid the server and took the coke-icer from the other's hand and bit into its richness, his eyes half-closing as he did so. It had been a rare treat in his boyhood – sometimes when he had scrounged the necessary credit to buy one with, sometimes when he had received a bite from a temporarily wealthy friend, most often when he had lifted one when nobody was watching. Now he could buy as many as he wished.

'Hey,' said a voice.

Raych opened his eyes. It was the man at the table, scowling at him.

Raych said gently, 'Are you speaking to me, bub?'

'Yeah. What'chuh doin'?'

'Eatin' a coke-icer. What's it to ya?' Automatically he had assumed the Billibotton way of talking. It was no strain at all.

'What'chuh doin' in Billibotton?'

'Born here. Raised here. In a bed. Not in a street, like you.' The insult came easily, as though he had never left home.

'That so? You dress pretty good for a Billibottoner. Pretty fancy-dancy. Got a perfume stink about ya.' And he held up a little finger to imply effeminacy.

'I won't talk about your stink. I went up in the world.'

'Up in the world? *La-dee-da*.' Two other men stepped into the bakery. Raych frowned slightly, for he wasn't sure whether they had been summoned or not. The man at the table said to the newcomers, 'This guy's gone up in the world. Says he's a Billibottoner.'

One of the two newcomers shambled a mock salute and grinned with no appearance of amiability. His teeth were discolored. 'Ain't that nice? It's always good to see a Billibottoner go up in the world. Gives 'em a chance to help their poor unfor'chnit sector people. Like, credits. You can always spare a credit or two for the poor, hey?'

'How many you got, mister?' said the other, the grin disappearing.

'Hey,' said the man behind the counter. 'All you guys get out of my store. I don't want no trouble in here.'

'There'll be no trouble,' said Raych. 'I'm leaving.'

He made to go, but the seated man put a leg in his way. 'Don't go, pal. We'd miss yer company.'

(The man behind the counter, clearly fearing the worst, disappeared into the rear.)

Raych smiled. He said, 'One time when I was in Billibotton, guys, I was with my old man and old lady and there were ten guys who stopped us. Ten. I counted them. We had to take care of them.'

'Yeah?' said the one who had been speaking. 'Yer old man took care of ten?'

'My old man? Nah. He wouldn't waste his time. My old lady did. And I can do it better than she can. And there are only three of you. So, if you don't mind, out of the way.'

'Sure. Just leave all your credits. Some of your clothes, too.'

The man at the table rose to his feet. There was a knife in his hand.

'There you are,' said Raych. 'Now you're going to waste my time.' He had finished his coke-icer and he half-turned. Then, as quickly as thought, he anchored himself to the table, while his right leg shot out and the point of his toe landed unerringly in the groin of the man with the knife.

Down he went with a loud cry. Up went the table, driving the second man toward the wall and keeping him there, while Raych's right arm flashed out, with the edge of the palm striking hard against the larynx of the third, who coughed and went down.

It had taken two seconds and Raych now stood there with a knife in each hand and said, 'Now which one of you wants to move?'

They glared at him but remained frozen in place and Raych said, 'In that case, I will now leave.'

But the server, who had retreated to the back room, must have summoned help, for three more men had now entered the store, while the server screeched, 'Trouble-makers! Nothing but troublemakers!'

The newcomers were dressed alike in what was obviously a uniform – but one that Raych had never seen. Trousers were tucked into boots, loose green T-shirts were belted, and odd semi-spherical hats that looked vaguely comic were perched on top of their heads. On the front of the left shoulder of each T-shirt were the letters JG.

They had the Dahlite look about them but not quite the Dahlite mustache. The mustaches were black and thick, but they were carefully trimmed at lip level and were kept from luxuriating too widely. Raych allowed himself an internal sneer. They lacked the vigor of his own wild mustache, but he had to admit they looked neat and clean.

The leader of these three men said, 'I'm Corporal Quinber. What's been going on here?'

The defeated Billibottoners were scrambling to their feet, clearly the worse for wear. One was still doubled over, one was rubbing his throat, and the third acted as though one of his shoulders had been wrenched.

The corporal stared at them with a philosophic eye, while his two men blocked the door. He turned to Raych – the one man who seemed untouched. 'Are you a Billibottoner, boy?'

'Born and bred, but I've lived elsewhere for eight years.' He let the Billibotton accent recede, but it was still there, at least to the extent that it existed in the corporal's speech as well. There were other parts of Dahl aside from Billibotton and some parts with considerable aspirations to gentility.

Raych said, 'Are you security officers? I don't seem to recall the uniform you're—'

'We're not security officers. You won't find security officers in Billibotton much. We're the Joranum Guard and we keep the peace here. We know these three and they've been warned. We'll take care of them. *You're* our problem, buster. Name. Reference number.'

Raych told them.

'And what happened here?'

Raych told them.

'And your business here?'

Raych said, 'Look here. Do you have the right to

82

question me? If you're not security officers—'

'Listen,' said the corporal in a hard voice, 'don't you question rights. We're all there is in Billibotton and we have the right because we take the right. You say you beat up these three men and I believe you. But you won't beat us up. We're not allowed to carry blasters—' And with that, the corporal slowly pulled out a blaster.

'Now tell me your business here.'

Raych sighed. If he had gone directly to a sector hall, as he should have done – if he had not stopped to drown himself in nostalgia for Billibotton and coke-icers—

He said, 'I have come on important business to see Mr Joranum, and since you seem to be part of his organi—'

'To see the leader?'

'Yes, Corporal.'

'With two knives on you?'

'For self-defense. I wasn't going to have them on me when I saw Mr Joranum.'

'So you say. We're taking you into custody, mister. We'll get to the bottom of this. It may take time, but we will.'

'But you don't have the right. You're not the legally const—'

'Well, find someone to complain to. Till then, you're ours.'

And the knives were confiscated and Raych was taken into custody.

15

Cleon was no longer quite the handsome young monarch that his holographs portrayed. Perhaps he still was – in the holographs – but his mirror told a different story. His most recent birthday had been celebrated with the usual pomp and ritual, but it was his fortieth just the same.

The Emperor could find nothing wrong with being forty. His health was perfect. He had gained a little weight but not much. His face would perhaps look older, if it were not for the microadjustments that were made periodically and that gave him a slightly enameled look.

He had been on the throne for eighteen years – already one of the longer reigns of the century – and he felt there was nothing that might necessarily keep him from reigning another forty years and perhaps having the longest reign in Imperial history as a result.

Cleon looked at the mirror again and thought he looked a bit better if he did not actualize the third dimension.

Now take Demerzel – faithful, reliable, necessary, *unbearable* Demerzel. No change in him. He maintained his appearance and, as far as Cleon knew, there had been no microadjustments, either. Of course, Demerzel was so close-mouthed about everything. And he had never been *young*. There had been no young look about him when he first served Cleon's father and Cleon had been the boyish Prince Imperial. And there was no young look about him now. Was it better to have looked old at the start and to avoid change afterward?

Change!

It reminded him that he had called Demerzel in for a

purpose and not just so that he might stand there while the Emperor ruminated. Demerzel would take too much Imperial rumination as a sign of old age.

'Demerzel,' he said.

'Sire?'

'This fellow Joranum. I tire of hearing of him.'

'There is no reason you should hear of him, Sire. He is one of those phenomena that are thrown to the surface of the news for a while and then disappears.'

'But he *doesn't* disappear.'

'Sometimes it takes a while, Sire.'

'What do you think of him, Demerzel?'

'He is dangerous but has a certain popularity. It is the popularity that increases the danger.'

'If you find him dangerous and if I find him annoying, why must we wait? Can't he simply be imprisoned or executed or something?'

'The political situation on Trantor, Sire, is delicate—'

'It is always delicate. When have you told me that it is anything but delicate?'

'We live in delicate times, Sire. It would be useless to move strongly against him if that would but exacerbate the danger.'

'I don't like it. I may not be widely read – an Emperor doesn't have the time to be widely read – but I know my Imperial history, at any rate. There have been a number of cases of these populists, as they are called, that have seized power in the last couple of centuries. In every case, they reduced the reigning Emperor to a mere figurehead. I do *not* wish to be a figurehead, Demerzel.'

'It is unthinkable that you would be, Sire.'

'It won't be unthinkable if you do nothing.'

'I am attempting to take measures, Sire, but cautious ones.'

'There's one fellow, at least, who isn't cautious. A month or so ago, a University professor – a *professor* – stopped a potential Joranumite riot single-handedly. He stepped right in and put a stop to it.'

85

'So he did, Sire. How did you come to hear of it?'

'Because he is a certain professor in whom I am interested. How is it that you didn't speak to me of this?'

Demerzel said, almost obsequiously, 'Would it be right for me to trouble you with every insignificant detail that crosses my desk?'

'Insignificant? This man who took action was Hari Seldon.'

'That was, indeed, his name.'

'And the name was a familiar one. Did he not present a paper, some years ago, at the last Decennial Convention that interested us?'

'Yes, Sire.'

Cleon looked pleased. 'As you see, I *do* have a memory. I need not depend on my staff for everything. I interviewed this Seldon fellow on the matter of his paper, did I not?'

'Your memory is indeed flawless, Sire.'

'What happened to his idea? It was a fortune-telling device. My flawless memory does not bring to mind what he called it.'

'Psychohistory, Sire. It was not precisely a fortune-telling device but a theory as to ways of predicting general trends in future human history.'

'And what happened to it?'

'Nothing, Sire. As I explained at the time, the idea turned out to be wholly impractical. It was a colorful idea but a useless one.'

'Yet he is capable of taking action to stop a potential riot. Would he have dared do this if he didn't know in advance he would succeed? Isn't that evidence that this – what? – psychohistory is working?'

'It is merely evidence that Hari Seldon is foolhardy, Sire. Even if the psychohistoric theory were practical, it would not have been able to yield results involving a single person or a single action.'

'You're not the mathematician, Demerzel. He is. I

86

think it is time I questioned him again. After all, it is not long before the Decennial Convention is upon us once more.'

'It would be a useless—'

'Demerzel, I desire it. See to it.'

'Yes, Sire.'

16

Raych was listening with an agonized impatience that he was trying not to show. He was sitting in an improvised cell, deep in the warrens of Billibotton, having been accompanied through alleys he no longer remembered. (*He*, who in the old days could have threaded those same alleys unerringly and lost any pursuer.)

The man with him, clad in the green of the Joranumite Guard, was either a missionary, a brainwasher, or a kind of theologian-*manqué*. At any rate, he had announced his name to be Sander Nee and he was delivering a long message in a thick Dahlite accent that he had clearly learned by heart.

'If the people of Dahl want to enjoy equality, they must show themselves worthy of it. Good rule, quiet behavior, seemly pleasures are all requirements. Aggressiveness and the bearing of knives are the accusations others make against us to justify their intolerance. We must be clean in word and—'

Raych broke in. 'I agree with you, Guardsman Nee, every word. – But I must see Mr Joranum.'

Slowly the guardsman shook his head. 'You can't 'less you got some appointment, some permission.'

'Look, I'm the son of an important professor at Streeling University, a mathematics professor.'

'Don't know no professor. – I thought you said you was from Dahl.'

'Of course I am. Can't you tell the way I talk?'

'And you got an old man who's a professor at a big University? That don't sound likely.'

'Well, he's my foster father.'

The guardsman absorbed that and shook his head. 'You know anyone in Dahl?'

'There's Mother Rittah. She'll know me.' (She had been very old when she had known him. She might be senile by now – or dead.)

'Never heard of her.'

(Who else? He had never known anyone likely to penetrate the dim consciousness of this man facing him. His best friend had been another youngster named Smoodgie – or at least that was the only name he knew him by. Even in his desperation, Raych could not see himself saying: 'Do you know someone my age named Smoodgie?')

Finally he said, 'There's Yugo Amaryl.'

A dim spark seemed to light Nee's eyes. 'Who?'

'Yugo Amaryl,' said Raych eagerly. 'He works for my foster father at the University.'

'He a Dahlite, too? Everyone at the University Dahlites?'

'Just he and I. He was a heatsinker.'

'What's he doing at the University?'

'My father took him out of the heatsinks eight years ago.'

'Well – I'll send someone.'

Raych had to wait. Even if he escaped, where would he go in the intricate alleyways of Billibotton without being picked up instantly?

Twenty minutes passed before Nee returned with the corporal who had arrested Raych in the first place. Raych felt a little hope; the corporal, at least, might conceivably have some brains.

The corporal said, 'Who is this Dahlite you know?'

'Yugo Amaryl, Corporal, a heatsinker who my father found here in Dahl eight years ago and took to Streeling University with him.'

'Why did he do that?'

'My father thought Yugo could do more important things than heatsink, Corporal.'

'Like what?'

'Mathematics. He—'

The corporal held up his hand. 'What heatsink did he work in?'

Raych thought for a moment. 'I was only a kid then, but it was at C-2, I think.'

'Close enough. C-3.'

'Then you know about him, Corporal?'

'Not personally, but the story is famous in the heatsinks and I've worked there, too. And maybe that's how you've heard of it. Have you any evidence that you really know Yugo Amaryl?'

'Look. Let me tell you what I'd like to do. I'm going to write down my name on a piece of paper and my father's name. Then I'm going to write down one word. Get in touch – any way you want – with some official in Mr Joranum's group – Mr Joranum will be here in Dahl tomorrow – and just read him my name, my father's name, and the one word. If nothing happens, then I'll stay here till I rot, I suppose, but I don't think that will happen. In fact, I'm sure that they will get me out of here in three seconds and that you'll get a promotion for passing along the information. If you refuse to do this, when they find out I am here – and they will – you will be in the deepest possible trouble. After all, if you know that Yugo Amaryl went off with a big-shot mathematician, just tell yourself that same big-shot mathematician is my father. His name is Hari Seldon.'

The corporal's face showed clearly that the name was not unknown to him.

He said, 'What's the one word you're going to write down?'

'Psychohistory.'

The corporal frowned. 'What's that?'

'That doesn't matter. Just pass it along and see what happens.'

The corporal handed him a small sheet of paper, torn out of a notebook. 'All right. Write it down and we'll see what happens.'

Raych realized that he was trembling. He wanted very much to know what would happen. It depended entirely on who it was that the corporal would talk to and what magic the word would carry with it.

17

Hari Seldon watched the raindrops form on the wrap-around windows of the Imperial ground-car and a sense of nostalgia stabbed at him unbearably.

It was only the second time in his eight years on Trantor that he had been ordered to visit the Emperor in the only open land on the planet – and both times the weather had been bad. The first time, shortly after he had arrived on Trantor, the bad weather had merely irritated him. He had found no novelty in it. His home world of Helicon had its share of storms, after all, particularly in the area where he had been brought up.

But now he had lived for eight years in make-believe weather, in which storms consisted of computerized cloudiness at random intervals, with regular light rains during the sleeping hours. Raging winds were replaced by zephyrs and there were no extremes of heat and cold – merely little changes that made you unzip the front of your shirt once in a while or throw on a light jacket. And he had heard complaints about even so mild a deviation.

But now Hari was seeing real rain coming down drearily from a cold sky – and he had not seen such a thing in years – and he loved it; that was the thing. It reminded him of Helicon, of his youth, of relatively carefree days, and he wondered if he might persuade the driver to take the long way to the Palace.

Impossible! The Emperor wanted to see him and it was a long enough trip by ground-car, even if one went in a straight line with no interfering traffic. The Emperor, of course, would not wait.

It was a different Cleon from the one Seldon had seen eight years before. He had put on about ten pounds and there was a sulkiness about his face. Yet the skin around his eyes and cheeks looked pinched and Hari recognized the results of one too many microadjustments. In a way, Seldon felt sorry for Cleon – for all his might and Imperial sway, the Emperor was powerless against the passage of time.

Once again Cleon met Hari Seldon alone – in the same lavishly furnished room of their first encounter. As was the custom, Seldon waited to be addressed.

After briefly assessing Seldon's appearance, the Emperor said in an ordinary voice, 'Glad to see you, Professor. Let us dispense with formalities, as we did on the former occasion on which I met you.'

'Yes, Sire,' said Seldon stiffly. It was not always safe to be informal, merely because the Emperor ordered you to be so in an effusive moment.

Cleon gestured imperceptibly and at once the room came alive with automation as the table set itself and dishes began to appear. Seldon, confused, could not follow the details.

The Emperor said casually, 'You will dine with me, Seldon?'

It had the formal intonation of a question but the force, somehow, of an order.

'I would be honored, Sire,' said Seldon. He looked around cautiously. He knew very well that one did not (or, at any rate, should not) ask questions of the Emperor, but he saw no way out of it. He said, rather quietly, trying to make it not sound like a question, 'The First Minister will not dine with us?'

'He will not,' said Cleon. 'He has other tasks at this moment and I wish, in any case, to speak to you privately.'

They ate quietly for a while, Cleon gazing at him fixedly and Seldon smiling tentatively. Cleon had no reputation for cruelty or even for irresponsibility, but he could, in theory, have Seldon arrested on some vague charge and, if the Emperor wished to exert his influence, the case might never come to trial. It was always best to avoid notice and at the moment Seldon couldn't manage it.

Surely it had been worse eight years ago, when he had been brought to the Palace under armed guard. – This fact did not make Seldon feel relieved, however.

Then Cleon spoke. 'Seldon,' he said. 'The First Minister is of great use to me, yet I feel that, at times, people may think I do not have a mind of my own. Do you think that?'

'Never, Sire,' said Seldon calmly. No use protesting too much.

'I don't believe you. However, I do have a mind of my own and I recall that when you first came to Trantor you had this psychohistory thing you were playing with.'

'I'm sure you also remember, Sire,' said Seldon softly, 'that I explained at the time it was a mathematical theory without practical application.'

'So you said. Do you still say so?'

'Yes, Sire.'

'Have you been working on it since?'

'On occasion I toy with it, but it comes to nothing. Chaos unfortunately interferes and predictability is not—'

The Emperor interrupted. 'There is a specific problem I wish you to tackle. – Do help yourself to the dessert, Seldon. It is very good.'

'What is the problem, Sire?'

'This man Joranum. Demerzel tells me – oh, so politely – that I cannot arrest this man and I cannot use armed force to crush his followers. He says it will simply make the situation worse.'

'If the First Minister says so, I presume it is so.'

'But I do not want this man Joranum . . . At any rate, I will *not* be his puppet. Demerzel does nothing.'

'I am sure that he is doing what he can, Sire.'

'If he is working to alleviate the problem, he certainly is not keeping me informed.'

'That may be, Sire, out of a natural desire to keep you

above the fray. The First Minister may feel that if Joranum should – if he should—'

'Take over,' said Cleon with a tone of infinite distaste.

'Yes, Sire. It would not be wise to have it appear that you were personally opposed to him. You must remain untouched for the sake of the stability of the Empire.'

'I would much rather assure the stability of the Empire without Joranum. What do you suggest, Seldon?'

'I, Sire?'

'You, Seldon,' said Cleon impatiently. 'Let me say that I don't believe you when you say that psychohistory is just a game. Demerzel stays friendly with you. Do you think I am such an idiot as not to know that? He *expects* something from you. He expects psychohistory from you and since I am no fool, I expect it, too. – Seldon, are you *for* Joranum? The truth!'

'No, Sire, I am not for him. I consider him an utter danger to the Empire.'

'Very well, I believe you. You stopped a potential Joranumite riot at your University grounds single-handedly, I understand.'

'It was pure impulse on my part, Sire.'

'Tell that to fools, not to me. You had worked it out by psychohistory.'

'*Sire!*'

'Don't protest. What are you doing about Joranum? You must be doing something if you are on the side of the Empire.'

'Sire,' said Seldon cautiously, uncertain as to how much the Emperor knew. 'I have sent my son to meet with Joranum in the Dahl Sector.'

'Why?'

'My son is a Dahlite – and shrewd. He may discover something of use to us.'

'May?'

'Only may, Sire.'

'You'll keep me informed?'

'Yes, Sire.'

'And, Seldon, do *not* tell me that psychohistory is just a game, that it does not exist. I do not want to hear that. I expect you to do something about Joranum. What it might be, I can't say, but you must do something. I will *not* have it otherwise. You may go.'

Seldon returned to Streeling University in a far darker mood than when he had left. Cleon had sounded as though he would not accept failure.

It all depended on Raych now.

18

Raych sat in the anteroom of a public building in Dahl into which he had never ventured – never *could* have ventured – as a ragamuffin youth. He felt, in all truth, a little uneasy about it now, as though he were trespassing.

He tried to look calm, trustworthy, lovable.

Dad had told him that this was a quality he carried around with him, but he had never been conscious of it. If it came about naturally, he would probably spoil it by trying too hard to *seem* to be what he really *was*.

He tried relaxing while keeping an eye on the official who was manipulating a computer at the desk. The official was not a Dahlite. He was, in fact, Gambol Deen Namarti, who had been with Joranum at the meeting with Dad that Raych had attended.

Every once in a while, Namarti would look up from his desk and glance at Raych with a hostile glare. This Namarti wasn't buying Raych's lovability. Raych could see that.

Raych did not try to meet Namarti's hostility with a friendly smile. It would have seemed too artificial. He simply waited. He had gotten this far. If Joranum arrived, as he was expected to, Raych would have a chance to speak to him.

Joranum did arrive, sweeping in, smiling his public smile of warmth and confidence. Namarti's hand came up and Joranum stopped. They spoke together in low voices while Raych watched intently and tried in vain to seem as if he wasn't. It seemed plain to Raych that Namarti was arguing against the meeting and Raych bridled a bit at that.

Then Joranum looked at Raych, smiled, and pushed

Namarti to one side. It occurred to Raych that, while Namarti was the brains of the team, it was Joranum who clearly had the charisma.

Joranum strode toward him and held out a plump, slightly moist hand. 'Well well. Professor Seldon's young man. How are you?'

'Fine, thank you, sir.'

'You had some trouble getting here, I understand.'

'Not too much, sir.'

'And you've come with a message from your father, I trust. I hope he is reconsidering his decision and has decided to join me in my great crusade.'

'I don't think so, sir.'

Joranum frowned slightly. 'Are you here without his knowledge?'

'No, sir. He sent me.'

'I see. – Are you hungry, lad?'

'Not at the moment, sir.'

'Then would you mind if I eat? I don't get much time for the ordinary amenities of life,' he said, smiling broadly.

'It's all right with me, sir.'

Together, they moved to a table and sat down. Joranum unwrapped a sandwich and took a bite. His voice slightly muffled, he said, 'And why did he send you, son?'

Raych shrugged. 'I think he thought I might find out something about you that he could use against you. He's heart and soul with First Minister Demerzel.'

'And you're not?'

'No, sir. I'm a Dahlite.'

'I know you are, Mr Seldon, but what does that mean?'

'It means I'm oppressed, so I'm on your side and I want to help you. Of course, I wouldn't want my father to know.'

'There's no reason he should know. How do you propose to help me?' He glanced quickly at Namarti, who was leaning against his desk, listening, with his arms folded and his expression lowering. 'Do you know anything about psychohistory?'

'No, sir. My father don't talk to me about that – and if he did, I wouldn't get it. I don't think he's getting anywhere with that stuff.'

'Are you sure?'

'Sure I'm sure. There's a guy there, Yugo Amaryl, also a Dahlite, who talks about it sometimes. I'm sure nothing is happening.'

'Ah! And can I see Yugo Amaryl sometime, do you suppose?'

'I don't think so. He ain't much for Demerzel, but he's all for my father. He wouldn't cross him.'

'But you would?'

Raych looked unhappy and he muttered stubbornly, 'I'm a Dahlite.'

Joranum cleared his throat. 'Then let me ask you again. How do you propose to help me, young man?'

'I've got something to tell you that maybe you won't believe.'

'Indeed? Try me. If I don't believe it, I will tell you so.'

'It's about First Minister Eto Demerzel.'

'Well?'

Raych looked around uneasily. 'Can anyone hear me?'

'Just Namarti and myself.'

'All right, then listen. This guy Demerzel ain't a guy. He's a robot.'

'What!' exploded Joranum.

Raych felt moved to explain. 'A robot is a mechanical man, sir. He ain't human. He's a machine.'

Namarti broke out passionately, 'Jo-Jo, don't believe that. It's ridiculous.'

But Joranum held up an admonitory hand. His eyes were gleaming. 'Why do you say that?'

'My father was in Mycogen once. He told me all about it. In Mycogen they talk about robots a lot.'

'Yes, I know. At least, I have heard so.'

'The Mycogenians believe that robots were once very

99

common among their ancestors, but they were wiped out.'

Namarti's eyes narrowed. 'But what makes you think that Demerzel is a robot? From what little I have heard of these fantasies, robots are made out of metal, aren't they?'

'That's so,' said Raych earnestly. 'But what I heard is that there were a few robots that look just like human beings and they live forever—'

Namarti shook his head violently. 'Legends! Ridiculous legends! Jo-Jo, why are we listening—'

But Joranum cut him off quickly. 'No, G.D. I want to listen. I've heard these legends, too.'

'But it's nonsense, Jo-Jo.'

'Don't be in such a rush to say "nonsense." And even if it were, people live and die by nonsense. It's not what *is* so much as what people *think* is. – Tell me, young man, putting legends to one side, what makes you think Demerzel is a robot? Let's suppose that robots exist. What is it, then, about Demerzel that makes you say *he* is a robot? Did he tell you so?'

'No, sir,' said Raych.

'Did your father tell you so?' asked Joranum.

'No, sir. It's just my own idea, but I'm sure of it.'

'Why? What makes you so sure?'

'It's just something about him. He doesn't change. He doesn't get older. He doesn't show emotions. Something about him *looks* like he's made of metal.'

Joranum sat back in his chair and looked at Raych for an extended time. It was almost possible to hear his thoughts buzzing.

Finally he said, 'Suppose he *is* a robot, young man. Why should you care? Does it matter to you?'

'Of course it matters to me,' said Raych. 'I'm a human being. I don't want no robot in charge of running the Empire.'

Joranum turned to Namarti with a gesture of eager approval. 'Do you hear that, G.D.? "I'm a human being.

I don't want no robot in charge of running the Empire." Put him on holovision and have him say it. Have him repeat it over and over till it's drummed into every person on Trantor—'

'Hey,' said Raych, finally catching his breath. 'I can't say that on holovision. I can't let my father find out—'

'No, of course not,' said Joranum quickly. 'We couldn't allow that. We'll just use the words. We'll find some other Dahlite. Someone from each of the sectors, each in his own dialect, but always the same message: "I don't want no robot in charge of running the Empire."'

Namarti said, 'And what happens when Demerzel proves he's *not* a robot?'

'Really,' said Joranum. 'How will he do that? It would be impossible for him to do so. Psychologically impossible. What? The great Demerzel, the power behind the throne, the man who has twitched the strings attached to Cleon I all these years and those attached to Cleon's father before him? Will he climb down now and whine to the public that he is, too, a human being? That would be almost as destructive to him as *being* a robot. G.D., we have the villain in a no-win situation and we owe it all to this fine young man here.'

Raych flushed.

Joranum said, 'Raych is your name, isn't it? Once our party is in a position to do so, we won't forget. Dahl will be treated well and you will have a good position with us. You're going to be Dahl's sector leader someday, Raych, and you're not going to regret you've done this. Are you, now?'

'Not on your life,' said Raych fervently.

'In that case, we'll see that you get back to your father. You let him know that we intend him no harm, that we value him greatly. You can tell him you found that out in any way you please. And if you find anything else you think we might be able to use – about psychohistory, in particular, you let us know.'

'You bet. But do you mean it when you say you'll

see to it that Dahl gets some breaks?'

'Absolutely. Equality of sectors, my boy. Equality of worlds. We'll have a new Empire with all the old villainies of privilege and inequality wiped out.'

And Raych nodded his head vigorously. 'That's what I want.'

19

Cleon, Emperor of the Galaxy, was walking hurriedly through the arcade that led from his private quarters in the Small Palace to the offices of the rather tremendous staff that lived in the various annexes of the Imperial Palace, which served as the nerve center of the Empire.

Several of his personal attachés walked after him, with looks of the deepest concern on their faces. The Emperor did not walk to others. He summoned them and they came to him. If he did walk, he never showed signs of haste or emotional trauma. How could he? He was the Emperor and, as such, far more a symbol of all the worlds than a human being.

Yet now he seemed to be a human being. He motioned everyone aside with an impatient wave of his right hand. In his left hand he held a gleaming hologram.

'The First Minister,' he said in an almost strangled voice, not at all like the carefully cultivated tones he had painstakingly assumed along with the throne. 'Where is he?'

And all the high functionaries who were in his way fumbled and gasped and found it impossible to manage coherence. He brushed past them angrily, making them all feel, undoubtedly, as though they were living through a waking nightmare.

Finally he burst into Demerzel's private office, panting slightly, and shouted – literally shouted – *'Demerzel!'*

Demerzel looked up with a trace of surprise and rose smoothly to his feet, for one did not sit in the presence of the Emperor unless specifically invited to. 'Sire?' he said.

And the Emperor slammed the hologram down on Demerzel's desk and said, 'What is this? Will you tell me that?'

Demerzel looked at what the Emperor had given him. It was a beautiful hologram, sharp and alive. One could almost hear the little boy – perhaps ten years old – speaking the words that were included in the caption: 'I don't want no robot in charge of running the Empire.'

Demerzel said quietly, 'Sire, I have received this, too.'

'And who else has?'

'I am under the impression, Sire, that it is a flier that is being widely spread over Trantor.'

'Yes, and do you see the person at whom that brat is looking?' He tapped his Imperial forefinger at it. 'Isn't that you?'

'The resemblance is striking, Sire.'

'Am I wrong in supposing that the whole intent of this *flier*, as you call it, is to accuse you of being a robot?'

'That does seem to be its intention, Sire.'

'And stop me if I'm wrong, but aren't robots the legendary mechanical human beings one finds in – in thrillers and children's stories?'

'The Mycogenians have it as an article of faith, Sire, that robots—'

'I'm not interested in the Mycogenians and their articles of faith. Why are they accusing you of being a robot?'

'Merely a metaphorical point, I'm sure, Sire. They wish to portray me as a man of no heart, whose views are the conscienceless calculations of a machine.'

'That's too subtle, Demerzel. I'm no fool.' He tapped the hologram again. 'They're trying to make people believe you are really a robot.'

'We can scarcely prevent it, Sire, if people choose to believe that.'

'We cannot afford it. It detracts from the dignity of your office. Worse than that, it detracts from the dignity of the Emperor. The implication is that I – *I* would choose as my First Minister a mechanical man. That is impossible to endure. See here, Demerzel, aren't there *laws* that forbid the denigration of public officers of the Empire?'

'Yes, there are – and quite severe ones, Sire, dating back to the great Law Codes of Aburamis.'

'And to denigrate the Emperor himself is a capital offense, is it not?'

'Death is the punishment, Sire. Yes.'

'Well, this not only denigrates you, it denigrates me – and whoever did it should be executed forthwith. It was this Joranum, of course, who is behind it.'

'Undoubtedly, Sire, but proving it might be rather difficult.'

'Nonsense! I have proof enough! I want an execution.'

'The trouble is, Sire, that the laws of denigration are virtually never enforced. Not in this century, certainly.'

'And that is why society is becoming so unstable and the Empire is being shaken to its roots. The laws are still in the books, so enforce them.'

Demerzel said, 'Consider, Sire, if that would be wise. It would make you appear to be a tyrant and a despot. Your rule has been a most successful one through kindness and mildness—'

'Yes and see where that got me. Let's have them fear me for a change, rather than love me – in this fashion.'

'I strongly recommend that you not do so, Sire. It may be the spark that will start a rebellion.'

'What would you do, then? Go before the people and say, "Look at me. I am no robot." '

'No, Sire, for as you say that would destroy my dignity and, worse yet, yours.'

'Then?'

'I am not certain, Sire. I have not yet thought it through.'

'Not yet thought it through? – Get in touch with Seldon.'

'Sire?'

'What is so difficult to understand about my order? *Get in touch with Seldon!*'

'You wish me to summon him to the Palace, Sire?'

'No, there's no time for that. I presume you can set up a sealed communication line between us that cannot be tapped.'

'Certainly, Sire.'

'Then do so. Now!'

20

Seldon lacked Demerzel's self-possession, being, as he was, only flesh and blood. The summons to his office and the sudden faint glow and tingle of the scrambler field was indication enough that something unusual was taking place. He had spoken by sealed lines before but never to the full extent of Imperial security.

He expected some government official to clear the way for Demerzel himself. Considering the slowly mounting tumult of the robot flier, he could expect nothing less.

But he did not expect anything more, either, and when the image of the Emperor himself, with the faint glitter of the scramble field outlining him, stepped into his office (so to speak), Seldon fell back in his seat, mouth wide open, and could make only ineffectual attempts to rise.

Cleon motioned him impatiently to keep his seat. 'You must know what's going on, Seldon.'

'Do you mean about the robot flier, Sire?'

'That's exactly what I mean. What's to be done?'

Seldon, despite the permission to remain seated, finally rose. 'There's more, Sire. Joranum is organizing rallies all over Trantor on the robot issue. At least, that's what I hear on the newscasts.'

'It hasn't reached *me* yet. Of course not. Why should the Emperor know what is going on?'

'It is not for the Emperor to be concerned, Sire. I'm sure that the First Minister—'

'The First Minister will do nothing, not even keep me informed. I turn to you and your psychohistory. *Tell me what to do.*'

'Sire?'

'I'm not going to play your game, Seldon. You've been working on psychohistory for eight years. The First

Minister tells me I must not take legal action against Joranum. What, then, do I do?'

Seldon stuttered. 'S-sire! Nothing!'

'You have nothing to tell me?'

'No, Sire. That is not what I mean. I mean you must do nothing. *Nothing!* The First Minister is quite right if he tells you that you must not take legal action. It will make things worse.'

'Very well. What will make things better?'

'For you to do nothing. For the First Minister to do nothing. For the government to allow Joranum to do just as he pleases.'

'How will that help?'

And Seldon said, trying to suppress the note of desperation in his voice, 'That will soon be seen.'

The Emperor seemed to deflate suddenly, as though all the anger and indignation had been drawn out of him. He said, 'Ah! I understand! You have the situation well in hand!'

'Sire! I have not said that—'

'You need not say. I have heard enough. You have the situation well in hand, but I want results. I still have the Imperial Guard and the armed forces. They will be loyal and, if it comes to actual disorders, I will not hesitate. But I will give you your chance first.'

His image flashed out and Seldon sat there, simply staring at the empty space where the image had been.

Ever since the first unhappy moment when he had mentioned psychohistory at the Decennial Convention eight years before, he had had to face the fact that he didn't have what he had incautiously talked about.

All he had was the wild ghost of some thoughts – and what Yugo Amaryl called intuition.

21

In two days Joranum had swept Trantor, partly by himself, mostly through his lieutenants. As Hari muttered to Dors, it was a campaign that had all the marks of military efficiency. 'He was born to be a war admiral in the old days,' he said. 'He's wasted on politics.'

And Dors said, 'Wasted? At this rate, he's going to make himself First Minister in a week and, if he wishes, Emperor in two weeks. There are reports that some of the military garrisons are cheering him.'

Seldon shook his head. 'It will collapse, Dors.'

'What? Joranum's party or the Empire?'

'Joranum's party. The story of the robot has created an instant stir, especially with the effective use of that flier, but a little thought, a little coolness, and the public will see it for the ridiculous accusation it is.'

'But, Hari,' said Dors tightly, 'you needn't pretend with *me*. It is *not* a ridiculous story. How could Joranum possibly have found out that Demerzel is a robot?'

'Oh, *that*! Why, Raych told him so.'

'Raych!'

'That's right. He did his job perfectly and got back safely with the promise of being made Dahl's sector leader someday. Of course he was believed. I knew he would be.'

'You mean you told Raych that Demerzel was a robot and had him pass on the news to Joranum?' Dors looked utterly horrified.

'No, I couldn't do that. You know I couldn't tell Raych – or anyone – that Demerzel was a robot. I told Raych as firmly as I could that Demerzel was *not* a robot – and even that much was difficult. But I did ask him to tell Joranum that he was. He is under the firm impression that he lied to Joranum.'

'But why, Hari? Why?'

'It's not psychohistory, I'll tell you that. Don't you join the Emperor in thinking I'm a magician. I just wanted Joranum to believe that Demerzel was a robot. He's a Mycogenian by birth, so he was filled from youth with his culture's tales of robots. Therefore, he was predisposed to believe and he was convinced that the public would believe with him.'

'Well, won't they?'

'Not really. After the initial shock is over, they will realize that it's madcap fiction – or they will think so. I've persuaded Demerzel that he must give a talk on sub-etheric holovision to be broadcast to key portions of the Empire and to every sector on Trantor. He is to talk about everything but the robot issue. There are enough crises, we all know, to fill such a talk. People will listen and will hear nothing about robots. Then, at the end, he will be asked about the flier and he need not answer a word. He need only laugh.'

'Laugh? I've never known Demerzel to laugh. He almost never smiles.'

'This time, Dors, he'll laugh. It is the one thing that no one ever visualizes a robot doing. You've seen robots in holographic fantasies, haven't you? They're always pictured as literal-minded, unemotional, inhuman – That's what people are sure to expect. So Demerzel need merely laugh. And on top of that – Do you remember Sunmaster Fourteen, the religious leader of Mycogen?'

'Of course I do. Literal-minded, unemotional, inhuman. He's never laughed, either.'

'And he won't this time. I've done a lot of work on this Joranum matter since I had that little set-to at the Field. I know Joranum's real name. I know where he was born, who his parents were, where he had his early training, and all of it, with documentary proof, has gone to Sunmaster Fourteen. I don't think Sunmaster likes Breakaways.'

110

'But I thought you said you don't wish to spark off bigotry.'

'I don't. If I had given the information to the holovision people, I would have, but I've given it to Sunmaster, where, after all, it belongs.'

'And he'll start off the bigotry.'

'Of course he won't. No one on Trantor would pay any attention to Sunmaster – whatever he might say.'

'Then what's the point?'

'Well, that's what we'll see, Dors. I don't have a psychohistorical analysis of the situation. I don't even know if one is possible. I just hope that my judgment is right.'

22

Eto Demerzel laughed.

It was not the first time. He sat there, with Hari Seldon and Dors Venabili in a tap-free room, and, every once in a while, at a signal from Hari, he would laugh. Sometimes he leaned back and laughed uproariously, but Seldon shook his head. 'That would never sound convincing.'

So Demerzel smiled and then laughed with dignity and Seldon made a face. 'I'm stumped,' he said. 'It's no use trying to tell you funny stories. You get the point only intellectually. You will simply have to memorize the sound.'

Dors said, 'Use a holographic laughtrack.'

'No! That would never be Demerzel. That's a bunch of idiots being paid to yak. It's not what I want. Try again, Demerzel.'

Demerzel tried again until Seldon said, 'All right, then, memorize that sound and reproduce it when you're asked the question. You've got to look amused. You can't make the sound of laughing, however proficient, with a grave face. Smile a little, just a little. Pull back the corner of your mouth.' Slowly Demerzel's mouth widened into a grin. 'Not bad. Can you make your eyes twinkle?'

'What do you mean, "twinkle," ' said Dors indignantly. 'No one makes their eyes twinkle. That's a metaphorical expression.'

'No, it's not,' said Seldon. 'There's the hint of tears in the eye – sadness, joy, surprise, whatever – and the reflection of light from that hint of fluid is what does it.'

'Well, do you seriously expect Demerzel to produce tears?'

And Demerzel said, matter-of-factly, 'My eyes do

produce tears for general cleansing – never in excess. Perhaps, though, if I imagine my eyes to be slightly irritated—'

'Try it,' said Seldon. 'It can't hurt.'

And so it was that when the talk on subetheric holovision was over and the words were streaking out to millions of worlds at thousands of times the effective speed of light – words that were grave, matter-of-fact, informative, and without rhetorical embellishment – and that discussed everything but robots – Demerzel declared himself ready to answer questions.

He did not have to wait long. The very first question was: 'Mr First Minister, are you a robot?'

Demerzel simply stared calmly and let the tension build. Then he smiled, his body shook slightly, and he laughed. It was not a loud uproarious laugh, but it was a rich one, the laugh of someone enjoying a moment of fantasy. It was infectious. The audience tittered and then laughed along with him.

Demerzel waited for the laughter to die down and then, eyes twinkling, said, 'Must I really answer that? Is it necessary to do so?' He was still smiling as the screen darkened.

23

'I'm sure it worked,' said Seldon. 'Naturally we won't have a complete reversal instantly. It takes time. But things are moving in the right direction now. I noticed that when I stopped Namarti's talk at the University Field. The audience was with him until I faced him and showed spunk against odds. The audience began to change sides at once.'

'Do you think this is an analogous situation?' asked Dors dubiously.

'Of course. If I don't have psychohistory, I can use analogy – and the brains I was born with, I suppose. There was the First Minister, beleaguered on all sides with the accusation, and he faced it down with a smile and a laugh, the most nonrobot thing he could have done, so that in itself was an answer to the question. Of course sympathy began to slide to his side. Nothing would stop that. But that's only the beginning. We have to wait for Sunmaster Fourteen and hear what he has to say.'

'Are you confident there, too?'

'Absolutely.'

24

Tennis was one of Hari's favorite sports, but he preferred to play rather than watch others. He watched with impatience, therefore, as the Emperor Cleon, dressed in sports fashion, loped across the court to return the ball. It was Imperial tennis, actually, so-called because it was a favorite of Emperors, a version of the game in which a computerized racket was used that could alter its angle slightly with appropriate pressures on the handle. Hari had tried to develop the technique on several occasions but found that mastering the computerized racket would take a great deal of practice – and Hari Seldon's time was far too precious for what was clearly a trivial pursuit.

Cleon placed the ball in a nonreturnable position and won the game. He trotted off the court to the careful applause of the functionaries who were watching and Seldon said to him, 'Congratulations, Sire. You played a marvelous game.'

Cleon said indifferently, 'Do you think so, Seldon? They're all so careful to let me win. I get no pleasure out of it.'

Seldon said, 'In that case, Sire, you might order your opponents to play harder.'

'It wouldn't help. They'd be careful to lose anyway. And if they did win, I would get even less pleasure out of losing than out of winning meaninglessly. Being an Emperor has its woes, Seldon. Joranum would have found that out – if he had ever succeeded in becoming one.'

He disappeared into his private shower facility and emerged in due time, scrubbed and dried and dressed rather more formally.

'And now, Seldon,' he said, waving all the others

away, 'the tennis court is as private a place as we can find and the weather is glorious, so let us not go indoors. I have read the Mycogenian message of this Sunmaster Fourteen. Will it do?'

'Entirely, Sire. As you have read, Joranum was denounced as a Mycogenian Breakaway and is accused of blasphemy in the strongest terms.'

'And does that finish him?'

'It diminishes his importance fatally, Sire. There are few who accept the mad story of the First Minister's robothood now. Furthermore, Joranum is revealed as a liar and a poseur and, worse, one who was caught at it.'

'Caught at it, yes,' said Cleon thoughtfully. 'You mean that merely to be underhanded is to be sly and that may be admirable, while to be caught is to be stupid and that is never admirable.'

'You put it succinctly, Sire.'

'Then Joranum is no longer a danger.'

'We can't be certain of that, Sire. He may recover, even now. He still has an organization and some of his followers will remain loyal. History yields examples of men and women who have come back after disasters as great as this one – or greater.'

'In that case, let us execute him, Seldon.'

Seldon shook his head. 'That would be inadvisable, Sire. You would not want to create a martyr or to make yourself appear to be a despot.'

Cleon frowned. 'Now you sound like Demerzel. Whenever I wish to take forceful action, he mutters the word "despot." There have been Emperors before me who have taken forceful action and who have been admired as a result and have been considered strong and decisive.'

'Undoubtedly, Sire, but we live in troubled times. Nor is execution necessary. You can accomplish your purpose in a way that will make you seem enlightened *and* benevolent.'

'*Seem* enlightened?'

116

'*Be* enlightened, Sire. I misspoke. To execute Joranum would be to take revenge, which might be regarded as ignoble. As Emperor, however, you have a kindly – even paternal – attitude toward the beliefs of all your people. You make no distinctions, for you are the Emperor of all alike.'

'What is it you're saying?'

'I mean, Sire, that Joranum has offended the sensibilities of the Mycogenians and you are horrified at his sacrilege, he having been born one of them. What better can you do but hand Joranum over to the Mycogenians and allow them to take care of him? You will be applauded for your proper Imperial concern.'

'And the Mycogenians will execute him, then?'

'They may, Sire. Their laws against blasphemy are excessively severe. At best, they will imprison him for life at hard labor.'

Cleon smiled. 'Very good. I get the credit for humanity and tolerance and they do the dirty work.'

'They would, Sire, if you actually handed Joranum over to them. That would, however, still create a martyr.'

'Now you confuse me. What would you have me do?'

'Give Joranum the choice. Say that your regard for the welfare of all the people in your Empire urges you to hand him over to the Mycogenians for trial but that your humanity fears the Mycogenians may be too severe. Therefore, as an alternative, he may choose to be banished to Nishaya, the small and secluded world from which he *claimed* to have come, to live the rest of his life in obscurity and peace. You'll see to it that he's kept under guard, of course.'

'And that will take care of things?'

'Certainly. Joranum would be committing virtual suicide if he chose to be returned to Mycogen – and he doesn't strike me as the suicidal type. He will certainly choose Nishaya, and though that is the sensible course of action, it is also an unheroic one. As a refugee in Nishaya, he can scarcely lead any movement designed to take over the Empire. His following is sure to disintegrate. They could follow a martyr with holy zeal, but it would be difficult, indeed, to follow a coward.'

'Astonishing! How did you manage all this, Seldon?' There was a distinct note of admiration in Cleon's voice.

Seldon said, 'Well, it seemed reasonable to suppose—'

'Never mind,' said Cleon abruptly. 'I don't suppose you'll tell me the truth or that I would understand you if you did, but I'll tell you this much. Demerzel is leaving office. This last crisis has proved to be too much for him and I agree with him that it is time for him to retire. But I can't do without a First Minister and, from this moment onward, you are he.'

'*Sire!*' exclaimed Seldon in mingled astonishment and horror.

'First Minister Hari Seldon,' said Cleon calmly, 'The Emperor wishes it.'

25

'Don't be alarmed,' said Demerzel. 'It was my suggestion. I've been here too long and the succession of crises has reached the point where the consideration of the Three Laws paralyzes me. You are the logical successor.'

'I am *not* the logical successor,' said Seldon hotly. 'What do *I* know about running an Empire? The Emperor is foolish enough to believe that I solved this crisis by psychohistory. Of course I didn't.'

'That doesn't matter, Hari. If he *believes* you have the psychohistorical answer, he will follow you eagerly and that will make you a good First Minister.'

'He may follow me straight into destruction.'

'I feel that your good sense – or *intuition* – will keep you on target . . . with or without psychohistory.'

'But what will I do without you – Daneel?'

'Thank you for calling me that. I am Demerzel no more, only Daneel. As to what you will do without me – Suppose you try to put into practice some of Joranum's ideas of equality and social justice? He may not have meant them – he may have used them only as ways of capturing allegiance – but they are not bad ideas in themselves. And find ways of having Raych help you in that. He clung to you against his own attraction to Joranum's ideas and he must feel torn and half a traitor. Show him he isn't. In addition, you can work all the harder on psychohistory, for the Emperor will be there with you, heart and soul.'

'But what will *you* do, Daneel?'

'I have other things in the Galaxy to which I must attend. There is still the Zeroth Law and I must labor for the good of humanity, insofar as I can determine what that might be. And, Hari—'

119

'Yes, Daneel.'

'You still have Dors.'

Seldon nodded. 'Yes, I still have Dors.' He paused for a moment before grasping Daneel's firm hand with his own. 'Good-bye, Daneel.'

'Good-bye, Hari,' Daneel replied.

And with that, the robot turned, his heavy First Minister's robe rustling as he walked away, head up, back ramrod straight, along the Palace hallway.

Seldon stood there for a few minutes after Daneel had gone, lost in thought. Suddenly he began moving in the direction of the First Minister's apartment. Seldon had one more thing to tell Daneel – the most important thing of all.

Seldon hesitated in the softly lit hallway before entering. But the room was empty. The dark robe was draped over a chair. The First Minister's chambers echoed Hari's last words to the robot: 'Good-bye, my friend.' Eto Demerzel was gone; R. Daneel Olivaw had vanished.

Part II

CLEON I

CLEON I – . . . Though often receiving panegyrics for being the last Emperor under whom the First Galactic Empire was reasonably united and reasonably prosperous, the quarter-century reign of Cleon I was one of continuous decline. This cannot be viewed as his direct responsibility, for the Decline of the Empire was based on political and economic factors too strong for anyone to deal with at the time. He was fortunate in his selection of First Ministers – Eto Demerzel and then Hari Seldon, in whose development of psychohistory the Emperor never lost faith. Cleon and Seldon, as the objects of the final Joranumite Conspiracy, with its bizarre climax—

ENCYCLOPEDIA GALACTICA

1

Mandell Gruber was a happy man. He seemed so to Hari Seldon, certainly. Seldon stopped his morning constitutional to watch him.

Gruber, perhaps in his late forties, a few years younger than Seldon, was a bit gnarled from his continuing work in the Imperial Palace grounds, but he had a cheerful, smoothly shaven face, topped by a pink skull, not much of which was hidden by his thin sandy hair. He whistled softly to himself as he inspected the leaves of the bushes for any signs of insect infestation.

He was not the Chief Gardener, of course. The Chief Gardener of the Imperial Palace grounds was a high functionary who had a palatial office in one of the buildings of the enormous Imperial complex, with an army of men and women under him. The chances are he did not inspect the Palace grounds more often than once or twice a year.

Gruber was but one of that army. His title, Seldon knew, was Gardener First-Class and it had been well earned, with thirty years of faithful service.

Seldon called to him as he paused on the perfectly level crushed gravel walk, 'Another marvelous day, Gruber.'

Gruber looked up and his eyes twinkled. 'Yes, indeed, First Minister, and it's sorry I am for those who be cooped up indoors.'

'You mean as I am about to be.'

'There's not much about you, First Minister, for people to sorrow over, but if you're disappearing into those buildings on a day like this, it's a bit of sorrow that we fortunate few can feel for you.'

'I thank you for your sympathy, Gruber, but you know we have forty billion Trantorians under the dome. Are you sorry for all of them?'

'Indeed, I am. I am grateful I am not of Trantorian extraction myself so that I could qualify as a gardener. There be few of us on this world that work in the open, but here I be, one of the fortunate few.'

'The weather isn't always this ideal.'

'That is true. And I have been out here in the sluicing rains and the whistling winds. Still, as long as you dress fittingly . . . Look—' And Gruber spread his arms open, wide as his smile, as if to embrace the vast expanse of the Palace grounds. 'I have my friends – the trees and the lawns and all the animal life forms to keep me company – and growth to encourage in geometric form, even in the winter. Have you ever *seen* the geometry of the grounds, First Minister?'

'I am looking at it right now, am I not?'

'I mean the plans spread out so you can really appreciate it all – and marvelous it is, too. It was planned by Tapper Savand, over a hundred years ago, and it has been little changed since. Tapper was a great horti-culturist, the greatest – and he came from my planet.'

'That was Anacreon, wasn't it?'

'Indeed. A far-off world near the edge of the Galaxy, where there is still wilderness and life can be sweet. I came here when I was still an ear-wet lad, when the present Chief Gardener took power under the old Emperor. Of course, now they're talking of redesigning the grounds.' Gruber sighed deeply and shook his head. 'That would be a mistake. They are just right as they are now properly proportioned, well balanced, pleasing to the eye and spirit. But it is true that in history, the grounds have oc-casionally been redesigned. Emperors grow tired of the old and are always seeking the new, as if new is somehow always better. Our present Emperor, may he live long, has been planning the redesign with the Chief Gardener. At least, that is the word that runs from gardener to gardener.' This last he added quickly, as if abashed at spreading Palace gossip.

'It might not happen soon.'

'I hope not, First Minister. Please, if you have the chance to take some time from all the heart-stopping work you must be after doing, study the design of the grounds. It is a rare beauty and, if I have my way, there should not be a leaf moved out of place, nor a flower, nor a rabbit, anywhere in all these hundreds of square kilometers.'

Seldon smiled. 'You are a dedicated man, Gruber. I would not be surprised if someday you were Chief Gardener.'

'May Fate protect me from that. The Chief Gardener breathes no fresh air, sees no natural sights, and forgets all he has learned of nature. He lives there' – Gruber pointed scornfully – 'and I think he no longer knows a bush from a stream unless one of his underlings leads him out and places his hand on one or dips it into the other.'

For a moment it seemed as though Gruber would expectorate his scorn, but he could not find any place on which he could bear to spit.

Seldon laughed quietly. 'Gruber, it's good to talk to you. When I am overcome with the duties of the day, it is pleasant to take a few moments to listen to your philosophy of life.'

'Ah, First Minister, it is no philosopher I am. My schooling was very sketchy.'

'You don't need schooling to be a philosopher. Just an active mind and experience with life. Take care, Gruber. I just might have you promoted.'

'If you but leave me as I am, First Minister, you will have my total gratitude.'

Seldon was smiling as he moved on, but the smile faded as his mind turned once more to his current problems. Ten years as First Minister – and if Gruber knew how heartily sick Seldon was of his position, his sympathy would rise to enormous heights. Could Gruber grasp the fact that Seldon's progress in the techniques of psychohistory showed the promise of facing him with an unbearable dilemma?

2

Seldon's thoughtful stroll across the grounds was the epitome of peace. It was hard to believe here, in the midst of the Emperor's immediate domain, that he was on a world that, except for this area, was totally enclosed by a dome. Here, in this spot, he might be on his home world of Helicon or on Gruber's home world of Anacreon.

Of course, the sense of peace was an illusion. The grounds were guarded – thick with security.

Once, a thousand years ago, the Imperial Palace grounds – much less palatial, much less differentiated from a world only beginning to construct domes over individual regions – had been open to all citizens and the Emperor himself could walk along the paths, unguarded, nodding his head in greeting to his subjects.

No more. Now security was in place and no one from Trantor itself could possibly invade the grounds. That did not remove the danger, however, for that, when it came, came from discontented Imperial functionaries and from corrupt and suborned soldiers. It was *within* the grounds that the Emperor and his staff were most in danger. What would have happened if, on that occasion, nearly ten years before, Seldon had not been accompanied by Dors Venabili?

It had been in his first year as First Minister and it was only natural, he supposed (after the fact), that there would be jealous heart-burning over his unexpected choice for the post. Many others, far better qualified in training – in years of service and, most of all, in their own eyes – could view the appointment with anger. They did not know of psychohistory or of the importance the Emperor attached to it and the easiest way to correct the situation was to corrupt one of the sworn protectors of the First Minister.

Dors must have been more suspicious than Seldon himself was. Or else, with Demerzel's disappearance from the scene, her instructions to guard Seldon had been strengthened. The truth was that, for the first few years of his First Ministership, she was at his side more often than not.

And on the late afternoon of a warm sunny day, Dors noted the glint of the westering sun – a sun never seen under Trantor's dome – on the metal of a blaster.

'Down, Hari!' she cried suddenly and her legs crushed the grass as she raced toward the sergeant.

'Give me that blaster, Sergeant,' she said tightly.

The would-be assassin, momentarily immobilized by the unexpected sight of a woman running toward him, now reacted quickly, raising the drawn blaster.

But she was already at him, her hand enclosing his right wrist in a steely grip and lifting his arm high. 'Drop it,' she said through clenched teeth.

The sergeant's face twisted as he attempted to yank his arm loose.

'Don't try, Sergeant,' said Dors. 'My knee is three inches from your groin and, if you so much as blink, your genitals will be history. So just freeze. That's right. Okay, now open your hand. If you don't drop the blaster right *now*, I will shatter your arm.'

A gardener came running up with a rake. Dors motioned him away. The sergeant dropped the blaster to the ground.

Seldon had arrived. 'I'll take over, Dors.'

'You will *not*. Get in among those trees and take the blaster with you. Others may be involved – and ready to act.'

Dors had not loosened her grip on the sergeant. She said, 'Now, Sergeant, I want the name of whoever it was who persuaded you to make an attempt on the First

Minister's life – and the name of everyone else who is in this with you.'

The sergeant was silent.

'Don't be foolish,' said Dors. 'Speak!' She twisted his arm and he sank down to his knees. She put her shoe on his neck. 'If you think silence becomes you, I can crush your larynx and you will be silent forever. And even before that, I am going to damage you *badly* – I won't leave one bone unbroken. You had better talk.'

The sergeant talked.

Later Seldon had said to her, 'How could you do that, Dors? I never believed you capable of such . . . *violence*.'

Dors said coolly, 'I did not actually hurt him much, Hari. The threat was sufficient. In any case, your safety was paramount.'

'You should have let me take care of him.'

'Why? To salvage your masculine pride? You wouldn't have been fast enough, for one thing. Secondly, no matter what you would have succeeded in doing, you are a man and it would have been expected. I am a woman and women, in popular thought, are not considered as ferocious as men and most, in general, do not have the strength to do what I did. The story will improve in the telling and everyone will be terrified of me. No one will dare to try to harm you for fear of me.'

'For fear of you and for fear of execution. The sergeant and his cohorts are to be killed, you know.'

At this, an anguished look clouded Dors's usually composed visage, as if she could not stand the thought of the traitorous sergeant being put to death, even though he would have cut down her beloved Hari without a second thought.

'But,' she exclaimed, 'there is no need to execute the conspirators. Exile will do the job.'

'No, it won't,' said Seldon. 'It's too late. Cleon will hear of nothing but executions. I can quote him – if you wish.'

'You mean he's already made up his mind?'

'At once. I told him that exile or imprisonment would be all that was necessary, but he said no. He said, "Every time I try to solve a problem by direct and forceful action, first Demerzel and then you talk of 'despotism' and 'tyranny.' But this is *my* Palace. These are *my* grounds. These are *my* guardsmen. My safety depends on the security of this place and the loyalty of my people. Do you think that any deviation from absolute loyalty can be met with anything but instant death? How else would you be safe? How else would *I* be safe?"'

'I said there would have to be a trial. "Of course," he said, "a short military trial and I don't expect a single vote for anything but execution. I shall make that quite clear."'

Dors looked appalled. 'You're taking this very quietly. Do you agree with the Emperor?'

Reluctantly Seldon nodded. 'I do.'

'Because there was an attempt on *your* life. Have you abandoned your principles for mere revenge?'

'Now, Dors, I'm not a vengeful person. However, it was not myself alone at risk or even the Emperor. If there is anything that the recent history of the Empire shows us, it is that Emperors come and go. It is psychohistory that must be protected. Undoubtedly, even if something happens to me, psychohistory will someday be developed, but the Empire is falling fast and we cannot wait – and only I have advanced far enough to obtain the necessary techniques in time.'

'Then you should teach what you know to others,' said Dors gravely.

'I'm doing so. Yugo Amaryl is a reasonable successor and I have gathered a group of technicians who will someday be useful, but they won't be as—' He paused.

'They won't be as good as you – as wise, as capable? Really?'

'I happen to think so,' said Seldon. 'And I happen to be human. Psychohistory is mine and, if I can possibly manage it, I want the credit.'

'Human,' sighed Dors, shaking her head almost sadly.

The executions went through. No such purge had been seen in over a century. Two Ministers, five officials of lower ranks, and four soldiers, including the hapless sergeant, met their deaths. Every guardsman who could not withstand the most rigorous investigation was relieved of duty and exiled to the remote Outer Worlds.

Since then, there had been no whisper of disloyalty and so notorious had become the care with which the First Minister was guarded, to say nothing of the terrifying woman – called 'The Tiger Woman' by many – who watched over him, that it was no longer necessary for Dors to accompany him everywhere. Her invisible presence was an adequate shield and the Emperor Cleon enjoyed nearly ten years of quiet and absolute security.

Now, however, psychohistory was finally reaching the point where predictions, of a sort, could be made and, as Seldon crossed the grounds in his passage from his office (First Minister) to his laboratory (psychohistorian), he was uneasily aware of the likelihood that this era of peace might be coming to an end.

3

Yet, even so, Hari Seldon could not repress the surge of satisfaction that he felt as he entered his laboratory.

How things had changed.

It had begun twenty years earlier with his own doodlings on his second-rate Heliconian computer. It was then that the first hint of what was to become parachaotic math came to him in a cloudy fashion.

Then there were the years at Streeling University, when he and Yugo Amaryl, working together, attempted to renormalize the equations, get rid of the inconvenient infinities, and find a way around the worst of the chaotic effects. They made very little progress, indeed.

But now, after ten years as First Minister, he had a whole floor of the latest computers and a whole staff of people working on a large variety of problems.

Of necessity, none of his staff – except for Yugo and himself, of course – could really know much more than the immediate problem they were dealing with. Each of them worked with only a small ravine or outcropping on the gigantic mountain range of psychohistory that only Seldon and Amaryl could see as a mountain range – and even they could see it only dimly, its peaks hidden in clouds, its slopes veiled by mist.

Dors Venabili was right, of course. He would have to begin initiating his people into the entire mystery. The technique was getting well beyond what only two men could handle. And Seldon was aging. Even if he could look forward to some additional decades, the years of his most fruitful breakthroughs were surely behind him.

Even Amaryl would be thirty-nine within a month and, though that was still young, it was perhaps not overly young for a mathematician – and he had been working on the problem almost as long as Seldon himself. His capacity for new and tangential thinking might be dwindling, too.

Amaryl had seen him enter and was now approaching. Seldon watched him fondly. Amaryl was as much a Dahlite as Seldon's foster son, Raych, was, and yet Amaryl, despite his muscular physique and short stature, did not seem Dahlite at all. He lacked the mustache, he lacked the accent, he lacked, it would seem, Dahlite consciousness of any kind. He had even been impervious to the lure of Jo-Jo Joranum, who had appealed so thoroughly to the people of Dahl.

It was as though Amaryl recognized no sectoral patriotism, no planetary patriotism, not even Imperial patriotism. He belonged – completely and entirely – to psychohistory.

Seldon felt a twinge of insufficiency. He himself remained conscious of his first two decades on Helicon and there was no way he could keep from thinking of himself as a Heliconian. He wondered if that consciousness was not sure to betray him by causing him to skew his thinking about psychohistory. Ideally, to use psychohistory properly, one should be above worlds and sectors and deal only with humanity in the faceless abstract – and this was what Amaryl did.

And Seldon didn't, he admitted to himself, sighing silently.

Amaryl said, 'We *are* making progress, Hari, I suppose.'

'You suppose, Yugo? Merely suppose?'

'I don't want to jump into outer space without a suit.' He said this quite seriously (he did not have much of a sense of humor, Seldon knew) and they moved into their private office. It was small, but it was also well shielded.

Amaryl sat down and crossed his legs. He said, 'Your latest scheme for getting around chaos may be working in part – at the cost of sharpness, of course.'

'Of course. What we gain in the straightaway, we lose

134

in the roundabouts. That's the way the Universe works. We've just got to fool it somehow.'

'We've fooled it a little bit. It's like looking through frosted glass.'

'Better than the years we spent trying to look through lead.'

Amaryl muttered something to himself, then said, 'We can catch glimmers of light and dark.'

'Explain!'

'I can't, but I have the Prime Radiant, which I've been working on like a – a—'

'Try lamec. That's an animal – a beast of burden – we have on Helicon. It doesn't exist on Trantor.'

'If the lamec works hard, then that is what my work on the Prime Radiant has been like.'

He pressed the security keypad on his desk and a drawer unsealed and slid open noiselessly. He took out a dark opaque cube that Seldon scrutinized with interest. Seldon himself had worked out the Prime Radiant's circuitry, but Amaryl had put it together – a clever man with his hands was Amaryl.

The room darkened and equations and relationships shimmered in the air. Numbers spread out beneath them, hovering just above the desk surface, as if suspended by invisible marionette strings.

Seldon said, 'Wonderful. Someday, if we live long enough, we'll have the Prime Radiant produce a river of mathematical symbolism that will chart past and future history. In it we can find currents and rivulets and work out ways of changing them in order to make them follow other currents and rivulets that we would prefer.'

'Yes,' said Amaryl dryly, 'if we can manage to live with the knowledge that the actions we take, which we will mean for the best, may turn out to be for the worst.'

'Believe me, Yugo, I never go to bed at night without that particular thought gnawing at me. Still, we haven't come to it yet. All we have is this – which, as you say, is no more than seeing light and dark fuzzily through frosted glass.'

'True enough.'

'And what is it you think you see, Yugo?' Seldon watched Amaryl closely, a little grimly. He was gaining weight, getting just a bit pudgy. He spent too much time bent over the computers (and now over the Prime Radiant) – and not enough in physical activity. And, though he saw a woman now and then, Seldon knew, he had never married. A mistake! Even a workaholic is forced to take time off to satisfy a mate, to take care of the needs of children.

Seldon thought of his own still-trim figure and of the manner in which Dors strove to make him keep it that way.

Amaryl said, 'What do I see? The Empire is in trouble.'

'The Empire is always in trouble.'

'Yes, but it's more specific. There's a possibility that we may have trouble at the center.'

'At Trantor?'

'I presume. Or at the Periphery. Either there will be a bad situation here – perhaps civil war – or the outlying Outer Worlds will begin to break away.'

'Surely it doesn't take psychohistory to point out these possibilities.'

'The interesting thing is that there seems a mutual exclusivity. One or the other. The likelihood of both together is very small. Here! Look! It's your own mathematics. Observe!'

They bent over the Prime Radiant display for a long time.

Seldon said finally, 'I fail to see *why* the two should be mutually exclusive.'

'So do I, Hari, but where's the value of psychohistory if it shows us only what we would see anyway? This is showing us something we *wouldn't* see. What it doesn't show us is, first, which alternative is better, and second,

136

what to do to make the better come to pass and depress the possibility of the worse.'

Seldon pursed his lips, then said slowly, 'I can tell you which alternative is preferable. Let the Periphery go and keep Trantor.'

'Really?'

'No question. We must keep Trantor stable, if for no other reason than that we're here.'

'Surely our own comfort isn't the decisive point.'

'No, but psychohistory is. What good will it do us to keep the Periphery intact if conditions on Trantor force us to stop work on psychohistory? I don't say that we'll be killed, but we may be unable to work. The development of psychohistory is on what our fate will depend. As for the Empire, if the Periphery secedes it will only begin a disintegration that may take a long time to reach the core.'

'Even if you're right, Hari, what do we do to keep Trantor stable?'

'To begin with, we have to think about it.'

A silence fell between them and then Seldon said, 'Thinking doesn't make me happy. What if the Empire is altogether on the wrong track and has been for all its history? I think of that every time I talk to Gruber.'

'Who's Gruber?'

'Mandell Gruber. A gardener.'

'Oh. The one who came running up with the rake to rescue you at the time of the assassination attempt?'

'Yes. I've always been grateful to him for that. He had only a rake against possibly other conspirators with blasters. That's loyalty. Anyhow, talking to him is like a breath of fresh air. I can't spend all my time talking to court officials and to psychohistorians.'

'Thank you.'

'Come! You know what I mean. Gruber likes the open. He wants the wind and the rain and the biting cold and everything else that raw weather can bring to him. I miss it myself sometimes.'

'I don't. I wouldn't care if I never go out there.'

'You were brought up under the dome – but suppose the Empire consisted of simple unindustrialized worlds, living by herding and farming, with thin populations and empty spaces. Wouldn't we all be better off?'

'It sounds horrible to me.'

'I found some spare time to check it as best I could. It seems to me it's a case of unstable equilibrium. A thinly populated world of the type I describe either grows moribund and impoverished, falling off into an uncultured near-animal level – or it industrializes. It is standing on a narrow point and topples over in either direction and, as it just so happens, almost every world in the Galaxy has fallen over into industrialization.'

'Because that's better.'

'Maybe. But it can't continue forever. We're watching the results of the overtoppling now. The Empire cannot exist for much longer because it has – it has overheated. I can't think of any other expression. What will follow we don't know. If, through psychohistory, we manage to prevent the Fall or, more likely, force a recovery after the Fall, is that merely to ensure another period of overheating? Is that the only future humanity has, to push the boulder, like Sisyphus, up to the top of a hill, only to see it roll to the bottom again?'

'Who's Sisyphus?'

'A character in a primitive myth. Yugo, you must do more reading.'

Amaryl shrugged. 'So I can learn about Sisyphus? Not important. Perhaps psychohistory will show us a path to an entirely new society, one altogether different from anything we have seen, one that would be stable and desirable.'

'I hope so,' sighed Seldon. 'I hope so, but there's no sign of it yet. For the near future, we will just have to labor to let the Periphery go. That will mark the beginning of the Fall of the Galactic Empire.'

138

4

'And so I said,' said Hari Seldon, '"That will mark the beginning of the Fall of the Galactic Empire." And so it will, Dors.'

Dors listened, tight-lipped. She accepted Seldon's First Ministership as she accepted everything – calmly. Her only mission was to protect him and his psychohistory, but that task, she well knew, was made harder by his position. The best security was to go unnoticed and, as long as the Spaceship-and-Sun, the symbol of the Empire, shone down upon Seldon, all of the physical barriers in existence would be unsatisfactory.

The luxury in which they now lived – the careful shielding from spy beams, as well as from physical interference; the advantages to her own historical research of being able to make use of nearly unlimited funds – did not satisfy her. She would gladly have exchanged it all for their old quarters at Streeling University. Or, better yet, for a nameless apartment in a nameless sector where no one knew them.

'That's all very well, Hari dear,' she said, 'but it's not enough.'

'What's not enough?'

'The information you're giving me. You say we might lose the Periphery. How? Why?'

Seldon smiled briefly. 'How nice it would be to know, Dors, but psychohistory is not yet at the stage where it could tell us.'

'In your opinion, then. Is it the ambition of local far-away governors to declare themselves independent?'

'That's a factor, certainly. It's happened in past history – as you know far better than I – but never for long. Maybe this time it will be permanent.'

'Because the Empire is weaker?'

'Yes, because trade flows less freely than it once did, because communications are stiffer than they once were, because the governors in the Periphery are, in actual fact, closer to independence than they have ever been. If one of them arises with particular ambitions—'

'Can you tell which one it might be?'

'Not in the least. All we can force out of psychohistory at this stage is the definite knowledge that *if* a governor of unusual ability and ambition arises, he would find conditions more suitable for his purposes than he would have in the past. It could be other things, too – some great natural disaster or some sudden civil war between two distant Outer World coalitions. None of that can be precisely predicted as of now, but we can tell that anything of the sort that happens will have more serious consequences than it would have had a century ago.'

'But if you don't know a little more precisely what will happen in the Periphery, how can you so guide actions as to make sure the Periphery goes, rather than Trantor?'

'By keeping a close eye on both and trying to stabilize Trantor and *not* trying to stabilize the Periphery. We can't expect psychohistory to order events automatically without much greater knowledge of its workings, so we have to make use of constant manual controls, so to speak. In days to come, the technique will be refined and the need for manual control will decrease.'

'But that,' said Dors, 'is in days to come. Right?'

'Right. And even that is only a hope.'

'And just what kind of instabilities threaten Trantor – if we hang on to the Periphery?'

'The same possibilities – economic and social factors, natural disasters, ambitious rivalries among high officials. And something more. I have described the Empire to Yugo as being overheated – and Trantor is the most overheated portion of all. It seems to be breaking down. The infrastructure – water supply, heating, waste disposal, fuel lines, everything – seems to be having unusual problems and that's something I've been turning my attention to more and more lately.'

'What about the death of the Emperor?'

Seldon spread his hands. 'That happens inevitably, but Cleon is in good health. He's only my age, which I wish was younger, but he isn't too old. His son is totally inadequate for the succession, but there will be enough claimants. More than enough to cause trouble and make his death distressing, but it might not prove a total catastrophe – in the historic sense.'

'Let's say his assassination, then.'

Seldon looked up nervously. 'Don't say that. Even if we're shielded, don't use the word.'

'Hari, don't be foolish. It's an eventuality that must be reckoned with. There was a time when the Joranumites might have taken power and, if they had, the Emperor, one way or another—'

'Probably not. He would have been more useful as a figurehead. And in any case, forget it. Joranum died last year on Nishaya, a rather pathetic figure.'

'He had followers.'

'Of course. Everyone has followers. Did you ever come across the Globalist party on my native world of Helicon in your studies of the early history of the Kingdom of Trantor and of the Galactic Empire?'

'No, I haven't. I don't want to hurt your feelings, Hari, but I don't recall coming across any piece of history in which Helicon played a role.'

'I'm not hurt, Dors. Happy the world without a history, I always say. – In any case, about twenty-four hundred years ago, there arose a group of people on Helicon who were quite convinced that Helicon was the only inhabited globe in the Universe. Helicon *was* the Universe and beyond it there was only a solid sphere of sky speckled with tiny stars.'

'How could they believe that?' said Dors. 'They were part of the Empire, I presume.'

'Yes, but Globalists insisted that all evidence to the

effect that the Empire existed was either illusion or deliberate deceit, that Imperial emissaries and officials were Heliconians playing a part for some reason. They were absolutely immune to reason.'

'And what happened?'

'I suppose it's always pleasant to think that your particular world is *the* world. At their peak, the Globalists may have persuaded 10 percent of the population of the planet to be part of the movement. Only 10 percent, but they were a vehement minority that drowned out the indifferent majority and threatened to take over.'

'But they didn't, did they?'

'No, they didn't. What happened was that Globalism caused a diminishing of Imperial trade and the Heliconian economy slid into the doldrums. When the belief began to affect the pocketbooks of the population, it lost popularity rapidly. The rise and fall puzzled many at the time, but psychohistory, I'm sure, would have shown it to be inevitable and would have made it unnecessary to give it any thought.'

'I see. But, Hari, what is the point of this story? I presume there's some connection with what we were discussing.'

'The connection is that such movements never completely die, no matter how ridiculous their tenets may seem to sane people. Right now, on Helicon, *right now* there are still Globalists. Not many, but every once in a while seventy or eighty of them get together in what they call a Global Congress and take enormous pleasure in talking to each other about Globalism. – Well, it is only ten years since the Joranumite movement seemed such a terrible threat on this world and it would not be at all surprising if there weren't still some remnants left. There may still be some remnants a thousand years from now.'

'Isn't it possible that a remnant may be dangerous?'

'I doubt it. It was Jo-Jo's charisma that made the movement dangerous – and he's dead. He didn't even die a heroic death or one that was in any way remarkable; he just withered away and died in exile, a broken man.'

Dors stood up and walked the length of the room quickly, swinging her arms at her sides and clenching her fists. She returned and stood before the seated Seldon.

'Hari,' she said, 'let me speak my mind. If psychohistory points to the possibility of serious disturbances on Trantor, then if there are Joranumites still left, they may still be plotting the Emperor's death.'

Seldon laughed nervously. 'You jump at shadows, Dors. Relax.'

But he found that he could not dismiss what she had said quite that easily.

5

The Wye Sector had a tradition of opposition to the Entun Dynasty of Cleon I that had been ruling the Empire for over two centuries. The opposition dated back to a time when the line of Mayors of Wye had contributed members who had served as Emperor. The Wyan Dynasty had neither lasted long nor had it been conspicuously successful, but the people and rulers of Wye found it difficult to forget that they had once been – however imperfectly and temporarily – supreme. The brief period when Rashelle, as the self-appointed Mayor of Wye, had challenged the Empire, eighteen years earlier, had added both to Wye's pride and to its frustration.

All this made it reasonable that the small band of leading conspirators should feel as safe in Wye as they would feel anywhere on Trantor.

Five of them sat around a table in a room in a run-down portion of the sector. The room was poorly furnished but well shielded.

In a chair, which by its marginal superiority in quality to the others, sat the man who might well be judged to be the leader. He had a thin face, a sallow complexion, and a wide mouth with lips so pale as to be nearly invisible. There was a touch of gray in his hair, but his eyes burned with an inextinguishable anger.

He was staring at the man seated exactly opposite him – distinctly older and softer, his hair almost white, his plump cheeks tending to quiver when he spoke.

The leader said sharply, 'Well? It is quite apparent that you have done nothing. Explain that!'

The older man said, 'I am an old Joranumite, Namarti. Why do I have to explain my actions?'

Gambol Deen Namarti, once the right-hand man of Laskin 'Jo-Jo' Joranum, said, 'There are many old Joranumites. Some are incompetent, some are soft, some have forgotten. Being an old Joranumite may mean no more than that one is an old fool.'

The older man sat back in his chair. 'Are you calling me an old fool? Me? Kaspal Kaspalov? I was with Jo-Jo when you had not yet joined the party, when you were a ragged nothing in search of a cause.'

'I am not calling you a fool,' said Namarti sharply. 'I say simply that some old Joranumites are fools. You have a chance now to show me that you are not one of them.'

'My association with Jo-Jo—'

'Forget that. He's dead!'

'I should think his spirit lives on.'

'If that thought will help us in our fight, then his spirit lives on. But to others – not to us. We know he made mistakes.'

'I deny that.'

'Don't insist on making a hero out of a mere man who made mistakes. He thought he could move the Empire by the strength of oratory alone, by words—'

'History shows that words have moved mountains in the past.'

'Not Joranum's words, obviously, because he made mistakes. He hid his Mycogenian origins far too clumsily. Worse, he let himself be tricked into accusing First Minister Eto Demerzel of being a robot. I warned him against that accusation, but he wouldn't listen – and it destroyed him. Now let's start fresh, shall we? Whatever use we make of Joranum's memory for outsiders, let us not ourselves be transfixed by it.'

Kaspalov sat silent. The other three transferred their gaze from Namarti to Kaspalov and back, content to let Namarti carry the weight of the discussion.

'With Joranum's exile to Nishaya, the Joranumite movement fell apart and seemed to vanish,' said Namarti harshly. 'It would, indeed, have vanished – but for me.

Bit by bit and rubble by rubble, I rebuilt it into a network that extends over all of Trantor. You know this, I take it.'

'I know it, Chief,' mumbled Kaspalov. The use of the title made it plain that Kaspalov was seeking reconciliation.

Namarti smiled tightly. He did not insist on the title, but he always enjoyed hearing it used. He said, 'You're part of this network and you have your duties.'

Kaspalov stirred. He was clearly debating with himself internally and finally he said slowly, 'You tell me, Chief, that you warned Joranum against accusing the old First Minister of being a robot. You say he didn't listen, but at least you had your say. May I have the same privilege of pointing out what I think is a mistake and have you listen to me as Joranum listened to you, even if you, like he, don't take the advice given you?'

'Of course you can speak your piece, Kaspalov. You are here in order that you might do so. What is your point?'

'These new tactics of ours, Chief, are a mistake. They create disruption and do damage.'

'Of course! They are designed to do that.' Namarti stirred in his seat, controlling his anger with an effort. 'Joranum tried persuasion. It didn't work. We will bring Trantor down by *action*.'

'For how long? And at what cost?'

'For as long as it takes – and at very little cost, actually. A power stoppage here, a water break there, a sewage backup, an air-conditioning halt. Inconvenience and discomfort – that's all it means.'

Kaspalov shook his head. 'These things are cumulative.'

'Of course, Kaspalov, and we want public dismay and resentment to be cumulative, too. Listen, Kaspalov. The Empire is decaying. Everyone knows that. Everyone capable of intelligent thought knows that. The technology will fail here and there, even if we do nothing. We're just helping it along a little.'

'It's dangerous, Chief. Trantor's infrastructure is incredibly complicated. A careless push may bring it down in ruins. Pull the wrong string and Trantor may topple like a house of cards.'

'It hasn't so far.'

'It may in the future. And what if the people find out that we are behind it? They would tear us apart. There would be no need to call in the security establishment or the armed forces. Mobs would destroy us.'

'How would they ever learn enough to blame us? The natural target for the people's resentment will be the government – the Emperor's advisers. They will never look beyond that.'

'And how do we live with ourselves, knowing what we have done?'

This last was asked in a whisper, the old man clearly moved by strong emotion. Kaspalov looked pleadingly across the table at his leader, the man to whom he had sworn allegiance. He had done so in the belief that Namarti would truly continue to bear the standard of freedom passed on by Jo-Jo Joranum; now Kaspalov wondered if this is how Jo-Jo would have wanted his dream to come to pass.

Namarti clucked his tongue, much as a reproving parent does when confronting an errant child.

'Kaspalov, you can't seriously be turning sentimental on us, are you? Once we are in power, we will pick up the pieces and rebuild. We will gather in the people with all of Joranum's old talk of popular participation in government, with greater representation, and when we are firmly in power we will establish a more efficient and forceful government. We will then have a better Trantor and a stronger Empire. We will set up some sort of discussion system whereby representatives of other worlds can talk themselves into a daze – but *we* will do the governing.'

Kaspalov sat there, irresolute.

Namarti smiled joylessly. 'You are not certain? We can't lose. It's been working perfectly and it will continue working perfectly. The Emperor doesn't know what's going on. He hasn't the faintest notion. And his First Minister is a mathematician. He ruined Joranum, true, but since then he has done nothing.'

'He has something called – called—'

'Forget it. Joranum attached a great deal of importance to it, but it was a part of his being Mycogenian, like his robot mania. This mathematician has *nothing*—'

'Historical psychoanalysis or something like that. I heard Joranum once say—'

'*Forget* it. Just do your part. You handle the ventilation in the Anemoria Sector, don't you? Very well, then. Have it misfunction in a manner of your choosing. It either shuts down so that the humidity rises or it produces a peculiar odor or something else. None of this will kill anyone, so don't get yourself into a fever of virtuous guilt. You will simply make people uncomfortable and raise the general level of discomfort and annoyance. Can we depend on you?'

'But what would only be discomfort and annoyance to the young and healthy may be more than that to infants, the aged, and the sick . . .'

'Are you going to insist that no one at all must be hurt?'

Kaspalov mumbled something.

Namarti said, 'It's impossible to do *anything* with a guarantee that no one at all will be hurt. You just do your job. Do it in such a way that you hurt as few as possible – if your conscience insists upon it – but *do it!*'

Kaspalov said, 'Look! I have one thing more to say, Chief.'

'Then say it,' said Namarti wearily.

'We can spend years poking at the infrastructure. The time must come when you take advantage of gathering dissatisfaction to seize the government. How do you intend to do that?'

'You want to know exactly how we'll do it?'

'Yes. The faster we strike, the more limited the damage, the more efficiently the surgery is performed.'

Namarti said slowly, 'I have not yet decided on the

nature of this "surgical strike." But it will come. Until then, will you do your part?'

Kaspalov nodded his head in resignation. 'Yes, Chief.'

'Well then, go,' said Namarti with a sharp gesture of dismissal.

Kaspalov rose, turned, and left. Namarti watched him go. He said to the man at his right, 'Kaspalov is not to be trusted. He has sold out and it's only so that he can betray us that he wants to know my plans for the future. Take care of him.'

The other nodded and all three left, leaving Namarti alone in the room. He switched off the glowing wall panels, leaving only a lonely square in the ceiling to provide the light that would keep him from being entirely in the darkness.

He thought: Every chain has weak links that must be eliminated. We have had to do this in the past and the result is that we have an organization that is untouchable.

And in the dimness, he smiled, twisting his face into a kind of feral joy. After all, the network extended even into the Palace itself – not quite firmly, not quite reliably, but it was there. And it would be strengthened.

6

The weather was holding up over the undomed area of the Imperial Palace grounds – warm and sunny.

It didn't often happen. Hari remembered Dors telling him once how this particular area with its cold winters and frequent rains had been chosen as the site.

'It wasn't actually *chosen*,' she said. 'It was a family estate of the Morovian family in the early days of the Kingdom of Trantor. When the Kingdom became an Empire, there were numerous sites where the Emperor could live – summer resorts, winter places, sports lodges, beach properties. And, as the planet was slowly domed, one reigning Emperor, living here, liked it so much that it remained undomed. And, just because it was the *only* area left undomed, it became special – a place apart – and that uniqueness appealed to the next Emperor . . . and the next . . . and the next . . . And so, a tradition was born.'

And as always, when hearing something like that, Seldon would think: And how would psychohistory handle this? Would it predict that one area would remain undomed but be absolutely unable to say which area? Could it go even so far? Could it predict that several areas would remain undomed or none – and be wrong? How could it account for the personal likes and dislikes of an Emperor who happened to be on the throne at the crucial time and who made a decision in a moment of whimsy and nothing more. That way lay chaos – and madness.

Cleon I was clearly enjoying the good weather.

'I'm getting old, Seldon,' he said. 'I don't have to tell you that. We're the same age, you and I. Surely it's a sign of age when I don't have the impulse to play tennis or go fishing, even though they've newly restocked the lake, but am willing to walk gently over the pathways.'

He was eating nuts as he spoke, which resembled what on Seldon's native world of Helicon would have been called pumpkin seeds, but which were larger and a little less delicate in taste. Cleon cracked them gently between his teeth, peeled the thin shells and popped the kernels into his mouth.

Seldon did not like the taste particularly but, of course, when he was offered some by the Emperor, he accepted them and ate a few.

The Emperor had a number of shells in his hand and looked vaguely around for a receptacle of some sort that he could use for disposal. He saw none, but he did notice a gardener standing not far away, his body at attention (as it should be in the Imperial presence) and his head respectfully bowed.

Cleon said, 'Gardener!'

The gardener approached quickly. 'Sire!'

'Get rid of these for me,' he said, tapping the shells into the gardener's hand.

'Yes, Sire.'

Seldon said, 'I have a few, too, Gruber.'

Gruber held out his hand and said, almost shyly, 'Yes, First Minister.'

He hurried away and the Emperor looked after him curiously. 'Do you know the fellow, Seldon?'

'Yes, indeed, Sire. An old friend.'

'The *gardener* is an old friend? What is he? A mathematical colleague fallen on hard times?'

'No, Sire. Perhaps you remember the story. It was the time when' – he cleared his throat, searching for the most tactful way to recall the incident – 'the sergeant threatened my life shortly after I was appointed to my present post through your kindness.'

'The assassination attempt.' Cleon looked up to heaven, as though seeking patience. 'I don't know why everyone is so afraid of that word.'

'Perhaps,' said Seldon smoothly, slightly despising himself for the ease with which he had become able to flatter, 'the rest of us are more perturbed at the possibility of something untoward happening to our Emperor than you yourself are.'

Cleon smiled ironically. 'I dare say. And what has this to do with Gruber? Is that his name?'

'Yes, Sire. Mandell Gruber. I'm sure you will recall, if you cast your mind back, that there was a gardener who came rushing up with a rake to defend me against the armed sergeant.'

'Ah yes. Was that fellow the gardener who did that?'

'He was the man, Sire. I've considered him a friend ever since and I meet him almost every time I am on the grounds. I think he watches for me, feels proprietary toward me. And, of course, I feel kindly toward him.'

'I don't blame you. – And while we're on the subject, how is your formidable lady, Dr Venabili? I don't see her often.'

'She's a historian, Sire. Lost in the past.'

'She doesn't frighten you? She'd frighten me. I've been told how she treated that sergeant. One could almost be sorry for him.'

'She grows savage on my behalf, Sire, but has not had occasion to do so lately. It's been very quiet.'

The Emperor looked after the disappearing gardener. 'Have we ever rewarded that man?'

'I have done so, Sire. He has a wife and two daughters and I have arranged that each daughter will have a sum of money put aside for the education of any children she may have.'

'Very good. But he needs a promotion, I think. – Is he a good gardener?'

'Excellent, Sire.'

'The Chief Gardener, Malcomber – I'm not quite sure I remember his name – is getting on and is, perhaps, not up to the job anymore. He is well into his late seventies. Do you think this Gruber might be able to take over?'

'I'm certain he can, Sire, but he likes his present job. It keeps him out in the open in all kinds of weather.'

'A peculiar recommendation for a job. I'm sure he can get used to administration and I *do* need someone for some sort of renewal of the grounds. Hmmm. I must think upon this. Your friend Gruber may be just the man I need. – By the way, Seldon, what did you mean by saying it's been very quiet?'

'I merely meant, Sire, that there has been no sign of discord at the Imperial Court. The unavoidable tendency to intrigue seems to be as near a minimum as it is ever likely to get.'

'You wouldn't say that if you were Emperor, Seldon, and had to contend with all these officials and their complaints. How can you tell me things are quiet when reports seem to reach me every other week of some serious breakdown here and there on Trantor?'

'These things are bound to happen.'

'I don't recall such things happening so frequently in previous years.'

'Perhaps that was because they didn't, Sire. The infrastructure grows older with time. To make the necessary repairs properly would take time, labor, and enormous expense. This is not a time when a rise in taxes will be looked on favorably.'

'There's never any such time. I gather that the people are experiencing serious dissatisfaction over these breakdowns. It must stop and you must see to it, Seldon. What does psychohistory say?'

'It says what common sense says, that everything is growing older.'

'Well, all this is quite spoiling the pleasant day for me. I leave it in your hands, Seldon.'

'Yes, Sire,' said Seldon quietly.

The Emperor strode off and Seldon thought that it was all spoiling the pleasant day for him, too. This breakdown at the center was the alternative he didn't want. But how was he to prevent it and switch the crisis to the Periphery?

Psychohistory didn't say.

7

Raych Seldon felt extraordinarily contented, for it was the first dinner *en famille* that he had had in some months with the two people he thought of as his father and mother. He knew perfectly well that they were not his parents in any biological sense, but it didn't matter. He merely smiled at them with complete love.

The surroundings were not as warm as they had been at Streeling in the old days, when their home had been small and intimate, a virtual gem in the larger setting of the University. Now, unfortunately, nothing could hide the grandeur of the First Minister's Palace suite.

Raych sometimes stared at himself in the mirror and wondered how it could be. He was not tall, only 163 centimeters in height, distinctly shorter than either parent. He was rather stocky but muscular – and not fat, with black hair and the distinctive Dahlite mustache that he kept as dark and as thick as possible.

In the mirror he could still see the street urchin he had once been before the chanciest of great chances had dictated his meeting with Hari and Dors. Seldon had been much younger then and his appearance now made it plain that Raych himself was almost as old now as Seldon had been when they met. Amazingly, Dors had hardly changed at all. She was as sleek and fit as the day Raych had first showed Hari and Dors the way to Mother Rittah's in Billibotton. And he, Raych, born to poverty and misery, was now a member of the civil service, a small cog in the Ministry of Population.

Seldon said, 'How are things going at the Ministry, Raych? Any progress?'

'Some, Dad. The laws are passed. The court decisions are made. Speeches are pronounced. Still, it's difficult to move people. You can preach brotherhood all you want, but no one feels like a brother. What gets me is that the Dahlites are as bad as any of the others. They want to be treated as equals, they say, and so they do, but, given a chance, they have no desire to treat others as equals.'

Dors said, 'It's all but impossible to change people's minds and hearts, Raych. It's enough to try and perhaps eliminate the worst of the injustices.'

'The trouble is,' said Seldon, 'that through most of history, no one's been working on this problem. Human beings have been allowed to fester in the delightful game of I'm-better-than-you and cleaning up that mess isn't easy. If we allow things to follow their own bent and grow worse for a thousand years, we can't complain if it takes, say, a hundred years to work an improvement.'

'Sometimes, Dad,' said Raych, 'I think you gave me this job to punish me.'

Seldon's eyebrows raised. 'What motivation could I have had to punish you?'

'For feeling attracted to Joranum's program of sector equality and for greater popular representation in government.'

'I don't blame you for that. These are attractive suggestions, but you know that Joranum and his gang were using it only as a device to gain power. Afterward—'

'But you had me entrap him, despite my attraction to his views.'

Seldon said, 'It wasn't easy for me to ask you to do that.'

'And now you keep me working at the implementation of Joranum's program, just to show me how hard the task is in reality.'

Seldon said to Dors, 'How do you like that, Dors? The boy attributes to me a kind of sneaky underhandedness that simply isn't part of my character.'

'Surely,' said Dors with the ghost of a smile playing at her lips, 'you are attributing no such thing to your father.'

'Not really. In the ordinary course of life, there's no one

155

straighter than you, Dad. But if you *have* to, you know you can stack the cards. Isn't that what you hope to do with psychohistory?'

Seldon said sadly, 'So far, I've done very little with psychohistory.'

'Too bad. I keep thinking that there is some sort of psychohistorical solution to the problem of human bigotry.'

'Maybe there is, but, if so, I haven't found it.'

When dinner was over, Seldon said, 'You and I, Raych, are going to have a little talk now.'

'Indeed?' said Dors. 'I take it I'm not invited.'

'Ministerial business, Dors.'

'Ministerial nonsense, Hari. You're going to ask the poor boy to do something I wouldn't want him to do.'

Seldon said firmly, 'I'm certainly not going to ask him to do anything *he* doesn't want to do.'

Raych said, 'It's all right, Mom. Let Dad and me have our talk. I promise I'll tell you all about it afterward.'

Dors's eyes rolled upward. 'You two will plead "state secrets." I know it.'

'As a matter of fact,' said Seldon firmly, 'that's exactly what I must discuss. And of the first magnitude. I'm serious, Dors.'

Dors rose, her lips tightening. She left the room with one final injunction. 'Don't throw the boy to the wolves, Hari.'

And after she was gone, Seldon said quietly, 'I'm afraid that throwing you to the wolves is exactly what I'll have to do, Raych.'

8

They faced each other in Seldon's private office, his 'thinking place,' as he called it. There, he had spent uncounted hours trying to think his way past and through the complexities of Imperial and Trantorian government.

He said, 'Have you read much about the recent breakdowns we've been having in planetary services, Raych?'

'Yes,' said Raych, 'but you know, Dad, we've got an old planet here. What we gotta do is get everyone off it, dig the whole thing up, replace everything, add the latest computerizations, and then bring everyone back – or at least half of everyone. Trantor would be much better off with only twenty billion people.'

'Which twenty billion?' asked Seldon, smiling.

'I wish I knew,' said Raych darkly. 'The trouble is, we can't redo the planet, so we just gotta keep patching.'

'I'm afraid so, Raych, but there are some peculiar things about it. Now I want you to check me out. I have some thoughts about this.'

He brought a small sphere out of his pocket.

'What's that?' asked Raych.

'It's a map of Trantor, carefully programmed. Do me a favor, Raych, and clear off this tabletop.'

Seldon placed the sphere more or less in the middle of the table and placed his hand on a keypad in the arm of his desk chair. He used his thumb to close a contact and the light in the room went out while the tabletop glowed with a soft ivory light that seemed about a centimeter deep. The sphere had flattened and expanded to the edges of the table.

The light slowly darkened in spots and took on a pattern. After some thirty seconds, Raych said in surprise, 'It *is* a map of Trantor.'

'Of course. I told you it was. You can't buy anything like this at a sector mall, though. This is one of those gadgets the armed forces play with. It could present Trantor as a sphere, but a planar projection would more clearly show what I want to show.'

'And what is it you want to show, Dad?'

'Well, in the last year or two, there have been breakdowns. As you say, it's an old planet and we've got to expect breakdowns, but they've been coming more frequently and they would seem, almost uniformly, to be the result of human error.'

'Isn't that reasonable?'

'Yes, of course. Within limits. This is true, even where earthquakes are involved.'

'Earthquakes? On Trantor?'

'I admit Trantor is a fairly nonseismic planet – and a good thing, too, because enclosing a world in a dome when the world is going to shake itself badly several times a year and smash a section of that dome would be highly impractical. Your mother says that one of the reasons Trantor, rather than some other world, became the Imperial capital is that is was geologically moribund – that's her unflattering expression. Still, it might be moribund, but it's not dead. There are occasional minor earthquakes – three of them in the last two years.'

'I wasn't aware of that, Dad.'

'Hardly anyone is. The dome isn't a single object. It exists in hundreds of sections, each one of which can be lifted and set ajar to relieve tensions and compressions in case of an earthquake. Since an earthquake, when one does occur, lasts for only ten seconds to a minute, the opening endures only briefly. It comes and goes so rapidly that the Trantorians beneath are not even aware of it. They are much more aware of a mild tremor and a faint rattling of crockery than of the opening and closing of the dome overhead and the slight intrusion of the outside weather – whatever it is.'

'That's good, isn't it?'

'It should be. It's computerized, of course. The onset of an earthquake anywhere sets off the key controls for the opening and closing of that section of the dome so that it opens just before the vibration becomes strong enough to do damage.'

'Still good.'

'But in the case of the three minor earthquakes over the last two years, the dome controls failed in each case. The dome never opened and, in each case, repairs were required. It took some time, it took some money, and the weather controls were less than optimum for a considerable period of time. Now, what, Raych, are the chances that the equipment would have failed in all three cases?'

'Not high?'

'Not high at all. Less than one in a hundred. One can suppose that someone had gimmicked the controls in advance of an earthquake. Now, about once a century, we have a magma leak, which is far more difficult to control – and I'd hate to think of the results if it went unnoticed until it was too late. Fortunately that hasn't happened and isn't likely to, but consider – Here on this map you will find the location of the breakdowns that have plagued us over the past two years and that seem to be attributable to human error, though we haven't once been able to tell to *whom* each might be attributed.'

'That's because everyone is busy protecting his back.'

'I'm afraid you're right. That's a characteristic of any bureaucracy and Trantor's is the largest in history. – But what do you think of the locations?'

The map had lit up with bright little red markings that looked like small pustules covering the land surface of Trantor.

'Well,' said Raych cautiously, 'they seem to be evenly spread.'

'Exactly – and *that's* what's interesting. One would expect that the older sections of Trantor, the longest-domed sections, would have the most decayed infrastructure and would be more liable to events requiring quick human decision and laying the groundwork for possible human error. – I'll superimpose the older sections of Trantor on the map in a bluish color and you'll notice that the breakdowns don't seem to be taking place any oftener on the blue areas.'

'And?'

'And what I think it means, Raych, is that the breakdowns are not of natural origin but are deliberately caused and spread out in this fashion to affect as many people as possible, thus creating a dissatisfaction that is as widespread as possible.'

'It don't seem likely.'

'No? Then let's look at the breakdowns as spread through time rather than through space.'

The blue areas and the red spots disappeared and, for a time, the map of Trantor was blank – and then the markings began to appear and disappear one at a time, here and there.

'Notice,' said Seldon, 'that they don't appear in clumps in time, either. One appears, then another, then another, and so on, almost like the steady ticking of a metronome.'

'Do ya think that's on purpose, too?'

'It must be. Whoever is bringing this about wants to cause as much disruption with as little effort as possible, so there's no use doing two at once, where one will partially cancel the other in the news and in the public consciousness. Each incident must stand out in full irritation.'

The map went out and the lights went on. Seldon returned the sphere, shrunken back to its original size, to his pocket.

Raych said, 'Who would be doing all this?'

Seldon said thoughtfully, 'A few days ago I received a report of a murder in Wye Sector.'

'That's not unusual,' said Raych. 'Even though Wye isn't one of your really lawless sectors, there must be lots of murders there every day.'

'Hundreds,' said Seldon, shaking his head. 'We've had

bad days when the number of deaths by violence on Trantor as a whole approaches the million-a-day mark. Generally there's not much chance of finding every culprit, every murderer. The dead just enter the books as statistics. This one, however, was unusual. The man had been knifed – but unskillfully. He was still alive when found, just barely. He had time to gasp out one word before he died and that word was "Chief."

'That roused a certain curiosity and he was actually identified. He works in Anemoria and we don't know what he was doing in Wye. But some worthy officer managed to dig up the fact that he was an old Joranumite. His name was Kaspal Kaspalov and he is well known to have been one of the intimates of Laskin Joranum. And now he's dead – knifed.'

Raych frowned. 'Do you suspect another Joranumite Conspiracy, Dad? There aren't any Joranumites around anymore.'

'It wasn't long ago that your mother asked me if I thought that the Joranumites were still active and I told her that any odd belief always retained a certain cadre, sometimes for centuries. They're usually not very important, just splinter groups that simply don't count. Still, what if the Joranumites have kept up an organization, what if they have retained a certain strength, what if they are capable of killing someone they consider a traitor in their ranks, and what if they are producing these breakdowns as a preliminary to seizing control?'

'That's an awful lot of "what ifs," Dad.'

'I know that. And I might be totally wrong. The murder happened in Wye and, as it so happens, there have been no infrastructure breakdowns in Wye.'

'What does that prove?'

'It might prove that the center of the conspiracy is in Wye and that the conspirators don't want to make themselves uncomfortable, only the rest of Trantor. It also might mean that it's not the Joranumites at all but members of the old Wyan family who still

161

dream of ruling the Empire once again.'

'Oh boy, Dad. You're building all this on very little.'

'I know. Now suppose it *is* another Joranumite Conspiracy. Joranum had, as his right-hand man, Gambol Deen Namarti. We have no record of Namarti's death, no record of his having left Trantor, no record of his life over the last decade or so. That's not terribly surprising. After all, it's easy to lose one person among forty billion. There was a time in my life when I tried to do just that. Of course, Namarti may be dead. That would be the easiest explanation, but he may not be.'

'What do we do about it?'

Seldon sighed. 'The logical thing would be to turn to the security establishment, but I can't. I don't have Demerzel's presence. He could cow people; I can't. He had a powerful personality; I'm just a – mathematician. I shouldn't be First Minister at all; I'm not cut out for it. And I wouldn't be – if the Emperor weren't fixated on psychohistory to a far greater extent than it deserves.'

'You're kinda whipping yourself, ain't you, Dad?'

'Yes. I suppose I am, but I have a picture of myself going to the security establishment, for instance, with what I have just shown you on the map' – he pointed to the now-empty tabletop – 'and arguing that we were in great danger of some conspiracy of unknown consequence and nature. They would listen solemnly and, after I had left, they would laugh among themselves about "the crazy mathematician" – and then do nothing.'

'Then what do we do about it?' said Raych, returning to the point.

'It's what *you* will do about it, Raych. I need more evidence and I want you to find it for me. I would send your mother, but she won't leave me under any circumstances. I myself can't leave the Palace grounds at this time. Next to Dors and myself, I trust you. More than Dors and myself, in fact. You're still quite young, you're strong, you're a better Heliconian Twister than I ever was, and you're smart.

162

'Mind you, now, I don't want you to risk your life. No heroism, no derring-do. I couldn't face your mother if anything happened to you. Just find out what you can. Perhaps you'll find that Namarti is alive and operating – or dead. Perhaps you'll find out that the Joranumites are an active group – or moribund. Perhaps you'll find out that the Wyan ruling family is active – or not. Any of that would be interesting – but not vital. What I want you to find out is whether the infrastructure breakdowns are of human manufacture, as I think they are, and, far more important still, if they are deliberately caused, what else the conspirators plan to do. It seems to me they must have plans for some major coup and, if so, I must know what that will be.'

Raych said cautiously, 'Do you have some kinda plan to get me started?'

'Yes indeed, Raych. I want you to go down to the area of Wye where Kaspalov was killed. Find out if you can if he was an active Joranumite and see if you can't join a Joranumite cell yourself.'

'Maybe that's possible. I can always pretend to be an old Joranumite. It's true that I was pretty young when Jo-Jo was sounding off, but I was very impressed by his ideas. It's even sorta true.'

'Well yes, but there's one important catch. You might be recognized. After all, you're the son of the First Minister. You have appeared on holovision now and then and you have been interviewed concerning your views on sector equality.'

'Sure, but—'

'No buts, Raych. You'll wear elevated shoes to add three centimeters to your height and we'll have someone show you how to change the shape of your eyebrows and make your face fuller and change the timbre of your voice.'

Raych shrugged. 'A lotta trouble for nothing.'

'*And*,' said Seldon with a distinct quaver, 'you will shave off your mustache.'

Raych's eyes widened and for a moment he sat there in appalled silence. Finally he said in a hoarse whisper, 'Shave my mustache?'

'Clean as a whistle. No one would recognize you without it.'

'But it can't be done. Like cutting off your – Like castration.'

Seldon shook his head. 'It's just a cultural curiosity. Yugo Amaryl is as Dahlite as you are and he wears no mustache.'

'Yugo is a *nut*. I don't think he's alive at all, except for his mathematics.'

'He's a great mathematician and the absence of a mustache does not alter that fact. Besides, it's *not* castration. Your mustache will grow back in two weeks.'

'Two weeks! It'll take two *years* to reach this – this—'

He put his hand up, as though to cover and protect it.

Seldon said inexorably, 'Raych, you have to do it. It's a sacrifice you must make. If you act as my spy *with* your mustache, you may – come to harm. I can't take that chance.'

'I'd *rather* die,' said Raych violently.

'Don't be melodramatic,' said Seldon severely. 'You would *not* rather die and this is something you *must* do. However' – and here he hesitated – 'don't say anything about it to your mother. I will take care of that.'

Raych stared at his father in frustration and then said in a low and despairing tone, 'All right, Dad.'

Seldon said, 'I will get someone to supervise your disguise and then you will go to Wye by air-jet. – Buck up, Raych, it's not the end of the world.'

Raych smiled wanly and Seldon watched him leave, a deeply troubled look on his face. A mustache could easily be regrown, but a son could not. Seldon knew perfectly well that he was sending Raych into danger.

9

We all have our small illusions and Cleon – Emperor of the Galaxy, King of Trantor, and a wide collection of other titles that on rare occasions could be called out in a long sonorous roll – was convinced that he was a person of democratic spirit.

It always angered him when he was warned off a course of action by Demerzel (or, later, by Seldon) on the grounds that such action would be looked on as 'tyrannical' or 'despotic.'

Cleon was not a tyrant or despot by disposition, he was certain; he only wanted to take firm and decisive action.

He spoke many times with nostalgic approval of the days when Emperors could mingle freely with their subjects, but now, of course, when the history of coups and assassinations – actual or attempted – had become a dreary fact of life, the Emperor had, of necessity, been shut off from the world.

It is doubtful that Cleon, who had never in his life met with people except under the most constricted of conditions, would really have felt at home in offhand encounters with strangers, but he always imagined he would enjoy it. He was excited therefore, for the rare chance of talking to one of the underlings on the grounds, to smile and to doff the trappings of Imperial rule for a few minutes. It made him feel democratic.

There was this gardener whom Seldon had spoken of, for instance. It would be fitting, even a pleasure, to reward him belatedly for his loyalty and bravery – and to . do so himself, rather than leaving it to some functionary.

He therefore arranged to meet the fellow in the spacious rose garden, which was in full bloom. That would be appropriate, Cleon thought, but, of course, they would have to bring the gardener there first. It was unthinkable for the Emperor to be made to wait. It is one thing to be democratic, quite another to be inconvenienced.

The gardener was waiting for him among the roses, his eyes wide, his lips trembling. It occurred to Cleon that it was possible that no one had told the man the exact reason for the meeting. Well, he would reassure him in kindly fashion – except that, now he came to think of it, he could not remember the fellow's name.

He turned to one of the officials at his side and said, 'What is the gardener's name?'

'Sire, it is Mandell Gruber. He has been a gardener here for thirty years.'

The Emperor nodded and said, 'Ah, Gruber. How glad I am to meet a worthy and hardworking gardener.'

'Sire,' mumbled Gruber, his teeth chattering. 'I am not a man of many talents, but it is always my best I try to do on behalf of your gracious self.'

'Of course, of course,' said the Emperor, wondering if the gardener suspected him of sarcasm. These men of the lower class lacked the finer feelings that came with refinement and manners, which always made any attempt at democratic display difficult.

Cleon said, 'I have heard from my First Minister of the loyalty with which you once came to his aid and of your skill in taking care of the grounds. The First Minister tells me that he and you are quite friendly.'

'Sire, the First Minister is most gracious to me, but I know my place. I never speak to him unless he speaks first.'

'Quite, Gruber. That shows good manners on your part, but the First Minister, like myself, is a man of democratic impulses and I trust his judgment of people.'

Gruber bowed low.

The Emperor said, 'As you know, Gruber, Chief Gardener Malcomber is quite old and longs to retire. The responsibilities are becoming greater than even he can bear.'

'Sire, the Chief Gardener is much respected by all the gardeners. May he be spared for many years so that we can all come to him for the benefit of his wisdom and judgment.'

'Well said, Gruber,' said the Emperor carelessly, 'but you very well know that that is just mumbo-jumbo. He is not going to be spared, at least not with the strength and wit necessary for the position. He himself requests retirement within the year and I have granted him that. It remains to find a replacement.'

'Oh, Sire, there are fifty men and women in this grand place who could be Chief Gardener.'

'I dare say,' said the Emperor, 'but my choice has fallen upon you.' The Emperor smiled graciously. This was the moment he had been waiting for. Gruber would now, he expected, fall to his knees in an ecstasy of gratitude.

He did not and the Emperor frowned.

Gruber said, 'Sire, it is an honor that is too great for me – entirely.'

'Nonsense,' said Cleon, offended that his judgment should be called into question. 'It is about time that your virtues are recognized. You will no longer have to be exposed to weather of all kinds at all times of the year. You will have the Chief Gardener's office, a fine place, which I will have redecorated for you, and where you can bring your family. – You do have a family, don't you, Gruber?'

'Yes, Sire. A wife and two daughters. And a son-in-law.'

'Very good. You will be very comfortable and you will enjoy your new life, Gruber. You will be indoors, Gruber, and out of the weather, like a true Trantorian.'

'Sire, consider that I am an Anacreonian by upbringing—'

'I have considered, Gruber. All worlds are alike to the

Emperor. It is done. The new job is what you deserved.'

He nodded his head and stalked off. Cleon was satisfied with this latest show of his benevolence. Of course, he could have used a little more gratitude from the fellow, a little more appreciation, but at least the task was done.

And it was much easier to have *this* done than to settle the matter of the failing infrastructure.

Cleon had, in a moment of testiness, declared that whenever a breakdown could be attributed to human error, the human being in question should forthwith be executed.

'Just a few executions,' he said, 'and it will be remarkable how careful everyone will become.'

'I'm afraid, Sire,' Seldon had said, 'that this type of despotic behavior would not accomplish what you wish. It would probably force the workers to go on strike – and if you try to force them back to work, there would then be an insurrection – and if you try to replace them with soldiers, you will find they do not know how to control the machinery, so that breakdowns will begin to take place much more frequently.'

It was no wonder that Cleon turned to the matter of appointing a Chief Gardener with relief.

As for Gruber, he gazed after the departing Emperor with the chill of sheer horror. He was going to be taken from the freedom of the open air and condemned to the constriction of four walls. – Yet how could one refuse the Emperor?

168

10

Raych looked in the mirror of his Wye hotel room somberly (it was a pretty run-down hotel room, but Raych was not supposed to have too many credits). He did not like what he saw. His mustache was gone; his sideburns were shortened; his hair was clipped at the sides and back.

He looked – plucked.

Worse than that. As a result of the change in his facial contours, he looked baby-faced.

It was disgusting.

Nor was he making any headway. Seldon had given him the security reports on Kaspal Kaspalov's death, which he had studied. There wasn't much there. Just that Kaspalov had been murdered and that the local security officers had come up with nothing of importance in connection with that murder. It seemed quite clear that the security officers attached little or no importance to it, anyway.

That was not surprising. In the last century, the crime rate had risen markedly in most worlds, *certainly* in the grandly complex world of Trantor, and nowhere were the local security officers up to the job of doing anything useful about it. In fact, the security establishment had declined in numbers and efficiency everywhere and (while this was hard to prove) had become more corrupt. It was inevitable this should be so, with pay refusing to keep pace with the cost of living. One must *pay* civil officials to keep them honest. Failing that, they would surely make up for their inadequate salaries in other ways.

Seldon had been preaching this doctrine for some years now, but it did no good. There was no way to increase wages without increasing taxes and the populace would not sit still for increased taxes. It seemed they would rather lose ten times the credits in graft.

It was all part (Seldon had said) of the general deterioration of Imperial society over the previous two centuries.

Well, what was Raych to do? He was here at the hotel where Kaspalov had lived during the days immediately before his murder. Somewhere in the hotel there might be someone who had something to do with that – or who knew someone who had.

It seemed to Raych that he must make himself conspicuous. He must show an interest in Kaspalov's death and then someone would get interested in *him* and pick *him* up. It was dangerous, but if he could make himself sound harmless enough, they might not attack him immediately.

Well—

Raych looked at his timeband. There would be people enjoying their predinner aperitifs in the bar. He might as well join them and see what would happen – if anything.

11

In some respects, Wye could be quite puritanical. (This
was true of all the sectors, though the rigidity of one sector might be completely different from the rigidity of
another.) Here, the drinks were not alcoholic but were
synthetically designed to stimulate in other ways. Raych
did not like the taste, finding himself utterly unused to it,
but it meant that he could sip his drink slowly and look
around.

He caught the eye of a young woman several tables
away and had difficulty in looking away. She was attractive and it was clear that Wye's ways were not puritanical in *every* fashion.

After a few moments, the young woman smiled
slightly and rose. She drifted toward Raych's table, while
Raych watched her speculatively. He could scarcely (he
thought with marked regret) afford a side adventure just
now.

She stopped for a moment when she reached Raych
and then let herself slide smoothly into an adjacent chair.

'Hello,' she said. 'You don't look like a regular here.'

Raych smiled. 'I'm not. Do you know all the regulars?'

'Just about,' she said, unembarrassed. 'My name is
Manella. What's yours?'

Raych was more regretful than ever. She was quite
tall, taller than he himself was without his heels –
something he always found attractive – had a milky complexion, and long, softly wavy hair that had distinct
glints of dark red in it. Her clothing was not too garish
and she might, if she had tried a little harder, have passed
as a respectable woman of the not-too-hardworking class.

Raych said, 'My name doesn't matter. I don't have
many credits.'

'Oh. Too bad.' Manella made a face. 'Can't you get a few?'

'I'd like to. I need a job. Do you know of any?'

'What kind of job?'

Raych shrugged. 'I don't have any experience in anything fancy, but I ain't proud.'

Manella looked at him thoughtfully. 'I'll tell you what, Mr Nameless. Sometimes it doesn't take any credits at all.'

Raych froze at once. He had been successful enough with women, but with his mustache – his mustache. What could she see in his baby face?

He said, 'Tell you what. I had a friend living here a couple of weeks ago and I can't find him. Since you know all the regulars, maybe you know him. His name is Kaspalov.' He raised his voice slightly. 'Kaspal Kaspalov.'

Manella stared at him blankly and shook her head. 'I don't know anybody by that name.'

'Too bad. He was a Joranumite and so am I.' Again, a blank look. 'Do you know what a Joranumite is?'

She shook her head. 'N-no. I've heard the word, but I don't know what it means. Is it some kind of job?'

Raych felt disappointed.

He said, 'It would take too long to explain.'

It sounded like a dismissal and, after a moment of uncertainty, Manella rose and drifted away. She did not smile and Raych was a little surprised that she had remained as long as she did.

(Well, Seldon had always insisted that Raych had the capacity to inspire affection – but surely not in a businesswoman of this sort. For them, payment was the thing.)

His eyes followed Manella automatically as she stopped at another table, where a man was seated by himself. He was of early middle age, with butter-yellow hair, slicked back. He was very smooth-shaven, but it seemed to Raych that he could have used a beard, his chin being too prominent and a bit asymmetric.

Apparently Manella had no better luck with this

beardless one. A few words were exchanged and she moved on. Too bad, but surely it was impossible for her to fail often. She was unquestionably desirable.

Raych found himself thinking, quite involuntarily, of what the upshot would be if he, after all, could – And then Raych realized that he had been joined by someone else. It was a man this time. It was, in fact, the man to whom Manella had just spoken. He was astonished that his own preoccupation had allowed him to be thus approached and, in effect, caught by surprise. He couldn't very well afford this sort of thing.

The man looked at him with a glint of curiosity in his eyes. 'You were just talking to a friend of mine.'

Raych could not help smiling broadly. 'She's a friendly person.'

'Yes, she is. And a *good* friend of mine. I couldn't help overhearing what you said to her.'

'Wasn't nothing wrong, I think.'

'Not at all, but you called yourself a Joranumite.'

Raych's heart jumped. His remark to Manella had hit dead-center after all. It had meant nothing to her, but it seemed to mean something to her 'friend.'

Did that mean he was on the road now? Or merely in trouble?

173

Raych did his best to size up his new companion, without
allowing his own face to lose its smooth naïveté. The man
had sharp greenish eyes and his right hand clenched
almost threateningly into a fist as it rested on the table.

Raych looked owlishly at the other and waited.

Again, the man said, 'I understand you call yourself a
Joranumite.'

Raych did his best to look uneasy. It was not difficult.
He said, 'Why do you ask, mister?'

'Because I don't think you're old enough.'

'I'm old enough. I used to watch Jo-Jo Joranum's
speeches on holovision.'

'Can you quote them?'

Raych shrugged. 'No, but I got the idea.'

'You're a brave young man to talk openly about being
a Joranumite. Some people don't like that.'

'I'm told there are lots of Joranumites in Wye.'

'That may be. Is that why you came here?'

'I'm looking for a job. Maybe another Joranumite
would help me.'

'There are Joranumites in Dahl, too. Where are you
from?'

There was no question that he recognized Raych's
accent. That could not be disguised.

He said, 'I was born in Millimaru, but I lived mostly
in Dahl when I was growing up.'

'Doing what?'

'Nothing much. Going to school some.'

'And why are you a Joranumite?'

Raych let himself heat up a bit. He couldn't have lived
in down-trodden, discriminated-against Dahl without
having obvious reasons for being a Joranumite. He said,

'Because I think there should be more representative government in the Empire, more participation by the people, and more equality among the sectors and the worlds. Doesn't anyone with brains and a heart think that?'

'And you want to see the Emperorship abolished?'

Raych paused. One could get away with a great deal in the way of subversive statements, but anything overtly anti-Emperor was stepping outside the bounds. He said, 'I ain't saying that. I believe in the Emperor, but ruling a whole Empire is too much for one man.'

'It isn't one man. There's a whole Imperial bureaucracy. What do you think of Hari Seldon, the First Minister?'

'Don't think nothing about him. Don't know about him.'

'All you know is that people should be more represented in the affairs of government. Is that right?'

Raych allowed himself to look confused. 'That's what Jo-Jo Joranum used to say. I don't know what you call it. I heard someone once call it "democracy," but I don't know what that means.'

'Democracy is something that some worlds have tried. Some still do. I don't know that those worlds are run better than other worlds. So you're a democrat?'

'Is that what you call it?' Raych let his head sink, as if in deep thought. 'I feel more at home as a Joranumite.'

'Of course, as a Dahlite—'

'I just lived there awhile.'

'—you're all for people's equalities and such things. The Dahlites, being an oppressed group, would naturally think in that fashion.'

'I hear that Wye is pretty strong in Joranumite thinking. *They're* not oppressed.'

'Different reason. The old Wye Mayors always wanted to be Emperors. Did you know that?'

Raych shook his head.

'Eighteen years ago,' said the man, 'Mayor Rashelle

175

nearly carried through a coup in that direction. So the Wyans are rebels, not so much Joranumite as anti-Cleon.'

Raych said, 'I don't know nothing about that. I ain't against the Emperor.'

'But you are for popular representation, aren't you? Do you think that some sort of elected assembly could run the Galactic Empire without bogging down in politics and partisan bickering? Without paralysis?'

Raych said, 'Huh? I don't understand.'

'Do you think a great many people could come to some decision quickly in times of emergency? Or would they just sit around and argue?'

'I don't know, but it doesn't seem right that just a few people should have all the say over all the worlds.'

'Are you willing to fight for your beliefs? Or do you just like to talk about them?'

'No one asked me to do any fighting,' said Raych.

'Suppose someone did. How important do you think your beliefs about democracy – or Joranumite philosophy – are?'

'I'd fight for them – if I thought it would do any good.'

'There's a brave lad. So you came to Wye to fight for your beliefs.'

'No,' said Raych uncomfortably, 'I can't say I did. I came to look for a job, sir. It ain't easy to find no jobs these days – and I ain't got no credits. A guy's gotta live.'

'I agree. What's your name?'

The question shot out without warning, but Raych was ready for it. 'Planchet, sir.'

'First or last name?'

'Only name, as far as I know.'

'You have no credits and, I gather, very little education.'

'Afraid so.'

'And no experience at any specialized job?'

'I ain't worked much, but I'm willing.'

'All right. I'll tell you what, Planchet.' He took a small

176

white triangle out of his pocket and pressed it in such a way as to produce a printed message on it. Then he rubbed his thumb across it, freezing it. 'I'll tell you where to go. You take this with you and it may get you a job.'

Raych took the card and glanced at it. The signals seemed to fluoresce, but Raych could not read them. He looked at the other man warily. 'What if they think I stole it?'

'It can't be stolen. It has my sign on it and now it has your name.'

'What if they ask me who you are?'

'They won't. – You say you want a job. There's your chance. I don't guarantee it, but there's your chance.' He gave him another card. 'This is where to go.' Raych could read this one.

'Thank you,' he mumbled.

The man made little dismissing gestures with his hand.

Raych rose and left – and wondered what he was getting into.

13

Up and down. Up and down. Up and down.

Gleb Andorin watched Gambol Deen Namarti trudging up and down. Namarti was obviously unable to sit still under the driving force of the violence of his passion.

Andorin thought: He's not the brightest man in the Empire or even in the movement, not the shrewdest, certainly not the most capable of rational thought. He has to be held back constantly – but he's driven as none of the rest of us are. We would give up, let go, but *he* won't. Push, pull, prod, kick. – Well, maybe we need someone like that. We *must* have someone like that or nothing will ever happen.

Namarti stopped, as though he felt Andorin's eyes boring into his back. He turned around and said, 'If you're going to lecture me again on Kaspalov, don't bother.'

Andorin shrugged lightly. 'Why bother lecturing you? The deed is done. The harm – if any – has been done.'

'What harm, Andorin? What harm? If I had not done it, *then* we would have been harmed. The man was on the edge of being a traitor. Within a month, he would have gone running—'

'I know. I was there. I heard what he said.'

'Then you understand there was no choice. No choice. You don't think I liked to have an old comrade killed, do you? I had no choice.'

'Very well. You had no choice.'

Namarti resumed his tramping, then turned again. 'Andorin, do you believe in gods?'

Andorin stared, 'In what?'

'In gods.'

'I never heard the word. What is it?'

Namarti said, 'It's not Galactic Standard. Supernatural influences. How's that?'

'Oh, supernatural influences. Why didn't you say so? No, I don't believe in that sort of thing. By definition, something is supernatural if it exists outside the laws of nature and nothing exists outside the laws of nature. Are you turning into a mystic?' Andorin asked it as though he were joking, but his eyes narrowed with sudden concern.

Namarti stared him down. Those blazing eyes of his could stare anyone down. 'Don't be a fool. I've been reading about it. Trillions of people believe in supernatural influences.'

'I know,' said Andorin. 'They always have.'

'They've done so since before the beginning of history. The word "gods" is of unknown origin. It is, apparently, a hangover from some primeval language of which no trace any longer exists, except that word. – Do you know how many different varieties of beliefs there are in various kinds of gods?'

'Approximately as many as the varieties of fools among the Galactic population, I should say.'

Namarti ignored that. 'Some people think the word dates back to the time when all humanity existed on but a single world.'

'Itself a mythological concept. That's just as lunatic as the notion of supernatural influences. There never was one original human world.'

'There would have to be, Andorin,' said Namarti, annoyed. 'Human beings can't have evolved on different worlds and ended as a single species.'

'Even so, there's no *effective* human world. It can't be located, it can't be defined, so it can't be spoken of sensibly, so it *effectively* doesn't exist.'

'These gods,' said Namarti, continuing to follow his own line of thought, 'are supposed to protect humanity and keep it safe or at least to care for those portions of humanity that know how to make use of the gods. At a time when there was only one human world, it makes

179

sense to suppose they would be particularly interested in caring for that one tiny world with a few people. They would care for such a world as though they were big brothers – or parents.'

'Very nice of them. I'd like to see them try to handle the entire Empire.'

'What if they could? What if they were infinite?'

'What if the Sun were frozen? What's the use of "what if?"'

'I'm just speculating. Just thinking. Haven't you ever let your mind wander freely? Do you always keep everything on a leash?'

'I should imagine that's the safest way, keeping it on a leash. What does your wandering mind tell you, Chief?'

Namarti's eyes flashed at the other, as though he suspected sarcasm, but Andorin's face remained good-natured and blank.

Namarti said, 'What my mind is telling me is this – If there are gods, they must be on our side.'

'Wonderful – if true. Where's the evidence?'

'Evidence? Without the gods, it would just be a co-incidence, I suppose, but a very useful one.' Suddenly Namarti yawned and sat down, looking exhausted.

Good, thought Andorin. His galloping mind has finally wound itself down and he may talk sense now.

'This matter of internal breakdown of the infra-structure—' said Namarti, his voice distinctly lower.

Andorin interrupted. 'You know, Chief, Kaspalov was not entirely wrong about this. The longer we keep it up, the greater the chance that Imperial forces will discover the cause. The whole program must, sooner or later, explode in our faces.'

'Not yet. So far, everything is exploding in the Imperial face. The unrest on Trantor is something I can feel.' He raised his hands, rubbing his fingers together. 'I can feel it. And we *are* almost through. We are ready for the next step.'

Andorin smiled humorlessly. 'I'm not asking for

details, Chief. Kaspalov did and look where that got him. I am not Kaspalov.'

'It's precisely because you're not Kaspalov that I can tell you. And because I know something now I didn't then.'

'I presume,' said Andorin, only half-believing what he was saying, 'that you intend a strike on the Imperial Palace grounds.'

Namarti looked up. 'Of course. What else is there to do? The problem, however, is how to penetrate the grounds effectively. I have my sources of information there, but they are only spies. I'll need men of action on the spot.'

'To get men of action into the most heavily guarded region in all the Galaxy will not be easy.'

'Of course not. That's what has been giving me an unbearable headache till now – and then the gods intervened.'

Andorin said gently (it was taking all his self-restraint to keep from showing his disgust), 'I don't think we need a metaphysical discussion. What has happened – leaving the gods to one side?'

'My information is that His Gracious and Ever to Be Beloved Emperor Cleon I has decided to appoint a new Chief Gardener. This is the first new appointee in nearly a quarter of a century.'

'And if so?'

'Do you see no significance?'

Andorin thought for a moment. 'I am not a favorite of your gods. I don't see any significance.'

'If you have a new Chief Gardener, Andorin, the situation is the same as having a new administrator of any other type – the same as if you had a new First Minister or a new Emperor. The new Chief Gardener will certainly want his own staff. He will force into retirement what he considers dead wood and will hire younger gardeners by the hundreds.'

'That's possible.'

181

'It's more than possible. It's certain. Exactly that happened when the present Chief Gardener was appointed and the same when his predecessor was appointed and so on. Hundreds of strangers from the Outer Worlds—'

'Why from the Outer Worlds?'

'Use your brains – if you have any, Andorin. What do Trantorians know about gardening when they've lived under domes all their lives, tending potted plants, zoos, and carefully arranged crops of grains and fruit trees? What do they know about life in the wild?'

'Ahhh. Now I understand.'

'So there will be these strangers flooding the grounds. They will be carefully checked, I presume, but they won't be as tightly screened as they would be if they were Trantorians. And that means, surely, that we should be able to supply just a few of our own people, with false identifications, and get them inside. Even if some are screened out, a few might make it – a few *must* make it. Our people will enter, despite the supertight security established since the failed coup in the early days of First Minister Seldon.' (He virtually spat out the name, as he always did.) 'We'll finally have our chance.'

Now it was Andorin who felt dizzy, as if he'd fallen into a spinning vortex. 'It seems odd for me to say so, Chief, but there is something to this "gods" business after all, because I have been waiting to tell you something that I now see fits in perfectly.'

Namarti stared at the other suspiciously and looked around the room, as though he suddenly feared for security. But such fear was groundless. The room was located deep in an old-fashioned residential complex and was well shielded. No one could overhear and no one, even with detailed directions, could find it easily – nor get through the layers of protection provided by loyal members of the organization.

Namarti said, 'What are you talking about?'

'I've found a man for you. A young man – very naïve.

182

A quite likable fellow, the kind you feel you can trust as soon as you see him. He's got an open face, wide-open eyes; he's lived in Dahl; he's an enthusiast for equality; he thinks Joranum was the greatest thing since Dahlite coke-icers; and I'm sure we can easily talk him into doing anything for the cause.'

'For the cause?' said Namarti, whose suspicions were not in the least alleviated. 'Is he one of us?'

'Actually, he's not one of anything. He's got some vague notions in his head that Joranum wanted sector equality.'

'That was his lure. Sure.'

'It's ours, too, but the kid *believes* it. He talks about equality and popular participation in government. He even mentioned democracy.'

Namarti snickered. 'In twenty thousand years, democracy has never been used for very long without falling apart.'

'Yes, but that's not our concern. It's what drives the young man and I tell you, Chief, I knew we had our tool just about the moment I saw him, but I didn't know how we could possibly use him. Now I know. We can get him onto the Imperial Palace grounds as a gardener.'

'How? Does he know anything about gardening?'

'No. I'm sure he doesn't. He's never worked at any-thing but unskilled labor. He's operating a hauler right now and I think that he had to be taught how to do that. Still, if we can get him in as a gardener's helper, if he just knows how to hold a pair of shears, then we've got it.'

'Got what?'

'Got someone who can approach anyone we wish – and do so without raising the flutter of a suspicion – and get close enough to strike. I'm telling you he simply exudes a kind of honorable stupidity, a kind of foolish virtue that inspires confidence.'

'And he'll do what we tell him to do?'

'Absolutely.'

'How did you meet this person?'

'It wasn't I. It was Manella who really spotted him.'

'Who?'

'Manella. Manella Dubanqua.'

'Oh. That friend of yours.' Namarti's face twisted into a look of prissy disapproval.

'She's the friend of many people,' said Andorin tolerantly. 'That's one of the things that makes her so useful. She can weigh a man quickly and with very little to go on. She talked to this fellow because she was attracted to him at sight – and I assure you that Manella is *not* one who is usually attracted by anything but the bottom line – so, you see, this man is rather unusual. She talked to this fellow – his name is Planchet, by the way – and then told me, "I have a live one for you, Gleb." I'll trust her on the matter of live ones any day of the week.'

Namarti said slyly, 'And what do you think this wonderful tool of yours would do once he had the run of the grounds, eh, Andorin?'

Andorin took a deep breath. 'What else? If we do everything right, he will dispose of our dear, Emperor Cleon, First of that Name, for us.'

Namarti's face blazed into anger. 'What? Are you mad? Why should we want to kill Cleon? He's our hold on the government. He's the façade behind which we can rule. He's our passport to legitimacy. Where are your brains? We need him as a figurehead. He won't interfere with us and we'll be stronger for his existence.'

Andorin's fair face turned blotchy red and his good humor finally exploded. 'What do you have in mind, then? What are you planning? I'm getting tired of always having to second-guess.'

Namarti raised his hand. 'All right. All right. Calm down. I meant no harm. But think a bit, will you? Who destroyed Joranum? Who destroyed our hopes ten years ago? It was that mathematician. And it is he who rules the Empire now with his idiotic talk about psychohistory. Cleon is nothing. It is Hari Seldon we must destroy. It is Hari Seldon whom I've been turning into an object of ridicule with these constant breakdowns. The miseries they entail are placed at *his* doorstep. It is all being interpreted as *his* inefficiency, *his* incapacity.' There was a trace of spittle in the corners of Namarti's mouth. 'When he's cut down, there will be a cheer from the Empire that will drown out every holovision report for hours. It won't even matter if they know who did it.' He raised his hand and let it drop, as if he were plunging a knife into someone's heart. 'We will be looked upon as heroes of the Empire, as saviors. – Eh? Eh? Do you think your youngster can cut down Hari Seldon?'

Andorin had recovered his sense of equanimity – at least outwardly.

'I'm sure he would,' he said with forced lightness. 'For Cleon, he might have some respect; the Emperor has a mystical aura about him, as you know.' (He stressed the 'you' faintly and Namarti scowled.) 'He would have no such feelings about Seldon.'

Inwardly, however, Andorin was furious. This was not what he wanted. He was being betrayed.

14

Manella brushed the hair out of her eyes and smiled up at Raych. 'I told you it wouldn't cost you any credits.'

Raych blinked and scratched at his bare shoulder. 'But are you going to ask me for some now?'

She shrugged and smiled rather impishly. 'Why should I?'

'Why shouldn't you?'

'Because I'm allowed to take my own pleasure sometimes.'

'With me?'

'There's no one else here.'

There was a long pause and then Manella said soothingly, 'Besides, you don't have that many credits anyway. How's the job?'

Raych said, 'Ain't much but better than nothing. Lots better. Did you tell that guy to get me one?'

Manella shook her head slowly. 'You mean Gleb Andorin? I didn't tell him to do anything. I just said he might be interested in you.'

'Is he going to be annoyed because you and I—'

'Why should he? None of *his* business. And none of *yours*, either.'

'What's he do? I mean, what does he work at?'

'I don't think he works at anything. He's rich. He's a relative of the old Mayors.'

'Of Wye?'

'Right. He doesn't like the Imperial government. None of those old Mayor people do. He says Cleon should—'

She stopped suddenly and said, 'I'm talking too much. Don't you go repeating anything I say.'

'Me? I ain't heard you say nothing at all. And I ain't going to.'

'All right.'

'But what about Andorin? Is he high up in Joranumite business? Is he an important guy there?'

'I wouldn't know.'

'Don't he ever talk about that kind of stuff?'

'Not to me.'

'Oh,' said Raych, trying not to sound annoyed.

Manella looked at him shrewdly. 'Why are you so interested?'

'I want to get in with them. I figure I'll get higher up that way. Better job. More credits. You know.'

'Maybe Andorin will help you. He likes you. I know that much.'

'Could you make him like me more?'

'I can try. I don't know why he shouldn't. *I* like you. I like you more than I like him.'

'Thank you, Manella. I like you, too. – A lot.' He ran his hand down the side of her body and wished ardently that he could concentrate more on her and less on his assignment.

15

'Gleb Andorin,' said Hari Seldon wearily, rubbing his eyes.

'And who is he?' asked Dors Venabili, her mood as cold as it had been every day since Raych had left.

'Until a few days ago I never heard of him,' said Seldon.

'That's the trouble with trying to run a world of forty billion people. You never hear of anyone, except for the few who obtrude themselves on your notice. With all the computerized information in the world, Trantor remains a planet of anonymities. We can drag up people with their reference numbers and their statistics, but *whom* do we drag up? Add twenty-five million Outer Worlds and the wonder is that the Galactic Empire has remained a working phenomenon for all these millennia. Frankly I think it has existed only because it very largely runs itself. And now it is finally running down.'

'So much for philosophizing, Hari,' said Dors. 'Who is this Andorin?'

'Someone I admit I *ought* to have known about. I managed to cajole the security establishment into calling up some files on him. He's a member of the Wyan Mayoralty family – the most prominent member, in fact – so the security people have kept tabs on him. They think he has ambitions but is too much of a playboy to do anything about them.'

'And is he involved with the Joranumites?'

Seldon made an uncertain gesture. 'I'm under the impression that the security establishment knows nothing about the Joranumites. That may mean that the Joranumites no longer exist or that, if they do, they are of no importance. It may also mean that the security establishment just isn't interested. Nor is there any way in which I can force it to be interested. I'm only thankful the officers give me any information at all. And I *am* the First Minister.'

'Is it possible that you're not a very good First Minister?' said Dors, dryly.

'That's more than possible. It's probably been generations since there's been an appointee less suited to the job than myself. But that has nothing to do with the security establishment. It's a totally independent arm of the government. I doubt that Cleon himself knows much about it, though, in theory, the security officers are supposed to report to him through their director. Believe me, if we only knew more about the security establishment, we'd be trying to stick its actions into our psychohistorical equations, such as they are.'

'Are the security officers on our side, at least?'

'I believe so, but I can't swear to it.'

'And why are you interested in this what's-his-name?'

'Gleb Andorin. Because I received a roundabout message from Raych.'

Dors's eyes flashed. 'Why didn't you tell me? Is he all right?'

'As far as I know, but I hope he doesn't try any further messages. If he's caught communicating, he *won't* be all right. In any case, he has made contact with Andorin.'

'And the Joranumites, too?'

'I don't think so. It would sound unlikely, for the connection is not something that would make sense. The Joranumite movement is predominantly lower-class – a proletarian movement, so to speak. And Andorin is an aristocrat of aristocrats. What would he be doing with the Joranumites?'

'If he's of the Wyan Mayoralty family, he might aspire to the Imperial throne, might he not?'

'They've been aspiring for generations. You remember Rashelle, I trust. She was Andorin's aunt.'

189

'Then he might be using the Joranumites as a stepping-stone, don't you think?'

'If they exist. And if they do – and if a stepping-stone is what Andorin wants – I think he'd find himself playing a dangerous game. The Joranumites – if they exist – would have their own plans and a man like Andorin may find he's simply riding a greti—'

'What's a greti?'

'Some extinct animal of a ferocious type, I think. It's just a proverbial phrase back on Helicon. If you ride a greti, you find you can't get off, for then it will eat you.'

Seldon paused. 'One more thing. Raych seems to be involved with a woman who knows Andorin and through whom, he thinks, he may get important information. I'm telling you this now so that you won't accuse me afterward of keeping anything from you.'

Dors frowned. 'A woman?'

'One, I gather, who knows a great many men who will talk to her unwisely, sometimes, under intimate circumstances.'

'One of *those*.' Her frown deepened. 'I don't like the thought of Raych—'

'Come, come. Raych is thirty years old and undoubtedly has much experience. You can leave this woman – or any woman, I think – safely to Raych's good sense.' He turned toward Dors with a look so worn, so weary, and said, 'Do you think I like this? Do you think I like *any* of this?'

And Dors could find nothing to say.

16

Gambol Deen Namarti was not, at even the best of times, noted for his politeness and suavity – and the approaching climax of a decade of planning had left his disposition sour.

He rose from his chair with some agitation and said, 'You've taken your time getting here, Andorin.'

Andorin shrugged. 'But I'm here.'

'And this young man of yours – this remarkable tool that you're touting. Where is he?'

'He'll be here eventually.'

'Why not now?'

Andorin's rather handsome head seemed to sink a bit, as though he were lost in thought or coming to a decision, and then he said abruptly, 'I don't want to bring him until I know where I stand.'

'What does that mean?'

'Simple words in Galactic Standard. How long has it been your aim to get rid of Hari Seldon?'

'Always! Always! Is that so hard to understand? We deserve revenge for what he did to Jo-Jo. Even if he hadn't done that, since he's the First Minister, we'd have to put him out of the way.'

'But it's Cleon – *Cleon* – who must be brought down. If not only he, then at least he, in addition to Seldon.'

'Why does a figurehead concern you?'

'You weren't born yesterday. I've never had to explain my part in this because you're not so ignorant a fool as not to know. What can I possibly care about your plans if they don't include a replacement on the throne?'

Namarti laughed. 'Of course. I've known for a long time that you look upon me as your footstool, your way of climbing up to the Imperial throne.'

'Would you expect anything else?'

'Not at all. I will do the planning, take the chances, and then, when all is quite done, you gather in the reward. It makes sense, doesn't it?'

'Yes, it does make sense, for the reward will be yours, too. Won't you become the First Minister? Won't you be able to count on the full support of a new Emperor, one who is filled with gratitude? Won't I be' – and his face twisted with irony as he spat out the words – 'the new figurehead?'

'Is that what you plan to be? A figurehead?'

'I plan to be the Emperor. I supplied advances of credit when you had none. I supplied the cadre when you had none. I supplied the respectability you needed to build a large organization here in Wye. I can still withdraw everything I've brought in.'

'I don't think so.'

'Do you want to risk it? Don't think you can treat me the way you treated Kaspalov, either. If anything happens to me, Wye will become uninhabitable for you and yours – and you will find that no other sector will supply you with what you need.'

Namarti sighed. 'Then you insist on having the Emperor killed.'

'I didn't say "killed." I said "brought down." The details I leave to you.' This last statement was accompanied with an almost dismissive wave of the hand, a flick of the wrist, as if Andorin were already sitting on the Imperial throne.

'And then you'll be Emperor?'

'Yes.'

'No, you won't. You'll be dead – and not at my hands, either. Andorin, let me teach you some of the facts of life. If Cleon is killed, then the matter of the succession comes up and, to avoid civil war, the Imperial Guard will at once kill every member of the Wyan Mayoral family they can find – you first of all. On the other hand, if only the First Minister is killed, you will be safe.'

'Why?'

'A First Minister is only a First Minister. They come and go. It is possible that Cleon himself may have grown tired of him and arranged the murder. Certainly we would see to it that rumors of this sort are spread. The Imperial Guard would hesitate and would give us a chance to put the new government into place. Indeed, it is quite possible that they themselves would be grateful for the end of Seldon.'

'And with the new government in place, what am I to do? Keep on waiting? Forever?'

'No. Once I'm First Minister, there will be ways of dealing with Cleon. I may even be able to do something with the Imperial Guard – and even with the security establishment – and use them all as my instruments. I will then manage to find some safe way of getting rid of Cleon and replacing him with you.'

Andorin burst out, 'Why should you?'

Namarti said, 'What do you mean, why should I?'

'You have a personal grudge against Seldon. Once he is gone, why should you run unnecessary risks at the highest level? You will make your peace with Cleon and I will have to retire to my crumbling estate and my impossible dreams. And perhaps, to play it safe, you will have me killed.'

Namarti said, 'No! Cleon was born to the throne. He comes from several generations of Emperors – the proud Entun Dynasty. He would be very difficult to handle, a plague. You, on the other hand, would come to the throne as a member of a new dynasty, without any strong ties to tradition, for the previous Wyan Emperors were, you will admit, totally undistinguished. You will be seated on a shaky throne and will need someone to support you – me. And I will need someone who is dependent upon me and whom I can therefore handle – *you*. – Come, Andorin, ours is not a marriage of love, which fades in a year; it is a marriage of convenience, which can last as long as we both live. Let us trust each other.'

'You swear I will be Emperor.'

'What good would swearing do if you couldn't trust my word? Let us say I would find you an extraordinarily useful Emperor and I would want you to replace Cleon as soon as that can safely be managed. Now introduce me to this man whom you think will be the perfect tool for your purposes.'

'Very well. And remember what makes him different. I have studied him. He's a not-very-bright idealist. He will do what he's told, unconcerned by danger, unconcerned by second thoughts. And he exudes a kind of trustworthiness so that his victim will trust him, even if he has a blaster in his hand.'

'I find that impossible to believe.'

'Wait till you meet him,' said Andorin.

17

Raych kept his eyes down. He had taken a quick look at Namarti and it was all he needed. He had met the man ten years before, when Raych had been sent to lure Jo-Jo Joranum to his destruction, and one look was more than enough.

Namarti had changed little in ten years. Anger and hatred were still the dominant characteristics one could see in him – or that Raych could see in him, at any rate, for he realized he was not an impartial witness – and those seemed to have marinated him into leathery permanence. His face was a trifle more gaunt, his hair was flecked with gray, but his thin-lipped mouth was set in the same harsh line and his dark eyes were as brilliantly dangerous as ever.

That was enough and Raych kept his eyes averted. Namarti, he felt, was not the type of person who would take to someone who could stare him straight in the face.

Namarti seemed to devour Raych with his own eyes, but the slight sneer his face always seemed to wear remained.

He turned to Andorin, who stood uneasily to one side, and said, quite as though the subject of conversation were not present, 'This is the man, then.'

Andorin nodded and his lips moved in a soundless 'Yes, Chief.'

Namarti said to Raych abruptly, 'Your name.'

'Planchet, sir.'

'You believe in our cause?'

'Yes, sir.' He spoke carefully, in accordance with Andorin's instructions. 'I am a democrat and want greater participation of the people in the governmental process.'

195

Namarti's eyes flicked in Andorin's direction. 'A speechmaker.'

He looked back at Raych. 'Are you willing to undertake risks for the cause?'

'Any risk, sir.'

'You will do as you are told? No questions? No hanging back?'

'I will follow orders.'

'Do you know anything about gardening?'

Raych hesitated. 'No, sir.'

'You're a Trantorian, then? Born under the dome?'

'I was born in Millimaru, sir, and I was brought up in Dahl.'

'Very well,' said Namarti. Then to Andorin, 'Take him out and deliver him temporarily to the men waiting there. They will take good care of him. Then come back, Andorin. I want to speak to you.'

When Andorin returned, a profound change had come over Namarti. His eyes were glittering and his mouth was twisted into a feral grin.

'Andorin,' he said, 'the gods we spoke of the other day are with us to an extent I couldn't have imagined.'

'I told you the man was suitable for our purposes.'

'Far more suitable than you think. You know, of course, the tale of how Hari Seldon, our revered First Minister, sent his son – or foster son, rather – to see Joranum and to set the trap into which Joranum, against my advice, fell.'

'Yes,' said Andorin, nodding wearily, 'I know the story.' He said it with the air of one who knew the story entirely too well.

'I saw that boy only that once, but his image burned into my brain. Do you suppose that ten years' passage and false heels and a shaved mustache could fool me? That Planchet of yours is Raych, the foster son of Hari Seldon.'

Andorin paled and held his breath for a moment. He said, 'Are you sure of that, Chief?'

'As sure as I am that you're standing here in front of me

and that you have introduced an enemy into our midst.'

'I had no idea—'

'Don't get nervous,' said Namarti. 'I consider it the best thing you have ever done in your idle aristocratic life. You have played the role that the gods have marked out for you. If I had not known who he was, he might have fulfilled the function for which he was undoubtedly intended: to be a spy in our midst and an informant of our most secret plans. But since I know who he is, it won't work that way. Instead, we now have *everything*.' Namarti rubbed his hands together in delight and, haltingly, as if he realized how far out of character it was for him, he smiled – and laughed.

18

Manella said thoughtfully, 'I guess I won't be seeing you anymore Planchet.'

Raych was drying himself after his shower. 'Why not?'

'Gleb Andorin doesn't want me to.'

'Why not?'

Manella shrugged her smooth shoulders. 'He says you have important work to do and no more time to fool around. Maybe he means you'll get a better job.'

Raych stiffened. 'What kind of work? Did he mention anything in particular?'

'No, but he said he would be going to the Imperial Sector.'

'Did he? Does he often tell you things like that?'

'You know how it is, Planchet. When a fellow's in bed with you, he talks a lot.'

'I know,' said Raych, who was always careful not to. 'What else does he say?'

'Why do you ask?' She frowned a bit. 'He always asks about you, too. I noticed that about men. They're curious about each other. Why is that, do you suppose?'

'What do you tell him about me?'

'Not much. Just that you're a very decent sort of guy. Naturally I don't tell him that I like you better than I like him. That would hurt his feelings – and it might hurt me, too.'

Raych was getting dressed. 'So it's good-bye, then.'

'For a while, I suppose. Gleb may change his mind. Of course, I'd like to go to the Imperial Sector – if he'd take me. I've never been there.'

Raych almost slipped, but he managed to cough, then said, 'I've never been there, either.'

'It's got the biggest buildings and the nicest places and

the fanciest restaurants – and that's where the rich people live. I'd like to meet some rich people – besides Gleb, I mean.'

Raych said, 'I suppose there's not much you can get out of a person like me.'

'You're all right. You can't think of credits all the time, but you've got to think of them some of the time. Especially since I think Gleb is getting tired of me.'

Raych felt compelled to say, 'No one could get tired of you,' and then found, a little to his own confusion, that he meant it.

Manella said, 'That's what men always say, but you'd be surprised. Anyway, it's been good, you and I, Planchet. Take care of yourself and, who knows, we may see each other again.'

Raych nodded and found himself at a loss for words. There was no way in which he could say or do anything to express his feelings.

He turned his mind in other directions. He had to find out what the Namarti people were planning. If they were separating him from Manella, the crisis must be rapidly approaching. All he had to go on was that odd question about gardening.

Nor could he get any further information back to Seldon. He had been kept under close scrutiny since his meeting with Namarti and all avenues of communication were cut off – surely another indication of an approaching crisis.

But if he were to find out what was going on only after it was done – and if he could communicate the news only after it was no longer news – he would have failed.

19

Hari Seldon was not having a good day. He had not heard from Raych since his first communique; he had no idea what was happening.

Aside from his natural concern for Raych's safety (surely he would hear if something really bad had happened), there was his uneasiness over what might be planned.

It would have to be subtle. A direct attack on the Palace itself was totally out of the question. Security there was far too tight. But if so, what else could be planned that would be sufficiently effective?

The whole thing was keeping him awake at night and distracted by day.

The signal light flashed.

'First Minister. Your two o'clock appointment, sir —'

'What two o'clock appointment is this?'

'Mandell Gruber, the gardener. He has the necessary certification.'

Seldon remembered. 'Yes. Send him in.'

This was no time to see Gruber, but he had agreed to it in a moment of weakness – the man had seemed distraught. A First Minister should not have such moments of weakness, but Seldon had been Seldon long before he had become First Minister.

'Come in, Gruber,' he said kindly.

Gruber stood before him, head ducking mechanically, eyes darting this way and that. Seldon was quite certain the gardener had never been in any room as magnificent as this one and he had the bitter urge to say: 'Do you like it? Please take it. *I* don't want it.'

But he only said, 'What is it, Gruber? Why are you so unhappy?'

There was no immediate answer; Gruber merely smiled vacantly.

Seldon said, 'Sit down, man. Right there in that chair.'

'Oh no, First Minister. It would not be fitting. I'll get it dirty.'

'If you do, it will be easy to clean. Do as I say. – Good! Now just sit there a minute or two and gather your thoughts. Then, when you are ready, tell me what's the matter.'

Gruber sat silent for a moment, then the words came out in a panting rush. 'First Minister. It is Chief Gardener I am to be. The blessed Emperor himself told me so.'

'Yes, I have heard of that, but that surely isn't what is troubling you. Your new post is a matter of congratulations and I do congratulate you. I may even have contributed to it, Gruber. I have never forgotten your bravery at the time I was nearly killed and you can be sure I mentioned it to His Imperial Majesty. It is a suitable reward, Gruber, and you would deserve the promotion in any case, for it is quite clear from your record that you are fully qualified for the post. So, now that that's out of the way, tell me what is troubling you.'

'First Minister, it is the very post and promotion that's troubling me. It is something I cannot manage, for I am not qualified.'

'We are convinced you are.'

Gruber grew agitated. 'And is it in an office I will have to sit? I can't sit in an office. I could not go out in the open air and work with the plants and animals. I would be in prison, First Minister.'

Seldon's eyes opened wide. 'No such thing, Gruber. You needn't stay in the office longer than you have to. You could wander around the grounds freely, supervising everything. You will have all the outdoors you want and you will merely spare yourself the hard work.'

'I want the hard work, First Minister, and it's no chance at all they will let me come out of the office. I have watched the present Chief Gardener. He couldn't leave his office, though he wanted to, ever so. There is too much administration, too much bookkeeping. Sure, if he wants to know what is going on, we must go to his office to tell him. He watches things on *holovision*' – he said with infinite contempt – 'as though you can tell anything about growing, living things from pictures. It is not for me, First Minister.'

'Come, Gruber, be a man. It's not all that bad. You'll get used to it. You'll work your way in slowly.'

Gruber shook his head. 'First off – at the very first – I will have to deal with all the new gardeners. I'll be buried.' Then, with sudden energy, 'It is a job I do not want and must not have, First Minister.'

'Right now, Gruber, perhaps you don't want the job, but you are not alone. I'll tell you that right now I wish I were not First Minister. This job is too much for me. I even have a notion that there are times when the Emperor himself is tired of his Imperial robes. We're all in this Galaxy to do our work and the work isn't always pleasant.'

'I understand that, First Minister, but the Emperor must be Emperor, for he was born to that. And you must be First Minister, for there is no one else who can do the job. But in my case, it is just Chief Gardener we are ruminating upon. There are fifty gardeners in the place who could do it as well as I could and who wouldn't mind the office. You say that you spoke to the Emperor about how I tried to help you. Can't you speak to him again and explain that if he wants to reward me for what I did, he can leave me as I am?'

Seldon leaned back in his chair and said solemnly, 'Gruber, I would do that for you if I could, but I must explain something to you and I can only hope that you will understand it. The Emperor, in theory, is absolute ruler of the Empire. In actual fact, there is very little he can do. I run the Empire right now much more than he does and there is very little I can do, too. There are millions and billions of people at all levels of government, all making decisions, all making mistakes, some acting wisely and heroically, some acting foolishly and thievishly. There's no controlling them. Do you understand me, Gruber?'

'I do, but what has this to do with my case?'

'Because there is only one place where the Emperor is really absolute ruler – and that is over the Imperial grounds. Here, his word is law and the layers of officials beneath him are few enough for him to handle. For him to be asked to rescind a decision he has made in connection with the Imperial Palace grounds would be to invade the only area that he would consider inviolate. If I were to say, "Take back your decision on Gruber, Your Imperial Majesty," he would be much more likely to relieve me of my duties than to take back his decision. That might be a good thing for me, but it wouldn't help you any.'

Gruber said, 'Does that mean there's no way things can be changed?'

'That's exactly what it means. But don't worry, Gruber, I'll help you all I can. I'm sorry. But now I have really spent all the time with you that I am able to spare.'

Gruber rose to his feet. In his hands he twisted his green gardening cap. There was more than a suspicion of tears in his eyes.

'Thank you, First Minister. I know you would like to help. You're – you're a good man, First Minister.'

He turned and left, sorrowing.

Seldon looked after him thoughtfully and shook his head. Multiply Gruber's woes by a quadrillion and you would have the woes of all the people of the twenty-five million worlds of the Empire and how was he, Seldon, to work out salvation for all of them, when he was helpless to solve the problem of one single man who had come to him for help?

Psychohistory could not save one man. Could it save a quadrillion?

He shook his head again, checked the nature and time of his next appointment, and then suddenly stiffened. He shouted into his communications wire in sudden wild abandon, quite unlike his usually strict control. 'Get that gardener back! Get him back here right now!'

20

'What's this about new gardeners?' exclaimed Seldon. This time he did not ask Gruber to sit down.

Gruber's eyes blinked rapidly. He was in a panic at having been recalled so unexpectedly. 'N-new g-gardeners?' he stammered.

'You said "all the new gardeners." Those were your words. *What* new gardeners?'

Gruber was astonished. 'Sure, if there is a new Chief Gardener, there will be new gardeners. It is the custom.'

'I have never heard of this.'

'The last time we had a change of Chief Gardeners, you were not First Minister. It is likely you were not even on Trantor.'

'But what's it all about?'

'Well, gardeners are never discharged. Some die. Some grow too old and are pensioned off and replaced. Still, by the time a new Chief Gardener is ready for his duties, at least half the staff is aged and beyond their best years. They are all pensioned off generously and new gardeners are brought in.'

'For youth.'

'Partly and partly because by that time there are usually new plans for the gardens and it is new ideas and new schemes we must have. There are almost five hundred square kilometers in the gardens and parklands and it usually takes some years to reorganize it and it is myself who will have to supervise it all. Please, First Minister.' Gruber was gasping. 'Surely a clever man like your own self can find a way to change the blessed Emperor's mind.'

Seldon paid no attention. His forehead was creased in

concentration. 'Where do the new gardeners come from?'

'There are examinations on all the worlds – there are always people waiting to serve as replacements. They'll be coming in by the hundreds in a dozen batches. It will take me a year, at the least—'

'From where do they come? From where?'

'From any of a million worlds. We want a variety of horticultural knowledge. Any citizen of the Empire can qualify.'

'From Trantor, too?'

'No, not from Trantor. There is no one from Trantor in the gardens.' His voice grew contemptuous. 'You can't get a gardener out of Trantor. The parks they have here under the dome aren't gardens. They are potted plants and the animals are in cages. Trantorians, poor specimens that they are, know nothing about open air, free water, and the true balance of nature.'

'All right, Gruber. I will now give you a job. It will be up to you to get me the names of every new gardener scheduled to arrive over the coming weeks. Everything about them. Name. World. Reference number. Education. Experience. Everything. I want it all here on my desk just as quickly as possible. I'm going to send people to help you. People with machines. What kind of a computer do you use?'

'Only a simple one for keeping track of plantings and species and things like that.'

'All right. The people I send will be able to do anything you can't do. I can't tell you how important this is.'

'If I should do this—'

'Gruber, this is not the time to make bargains. Fail me and you will not be Chief Gardener. Instead, you will be discharged without a pension.'

Alone again, Seldon barked into his communication wire, 'Cancel all appointments for the rest of the afternoon.'

He then let his body flop in his chair, feeling every bit

of his fifty years and feeling his headache worsen. For years, for decades, security had been built up around the Imperial Palace grounds, thicker, more solid, more impenetrable, as each new layer and each new device was added.

—And every once in a while, hordes of strangers were let into the grounds. No questions asked, probably, but one: 'Can you garden?'

The stupidity involved was too colossal to grasp.

And he had barely caught it in time. Or had he? Was he, even now, too late?

21

Gleb Andorin gazed at Namarti through half-closed eyes. He never liked the man, but there were times when he liked him less than he usually did and this was one of those times. Why should Andorin, a Wyan of royal birth (that's what it amounted to, after all) have to work with this parvenu, this near-psychotic paranoid?

Andorin knew why and he had to endure, even when Namarti was once again in the process of telling the story of how he had built up the movement during a period of ten years to its present pitch of perfection. Did he tell this to everyone, over and over? Or was it just Andorin who was his chosen vessel?

Namarti's face seemed to shine with malignant glee as he said, in an odd singsong, as though it were a matter of rote, 'Year after year, I worked on those lines, even through hopelessness and uselessness, building an organization, chipping away at confidence in the government, creating and intensifying dissatisfaction. When there was the banking crisis and the week of the moratorium, I—'

He paused suddenly. 'I've told you this many times and you're sick of hearing it, aren't you?'

Andorin's lips twitched in a brief dry smile. Namarti was not such an idiot as not to know what a bore he was; he just couldn't help it. Andorin said, 'You've told me this many times.' He allowed the remainder of the question to hang in the air, unanswered. The answer, after all, was an obvious affirmative. There was no need to face him with it.

A slight flush crossed Namarti's sallow face. He said, 'But it could have gone on forever – the building, the chipping, without ever coming to a point – if I hadn't had the proper tool in my hands. And without any effort on my part, the tool came to me.'

'The gods brought you Planchet,' said Andorin neutrally.

'You're right. There will be a group of gardeners entering the Imperial Palace grounds soon.' He paused and seemed to savor the thought. 'Men and women. Enough to serve as a mask for the handful of our operatives who will accompany them. Among them will be you – and Planchet. And what will make you and Planchet unusual is that you will be carrying blasters.'

'Surely,' said Andorin with deliberate malice behind a polite expression, 'we'll be stopped at the gates and held for questioning. Bringing an illicit blaster onto the Palace grounds—'

'You won't be stopped,' said Namarti, missing the malice. 'You won't be searched. That's been arranged. You will all be greeted as a matter of course by some Palace official. I don't know who would ordinarily be in charge of that task – the Third Assistant Chamberlain in Charge of Grass and Leaves, for all I know – but in this case, it will be Seldon himself. The great mathematician will hurry out to greet the new gardeners and welcome them to the grounds.'

'You're sure of that, I suppose.'

'Of course, I am. It's all been arranged. He will learn, at more or less the last minute, that his foster son is among those listed as new gardeners and it will be impossible for him to refrain from coming out to see him. And when Seldon appears, Planchet will raise his blaster. Our people will raise the cry of "Treason!" In the confusion and hurly-burly, Planchet will kill Seldon and then you will kill Planchet. You will then drop your blaster and leave. There are those who will help you leave. It's been arranged.'

'Is it absolutely necessary to kill Planchet?'

Namarti frowned. 'Why? Do you object to one killing and not to another? When Planchet recovers, do you wish him to tell the authorities all he knows about us? Besides, this is a family feud we are arranging. Don't forget that Planchet is, in actual fact, Raych Seldon. It will look as though the two had fired simultaneously – or as though Seldon had given orders that if his son made any hostile move, he was to be shot down. We will see to it that the family angle will be given full publicity. It will be reminiscent of the bad old days of the Bloody Emperor Manowell. The people of Trantor will surely be repelled by the sheer wickedness of the deed. That, piled on top of all the inefficiencies and breakdowns they've been witnessing and living through, will raise the cry for a new government – and no one will be able to refuse them, least of all the Emperor. And then we'll step in.'

'Just like that?'

'No, not just like that. I don't live in a dream world. There is likely to be some interim government, but it will fail. We'll see to it that it fails and we'll come out in the open and revive the old Joranumite arguments that the Trantorians have never forgotten. And in time – in not too much time – I will be First Minister.'

'And I?'

'Will eventually be the Emperor.'

Andorin said, 'The chance of all this working is small. – This is arranged. That is arranged. The other thing is arranged. All of it has to come together and mesh perfectly or it will fail. Somewhere, someone is bound to mess up. It's an unacceptable risk.'

'Unacceptable? For whom? For you?'

'Certainly. You expect me to make certain that Planchet will kill his father and you expect me to then kill Planchet. Why me? Aren't there tools worth less than I who might more easily be risked?'

'Yes, but to choose anyone else would make failure certain. Who but you has so much riding on this mission that there is no chance you will turn back in a fit of vapors at the last minute?'

'The risk is enormous.'

'Isn't it worth it to you? You're playing for the Imperial throne.'

'And what risk are you taking, Chief. You will remain here, quite comfortable, and wait to hear the news.'

Namarti's lip curled. 'What a fool you are, Andorin! What an Emperor you will make! Do you suppose I take no risk because I will be here? If the gambit fails, if the plot miscarries, if some of our people are taken, do you think they won't tell everything they know? If you were somehow caught, would you face the tender treatment of the Imperial Guard without ever telling them about me?

'And with a failed assassination attempt at hand, do you suppose they won't comb Trantor to find me? Do you suppose that, in the end they will fail to find me? And when they do find me, what do you suppose I will have to face at their hands? – Risk? I run a worse risk than any of you, just sitting here doing nothing. It boils down to this, Andorin. Do you or do you not wish to be Emperor?'

Andorin said in a low voice, 'I wish to be Emperor.'

And so things were set in motion.

22

Raych had no trouble seeing that he was being treated with special care. The whole group of would-be gardeners was now quartered in one of the hotels in the Imperial Sector, although not one of the prime hotels, of course.

The gardeners were an odd lot, from fifty different worlds, but Raych had little chance to speak to any of them. Andorin, without being too obvious about it, had managed to keep him apart from the others.

Raych wondered why. It depressed him. In fact, he had been feeling somewhat depressed since he had left Wye. It interfered with his thinking process and he fought it – but not with entire success.

Andorin was himself wearing rough clothes and was attempting to look like a workman. He would be playing the part of a gardener as a way of running the 'show' – whatever the 'show' might be.

Raych felt ashamed that he had not been able to penetrate the nature of that 'show.' They had closed in on him and prevented all communication, so he hadn't even had the chance to warn his father. They might be doing this for every Trantorian who had been pushed into the group, for all he knew, just as an extreme precaution. Raych estimated that there might be a dozen Trantorians among them, all of them Namarti's people, of course, men and women both.

What puzzled him was that Andorin treated him with what was almost affection. He monopolized him, insisted on having all his meals with him, treated him quite differently from the way in which he treated anyone else.

Could it be because they had shared Manella? Raych

did not know enough about the mores of the Wye Sector to be able to tell whether there might not be a polyandrous touch to their society. If two men shared a woman, did that make them, in a way, fraternal? Did it create a bond?

Raych had never heard of such a thing, but he knew better than to suppose he had a grasp of even a tiny fraction of the infinite subtleties of Galactic societies – even of Trantorian societies.

But now that his mind had brought him back to Manella, he dwelled on her for a while. He missed her terribly and it occurred to him that missing her might be the cause of his depression, though, to tell the truth, what he was feeling now, as he was finishing lunch with Andorin, was almost despair – though he could think of no cause for it.

Manella!

She had said she wanted to visit the Imperial Sector and presumably she could wheedle Andorin to her liking. He was desperate enough to ask a foolish question. 'Mr Andorin, I keep wondering if maybe you brought Miss Dubanqua along with you. Here, to the Imperial Sector.'

Andorin looked utterly astonished. Then he laughed gently. 'Manella? Do you see her doing any gardening? Or even pretending she could? No no, Manella is one of those women invented for our quiet moments. She has no function at all, otherwise.' Then 'Why do you ask, Planchet?'

Raych shrugged. 'I don't know. It's sort of dull around here. I sort of thought—' His voice trailed away.

Andorin watched him carefully. Finally he said, 'Surely you're not of the opinion that it matters much which woman you are involved with? I assure you it doesn't matter to her which man she's involved with. Once this is over, there will be other women. Plenty of them.'

'When will this be over?'

'Soon. And you're going to be part of it in a very

212

important way.' Andorin watched Raych narrowly.

Raych said, 'How important? Aren't I gonna be just – a gardener?' His voice sounded hollow and he found himself unable to put a spark in it.

'You'll be more than that, Planchet. You'll be going in with a blaster.'

'With a what?'

'A blaster.'

'I never held a blaster. Not in my whole life.'

'There's nothing to it. You lift it. You point it. You close the contact and someone dies.'

'I can't kill anyone.'

'I thought you were one of us, that you would do anything for the cause.'

'I didn't mean – kill.' Raych couldn't seem to collect his thoughts. Why must he kill? What did they really have in mind for him? And how would he be able to alert the Imperial Guard before the killing would be carried out?

Andorin's face hardened suddenly, an instant conversion from friendly interest to stern decision. He said, 'You *must* kill.'

Raych gathered all his strength. 'No. I ain't gonna kill nobody. That's final.'

Andorin said, 'Planchet, you will do as you are told.'

'Not murder.'

'Even murder.'

'How you gonna make me?'

'I shall simply tell you to.'

Raych felt dizzy. What made Andorin so confident? He shook his head. 'No.'

Andorin said, 'We've been feeding you, Planchet, ever since you left Wye. I made sure you ate with me. I supervised your diet. Especially the meal you just ate.'

Raych felt the horror rise within him. He suddenly understood. 'Desperance!'

'Exactly,' said Andorin. 'You're a sharp devil, Planchet.'

'It's illegal.'

213

'Yes, of course. So's murder.'

Raych knew about desperance. It was a chemical modification of a perfectly harmless tranquilizer. The modified form, however, did not produce tranquillity but despair. It had been outlawed because of its use in mind control, though there were persistent rumors that the Imperial Guard used it.

Andorin said, as though it were not hard to read Raych's mind, 'It's called desperance because that's an old word meaning "hopelessness." I think you're feeling hopeless.'

'Never,' whispered Raych.

'Very resolute of you, but you can't fight the chemical. And the more hopeless you feel, the more effective the drug.'

'No chance.'

'Think about it, Planchet. Namarti recognized you at once, even without your mustache. He knows you are Raych Seldon and, at my direction, you are going to kill your father.'

Raych muttered, 'Not before I kill you.'

He rose from his chair. There should be no problem at all in this. Andorin might be taller, but he was slender and clearly no athlete. Raych would break him in two with one arm – but he swayed as he rose. He shook his head, but it wouldn't clear.

Andorin rose, too, and backed away. He drew his right hand from where it had been resting within his left sleeve. He was holding a weapon.

He said pleasantly, 'I came prepared. I have been informed of your prowess as a Heliconian Twister and there will be no hand-to-hand combat.'

He looked down at his weapon. 'This is not a blaster,' he said. 'I can't afford to have you killed before you accomplish your task. It's a neuronic whip. Much worse, in a way. I will aim at your left shoulder and, believe me, the pain will be so excruciating that the world's greatest stoic would not be able to endure it.'

Raych, who had been advancing slowly and grimly, stopped abruptly. He had been twelve years old when he had had a taste – a small one – of a neuronic whip. Once struck, no one ever forgets the pain, however long he lives, however full of incidents his life is.

Andorin said, 'Moreover, I will use full strength so that the nerves in your upper arms will be stimulated first into unbearable pain and then damaged into uselessness. You will never use your left arm again. I will spare the right so you can handle the blaster. – Now if you sit down and accept matters, as you must, you may keep both arms. Of course, you must eat again so your desperance level increases. Your situation will only worsen.'

Raych felt the drug-induced despair settle over him and that despair served, in itself, to deepen the effect. His vision was turning double and he could think of nothing to say.

Raych only knew that he would have to do what Andorin would tell him to do. He had played the game and he had lost.

23

'No!' Hari Seldon was almost violent. 'I don't want you out there, Dors.'

Dors Venabili stared back at him with an expression as firm as his own. 'Then I won't let you go, either, Hari.'

'I must be there.'

'It is *not* your place. It is the Gardener First-Class who must greet these new people.'

'So it is. But Gruber can't do it. He's a broken man.'

'He must have an assistant of some sort. Or let the old Chief Gardener do it. He holds the office till the end of the year.'

'The old Chief Gardener is too ill. Besides' – Seldon hesitated – 'there are ringers among the gardeners. Trantorians. They're here, for some reason. I have the names of every one of them.'

'Have them taken into custody, then. Every last one of them. It's simple. Why are you making it so complex?'

'Because we don't know *why* they're here. Something's up. I don't see what twelve gardeners can do, but – No, let me rephrase that. I can see a dozen things they can do, but I don't know which one of those things they've planned. We will, indeed, take them into custody, but I must know more about everything before it's done.

'We have to know enough to winkle out everyone in the conspiracy from top to bottom and we must know enough of what they're doing to be able to make the proper punishment stick. I don't want to get twelve men and women on what is essentially a misdemeanor charge. They'll plead desperation, the need for a job. They'll complain that it isn't fair for Trantorians to be excluded. They'll get plenty of sympathy and we'll be left looking like fools. We must give them a chance to convict themselves of more than that. Besides—'

There was a long pause and Dors said wrathfully, 'Well, what's the new "besides"?'

Seldon's voice lowered. 'One of the twelve is Raych, using the alias Planchet.'

'*What?*'

'Why are you surprised? I sent him to Wye to infiltrate the Joranumite movement and he's succeeded in infiltrating something. I have every faith in him. If he's there, he knows why he's there and he must have some sort of plan to put a spoke in the wheel. But I want to be there, too. I want to see him. I want to be in a position to help him if I can.'

'If you want to help him, have fifty guards of the Palace standing shoulder to shoulder on either side of your gardeners.'

'No. Again, we'll end up with nothing. The Imperial Guard will be in place but not in evidence. The gardeners in question must think they have a clear hand to do whatever it is they plan to do. Before they can do so, but after they have made it quite plain what they intend – we'll have them.'

'That's risky. It's risky for Raych.'

'Risks are something we have to take. There's more riding on this than individual lives.'

'That is a heartless thing to say.'

'You think I have no heart? Even if it broke, my concern would have to be with psycho—'

'Don't say it.' She turned away, as if in pain.

'I understand,' said Seldon, 'but you mustn't be there. Your presence would be so inappropriate that the conspirators will suspect we know too much and will abort their plan. I don't want their plan aborted.'

He paused, then said softly, 'Dors, you say your job is to protect *me*. That comes before protecting Raych and you know that. I wouldn't insist on it, but to protect me is to protect psychohistory and the entire human species. That must come first. What I have of psychohistory tells

217

me that I, in turn, must protect the center at all costs and that is what I am trying to do. – Do you understand?'

Dors said, 'I understand,' then turned away from him.

Seldon thought: And I hope I'm right.

If he weren't, she would never forgive him. Far worse, he would never forgive himself – psychohistory or not.

24

They were lined up beautifully, feet spread apart, hands behind their backs, every one in a natty green uniform, loosely fitted and with wide pockets. There was very little gender differential and one could only guess that some of the shorter ones were women. The hoods covered whatever hair they had, but then, gardeners were supposed to clip their hair quite short – either sex – and there could be no facial hair.

Why that should be, one couldn't say. The word 'tradition' covered it all, as it covered so many things, some useful, some foolish.

Facing them was Mandell Gruber, flanked on either side by an assistant. Gruber was trembling, his wide-opened eyes glazed.

Hari Seldon's lips tightened. If Gruber could but manage to say, 'The Emperor's gardeners greet you all,' that would be enough. Seldon himself would then take over.

His eyes swept over the new contingent and he located Raych.

His heart jumped a bit. It was the mustacheless Raych in the front row, standing more rigid than the rest, staring straight ahead. His eyes did not move to meet Seldon's; he showed no sign of recognition, however subtle.

Good, thought Seldon. He's not supposed to. He's giving nothing away.

Gruber muttered a weak welcome and Seldon jumped in.

He advanced with an easy stride, putting himself immediately before Gruber, and said, 'Thank you, Gardener First-Class. Men and women, gardeners of the

Emperor, you are to undertake an important task. You will be responsible for the beauty and health of the only open land on our great world of Trantor, capital of the Galactic Empire. You will see to it that if we don't have the endless vistas of open undomed worlds, we will have a small jewel here that will outshine anything else in the Empire.

'You will all be under Mandell Gruber, who will shortly become Chief Gardener. He will report to me, when necessary, and I will report to the Emperor. This means, as you can all see, that you will be only three levels removed from the Imperial presence and you will always be under his benign watch. I am certain that even now he is surveying us from the Small Palace, his personal home, which is the building you see to the right – the one with the opal-layered dome – and that he is pleased with what he sees.

'Before you start work, of course, you will all undertake a course of training that will make you entirely familiar with the grounds and its needs. You will—'

He had, by this time, moved, almost stealthily,, to a point directly in front of Raych, who still remained motionless, unblinking.

Seldon tried not to look unnaturally benign and then a slight frown crossed his face. The person directly behind Raych looked familiar. He might have gone unrecognized if Seldon had not studied his hologram. Wasn't that Gleb Andorin of Wye? Raych's patron in Wye, in fact? What was he doing here?

Andorin must have noticed Seldon's sudden regard, for he muttered something between scarcely opened lips and Raych's right arm, moving forward from behind his back, plucked a blaster out of the wide pocket of his green doublet. So did Andorin.

Seldon felt himself going into near-shock. How could blasters have been allowed onto the grounds? Confused, he barely heard the cries of 'Treason!' and the sudden noise of running and shouting.

All that really occupied Seldon's mind was Raych's blaster pointing directly at him and Raych looking at him without any sign of recognition. Seldon's mind filled with horror as he realized that his son was going to shoot and that he himself was only seconds from death.

25

A blaster, despite its name, does not 'blast' in the proper sense of the term. It vaporizes and blows out an interior and – if anything – causes an implosion. There is a soft sighing sound, leaving what appears to be a 'blasted' object.

Hari Seldon did not expect to hear that sound. He expected only death. It was, therefore, with surprise that he heard the distinctive soft sighing sound and he blinked rapidly as he looked down at himself, slack-jawed.

He was alive? (He thought it as a question, not a statement.)

Raych was still standing there, his blaster pointing forward, his eyes glazed. He was absolutely motionless, as though some motive power had ceased.

Behind him was the crumpled body of Andorin, fallen in a pool of blood, and standing next to him, blaster in hand, was a gardener. The hood had slipped away; the gardener was clearly a woman with freshly clipped hair.

She allowed herself a glance at Seldon and said, 'Your son knows me as Manella Dubanqua. I'm a security officer. Do you want my reference number, First Minister?'

'No,' said Seldon faintly. Imperial Guard had converged on the scene. 'My son! What's wrong with my son?'

'Desperance, I think,' said Manella. 'That can be washed out eventually.' She reached forward to take the blaster out of Raych's hand. 'I'm sorry I didn't act sooner. I had to wait for an overt move and, when it came, it almost caught me napping.'

'I had the same trouble. We must take Raych to the Palace hospital.'

A confused noise suddenly emanated from the Small Palace. It occurred to Seldon that the Emperor was, indeed, watching the proceedings and, if so, he must be grandly furious, indeed.

'Take care of my son, Miss Dubanqua,' said Seldon. 'I must see the Emperor.'

He set off at an undignified run through the chaos on the Great Lawns and dashed into the Small Palace without ceremony. Cleon could scarcely grow any angrier over that.

And there, with an appalled group watching in stupor – there, on the semicircular stairway – was the body of His Imperial Majesty, Cleon I, smashed all but beyond recognition. His rich Imperial robes now served as a shroud. Cowering against the wall, staring stupidly at the horrified faces surrounding him, was Mandell Gruber.

Seldon felt he could take no more. He took in the blaster lying at Gruber's feet. It had been Andorin's, he was sure. He asked softly, 'Gruber, what have you done?'

Gruber, staring at him, babbled, 'Everyone screaming and yelling. I thought, Who would know? They would think someone else had killed the Emperor. But then I couldn't run.'

'But, Gruber. Why?'

'So I wouldn't have to be Chief Gardener.' And he collapsed.

Seldon stared in shock at the unconscious Gruber.

Everything had worked out by the narrowest of margins. He himself was alive. Raych was alive. Andorin was dead and the Joranumite Conspiracy would now be hunted down to the last person.

The center would have held, just as psychohistory had dictated.

And then one man, for a reason so trivial as to defy analysis, had killed the Emperor.

And now, thought Seldon in despair, what do we do? What happens next?

Part III

DORS VENABILI

VENABILI, DORS – The life of Hari Seldon is well encrusted with legend and uncertainty, so that little hope remains of ever obtaining a biography that can be thoroughly factual. Perhaps the most puzzling aspect of his life deals with his consort, Dors Venabili. There is no information whatever concerning Dors Venabili, except for her birth on the world of Cinna, prior to her arrival at Streeling University to become a member of the history faculty. Shortly after that, she met Seldon and remained his consort for twenty-eight years. If anything, her life is more interlarded with legend than Seldon's is. There are quite unbelievable tales of her strength and speed and she was widely spoken of, or perhaps whispered of, as 'The Tiger Woman.' Still more puzzling than her coming, however, is her going, for after a certain time, we hear of her no more and there is no indication as to what happened.

Her role as a historian is evidenced by her works on—

ENCYCLOPEDIA GALACTICA

1

Wanda was almost eight years old now, going by Galactic Standard Time – as everyone did. She was quite the little lady – grave in manner, with straight light-brown hair. Her eyes were blue but were darkening and she might well end with the brown eyes of her father.

She sat there, lost in thought. – Sixty.

That was the number that preoccupied her. Grandfather was going to have a birthday and it was going to be his sixtieth – and sixty was a large number. It bothered her because yesterday she had had a bad dream about it.

She went in search of her mother. She would have to ask.

Her mother was not hard to find. She was talking to Grandfather – about the birthday surely. Wanda hesitated. It wouldn't be nice to ask in front of Grandfather.

Her mother had no trouble whatever sensing Wanda's consternation. She said, 'One minute, Hari, and let's see what's bothering Wanda. What is it, dear?'

Wanda pulled at her hand. 'Not here, Mother. Private.'

Manella turned to Hari Seldon. 'See how early it starts? Private lives. Private problems. Of course, Wanda, shall we go to your room?'

'Yes, Mother.' Wanda was clearly relieved.

Hand in hand, they went and then her mother said, 'Now what is the problem, Wanda?'

'It's Grandfather, Mother.'

'Grandfather! I can't imagine him doing anything to bother you.'

'Well, he is.' Wanda's eyes filled with sudden tears. 'Is he going to die?'

229

'Your grandfather? What put that into your head, Wanda?'

'He's going to be sixty. That's so old.'

'No, it isn't. It's not young, but it's not old, either. People live to be eighty, ninety, even a hundred – and your grandfather is strong and healthy. He'll live a long time.'

'Are you sure?' She was sniffing.

Manella grasped her daughter by the shoulders and looked her straight in the eyes. 'We must all die someday, Wanda. I've explained that to you before. Just the same, we don't worry about it till the someday is much closer.' She wiped Wanda's eyes gently. 'Grandfather is going to stay alive till you're all grown up and have babies of your own. You'll see. Now come back with me. I want you to talk to Grandfather.'

Wanda sniffed again.

Seldon looked at the little girl with a sympathetic expression on her return and said, 'What is it, Wanda? Why are you unhappy?'

Wanda shook her head.

Seldon turned his gaze to the girl's mother. 'Well, what is it, Manella?'

Manella shook her head. 'She'll have to tell you herself.'

Seldon sat down and tapped his lap. 'Come, Wanda. Have a seat and tell me your troubles.'

She obeyed and wriggled a bit, then said, 'I'm scared.'

Seldon put his arm around her. 'Nothing to be scared of in your old grandfather.'

Manella made a face. 'Wrong word.'

Seldon looked up at her. 'Grandfather?'

'No. Old.'

That seemed to break the dike. Wanda burst into tears. 'You're old, Grandfather.'

'I suppose so. I'm sixty.' He bent his face down to Wanda's and whispered, 'I don't like it, either, Wanda. That's why I'm glad you're only seven going on eight.'

'Your hair is white, Grandpa.'

'It wasn't always. It just turned white recently.'

'White hair means you're going to die, Grandpa.'

Seldon looked shocked. He said to Manella, 'What is all this?'

'I don't know, Hari. It's her own idea.'

'I had a bad dream,' said Wanda.

Seldon cleared his throat. 'We all have bad dreams now and then, Wanda. It's good we do. Bad dreams get rid of bad thoughts and then we're better off.'

'It was about you dying, Grandfather.'

'I know. I know. Dreams can be about dying, but that doesn't make them important. Look at me. Don't you see how alive I am – and cheerful – and laughing? Do I look as though I'm dying? Tell me.'

'N-no.'

'There you are, then. Now you go out and play and forget all about this. I'm just having a birthday and everyone will have a good time. Go ahead, dear.'

Wanda left in reasonable cheer, but Seldon motioned to Manella to stay.

2

Seldon said, 'Wherever do you think Wanda got such a notion?'

'Come now, Hari. She had a Salvanian gecko that died, remember? One of her friends had a father who died in an accident and she sees deaths on holovision all the time. It is impossible for any child to be so protected as not to be aware of death. Actually I wouldn't want her to be so protected. Death is an essential part of life; she must learn that.'

'I don't mean death in general, Manella. I mean my death in particular. What has put that into her head?'

Manella hesitated. She was very fond, indeed, of Hari Seldon. She thought, Who would not be, so how can I say this?

But how could she *not* say this? So she said, 'Hari, you yourself put it into her head.'

'I?'

'Of course, you've been speaking for months of turning sixty and complaining loudly of growing old. The only reason people are setting up this party is to console you.'

'It's no fun turning sixty,' said Seldon indignantly. 'Wait! Wait! You'll find out.'

'I will – if I'm lucky. Some people don't make it to sixty. Just the same, if turning sixty and being old are all you talk about, you end up frightening an impressionable little girl.'

Seldon sighed and looked troubled. 'I'm sorry, but it's hard. Look at my hands. They're getting spotted and soon they'll be gnarled. I can do hardly anything in the way of Twisting any longer. A child could probably force me to my knees.'

'In what way does that make you different from other

sixty-year-olds? At least your brain is working as well as ever. How often have you said that that's all that counts?'

'I know. But I miss my body.'

Manella said with just a touch of malice, 'Especially when Dors doesn't seem to get any older.'

Seldon said uneasily, 'Well yes, I suppose – He looked away, clearly unwilling to talk about the matter.

Manella looked at her father-in-law gravely. The trouble was, he knew nothing about children – or about people generally. It was hard to think that he had spent ten years as First Minister under the old Emperor and yet ended up knowing as little about people as he did.

Of course, he was entirely wrapped up in this psycho-history of his, that dealt with quadrillions of people, which ultimately meant dealing with no people at all – as individuals. And how could he know about children when he had had no contact with any child except Raych, who had entered his life as a twelve-year-old? Now he had Wanda, who was – and would probably remain to him – an utter mystery.

Manella thought all this lovingly. She had the incredible desire to protect Hari Seldon from a world he did not understand. It was the only point at which she and her mother-in-law, Dors Venabili, met and coalesced – this desire to protect Hari Seldon.

Manella had saved Seldon's life ten years before. Dors, in her strange way, had considered this an invasion of her prerogative and had never quite forgiven Manella.

Seldon, in his turn, had then saved Manella's life. She closed her eyes briefly and the whole scene returned to her, almost as though it were happening to her right now.

3

It was a week after the assassination of Cleon – and a horrible week it had been. All of Trantor was in chaos.

Hari Seldon still kept his office as First Minister, but it was clear he had no power. He called in Manella Dubanqua.

'I want to thank you for saving Raych's life and my own. I haven't had a chance to do so yet.' Then with a sigh, 'I have scarcely had a chance to do anything this past week.'

Manella asked, 'What happened to the mad gardener?'

'Executed! At once! No trial! I tried to save him by pointing out that he was insane. But there was no question about it. If he had done anything else, committed any other crime, his madness would have been recognized and he would have been spared. Committed – locked up and treated – but spared, nonetheless. But to kill the Emperor—' Seldon shook his head sadly.

Manella said, 'What's going to happen now, First Minister?'

'I'll tell you what I think. The Entun Dynasty is finished. Cleon's son will not succeed. I don't think he wants to. He fears assassination in his turn and I don't blame him one bit. It would be much better for him to retire to one of the family estates on some Outer World and live a quiet life there. Because he is a member of the Imperial House, he will undoubtedly be allowed to do this. You and I may be less fortunate.'

Manella frowned. 'In what way, sir?'

Seldon cleared his throat. 'It is possible to argue that because you killed Gleb Andorin, he dropped his blaster, which became available to Mandell Gruber, who used it to kill Cleon. Therefore you bear a strong share of the responsibility of the crime and it may even be said that it was all prearranged.'

'But that's ridiculous. I am a member of the security establishment, fulfilling my duties – doing what I was ordered to do.'

Seldon smiled sadly. 'You're arguing rationally and rationality is not going to be in fashion for a while. What's going to happen now, in the absence of a legitimate successor to the Imperial throne, is that we are bound to have a military government.'

(In later years, when Manella came to understand the workings of psychohistory, she wondered if Seldon had used the technique to work out what was going to happen, for the military rule certainly came to pass. At the time, however, he made no mention of his fledgling theory.)

'If we do have a military government,' he went on, 'then it will be necessary for them to establish a firm rule at once, crush any signs of disaffection, act vigorously and cruelly, even in defiance of rationality and justice. If they accuse you, Miss Dubanqua, of being part of a plot to kill the Emperor, you will be slaughtered, not as an act of justice but as a way of cowing the people of Trantor.

'For that matter, they might say that I was part of the plot, too. After all, I went out to greet the new gardeners when it was not my place to do so. Had I not done so, there would have been no attempt to kill me, you would not have struck back, and the Emperor would have lived. – Do you see how it all fits?'

'I can't believe they will do this.'

'Perhaps they won't. I'll make them an offer that, just perhaps, they may not wish to refuse.'

'What would that be?'

'I will offer to resign as First Minister. They don't want me, they won't have me. But the fact is that I do have supporters at the Imperial Court and, even more important, people in the Outer Worlds who find me acceptable. That means that if the members of the Imperial Guard force me out, then even if they don't execute me, they will have some trouble. If, on the other hand, I resign, stating that I believe the military government is what Trantor and the Empire needs, then I actually help them, you see?'

He mused a little and said, 'Besides, there is the little matter of psychohistory.'

(That was the first time Manella had ever heard the word.)

'What's that?'

'Something I'm working on. Cleon believed in its powers very strongly – more strongly than I did at the time – and there's a considerable feeling in the court that psychohistory is, or might be, a powerful tool that could be made to work on the side of the government – whatever the government might be.

'Nor does it matter if they know nothing about the details of the science. I'd rather they didn't. Lack of knowledge can increase what we might call the superstitious aspect of the situation. In which case, they will let me continue working on my research as a private citizen. At least, I hope so. – And that brings me to you.'

'What about me?'

'I'm going to ask as part of the deal that you be allowed to resign from the security establishment and that no action be taken against you over the events in connection with the assassination. I ought to be able to get that.'

'But you're talking about ending my career.'

'Your career is, in any case, over. Even if the Imperial Guard doesn't work up an order of execution against you, can you imagine that you will be allowed to continue working as a security officer?'

'But what do I do? How do I make a living?'

'I'll take care of that, Miss Dubanqua. In all likelihood, I'll go back to Streeling University, with a large grant for my psychohistorical research, and I'm sure that I can find a place for you.'

Manella, round-eyed, said, 'Why should you—'

Seldon said, 'I can't believe you're asking. You saved Raych's life and my own. Is it conceivable that I don't owe you anything?'

And it was as he said. Seldon resigned gracefully from the post he had held for ten years. He was given a fulsome letter of appreciation for his services by the just-formed military government, a junta led by certain members of the Imperial Guard and the armed forces. He returned to Streeling University and Manella Dubanqua, relieved of her own post as a security officer, went with Seldon and his family.

4

Raych came in, blowing on his hands. 'I'm all for deliberate variety in the weather. You don't want things under a dome to always be the same. Today, though, they made it just a little too cold and worked up a wind, besides. I think it's about time someone complained to weather control.'

'I don't know that it's weather control's fault,' said Seldon. 'It's getting harder to control things in general.'

'I know. Deterioration.' Raych brushed his thick black mustache with the back of his hand. He did that often, as though he had never quite managed to get over the few months during which he had been mustacheless in Wye. He had also put on a little weight around the middle and, overall, had come to seem very comfortable and middle-class. Even his Dahl accent had faded somewhat.

He took off his light coverall and said, 'And how's the old birthday boy?'

'Resenting it. Wait, wait, my son. One of these days, you'll be celebrating your fortieth birthday. We'll see how funny you'll think that is.'

'Not as funny as sixty.'

'Stop joking,' said Manella, who had been chafing Raych's hands, trying to warm them.

Seldon spread his own hands. 'We're doing the wrong thing, Raych. Your wife is of the opinion that all this talk about my turning sixty has sent little Wanda into a decline over the possibility of my dying.'

'Really?' said Raych. 'That accounts for it, then. I stopped in to see her and she told me at once, before I even had a chance to say a word, that she had had a bad dream. Was it about your dying?'

'Apparently,' said Seldon.

'Well, she'll get over that. No way of stopping bad dreams.'

'I'm not dismissing it that easily,' said Manella. 'She's brooding over it and that's not healthy. I'm going to get to the bottom of this.'

'As you say, Manella,' said Raych agreeably. 'You're my dear wife and whatever you say – about Wanda – goes.' And he brushed his mustache again.

His dear wife! It hadn't been so easy to make her his dear wife. Raych remembered his mother's attitude toward the possibility. Talk about nightmares. It was he who had the periodic nightmares in which he had to face down the furious Dors Venabili once more.

5

Raych's first clear memory, after emerging from his desperance-induced ordeal, was that of being shaved.

He felt the vibrorazor moving along his cheek and he said weakly, 'Don't cut anywhere near my upper lip, barber. I want my mustache back.'

The barber, who had already received his instructions from Seldon, held up a mirror to reassure him.

Dors Venabili, who was sitting at his bedside, said, 'Let him work, Raych. Don't excite yourself.'

Raych's eyes turned toward her momentarily and he was quiet. When the barber left, Dors said, 'How do you feel, Raych?'

'Rotten,' he muttered. 'I'm so depressed, I can't stand it.'

'That's the lingering effect of the desperance you've been dosed with. The effects will wash out.'

'I can't believe it. How long has it been?'

'Never mind. It will take time. You were pumped full of it.'

He looked around restlessly. 'Has Manella been to see me?'

'That woman?' (Raych was getting used to hearing Dors speak of Manella with those words and in that tone of voice.) 'No. You're not fit for visitors yet.'

Interpreting the look on Raych's face, Dors quickly added, 'I'm an exception because I'm your mother, Raych. Why would you want that woman to see you, anyway? You're in no condition to be seen.'

'All the more reason to see her,' muttered Raych. 'I want her to see me at my worst.' He then turned to one side dispiritedly. 'I want to sleep.'

Dors Venabili shook her head. Later that day she said

to Seldon, 'I don't know what we're going to do about Raych, Hari. He's quite unreasonable.'

Seldon said, 'He's not well, Dors. Give the young man a chance.'

'He keeps muttering about that woman. Whatever her name is.'

'Manella Dubanqua. It's not a hard name to remember.'

'I think he wants to set up housekeeping with her. Live with her. *Marry* her.'

Seldon shrugged. 'Raych is thirty – old enough to make up his own mind.'

'As his parents, we have something to say – surely.'

Hari sighed. 'And I'm sure you've said it, Dors. And once you've said it, I'm sure he'll do as he wishes.'

'Is that your final word? Do you intend to do nothing while he makes plans to marry a woman like that?'

'What do you expect me to do, Dors? Manella saved Raych's life. Do you expect him to forget that? She saved mine, too, for that matter.'

That seemed to feed Dors's anger. She said, 'And you also saved her. The score is even.'

'I didn't exactly—'

'Of course you did. The military rascals who now run the Empire would have slaughtered her if you didn't step in and sell them your resignation and your support in order to save her.'

'Though I may have evened the score, which I don't think I have, Raych has not. And, Dors dear, I would be very careful when it came to using unfortunate terms to describe our government. These times are not going to be as easy as the times when Cleon ruled and there will always be informers to repeat what they hear you say.'

'Never mind that. I don't like that woman. I presume that, at least, is permissible.'

'Permissible, certainly, but of no use.'

Hari looked down at the floor, deep in thought. Dors's

usually unfathomable black eyes were positively flashing in anger. Hari looked up.

'What I'd like to know, Dors, is *why?* Why do you dislike Manella so? She saved our lives. If it had not been for her quick action, both Raych and I would be dead.'

Dors snapped back, 'Yes, Hari. I know that better than anyone. And if she had not been there, I would not have been able to do a thing to prevent your murder. I suppose you think I should be grateful. But every time I look at that woman, I am reminded of *my* failure. I know these feelings are not truly rational – and that is something I can't explain. So do not ask me to like her, Hari. I cannot.'

But the next day even Dors had to back down when the doctor said, 'Your son wishes to see a woman named Manella.'

'He's in no condition to see visitors,' snapped Dors.

'On the contrary. He is. He's doing quite well. Besides, he insists and is doing so most strenuously. I don't know that we'd be wise to refuse him.'

So they brought in Manella and Raych greeted her effusively and with the first faint sign of happiness since he had arrived at the hospital.

He made an unmistakable small gesture of dismissal at Dors. Lips tightened, she left.

And the day came when Raych said, 'She'll have me, Mom.'

Dors said, 'Do you expect me to be surprised, you foolish man? Of course she'll have you. You're her only chance, now that she's been disgraced, ousted from the security establishment . . .'

Raych said, 'Mom, if you're trying to lose me, this is exactly the way of doing it. Don't say things like that.'

'I'm only thinking of your welfare.'

'I'll think of my own good, thank you. I'm no one's ticket to respectability – if you'll stop to think of it. I'm not exactly handsome. I'm short. Dad isn't First Minister anymore and I talk solid lower-class. What's there for her to be proud of in me? She can do a lot better, but she wants me. And let me tell you, I want her.'

'But you know what she is.'

'Of course I know what she is. She's a woman who loves me. She's the woman I love. That's what she is.'

'And before you fell in love with her, what was she? You know some of what she had to do while undercover in Wye – *you* were one of her "assignments." How many others were there? Are you able to live with her past? With what she did in the name of duty? Now you can afford to be idealistic. But someday you will have your first quarrel with her – or your second or your nineteenth – and you'll break down and say, "You wh— !"'

Raych shouted angrily, 'Don't say that! When we fight, I'll call her unreasonable, irrational, nagging, whining, inconsiderate – a million adjectives that will fit the situation. And she'll have words for me. But they'll all be sensible words that can be withdrawn when the fight is over.'

'You think so – but just wait till it happens.'

Raych had turned white. He said, 'Mother, you've been with Father now for almost twenty years. Father is a hard man to disagree with, but there have been times when you two have argued. I've heard you. In all those twenty years, has he ever called you by any name that would in any way compromise your role as human being? For that matter, have I done so? Can you conceive of me doing so now – no matter how angry I get?'

Dors struggled. Her face did not show emotion in quite the same way that Raych's did or Seldon's would, but it was clear that she was momentarily incapable of speech.

'In fact,' said Raych, pushing his advantage (and feeling horrible at doing so) 'the fact of the matter is that you are jealous because Manella saved Dad's life. You don't want anyone to do that but you. Well, you had no chance to do so. Would you prefer it if Manella had not shot Andorin – if Dad had *died*? And me, too?'

Dors said in a choked voice, 'He insisted on going out

243

to meet the gardeners alone. He would not allow me to come.'

'But that wasn't Manella's fault.'

'Is that why you want to marry her? Gratitude?'

'No. Love.'

And so it was, but Manella said to Raych after the ceremony, 'Your mother may have attended the wedding because you insisted, Raych, but she looked like one of those thunderclouds they sometimes send sailing under the dome.'

Raych laughed. 'She doesn't have the face to be a thundercloud. You're just imagining it.'

'Not at all. How will we ever get her to give us a chance?'

'We'll just be patient. She'll get over it.'

But Dors Venabili didn't.

Two years after the wedding, Wanda was born. Dors's attitude toward the child was all Raych and Manella could have wanted, but Wanda's mother remained 'that woman' to Raych's mother.

6

Hari Seldon was fighting off melancholy. He was lectured in turn by Dors, by Raych, by Yugo, and by Manella. All united to tell him that sixty was not old.

They simply did not understand. He had been thirty when the first hint of psychohistory had come to him, thirty-two when he delivered his famous lecture at the Decennial Convention, following which everything seemed to happen to him at once. After his brief interview with Cleon, he had fled across Trantor and met Demerzel, Dors, Yugo, and Raych, to say nothing of the people of Mycogen, of Dahl, and of Wye.

He was forty when he became First Minister and fifty when he had relinquished the post. Now he was sixty.

He had spent thirty years on psychohistory. How many more years would he require? How many more years would he live? Would he die with the Psychohistory Project unfinished after all?

It was not the dying that bothered him, he told himself. It was the matter of leaving the Psychohistory Project unfinished.

He went to see Yugo Amaryl. In recent years they had somehow drifted apart, as the Psychohistory Project had steadily increased in size. In the first years at Streeling, it had merely been Seldon and Amaryl working together – no one else. Now—

Amaryl was nearly fifty – not exactly a young man – and he had somehow lost his spark. In all these years, he had developed no interest in anything *but* psychohistory: no woman, no companion, no hobby, no subsidiary activity.

Amaryl blinked at Seldon, who couldn't help but note the changes in the man's appearance. Part of it may have

245

been because Yugo had had to have his eyes recon-structed. He saw perfectly well, but there was an unnatural look about them and he tended to blink slowly. It made him appear sleepy.

'What do you think, Yugo?' said Seldon. 'Is there any light at the end of the tunnel?'

'Light? Yes, as a matter of fact,' said Amaryl. 'There's this new fellow, Tamwile Elar. You know him, of course.'

'Oh yes. I'm the one who hired him. Very vigorous and aggressive. How's he doing?'

'I can't say I'm really comfortable with him, Hari. His loud laughter gets on my nerves. But he's brilliant. The new system of equations fits right into the Prime Radiant and they seem to make it possible to get around the problem of chaos.'

'Seem? Or will?'

'Too early to say, but I'm very hopeful. I have tried a number of things that would have broken them down if they were worthless and the new equations survived them all. I'm beginning to think of them as "the achaotic equations."'

'I don't imagine,' said Seldon, 'we have anything like a rigorous demonstration concerning these equations?'

'No, we don't, though I've put half a dozen people on it, including Elar, of course.' Amaryl turned on his Prime Radiant – which was every bit as advanced as Seldon's was – and he watched as the curving lines of luminous equations curled in midair – too small, too fine to be read without amplification. 'Add the new equations and we may be able to begin to predict.'

'Each time I study the Prime Radiant now,' said Seldon thoughtfully, 'I wonder at the Electro-Clarifier and how tightly it squeezes material into the lines and curves of the future. Wasn't that Elar's idea, too?'

'Yes. With the help of Cinda Monay, who designed it.'

'It's good to have new and brilliant men and women in the Project. Somehow it reconciles me to the future.'

'You think someone like Elar may be heading the

Project someday?' asked Amaryl, still studying the Prime Radiant.

'Maybe. After you and I have retired – or died.'

Amaryl seemed to relax and turned off the device. 'I would like to complete the task before we retire or die.'

'So would I, Yugo. So would I.'

'Psychohistory has guided us pretty well in the last ten years.'

That was true enough, but Seldon knew that one couldn't attach too much triumph to that. Things had gone smoothly and without major surprises.

Psychohistory had predicted that the center would hold after Cleon's death – predicted it in a very dim and uncertain way – and it did hold. Trantor was reasonably quiet. Even with an assassination and the end of a dynasty, the center had held.

It did so under the stress of military rule – Dors was quite right in speaking of the junta as 'those military rascals.' She might have even gone farther in her accusations without being wrong. Nevertheless, they were holding the Empire together and would continue to do so for a time. Long enough, perhaps, to allow psychohistory to play an active role in the events that were to transpire.

Lately Yugo had been speaking about the possible establishment of Foundations – separate, isolated, independent of the Empire itself – serving as seeds for developments through the forthcoming dark ages and into a new and better Empire. Seldon himself had been working on the consequences of such an arrangement.

But he lacked the time and, he felt (with a certain misery), he lacked the youth as well. His mind, however firm and steady, did not have the resiliency and creativity that it had had when he was thirty and with each passing year, he knew he would have less.

Perhaps he ought to put the young and brilliant Elar on the task, taking him off everything else. Seldon had to admit to himself, shamefacedly, that the possibility did not excite him. He did not want to have invented psychohistory so that some stripling could come in and reap the final fruits of fame. In fact, to put it at its most disgraceful, Seldon felt jealous of Elar and realized it just sufficiently to feel ashamed of the emotion.

Yet, regardless of his less rational feelings, he would have to depend on other younger men – whatever his discomfort over it. Psychohistory was no longer the private preserve of himself and Amaryl. The decade of his being First Minister had converted it into a large government-sanctioned and -budgeted undertaking and, quite to his surprise, after resigning from his post as First Minister and returning to Streeling University, it had grown still larger. Hari grimaced at its ponderous – and pompous – official name: the Seldon Psychohistory Project at Streeling University. But most people simply referred to it as the Project.

The military junta apparently saw the Project as a possible political weapon and while that was so, funding was no problem. Credits poured in. In return, it was necessary to prepare annual reports, which, however, were quite opaque. Only fringe matters were reported on and even then the mathematics was not likely to be within the purview of any of the members of the junta.

It was clear as he left his old assistant that Amaryl, at least, was more than satisfied with the way psychohistory was going and yet Seldon felt the blanket of depression settle over him once more.

He decided it was the forthcoming birthday celebration that was bothering him. It was meant as a celebration of joy, but to Hari it was not even a gesture of consolation – it merely emphasized his age.

Besides, it was upsetting his routine and Hari was a creature of habit. His office and a number of those adjoining had been cleared out and it had been days since he had been able to work normally. His proper offices would be converted into halls of glory, he supposed, and it would be many days before he could get back to work.

Only Amaryl absolutely refused to budge and was able to maintain his office.

Seldon had wondered, peevishly, who had thought of doing all this. It wasn't Dors, of course. She knew him entirely too well. Not Amaryl or Raych, who never even remembered their own birthdays. He had suspected Manella and had even confronted her on the matter.

She admitted that she was all for it and had given orders for the arrangements to take place, but she said that the idea for the birthday party had been suggested to her by Tamwile Elar.

The brilliant one, thought Seldon. Brilliant in everything.

He sighed. If only the birthday were all over.

7

Dors poked her head through the door. 'Are you going to keep me out?'

'No, of course not. Why should you think I would?'

'This is not your usual place.'

'I know,' sighed Seldon. 'I have been evicted from my usual place because of the stupid birthday party. How I wish it were over.'

'There you are. Once that woman gets an idea in her head, it takes over and grows like the big bang.'

Seldon changed sides at once. 'Come. She means well, Dors.'

'Save me from the well-meaning,' said Dors. 'In any case, I'm here to discuss something else. Something which may be important.'

'Go ahead. What is it?'

'I've been talking to Wanda about her dream—' She hesitated.

Seldon made a gargling sound in the back of his throat, then said, 'I can't believe it. Just let it go.'

'No. Did you bother to ask her for the details of the dream?'

'Why should I put the little girl through that?'

'Neither did Raych, nor Manella. It was left up to me.'

'But why should you torture her with questions about it?'

'Because I had the feeling I should,' said Dors grimly. 'In the first place, she didn't have the dream when she was home in her bed.'

'Where was she, then?'

'In your office.'

'What was she doing in my office?'

'She wanted to see the place where the party would be

250

and she walked into your office and, of course, there was nothing to see, as it's been cleared out in preparation. But your chair was still there. The large one – tall back, tall wings, broken-down – the one you won't let me replace.'

Hari sighed, as if recalling a longstanding disagreement. 'It's *not* broken-down. I don't *want* a new one. Go on.'

'She curled up in your chair and began to brood over the fact that maybe you weren't really going to have a party and she felt bad. Then, she tells me, she must have fallen asleep because nothing is clear in her mind, except that in her dream there were two men – not women, she was sure about that – two men, talking.'

'And what were they talking about?'

'She doesn't know exactly. You know how difficult it is to remember details under such circumstances. But she says it was about dying and she thought it was you because you were so old. And she remembers two words clearly. They were "lemonade death."'

'What?'

'Lemonade death.'

'What does that mean?'

'I don't know. In any case, the talking ceased, the men left, and there she was in the chair, cold and frightened – and she's been upset about it ever since.'

Seldon mulled over Dors's report. Then he said, 'Look, dear, what importance can we attach to a child's dream?'

'We can ask ourselves first, Hari, if it even was a dream.'

'What do you mean?'

'Wanda doesn't say outright it was. She says she "must have fallen asleep." Those are her words. She didn't say she fell asleep, she said she *must have* fallen asleep.'

'What do you deduce from that?'

'She may have drifted off into a half-doze and, in that state, heard two men – two real men, not two dream men – talking.'

'Real men? Talking about killing me with lemonade death?'

'Something like that, yes.'

'Dors,' said Seldon forcefully, 'I know that you're forever foreseeing danger for me, but this is going too far. Why should anyone want to kill me?'

'It's been tried twice before.'

'So it has, but consider the circumstances. The first attempt came shortly after Cleon appointed me First Minister. Naturally this was an offense to the well-established court hierarchy and I was very resented. A few thought they might settle matters by getting rid of me. The second time was when the Joranumites were trying to seize power and they thought I was standing in their way – plus Namarti's distorted dream of revenge.

'Fortunately neither assassination attempt succeeded, but why should there now be a third? I am no longer First Minister and haven't been for ten years. I am an aging mathematician in retirement and surely no one has anything to fear from me. The Joranumites have been rooted out and destroyed and Namarti was executed long ago. There is absolutely no motivation for anyone to want to kill me.

'So please, Dors, relax. When you're nervous about me, you get unsettled, which makes you more nervous still, and I don't want that to happen.'

Dors rose from her seat and leaned across Hari's desk. 'It's easy for you to say that there is no motive to kill you, but none is needed. Our government is now a completely irresponsible one and if they wish—'

'Stop!' commanded Seldon loudly. Then, very quietly, 'Not a word, Dors. Not a word against the government. That could get us in the very trouble you're foreseeing.'

'I'm only talking to you, Hari.'

'Right now you are, but if you get into the habit of saying foolish things, you don't know when something will slip out in someone else's presence – someone who will then be glad to report you. Just learn, as a matter of

252

necessity, to refrain from political commentary.'

'I'll try, Hari,' said Dors, but she could not keep the indignation out of her voice. She turned on her heel and left.

Seldon watched her go. Dors had aged gracefully, so gracefully that at times she seemed not to have aged at all. Though she was two years younger than Seldon, her appearance had not changed nearly as much as his had in the twenty-eight years they had been together. Naturally.

Her hair was frosted with gray, but the youthful luster beneath the gray still shone through. Her complexion had grown more sallow; her voice was a bit huskier, and, of course, she wore clothes that were suitable for middle age. However, her movements were as agile and as quick as ever. It was as if nothing could be allowed to interfere with her ability to protect Hari in case of an emergency.

Hari sighed. This business of being protected – more or less against his will, at all times – was sometimes a heavy burden.

8

Manella came to see Seldon almost immediately afterward.

'Pardon me, Hari, but what has Dors been saying?'

Seldon looked up again. Nothing but interruptions.

'It wasn't anything important. Wanda's dream.'

Manella's lips pursed. 'I knew it. Wanda said Dors was asking her questions about it. Why doesn't she leave the girl alone? You would think that having a bad dream was some sort of felony.'

'As a matter of fact,' said Seldon soothingly, 'it's just a matter of something Wanda remembered as part of the dream. I don't know if Wanda told you, but apparently in her dream she heard something about "lemonade death."'

'Hmm!' Manella was silent for a moment. Then she said, 'That doesn't really matter so much. Wanda is crazy about lemonade and she's expecting lots of it at the party. I promised she'd have some with Mycogenian drops in it and she's looking forward to it.'

'So that if she heard something that sounded anything like lemonade, it would be translated into lemonade in her mind.'

'Yes. Why not?'

'Except that, in that case, what do you suppose it was that was *actually* said? She must have heard something in order to misinterpret it.'

'I don't think that's necessarily so. But why are we attaching so much importance to a little girl's dream? Please, I don't want anyone talking to her about it anymore. It's too upsetting.'

'I agree. I'll see to it that Dors drops the subject – at least with Wanda.'

'All right. I don't care if she is Wanda's grandmother, Hari. I'm her mother, after all, and my wishes come first.'

'Absolutely,' said Seldon soothingly and looked after Manella as she left. That was another burden – the unending competition between those two women.

9

Tamwile Elar was thirty-six years old and had joined Seldon's Psychohistory Project as Senior Mathematician four years earlier. He was a tall man, with a habitual twinkle in his eye and with more than a touch of self-assurance as well.

His hair was brown and had a loose wave in it, the more noticeable because he wore it rather long. He had an abrupt way of laughing, but there was no fault to be found with his mathematical ability.

Elar had been recruited from the West Mandanov University and Seldon always had to smile when he remembered how suspicious Yugo Amaryl had been of him at first. But then, Amaryl was suspicious of everyone. Deep in his heart (Seldon felt sure), Amaryl felt that psychohistory ought to have remained his and Hari's private province.

But even Amaryl was now willing to admit that Elar's membership in the group had eased his own situation tremendously. Yugo said, 'His techniques for avoiding chaos are unique and fascinating. No one else in the Project could have worked it out the way he did. Certainly nothing of this sort ever occurred to me. It didn't occur to you, either, Hari.'

'Well,' said Seldon grumpily, 'I'm getting old.' —

'If only,' said Amaryl, 'he didn't laugh so loud.'

'People can't help the way they laugh.'

Yet the truth was that Seldon found himself having a little trouble accepting Elar. It was rather humiliating that he himself had come nowhere near the 'achaotic equations,' as they were now called. It didn't bother Seldon that he had never thought of the principle behind the Electro-Clarifier — that was not really his field. The achaotic equations, however, he should, indeed, have thought of – or at least gotten close to.

He tried reasoning with himself. Seldon had worked out the entire basis for psychohistory and the achaotic equations grew naturally out of that basis. Could Elar have done Seldon's work three decades earlier? Seldon was convinced that Elar couldn't have. And was it so remarkable that Elar had thought up the principle of achaotism once the basis was in place?

All this was very sensible and very true, yet Seldon still found himself uneasy when facing Elar. Just slightly edgy. Weary age facing flamboyant youth.

Yet Elar never gave him obvious cause for feeling the difference in years. He never failed to show Seldon full respect or in any way to imply that the older man had passed his prime.

Of course, Elar was interested in the forthcoming festivities and had even, as Seldon had discovered, been the first to suggest that Seldon's birthday be celebrated. (Was this a nasty emphasis on Seldon's age? Seldon dismissed the possibility. If he believed *that*, it would mean he was picking up some of Dors's tricks of suspicion.)

Elar strode toward him and said, 'Maestro—' And Seldon winced, as always. He much preferred to have the senior members of the Project call him Hari, but it seemed such a small point to make a fuss over.

'Maestro,' said Elar. 'The word is out that you've been called in for a conference with General Tennar.'

'Yes. He's the new head of the military junta and I suppose he wants to see me to ask what psychohistory is all about. They've been asking me that since the days of Cleon and Demerzel.' (The new head! The junta was like a kaleidoscope, with some of its members periodically falling from grace and others rising from nowhere.)

'But it's my understanding he wants it now – right in the middle of the birthday celebration.'

'That doesn't matter. You can all celebrate without me.'

257

'No, we can't, Maestro. I hope you don't mind, but some of us got together and put in a call to the Palace and put the appointment off for a week.'

'What?' said Seldon, annoyed. 'Surely that was presumptuous of you – and risky, besides.'

'It worked out well. They've put it off and you'll need that time.'

'Why would I need a week?'

Elar hesitated. 'May I speak frankly, Maestro?'

'Of course you can. When have I ever asked that anyone speak to me in any way but frankly?'

Elar flushed slightly, his fair skin reddening, but his voice remained steady. 'It's not easy to say this, Maestro. You're a genius at mathematics. No one on the Project has any doubt of that. No one in the Empire – if they knew you and understood mathematics – would have any doubt about it. However, it is not given to anybody to be a universal genius.'

'I know that as well as you do, Elar.'

'I know you do. Specifically, though, you lack the ability to handle ordinary people – shall we say, stupid people. You lack a certain deviousness, a certain ability to sidestep, and if you are dealing with someone who is both powerful in government and somewhat stupid, you can easily endanger the Project and, for that matter, your own life, simply because you are too frank.'

'What is this? Am I suddenly a child? I've been dealing with politicians for a long time. I was First Minister for ten years, as perhaps you may remember.'

'Forgive me, Maestro, but you were not an extraordinarily effective one. You dealt with First Minister Demerzel, who was very intelligent, by all accounts, and with the Emperor Cleon, who was very friendly. Now you will encounter military people who are neither intelligent nor friendly – another matter entirely.'

'I've even dealt with military people and survived.'

'Not with General Dugal Tennar. He's another sort of thing altogether. I know him.'

258

'You know him? You have met him?'

'I don't know him personally, but he's from Mandanov, which, as you know, is my sector, and he was a power there before he joined the junta and rose through its ranks.'

'And what do you know about him?'

'Ignorant, superstitious, violent. He is not someone you can handle easily – or safely. You can use the week to work out methods for dealing with him.'

Seldon bit his lower lip. There was something to what Elar said and Seldon recognized the fact that, while he had plans of his own, it would still be difficult to try to manipulate a stupid, self-important, short-tempered person with overwhelming force at his disposal.

He said uneasily, 'I'll manage somehow. The whole matter of a military junta is, in any case, an unstable situation in the Trantor of today. It has already lasted longer than might have seemed likely.'

'Have we been testing that? I was not aware that we were making stability decisions on the junta.'

'Just a few calculations by Amaryl, making use of your achaotic equations.' He paused. 'By the way, I've come across some references to them as the Elar Equations.'

'Not by me, Maestro.'

'I hope you don't mind, but I don't want that. Psychohistoric elements are to be described functionally and not personally. As soon as personalities intervene, bad feelings arise.'

'I understand and quite agree, Maestro.'

'In fact,' said Seldon with a touch of guilt, 'I have always felt it wrong that we speak of the basic Seldon Equations of Psychohistory. The trouble is that's been in use for so many years, it's not practical to try to change it.'

'If you'll excuse my saying so, Maestro, you're an exceptional case. No one, I think, would quarrel with your receiving full credit for inventing the science of psychohistory. – But, if I may, I wish to get back to your meeting with General Tennar.'

'Well, what else is there to say?'

'I can't help but wonder if it might be better if you did not see him, did not speak to him, did not deal with him.'

'How am I to avoid that if he calls me in for a conference?'

'Perhaps you can plead illness and send someone in your place.'

'Whom?'

Elar was silent for a moment, but his silence was eloquent.

Seldon said, 'You, I take it.'

'Might that not be the thing to do? I am a fellow sectoral citizen of the General, which may carry some weight. You are a busy man, getting on in years, and it would be easy to believe that you are not entirely well. And if I see him, rather than yourself – please excuse me, Maestro – I can wiggle and maneuver more easily than you can.'

'Lie, you mean.'

'If necessary.'

'You'll be taking a huge chance.'

'Not too huge. I doubt that he will order my execution. If he becomes annoyed with me, as he well might, then I can plead – or you can plead on my behalf – youth and inexperience. In any case, if I get into trouble, that will be far less dangerous than if you were to do so. I'm thinking of the Project, which can do without me a great deal more easily than it can do without you.'

Seldon said with a frown, 'I'm not going to hide behind you, Elar. If the man wants to see me, he will see me. I refuse to shiver and shake and ask you to take chances for me. What do you think I am?'

'A frank and honest man – when the need is for a devious one.'

'I will manage to be devious – if I must. Please don't underestimate me, Elar.'

Elar shrugged hopelessly. 'Very well. I can only argue with you up to a certain point.'

'In fact, Elar, I wish you had not postponed the meeting. I would rather skip my birthday and see the General than the reverse. This birthday celebration was not my idea.' His voice died away in a grumble.

Elar said, 'I'm sorry.'

'Well,' said Seldon with resignation, 'we'll see what happens.'

He turned and left. Sometimes he wished ardently that he could run what was called a 'tight ship,' making sure that everything went as he wished it to, leaving little or no room for maneuvering among his subordinates. To do that, however, would take enormous time, enormous effort, would deprive him of any chance of working on psychohistory himself – and, besides, he simply lacked the temperament for it.

He sighed. He would have to speak to Amaryl.

10

Seldon strode into Amaryl's office, unannounced.

'Yugo,' he said abruptly, 'the session with General Tennar has been postponed.' He seated himself in a rather pettish manner.

It took Amaryl his usual few moments to disconnect his mind from his work. Looking up finally, he said, 'What was his excuse?'

'It wasn't he. Some of our mathematicians arranged a week's postponement so that it wouldn't interfere with the birthday celebration. I find all of this to be extremely annoying.'

'Why did you let them do that?'

'I didn't. They just went ahead and *arranged* things.' Seldon shrugged. 'In a way, it's my fault. I've whined so long about turning sixty that everyone thinks they have to cheer me up with festivities.'

Amaryl said, 'Of course, we can use the week.'

Seldon sat forward, immediately tense. 'Is something wrong?'

'No. Not that I can see, but it won't hurt to examine it further. Look, Hari, this is the first time in nearly thirty years that psychohistory has reached the point where it can actually make a prediction. It's not much of one – it's just a small pinch of the vast continent of humanity – but it's the best we've had so far. All right. We want to take advantage of that, see how it works, prove to ourselves that psychohistory is what we think it is: a predictive science. So it won't hurt to make sure that we haven't overlooked anything. Even this tiny bit of prediction is complex and I welcome another week of study.'

'Very well, then. I'll consult you on the matter before I go to see the General for any last-minute modifications that have to be made. Meanwhile, Yugo, do not allow any information concerning this to leak out to the others – not to *anyone*. If it fails, I don't want the people of the Project to grow downhearted. You and I will absorb the failure ourselves and keep on trying.'

A rare wistful smile crossed Amaryl's face. 'You and I. Do you remember when it really was just the two of us?'

'I remember it very well and don't think that I don't miss those days. We didn't have much to work with—'

'Not even the Prime Radiant, let alone the Electro-Clarifier.'

'But those were happy days.'

'Happy,' said Amaryl, nodding his head.

11

The University had been transformed and Hari Seldon could not refrain from being pleased.

The central rooms of the Project complex had suddenly sprouted in color and light, with holography filling the air with shifting three-dimensional images of Seldon at different places and different times. There was Dors Venabili smiling, looking somewhat younger – Raych as a teenager, still unpolished – Seldon and Amaryl, looking unbelievably young, bent over their computers. There was even a fleeting sight of Eto Demerzel, which filled Seldon's heart with yearning for his old friend and the security he had felt before Demerzel's departure.

The Emperor Cleon appeared nowhere in the holographics. It was not because holographs of him did not exist, but it was not wise, under the rule of the junta, to remind people of the past Imperium.

It all poured outward, overflowing, filling room after room, building after building. Somehow, time had been found to convert the entire University into a display the likes of which Seldon had never seen or even imagined. Even the dome lights were darkened to produce an artificial night against which the University would sparkle for three days.

'Three days!' said Seldon, half-impressed, half-horrified.

'Three days,' said Dors Venabili, nodding her head. 'The University would consider nothing less.'

'The expense! The labor!' said Seldon, frowning.

'The expense is minimal,' said Dors, 'compared to what you have done for the University. And the labor is all voluntary. The students turned out and took care of everything.'

A from-the-air view of the University appeared now, panoramically, and Seldon stared at it with a smile forcing itself onto his countenance.

Dors said, 'You're pleased. You've done nothing but grouse these past few months about how you didn't want any celebration for being an old man – and now look at you.'

'Well, it is flattering. I had no idea that they would do anything like this.'

'Why not? You're an icon, Hari. The whole world – the whole Empire – knows about you.'

'They do not,' said Seldon, shaking his head vigorously. 'Not one in a billion knows anything at all about me – and certainly not about psychohistory. No one outside the Project has the faintest knowledge of how psychohistory works and not everyone inside does, either.'

'That doesn't matter, Hari. It's *you*. Even the quadrillions who don't know anything about you or your work know that Hari Seldon is the greatest mathematician in the Empire.'

'Well,' said Seldon, looking around, 'they certainly are making me feel that way right now. But three days and three nights! The place will be reduced to splinters.'

'No, it won't. All the records have been stored away. The computers and other equipment have been secured. The students have set up a virtual security force that will prevent anything from being damaged.'

'You've seen to all of that, haven't you, Dors?' said Seldon, smiling at her fondly.

'A number of us have. It's by no means all me. Your colleague Tamwile Elar has worked with incredible dedication.'

Seldon scowled.

'What's the matter with Elar?' said Dors.

Seldon said, 'He keeps calling me "Maestro."'

Dors shook her head. 'Well, there's a terrible crime.'

Seldon ignored that and said, 'And he's young.'

'Worse and worse. Come, Hari, you're going to have to learn to grow old gracefully – and to begin with you'll have to show that you're enjoying yourself. That will please others and increase their enjoyment and surely you would want to do that. Come on. Move around. Don't hide here with me. Greet everyone. Smile. Ask after their health. And remember that, after the banquet, you're going to have to make a speech.'

'I dislike banquets and I doubly dislike speeches.'

'You'll have to, anyway. Now move!'

Seldon sighed dramatically and did as he was told. He cut quite an imposing figure as he stood in the archway leading into the main hall. The voluminous First Minister's robes of yesteryear were gone, as were the Heliconian-style garments he had favored in his youth. Now Seldon wore an outfit that bespoke his elevated status: straight pants, crisply pleated, a modified tunic on top. Embroidered in silver thread above his heart was the insignia: SELDON PSYCHOHISTORY PROJECT AT STREELING UNIVERSITY. It sparkled like a beacon against the dignified titanium-gray hue of his clothing. Seldon's eyes twinkled in a face now lined by age, his sixty years given away as much by his wrinkles as by his white hair.

He entered the room in which the children were feasting. The room had been entirely cleared, except for trestles with food upon them. The children rushed up to him as soon as they saw him – knowing, as they did, that he was the reason for the feast – and Seldon tried to avoid their clutching fingers.

'Wait, wait, children,' he said. 'Now stand back.'

He pulled a small computerized robot from his pocket and placed it on the floor. In an Empire without robots, this was something that he could expect to be eye-popping. It had the shape of a small furry animal, but it also had the capacity to change shapes without warning (eliciting squeals of children's laughter each time) and when it did so, the sounds and motions it made changed as well.

'Watch it,' said Seldon, 'and play with it, and try not to break it. Later on, there'll be one for each of you.'

He slipped out into the hallway leading back to the main hall and realized, as he did so, that Wanda was following him.

'Grandpa,' she said.

Well, of course, Wanda was different. He swooped down and lifted her high in the air, turned her over, and put her down.

'Are you having a good time, Wanda?' he asked.

'Yes,' she said, 'but don't go into that room.'

'Why not, Wanda? It's my room. It's the office where I work.'

'It's where I had my bad dream.'

'I know, Wanda, but that's all over, isn't it?' He hesitated, then he led Wanda to one of the chairs lining the hallway. He sat down and placed her in his lap.

'Wanda,' he said, 'are you sure it was a dream?'

'I think it was a dream.'

'Were you really sleeping?'

'I think I was.'

She seemed uncomfortable talking about it and Seldon decided to let it go. There was no use pushing her any further.

He said, 'Well, dream or not, there were two men and they talked of lemonade death, didn't they?'

Wanda nodded reluctantly.

Seldon said, 'You're sure they said lemonade?'

Wanda nodded again.

'Might they have said something else and you thought they said lemonade?'

'Lemonade is what they said.'

Seldon had to be satisfied with that. 'Well, run off and have a good time, Wanda. Forget about the dream.'

'All right, Grandpa.' She cheered up as soon as the matter of the dream was dismissed and off she went to join the festivities.

Seldon went to search for Manella. It took him an

extraordinarily long time to find her, since, at every step, he was stopped, greeted, and conversed with.

Finally he saw her in the distance. Muttering, 'Pardon me – Pardon me – There's someone I must – Pardon me–' he worked his way over to her with considerable trouble.

'Manella,' he said and drew her off to one side, smiling mechanically in all directions.

'Yes, Hari,' she said. 'Is something wrong?'

'It's Wanda's dream.'

'Don't tell me she's still talking about it.'

'Well, it's still bothering her. Listen, we have lemonade at the party, haven't we?'

'Of course, the children adore it. I've added a couple of dozen different Mycogenian taste buds to very small glasses of different shapes and the children try them one after the other to see which taste best. The adults have been drinking it, too. I have. Why don't you taste it, Hari? It's great.'

'I'm thinking. If it wasn't a dream, if the child really heard two men speak of lemonade death–' He paused, as though ashamed to continue.

Manella said, 'Are you thinking that someone poisoned the lemonade? That's ridiculous. By now every child in the place would be sick or dying.'

'I know,' muttered Seldon. 'I know.'

He wandered off and almost didn't see Dors when he passed her. She seized his elbow.

'Why the face?' she said. 'You look concerned.'

'I've been thinking of Wanda's lemonade death.'

'So have I, but I can't make anything of it so far.'

'I can't help but think of the possibility of poisoning.'

'Don't. I assure you that every bit of food that came into this party has been molecularly checked. I know you'll think that's my typical paranoia, but my task is guarding you and that is what I must do.'

'And everything is–'

'No poison. I promise you.'

Seldon smiled, 'Well, good. That's a relief. I didn't really think—'

'Let's hope not,' said Dors dryly. 'What concerns me far more than this myth of poison is that I have heard that you're going to be seeing that monster Tennar in a few days.'

'Don't call him a monster, Dors. Be careful. We're surrounded by ears and tongues.'

Dors immediately lowered her voice. 'I suppose you're right. Look around. All these smiling faces – and yet who knows which of our "friends" will be reporting back to the head and his henchmen when the night is over? Ah, humans! Even after all these thousands of centuries, to think that such base treachery still exists. It seems to me to be so unnecessary. Yet I know the harm it can do. That is why I must go with you, Hari.'

'Impossible, Dors. It would just complicate matters for me. I'll go myself and I'll have no trouble.'

'You would have no idea how to handle the General.'

Seldon looked grave. 'And *you* would? You sound exactly like Elar. He, too, is convinced that I am a helpless old fool. He, too, wants to come with me – or, rather, to go in my place. – I wonder how many people on Trantor are willing to take my place,' he added with clear sarcasm. 'Dozens? Millions?'

12

For ten years the Galactic Empire had been without an Emperor, but there was no indication of that fact in the way the Imperial Palace grounds were operated. Millennia of custom made the absence of an Emperor meaningless.

It meant, of course, that there was no figure in Imperial robes to preside over formalities of one sort or another. No Imperial voice gave orders; no Imperial wishes made themselves known; no Imperial gratifications or annoyances made themselves felt; no Imperial pleasures warmed either Palace; no Imperial sicknesses cast them in gloom. The Emperor's own quarters in the Small Palace were empty – the Imperial family did not exist.

And yet the army of gardeners kept the grounds in perfect condition. An army of service people kept the buildings in top shape. The Emperor's bed – never slept in – was made with fresh sheets every day; the rooms were cleaned; everything worked as it always worked; and the entire Imperial staff, from top to bottom, worked as they had always worked. The top officials gave commands as they would have done if the Emperor had lived, commands that they knew the Emperor would have given. In many cases, in particular in the higher echelons, the personnel were the same as those who had been there on Cleon's last day of life. The new personnel who had been taken on were carefully molded and trained into the traditions they would have to serve.

It was as though the Empire, accustomed to the rule of an Emperor, insisted on this 'ghost rule' to hold the Empire together.

The junta knew this – or, if they didn't, they felt it

vaguely. In ten years none of those military men who had commanded the Empire had moved into the Emperor's private quarters in the Small Palace. Whatever these men were, they were not Imperial and they knew they had no rights there. A populace that endured the loss of liberty would not endure any sign of irreverence to the Emperor – alive or dead.

Even General Tennar had not moved into the graceful structure that had housed the Emperors of a dozen different dynasties for so long. He had made his home and office in one of the structures built on the outskirts of the grounds – eyesores, but eyesores that were built like fortresses, sturdy enough to withstand a siege, with outlying buildings in which an enormous force of guards was housed.

Tennar was a stocky man, with a mustache. It was not a vigorous overflowing Dahlite mustache but one that was carefully clipped and fitted to the upper lip, leaving a strip of skin between the hair and the line of the lip. It was a reddish mustache and Tennar had cold blue eyes. He had probably been a handsome man in his younger days, but his face was pudgy now and his eyes were slits that expressed anger more often than any other emotion.

So he said angrily – as one would, who felt himself to be absolute master of millions of worlds and yet who dared not call himself an Emperor – to Hender Linn, 'I can establish a dynasty of my own.' He looked around with a scowl. 'This is not a fitting place for the master of the Empire.'

Linn said softly, 'To be master is what is important. Better to be a master in a cubicle than a figurehead in a palace.'

'Best yet, to be master in a palace. Why not?'

Linn bore the title of colonel, but it is quite certain that he had never engaged in any military action. His function was that of telling Tennar what he wanted to hear – and of carrying his orders, unchanged, to others. On occasion – if it seemed safe – he might try to

271

steer Tennar into more prudent courses.

Linn was well known as 'Tennar's lackey' and knew that was how he was known. It did not bother him. As lackey he was safe – and he had seen the downfall of those who had been too proud to be lackeys.

The time might, of course, come when Tennar himself would be buried in the ever-changing junta panorama, but Linn felt, with a certain amount of philosophy, that he would be aware of it in time and save himself. – Or he might not. There was a price for everything.

'No reason why you can't found a dynasty, General,' said Linn. 'Many others have done it in the long Imperial history. Still, it takes time. The people are slow to adapt. It is usually only the second or even third of the dynasty who is fully accepted as Emperor.'

'I don't believe that. I need merely announce myself as new Emperor. Who will dare quarrel with that? My grip is tight.'

'So it is, General. Your power is unquestioned on Trantor and in most of the Inner Worlds, yet it is possible that many in the farther Outer Worlds will not – just yet – accept a new Imperial dynasty.'

'Inner Worlds or Outer Worlds, military force rules all. That is an old Imperial maxim.'

'And a good one,' said Linn, 'but many of the provinces have armed forces of their own, nowadays, that they may not use on your behalf. These are difficult times.'

'You counsel caution, then.'

'I always counsel caution, General.'

'And someday you may counsel it once too often.'

Linn bent his head. 'I can only counsel what seems to me to be good and useful to you, General.'

'As in your constant harping to me about this Hari Seldon.'

'He is your greatest danger, General.'

'So you keep saying, but I don't see it. He's just a college professor.'

Linn said, 'So he is, but he was once First Minister.'

'I know, but that was in Cleon's time. Has he done anything since? With times being difficult and with the governors of the provinces being fractious, why is a professor my greatest danger?'

'It is sometimes a mistake,' said Linn carefully (for one had to be careful in educating the General), 'to suppose that a quiet unobtrusive man can be harmless. Seldon has been anything but harmless to those he has opposed. Twenty years ago the Joranumite movement almost destroyed Cleon's powerful First Minister, Eto Demerzel.'

Tennar nodded, but the slight frown on his face betrayed his effort to remember the matter.

'It was Seldon who destroyed Joranum and who succeeded Demerzel as First Minister. The Joranumite movement survived, however, and Seldon engineered its destruction, too, but not before it succeeded in bringing about the assassination of Cleon.'

'But Seldon survived that, didn't he?'

'You are perfectly correct. Seldon survived.'

'That is strange. To have permitted an Imperial assassination should have meant death for a First Minister.'

'So it should have. Nevertheless, the junta has allowed him to live. It seemed wiser to do so.'

'Why?'

Linn sighed internally. 'There is something called psychohistory, General.'

'I know nothing about that,' said Tennar flatly.

Actually he had a vague memory of Linn trying to talk to him on a number of occasions concerning this strange collection of syllables. He had never wanted to listen and Linn had known better than to push the matter. Tennar didn't want to listen now, either, but there seemed to be a hidden urgency in Linn's words. Perhaps, Tennar thought, he had now better listen.

'Almost no one knows anything about it,' said Linn, 'yet there are a few – uh – intellectuals, who find it of interest.'

'And what is it?'

'It is a complex system of mathematics.'

Tennar shook his head. 'Leave me out of that, please. I can count my military divisions. That's all the mathematics I need.'

'The story is,' said Linn, 'that psychohistory may make it possible to predict the future.'

The General's eyes bulged. 'You mean this Seldon is a fortune-teller?'

'Not in the usual fashion. It is a matter of science.'

'I don't believe it.'

'It is hard to believe, but Seldon has become something of a cult figure here on Trantor – and in certain places in the Outer Worlds. Now psychohistory – if it can be used to predict the future or if even people merely think it can be so used – can be a powerful tool with which to uphold the regime. I'm sure you have already seen this, General. One need merely predict our regime will endure and bring forth peace and prosperity for the Empire. People, believing this, will help make it a self-fulfilling prophecy. On the other hand, if Seldon wishes the reverse, he can predict civil war and ruin. People will believe that, too, and that would destabilize the regime.'

'In that case, Colonel, we simply make sure that the predictions of psychohistory are what we want them to be.'

'It would be Seldon who would have to make them and he is not a friend of the regime. It is important, General, that we differentiate between the Project that is working at Streeling University to perfect psychohistory and Hari Seldon. Psychohistory can be extremely useful to us, but it will be so only if someone other than Seldon were in charge.'

'Are there others who could be?'

'Oh yes. It is only necessary to get rid of Seldon.'

'What is so difficult with that? An order of execution – and it is done.'

'It would be better, General, if the government was

274

not seen to be directly involved in such a thing.'

'Explain!'

'I have arranged to have him meet with you, so that you can use your skill to probe his personality. You would then be able to judge whether certain suggestions I have in mind are worthwhile or not.'

'When is the meeting to take place?'

'It was to take place very soon, but his representatives at the Project asked for a few days leeway, because they were in the process of celebrating his birthday – his sixtieth, apparently. It seemed wise to allow that and to permit a week's delay.'

'Why?' demanded Tennar. 'I dislike any display of weakness.'

'Quite right, General. Quite right. Your instincts are, as always, correct. However, it seemed to me that the needs of the state might require us to know what and how the birthday celebration – which is taking place right now – might involve.'

'Why?'

'All knowledge is useful. Would you care to see some of the festivities?'

General Tennar's face remained dark. 'Is that necessary?'

'I think you will find it interesting, General.'

The reproduction – sight and sound – was excellent and for quite a while the hilarity of the birthday celebration filled the rather stark room in which the General sat.

Linn's low voice served as commentary. 'Most of this, General, is taking place in the Project complex, but the rest of the University is involved. We will have an air view in a few moments and you will see that the celebration covers a wide area. In fact, though I don't have the evidence available right now, there are corners of the planet here and there, in various University and sectoral settings mostly, where what we might call "sympathy celebrations" of one sort or another are taking place. The

275

celebrations are still continuing and will endure for another day at least.'

'Are you telling me that this is a Trantor-wide celebration?'

'In a specialized way. It affects mostly the intellectual classes, but it is surprisingly widespread. It may even be that there is some shouting on worlds other than Trantor.'

'Where did you get this reproduction?'

Linn smiled. 'Our facilities in the Project are quite good. We have reliable sources of information, so that little can happen that doesn't come our way at once.'

'Well then, Linn, what are all your conclusions about this?'

'It seems to me, General, and I'm sure that it seems so to you, that Hari Seldon is the focus of a personality cult. He has so identified himself with psychohistory that if we were to get rid of him in too open a manner, we would entirely destroy the credibility of the science. It would be useless to us.

'On the other hand, General, Seldon is growing old and it is not difficult to imagine him being replaced by another man: someone we could choose and who would be friendly to our great aims and hopes for the Empire. If Seldon could be removed in such a way that it is made to seem natural, then that is all we need.'

The General said, 'And you think I ought to see him?'

'Yes, in order to weigh his quality and decide what we ought to do. But we must be cautious, for he is a popular man.'

'I have dealt with popular people before,' said Tennar darkly.

13

'Yes,' said Hari Seldon wearily, 'it was a great triumph. I had a wonderful time. I can hardly wait until I'm seventy so I can repeat it. But the fact is, I'm exhausted.'

'So get yourself a good night's sleep, Dad,' said Raych, smiling. 'That's an easy cure.'

'I don't know how well I can relax when I have to see our great leader in a few days.'

'Not alone, you won't see him,' said Dors Venabili grimly.

Seldon frowned. 'Don't say that again, Dors. It is important for me to see him alone.'

'It won't be safe with you alone. Do you remember what happened ten years ago when you refused to let me come with you to greet the gardeners?'

'There is no danger of my forgetting when you remind me of it twice a week, Dors. In this case, though, I intend to go alone. What can he want to do to me if I come in as an old man, utterly harmless, to find out what he wants?'

'What do you imagine he wants?' said Raych, biting at his knuckle.

'I suppose he wants what Cleon always wanted. It will turn out that he has found out that psychohistory can, in some way, predict the future and he will want to use it for his own purposes. I told Cleon the science wasn't up to it nearly thirty years ago and I kept telling him that all through my tenure as First Minister – and now I'll have to tell General Tennar the same thing.'

'How do you know he'll believe you?' said Raych.

'I'll think of some way of being convincing.'

Dors said, 'I do not wish you to go alone.'

'Your wishing, Dors, makes no difference.'

At this point, Tamwile Elar interrupted. He said, 'I'm the only nonfamily person here. I don't know if a comment from me would be welcome.'

'Go ahead,' said Seldon. 'Come one, come all.'

'I would like to suggest a compromise. Why don't a number of us go with the Maestro. Quite a few of us. We can act as his triumphal escort, a kind of finale to the birthday celebration. – Now wait, I don't mean that we will all crowd into the General's offices. I don't even mean entering the Imperial Palace grounds. We can just take hotel rooms in the Imperial Sector at the edge of the grounds – the Dome's Edge Hotel would be just right – and we'll give ourselves a day of pleasure.'

'That's *just* what I need,' snorted Seldon. 'A day of pleasure.'

'Not you, Maestro,' said Elar at once. 'You'll be meeting with General Tennar. The rest of us, though, will give the people of the Imperial Sector a notion of your popularity – and perhaps the General will take note also. And if he knows we're all waiting for your return, it may keep him from being unpleasant.'

There was a considerable silence after that. Finally Raych said, 'It sounds too showy to me. It don't fit in with the image the world has of Dad.'

But Dors said, 'I'm not interested in Hari's *image*. I'm interested in Hari's *safety*. It strikes me that if we cannot invade the General's presence or the Imperial grounds, then allowing ourselves to accumulate, so to speak, as near the General as we can, might do us well. Thank you, Dr Elar, for a very good suggestion.'

'I don't want it done,' said Seldon.

'But I do,' said Dors, 'and if that's as close as I can get to offering you personal protection, then that much I will insist on.'

Manella, who had listened to it all without comment till then, said, 'Visiting the Dome's Edge Hotel could be a lot of fun.'

'It's not fun I'm thinking of,' said Dors, 'but I'll accept your vote in favor.'

And so it was. The following day some twenty of the higher echelon of the Psychohistory Project descended on the Dome's Edge Hotel, with rooms overlooking the open spaces of the Imperial Palace grounds.

The following evening Hari Seldon was picked up by the General's armed guards and taken off to the meeting.

At almost the same time Dors Venabili disappeared, but her absence was not noted for a long time. And when it was noted, no one could guess what had happened to her and the gaily festive mood turned rapidly into apprehension.

14

Dors Venabili had lived on the Imperial Palace grounds for ten years. As wife of the First Minister, she had entry to the grounds and could pass freely from the dome to the open, with her fingerprints as the pass.

In the confusion that followed Cleon's assassination, her pass had never been removed and now when, for the first time since that dreadful day, she wanted to move from the dome into the open spaces of the grounds, she could do so.

She had always known that she could do so easily only once, for, upon discovery, the pass would be canceled – but this was the one time to do it.

There was a sudden darkening of the sky as she moved into the open and she felt a distinct lowering of the temperature. The world under the dome was always kept a little lighter during the night period than natural night would require and was kept a little dimmer during the day period. And, of course, the temperature beneath the dome was always a bit milder than the outdoors.

Most Trantorians were unaware of this, for they spent their entire lives under the dome. To Dors it was expected, but it didn't really matter.

She took the central roadway, into which the dome opened at the site of the Dome's Edge Hotel. It was, of course, brightly lit, so that the darkness of the sky didn't matter at all.

Dors knew that she would not advance a hundred meters along the roadway without being stopped, less perhaps in the present paranoid days of the junta. Her alien presence would be detected at once.

Nor was she disappointed. A small ground-car skittered up and the guardsman shouted out the window,

'What are you doing here? Where are you going?'

Dors ignored the question and continued to walk.

The guardsman called out, 'Halt!' Then he slammed on the brakes and stepped out of the car, which was exactly what Dors had wanted him to do.

The guardsman was holding a blaster loosely in his hand – not threatening to use it, merely demonstrating its existence. He said, 'Your reference number.'

Dors said, 'I want your car.'

'What!' The guardsman sounded outraged. 'Your reference number. Immediately!' And now the blaster came up.

Dors said quietly, 'You don't need my reference number,' then she walked toward the guardsman.

The guardsman took a backward step. 'If you don't stop and present your reference number, I'll blast you.'

'No! Drop your blaster.'

The guardsman's lips tightened. His finger began to edge toward the contact, but before he could reach it, he was lost.

He could never describe afterward what happened in any accurate way. All he could say was 'How was I to know it was The Tiger Woman?' (The time came when he would be proud of the encounter.) 'She moved so fast, I didn't see exactly what she did or what happened. One moment I was going to shoot her down – I was sure she was some sort of madwoman – and the next thing I knew, I was completely overwhelmed.'

Dors held the guardsman in a firm grip, the hand with the blaster forced high. She said, 'Either drop the blaster at once or I will break your arm.'

The guardsman felt a kind of death grip around his chest that all but prevented him from breathing. Realizing he had no choice, he dropped the blaster.

Dors Venabili released him, but before the guardsman could make a move to recover, he found himself facing his own blaster in Dors's hand.

Dors said, 'I hope you've left your detectors in place.

Don't try to report what's happened too quickly. You had better wait and decide what it is you plan to tell your superiors. The fact that an unarmed woman took your blaster and your car may well put an end to your usefulness to the junta.'

Dors started the car and began to speed down the central roadway. A ten-year stay on the grounds told her exactly where she was going. The car she was in – an official ground-car – was not an alien intrusion into the grounds and would not be picked up as a matter of course. However, she had to take a chance on speed, for she wanted to reach her destination rapidly. She pushed the car to a speed of two hundred kilometers per hour.

The speed, at least, eventually did attract attention. She ignored radioed cries, demanding to know why she was speeding, and before long the car's detectors told her that another ground-car was in hot pursuit.

She knew that there would be a warning sent up ahead and that there would be other ground-cars waiting for her to arrive, but there was little any of them could do, short of trying to blast her out of existence – something apparently no one was willing to try, pending further investigation.

When she reached the building she had been heading for, two ground-cars were waiting for her. She climbed serenely out of her own car and walked toward the entrance.

Two men at once stood in her way, obviously astonished that the driver of the speeding car was not a guardsman but a woman dressed in civilian clothes.

'What are you doing here? What was the rush?'

Dors said quietly, 'Important message for Colonel Hender Linn.'

'Is that so?' said the guardsman harshly. There were now four men between her and the entrance. 'Reference number, please.'

Dors said, 'Don't delay me.'

'Reference number, I said.'

'You're wasting my time.'

One of the guardsmen said suddenly, 'You know who she looks like? The old First Minister's wife. Dr Venabili. The Tiger Woman.'

There was an odd backward step on the part of all four, but one of them said, 'You're under arrest.'

'Am I?' said Dors. 'If I'm The Tiger Woman, you must know that I am considerably stronger than any of you and that my reflexes are considerably faster. Let me suggest that all four of you accompany me quietly inside and we'll see what Colonel Linn has to say.'

'You're under arrest' came the repetition and four blasters were aimed at Dors.

'Well,' said Dors. 'If you insist.'

She moved rapidly and two of the guardsmen were suddenly on the ground, groaning, while Dors was standing with a blaster in each hand.

She said, 'I have tried not to hurt them, but it is quite possible that I have broken their wrists. That leaves two of you and I can shoot faster than you can. If either of you makes the slightest move – the slightest – I will have to break the habit of a lifetime and kill you. It will sicken me to do so and I beg you not to force me into it.'

There was absolute silence from the two guardsmen still standing – no motion.

'I would suggest,' said Dors, 'that you two escort me into the colonel's presence and that you then seek medical help for your comrades.'

The suggestion was not necessary. Colonel Linn emerged from his office. 'What is going on here? What is—'

Dors turned to him. 'Ah! Let me introduce myself. I am Dr Dors Venabili, the wife of Professor Hari Seldon. I have come to see you on important business. These four tried to stop me and, as a result, two are badly hurt. Send them all about their business and let me talk to you. I mean you no harm.'

Linn stared at the four guardsmen, then at Dors. He

said calmly, 'You mean me no harm? Though four guardsmen have not succeeded in stopping you, I have four thousand at my instant call.'

'Then call them,' said Dors. 'However quickly they come, it will not be in time to save you, should I decide to kill you. Dismiss your guardsmen and let us talk civilly.'

Linn dismissed the guardsmen and said, 'Well, come in and we will talk. Let me warn you, though, Dr Venabili – I have a long memory.'

'And I,' said Dors. They walked into Linn's quarters together.

15

Linn said with utmost courtesy, 'Tell me exactly why you are here, Dr Venabili.'

Dors smiled without menace – and yet not exactly pleasantly, either. 'To begin with,' she said, 'I have come here to show you that I *can* come here.'

'Ah?'

'Yes. My husband was taken to his interview with the General in an official ground-car under armed guard. I myself left the hotel at about the same time he did, on foot and unarmed – and here I am – and I believe I got here before he did. I had to wade through five guardsmen, including the guardsman whose car I appropriated, in order to reach you. I would have waded through fifty.'

Linn nodded his head phlegmatically. 'I understand that you are sometimes called The Tiger Woman.'

'I have been called that. – Now, having reached you, my task is to make certain that no harm comes to my husband. He is venturing into the General's lair – if I can be dramatic about it – and I want him to emerge unharmed and unthreatened.'

'As far as I am concerned, I know that no harm will come to your husband as a result of this meeting. But if you are concerned, why do you come to me? Why didn't you go directly to the General?'

'Because, of the two of you, it is you that has the brains.'

There was a short pause and Linn said, 'That would be a most dangerous remark – if overheard.'

'More dangerous for you than for me, so make sure it is not overheard. – Now, if it occurs to you that I am to be simply soothed and put off and that, if my husband is imprisoned or marked for execution, that there will really be nothing I can do about it, disabuse yourself.'

She indicated the two blasters that lay on the table before her. 'I entered the grounds with nothing. I arrived in your immediate vicinity with two blasters. If I had no blasters, I might have had knives, with which I am an expert. And if I had neither blasters nor knives, I would still be a formidable person. This table we're sitting at is metal – obviously – and sturdy.'

'It is.'

Dors held up her hands, fingers splayed, as if to show that she held no weapon. Then she dropped them to the table and, palms down, caressed its surface.

Abruptly Dors raised her fist and then brought it down on the table with a loud crash, which sounded almost as if metal were striking metal. She smiled and lifted her hand.

'No bruise,' Dors said. 'No pain. But you'll notice that the table is slightly bent where I struck it. If that same blow had come down with the same force on a person's head, the skull would have exploded. I have never done such a thing; in fact, I have never killed anyone, though I have injured several. Nevertheless, if Professor Seldon is harmed—'

'You are still threatening.'

'I am promising. I will do nothing if Professor Seldon is unharmed. Otherwise, Colonel Linn, I will be forced to maim or kill you and – I promise you again – I will do the same to General Tennar.'

Linn said, 'You cannot withstand an entire army, no matter how tigerish a woman you are. What then?'

'Stories spread,' said Dors, 'and are exaggerated. I have not really done much in the way of tigerishness, but many more stories are told of me than are true. Your guardsmen fell back when they recognized me and they themselves will spread the story, with advantage, of how I made my way to you. Even an army might hesitate to attack me, Colonel Linn, but even if they did and even if they destroyed me, beware the indignation of the people. The junta is maintaining order, but it is doing so only barely and you don't want anything to upset matters. Think, then, of how easy the alternative is. Simply do not harm Professor Hari Seldon.'

'We have no intention of harming him.'

'Why the interview, then?'

'What's the mystery? The General is curious about psychohistory. The government records are open to us. The old Emperor Cleon was interested. Demerzel, when he was First Minister, was interested. Why should we not be in our turn? In fact, more so.'

'Why more so?'

'Because time has passed. As I understand it, psychohistory began as a thought in Professor Seldon's mind. He has been working on it, with increasing vigor and with larger and larger groups of people, for nearly thirty years. He has done so almost entirely with government support, so that, in a way, his discoveries and techniques belong to the government. We intend to ask him about psychohistory, which, by now, must be far advanced beyond what existed in the times of Demerzel and Cleon, and we expect him to tell us what we want to know. We want something more practical than the vision of equations curling their way through air. Do you understand me?'

'Yes,' said Dors, frowning.

'And one more thing. Do not suppose that the danger to your husband comes from the government only and that any harm that reaches him will mean that you must attack us at once. I would suggest that Professor Seldon may have purely private enemies. I have no knowledge of such things, but surely it is possible.'

'I shall keep that in mind. Right now, I want to have you arrange that I join my husband during his interview with the General. I want to know, beyond doubt, that he is safe.'

'That will be hard to arrange and will take some time. It would be impossible to interrupt the conversation, but if you wait till it is ended—'

'Take the time and arrange it. Do not count on double-crossing me and remaining alive.'

16

General Tennar stared at Hari Seldon in a rather pop-eyed manner and his fingers tapped lightly at the desk where he sat.

'Thirty years,' he said. 'Thirty years and you are telling me you still have nothing to show for it?'

'Actually, General, twenty-eight years.'

Tennar ignored that. 'And all at government expense. Do you know how many billions of credits have been invested in your Project, Professor?'

'I haven't kept up, General, but we have records that could give me the answer to your question in seconds.'

'And so have we. The government, Professor, is not an endless source of funds. These are not the old times. We don't have Cleon's old free-and-easy attitude toward finances. Raising taxes is hard and we need credits for many things. I have called you here, hoping that you can benefit us in some way with your psychohistory. If you cannot, then I must tell you, quite frankly, that we will have to shut off the faucet. If you can continue your research without government funding, do so, for unless you show me something that would make the expense worth it, you will have to do just that.'

'General, you make a demand I cannot meet, but, if in response, you end government support, you will be throwing away the future. Give me time and eventually—'

'Various governments have heard that "eventually" from you for decades. Isn't it true, Professor, that you say your psychohistory predicts that the junta is unstable, that my rule is unstable, that in a short time it will collapse?'

Seldon frowned. 'The technique is not yet firm enough

for me to say that this is something that psychohistory states.'

'I put it to you that psychohistory does state it and that this is common knowledge within your Project.'

'No,' said Seldon warmly. 'No such thing. It is possible that some among us have interpreted some relationships to indicate that the junta may be an unstable form of government, but there are other relationships that may easily be interpreted to show it is stable. That is the reason why we must continue our work. At the present moment it is all too easy to use incomplete data and imperfect reasoning to reach any conclusion we wish.'

'But if you decide to present the conclusion that the government is unstable and say that psychohistory warrants it – even if it does not actually do so – will it not add to the instability?'

'It may very well do that, General. And if we announced that the government is stable, it may well add to the stability. I have had this very same discussion with Emperor Cleon on a number of occasions. It is possible to use psychohistory as a tool to manipulate the emotions of the people and achieve short-term effects. In the long run, however, the predictions are quite likely to prove incomplete or downright erroneous and psychohistory will lose all its credibility and it will be as though it had never existed.'

'Enough! Tell me straight out! What do you think psychohistory shows about my government?'

'It shows, we think, that there are elements of instability in it, but we are not certain – and cannot be certain – exactly in what way this can be made worse or made better.'

'In other words, psychohistory simply tells you what you would know without psychohistory and it is that in which government has invested uncounted piles of credits.'

'The time will come when psychohistory will tell us what we could not know without it and then the investment will pay itself back many, many times over.'

'And how long will it be before that time comes?'

'Not too long, I hope. We have been making rather gratifying progress in the last few years.'

Tennar was tapping his fingernail on his desk again. 'Not enough. Tell me something helpful now. Something useful.'

Seldon pondered, then said, 'I can prepare a detailed report for you, but it will take time.'

'Of course it will. Days, months, years – and somehow it will never be written. Do you take me for a fool?'

'No, of course not, General. However, I don't want to be taken for a fool, either. I can tell you something that I will take sole responsibility for. I have seen it in my psychohistorical research, but I may have misinterpreted what I saw. However, since you insist—'

'I insist.'

'You mentioned taxes a little while ago. You said raising taxes was difficult. Certainly. It is always difficult. Every government must do its work by collecting wealth in one form or another. The only two ways in which such credits can be obtained are, first, by robbing a neighbor, or second, persuading a government's own citizens to grant the credits willingly and peaceably.

'Since we have established a Galactic Empire that has been conducting its business in reasonable fashion for thousands of years, there is no possibility of robbing a neighbor, except as the result of an occasional rebellion and its repression. This does not happen often enough to support a government – and, if it did, the government would be too unstable to last long, in any case.'

Seldon drew a deep breath and went on. 'Therefore, credits must be raised by asking the citizens to hand over part of their wealth for government use. Presumably, since the government will then work efficiently, the citizens can better spend their credits in this way than to hoard it – each man to himself – while living in a dangerous and chaotic anarchy.

'However, though the request is reasonable and the citizenry is better off paying taxes as their price for maintaining a stable and efficient government, they are nevertheless reluctant to do so. In order to overcome this reluctance, governments must make it appear that they are not taking too many credits, and that they are considering each citizen's rights and benefits. In other words, they must lower the percentage taken out of low incomes; they must allow deductions of various kinds to be made before the tax is assessed, and so on.

'As time goes on, the tax situation inevitably grows more and more complex as different worlds, different sectors within each world, and different economic divisions all demand and require special treatment. The result is that the tax-collecting branch of the government grows in size and complexity and tends to become uncontrollable. The average citizen cannot understand why or how much he is being taxed; what he can get away with and what he can't. The government and the tax agency itself are often in the dark as well.

'What's more, an ever-larger fraction of the funds collected must be put into running the overelaborate tax agency – maintaining records, pursuing tax delinquents – so the amount of credits available for good and useful purposes declines despite anything we can do.

'In the end, the tax situation becomes overwhelming. It inspires discontent and rebellion. The history books tend to ascribe these things to greedy businessmen, to corrupt politicians, to brutal warriors, to ambitious viceroys – but these are just the individuals who take advantage of the tax overgrowth.'

The General said harshly, 'Are you telling me that our tax system is overcomplicated?'

Seldon said, 'If it were not, it would be the only one in history that wasn't, as far as I know. If there is one thing that psychohistory tells me is inevitable, it is tax overgrowth.'

'And what do we do about it?'

'That I cannot tell you. It is that for which I would like to prepare a report that – as you say – may take a while to get ready.'

'Never mind the report. The tax system is over-complicated, isn't it? Isn't that what you are saying?'

'It is possible that it is,' said Seldon cautiously.

'And to correct that, one must make the tax system simpler – as simple as possible, in fact.'

'I would have to study—'

'Nonsense. The opposite of great complication is great simplicity. I don't need a report to tell me that.'

'As you say, General,' said Seldon.

At this point the General looked up suddenly, as though he had been called – as, indeed, he had been. His fists clenched and holovision images of Colonel Linn and Dors Venabili suddenly appeared in the room.

Thunderstruck, Seldon exclaimed, 'Dors! What are you doing here?'

The General said nothing, but his brow furrowed into a frown.

17

The General had had a bad night and so, out of apprehension, had the colonel. They faced each other now – each at a loss.

The General said, 'Tell me again what this woman did.'

Linn seemed to have a heavy weight on his shoulders. 'She's The Tiger Woman. That's what they call her. She doesn't seem to be quite human, somehow. She's some sort of impossibly trained athlete, full of self-confidence, and, General, she's quite frightening.'

'Did she frighten *you*? A single woman?'

'Let me tell you exactly what she did and let me tell you a few other things about her. I don't know how true all the stories about her are, but what happened yesterday evening is true enough.'

He told the story again and the General listened, puffing out his cheeks.

'Bad,' he said. 'What do we do?'

'I think our course is plain before us. We want psychohistory—'

'Yes, we do,' said the General. 'Seldon told me something about taxation that – But never mind. That is beside the point at the moment. Go on.'

Linn, who, in his troubled state of mind, had allowed a small fragment of impatience to show on his face, continued, 'As I say, we want psychohistory without Seldon. He is, in any case, a used-up man. The more I study him, the more I see an elderly scholar who is living on his past deeds. He has had nearly thirty years to make a success of psychohistory and he has failed. Without him, with new men at the helm, psychohistory may advance more rapidly.'

'Yes, I agree. Now what about the woman?'

'Well, there you are. We haven't taken her into consideration because she has been careful to remain in the background. But I strongly suspect now that it will be difficult, perhaps impossible, to remove Seldon quietly and without implicating the government, as long as the woman remains alive.'

'Do you really believe that she will mangle you and me – if she thinks we have harmed her man?' said the General, his mouth twisting in contempt.

'I really think she will and that she will start a rebellion as well. It will be exactly as she promised.'

'You are turning into a coward.'

'General, please. I am trying to be sensible. I'm not backing off. We must take care of this Tiger Woman.' He paused thoughtfully. 'As a matter of fact, my sources have told me this and I admit to having paid far too little attention to the matter.'

'And how do you think we can get rid of her?'

Linn said, 'I don't know.' Then more slowly, 'But someone else might.'

18

Seldon had had a bad night also, nor was the new day promising to be much better. There weren't too many times when Hari felt annoyed with Dors. But this time, he was *very* annoyed.

He said, 'What a foolish thing to do! Wasn't it enough that we were all staying at the Dome's Edge Hotel? That alone would have been sufficient to drive a paranoid ruler into thoughts of some sort of conspiracy.'

'How? We were unarmed, Hari. It was a holiday affair, the final touch of your birthday celebration. We posed no threat.'

'Yes, but then you carried out your invasion of the Palace grounds. It was unforgivable. You raced to the Palace to interfere with my session with the General, when I had specifically – and several times – made it plain that I didn't want you there. I had my own plans, you know.'

Dors said, 'Your desires and your orders and your plans all take second place to your safety. I was primarily concerned about that.'

'I was in no danger.'

'That is not something I can carelessly assume. There have been two attempts on your life. What makes you think there won't be a third?'

'The two attempts were made when I was First Minister. I was probably worth killing then. Who would want to kill an elderly mathematician?'

Dors said, 'That's exactly what I want to find out and that's what I want to stop. I must begin by doing some questioning right here at the Project.'

'No. You will simply be upsetting my people. Leave them alone.'

'That's exactly what I can't do. Hari, my job is to protect you and for twenty-eight years I've been working at that. You cannot stop me now.'

Something in the blaze of her eyes made it quite clear that, whatever Seldon's desires or orders might be, Dors intended to do as she pleased.

Seldon's safety came first.

19

'May I interrupt you, Yugo?'

'Of course, Dors,' said Yugo Amaryl with a large smile. 'You are never an interruption. What can I do for you?'

'I am trying to find out a few things, Yugo, and I wonder if you would humor me in this.'

'If I can.'

'You have something in the Project called the Prime Radiant. I hear of it now and then. Hari speaks of it, so I imagine I know what it looks like when it is activated, but I have never actually seen it in operation. I would like to.'

Amaryl looked uncomfortable. 'Actually the Prime Radiant is just about the most closely guarded part of the Project and you aren't on the list of the members who have access.'

'I know that, but we've known each other for twenty-eight years—'

'And you're Hari's wife. I suppose we can stretch a point. We only have two full Prime Radiants. There's one in Hari's office and one here. Right there, in fact.'

Dors looked at the squat black cube on the central desk. It looked utterly undistinguished. 'Is that it?'

'That's it. It stores the equations that describe the future.'

'How do you get at those equations?'

Amaryl moved a contact and at once the room darkened and then came to life in a variegated glow. All around Dors were symbols, arrows, lines, mathematical signs of one sort or another. They seemed to be moving, spiraling, but when she focused her eyes on any particular portion, it seemed to be standing still.

She said, 'Is that the future, then?'

'It may be,' said Amaryl, turning off the instrument. 'I had it at full expansion so you could see the symbols. Without expansion, nothing is visible but patterns of light and dark.'

'And by studying those equations, you are able to judge what the future holds in store for us?'

'In theory.' The room was now back to its mundane appearance. 'But there are two difficulties.'

'Oh? What are they?'

'To begin with, no human mind has created those equations directly. We have merely spent decades programming more powerful computers and they have devised and stored the equations, but, of course, we don't know if they are valid and have meaning. It depends entirely on how valid and meaningful the programming is in the first place.'

'They could be all wrong, then?'

'They could be.' Amaryl rubbed his eyes and Dors could not help thinking how old and tired he seemed to have grown in the last couple of years. He was younger than Hari by nearly a dozen years, but he seemed much older.

'Of course,' Amaryl went on in a rather weary voice, 'we hope that they aren't all wrong, but that's where the second difficulty comes in. Although Hari and I have been testing and modifying them for decades, we can never be sure what the equations mean. The computer has constructed them, so it is to be presumed they must mean something – but what? There are portions that we think we have worked out. In fact, right now, I'm working on what we call Section A-23, a particularly knotty system of relationships. We have not yet been able to match it with anything in the real Universe. Still, each year sees us further advanced and I look forward confidently to the establishment of psychohistory as a legitimate and useful technique for dealing with the future.'

'How many people have access to these Prime Radiants?'

'Every mathematician in the Project has access but not at will. There have to be applications and time allotted and the Prime Radiant has to be adjusted to the portion of the equations a mathematician wishes to refer to. It gets a little complicated when everyone wants to use the Prime Radiant at the same time. Right now, things are slow, possibly because we're still in the aftermath of Hari's birthday celebration.'

'Is there any plan for constructing additional Prime Radiants?'

Amaryl thrust out his lips. 'Yes and no. It would be very helpful if we had a third, but someone would have to be in charge of it. It can't just be a community possession. I have suggested to Hari that Tamwile Elar – you know him, I think—'

'Yes, I do.'

'That Elar have a third Prime Radiant. His achaotic equations and the Electro-Clarifier he thought up make him clearly the third man in the Project after Hari and myself. Hari hesitates, however.'

'Why? Do you know?'

'If Elar gets one, he is openly recognized as the third man, over the head of other mathematicians who are older and who have more senior status in the Project. There might be some political difficulties, so to speak. I think that we can't waste time in worrying about internal politics, but Hari – Well, you know Hari.'

'Yes, I know Hari. Suppose I tell you that Linn has seen the Prime Radiant.'

'Linn?'

'Colonel Hender Linn of the junta. Tennar's lackey.'

'I doubt that very much, Dors.'

'He has spoken of spiraling equations and I have just seen them produced by the Prime Radiant. I can't help but think he's been here and seen it working.'

Amaryl shook his head, 'I can't imagine anyone bringing a member of the junta into Hari's office – or mine.'

'Tell me, who in the Project do you think is capable of

working with the junta in this fashion?'

'No one,' said Amaryl flatly and with clearly unlimited faith. 'That would be unthinkable. Perhaps Linn never saw the Prime Radiant but was merely told about it.'

'Who would tell him about it?'

Amaryl thought a moment and said, 'No one.'

'Well now, you talked about internal politics a while ago in connection with the possibility of Elar having a third Prime Radiant. I suppose in a Project such as this one with hundreds of people, there are little feuds going on all the time – friction – quarrels.'

'Oh yes. Poor Hari talks to me about it every once in a while. He has to deal with them in one way or another and I can well imagine what a headache it must be for him.'

'Are these feuds so bad that they interfere with the working of the Project?'

'Not seriously.'

'Are there any people who are more quarrelsome than others or any who draw more resentment than others? In short, are there people you can get rid of and perhaps remove 90 percent of the friction at the cost of 5 or 6 percent of the personnel?'

Amaryl raised his eyebrows. 'It sounds like a good idea, but I don't know whom to get rid of. I don't really participate in all the minutiae of internal politics. There's no way of stopping it, so for my part, I merely avoid it.'

'That's strange,' said Dors. 'Aren't you in this way denying any credibility to psychohistory?'

'In what way?'

'How can you pretend to reach a point where you can predict and guide the future, when you cannot analyze and correct something as homegrown as personal frictions in the very Project that promises so much?'

Amaryl chuckled softly. It was unusual, for he was not a man who was given to humor and laughter. 'I'm sorry, Dors, but you picked on the one problem that we have solved, after a manner of speaking. Hari himself identified the equations that represented the difficulties of personal friction years ago and I myself then added the final touch last year.

'I found that there were ways in which the equations could be changed so as to indicate a reduction in friction. In every such case, however, a reduction in friction here meant an increase in friction there. Never at any time was there a total decrease or, for that matter, a total increase in the friction within a closed group – that is, one in which no old members leave and no new members come in. What I proved, with the help of Elar's achaotic equations, was that this was true despite any conceivable action anyone could take. Hari calls it "the law of conservation of personal problems."

'It gave rise to the notion that social dynamics has its conservation laws as physics does and that, in fact, it is these laws that offer us the best possible tools for solving the truly troublesome aspects of psychohistory.'

Dors said, 'Rather impressive, but what if you end up finding that nothing at all can be changed, that everything that is bad is conserved, and that to save the Empire from destruction is merely to increase destruction of another kind?'

'Actually some have suggested that, but I don't believe it.'

'Very well. Back to reality. Is there anything in the frictional problems within the Project that threaten Hari? I mean, with physical harm.'

'Harm Hari? Of course not. How can you suggest such a thing?'

'Might there not be some who resent Hari, for being too arrogant, too pushy, too self-absorbed, too eager to grab all the credit? Or, if none of these things apply, might they not resent him simply because he has run the Project for so long a time?'

'I never heard anyone say such a thing about Hari.'

Dors seemed dissatisfied. 'I doubt that anyone would say such things in your hearing, of course. But thank you,

Yugo, for being so helpful and for giving me so much of your time.'

Amaryl stared after her as she left. He felt vaguely troubled, but then returned to his work and let other matters drift away.

20

One way Hari Seldon had (out of not too many ways) for pulling away from his work for a time was to visit Raych's apartment, just outside the University grounds. To do this invariably filled him with love for his foster son. There were ample grounds. Raych had been good, capable, and loyal – but besides that was the strange quality Raych had of inspiring trust and love in others.

Hari had observed it when Raych was a twelve-year-old street boy, who somehow pulled at his own and at Dors's heartstrings. He remembered how Raych had affected Rashelle, the onetime Mayor of Wye. Hari remembered how Joranum had trusted Raych, which led to his own destruction. Raych had even managed to win the heart of the beautiful Manella. Hari did not completely understand this particular quality that Raych embodied, but he enjoyed whatever contact he had with his foster son.

He entered the apartment with his usual 'All well here?'

Raych put aside the holographic material he was working with and rose to greet him, 'All well, Dad.'

'I don't hear Wanda.'

'For good reason. She's out shopping with her mother.'

Seldon seated himself and looked good-humoredly at the chaos of reference material. 'How's the book coming?'

'It's doing fine. It's me who might not survive.' He sighed. 'But for once, we'll get the straight poop on Dahl. Nobody's ever written a book devoted to that section, wouldja believe?'

Seldon had always noted that, whenever Raych

talked of his home sector, his Dahlite accent always strengthened.

Raych said, 'And how are you, Dad? Glad the festivities are over?'

'Enormously. I hated just about every minute of it.'

'Not so anyone could notice.'

'Listen, I had to wear a mask of sorts. I didn't want to spoil the celebration for everyone else.'

'You must have hated it when Mom chased after you onto the Palace grounds. Everyone I know has been talking about that.'

'I certainly did hate it. Your mother, Raych, is the most wonderful person in the world, but she is very difficult to handle. She might have spoiled my plans.'

'What plans are those, Dad?'

Seldon settled back. It was always pleasant to speak to someone in whom he had total trust and who knew nothing about psychohistory. More than once he had bounced thoughts off Raych and had worked them out into more sensible forms than would have been the case if those same thoughts had been mulled over in his mind. He said, 'Are we shielded?'

'Always.'

'Good. What I did was to set General Tennar thinking along curious lines.'

'What lines?'

'Well, I discussed taxation a bit and pointed out that, in the effort to make taxation rest evenly on the population, it grew more and more complex, unwieldy, and costly. The obvious implication was that the tax system must be simplified.'

'That seems to make sense.'

'Up to a point, but it is possible that, as a result of our little discussion, Tennar may oversimplify. You see, taxation loses effectiveness at both extremes. Overcomplicate it and people cannot understand it and pay for an overgrown and expensive tax organization. Oversimplify it and people consider it unfair and grow bitterly resentful.

The simplest tax is a poll tax, in which every individual pays the same amount, but the unfairness of treating rich and poor alike in this way is too evident to overlook.'

'And you didn't explain this to the General?'

'Somehow, I didn't get a chance.'

'Do you think the General will try a poll tax?'

'I think he will plan one. If he does, the news is bound to leak out and that alone would suffice to set off riots and possibly upset the government.'

'And you've done this on purpose, Dad?'

'Of course.'

Raych shook his head. 'I don't quite understand you, Dad. In your personal life, you're as sweet and gentle as any person in the Empire. Yet you can deliberately set up a situation in which there will be riots, suppression, deaths. There'll be a lot of damage done, Dad. Have you thought of that?'

Seldon leaned back in his chair and said sadly, 'I think of nothing else, Raych. When I first began my work on psychohistory, it seemed a purely academic piece of research to me. It was something that could not be worked out at all, in all likelihood, and, if it was, it would not be something that could be practically applied. But the decades pass and we know more and more and then comes the terrible urge to apply it.'

'So that people can die?'

'No, so that fewer people can die. If our psycho-historical analyses are correct now, then the junta cannot survive for more than a few years and there are various alternative ways in which it can collapse. They will all be fairly bloody and desperate. This method – the taxation gimmick – should do it more smoothly and gently than any other if – I repeat – our analyses are correct.'

'If they're not correct, what then?'

'In that case, we don't know what might happen. Still, psychohistory must reach the point where it can be used and we've been searching for years for something in which we have worked out the consequences with a certain assuredness and can find those consequences tolerable as compared with alternatives. In a way, this taxation gimmick is the first great psychohistoric experiment.'

'I must admit, it sounds like a simple one.'

'It isn't. You have no idea how complex psychohistory is. Nothing is simple. The poll tax has been tried now and then throughout history. It is never popular and it invariably gives rise to resistance of one form or another, but it almost never results in the violent overthrow of a government. After all, the powers of governmental oppression may be too strong or there may be methods whereby the people can bring to bear their opposition in a peaceful manner and achieve redress. If a poll tax were invariably or even just sometimes fatal, then no government would ever try it. It is only because it isn't fatal that it is tried repeatedly. The situation on Trantor is, however, not exactly normal. There are certain instabilities that seem clear in psychohistorical analysis, which make it seem that resentment will be particularly strong and repression particularly weak.'

Raych sounded dubious. 'I hope it works, Dad, but don't you think that the General will say that he was working under psychohistorical advice and bring you down with him?'

'I suppose he recorded our little session together, but if he publicizes that, it will show clearly that I urged him to wait till I could analyze the situation properly and prepare a report – and he refused to wait.'

'And what does Mom think of all this?'

Seldon said, 'I haven't discussed it with her. She's off on another tangent altogether.'

'Really?'

'Yes. She's trying to sniff out some deep conspiracy in the Project – aimed at me! I imagine she thinks there are many people in the Project who would like to get rid of me.' Seldon sighed. 'I'm one of them, I think. I would like to get rid of me as director of the Project and leave the gathering responsibilities of psychohistory to others.'

Raych said, 'What's bugging Mom is Wanda's dream. You know how Mom feels about protecting you. I'll bet even a dream about your dying would be enough to make her think of a murder conspiracy against you.'

'I certainly hope there isn't one.'

And at the idea of it both men laughed.

21

The small Electro-Clarification Laboratory was, for some reason, maintained at a temperature somewhat lower than normal and Dors Venabili wondered idly why that might be. She sat quietly, waiting for the one occupant of the lab to finish whatever it was she was doing.

Dors eyed the woman carefully. Slim, with a long face. Not exactly attractive, with her thin lips and receding jawline, but a look of intelligence shone in her dark brown eyes. The glowing nameplate on her desk said: CINDA MONAY.

She turned to Dors at last and said, 'My apologies, Dr Venabili, but there are some procedures that can't be interrupted even for the wife of the director.'

'I would have been disappointed in you if you had neglected the procedure on my behalf. I have been told some excellent things about you.'

'That's always nice to hear. Who's been praising me?'

'Quite a few,' said Dors. 'I gather that you are one of the most prominent nonmathematicians in the Project.'

Monay winced. 'There's a certain tendency to divide the rest of us from the aristocracy of mathematics. My own feeling is that, if I'm prominent, then I'm a prominent member of the Project. It makes no difference that I'm a nonmathematician.'

'That certainly sounds reasonable to me. – How long have you been with the Project?'

'Two and a half years. Before that I was a graduate student in radiational physics at Streeling and, while I was doing that, I served a couple of years with the Project as an intern.'

'You've done well at the Project, I understand.'

'I've been promoted twice, Dr Venabili.'

'Have you encountered any difficulties here, Dr Monay? – Whatever you say will be held confidential.'

'The work is difficult, of course, but if you mean, have I run into any social difficulties, the answer is no. At least not any more than one would expect in any large and complex project, I imagine.'

'And by that you mean?'

'Occasional spats and quarrels. We're all human.'

'But nothing serious?'

Monay shook her head. 'Nothing serious.'

'My understanding, Dr Monay,' said Dors, 'is that you have been responsible for the development of a device important to the use of the Prime Radiant. It makes it possible to cram much more information into the Prime Radiant.'

Monay broke into a radiant smile. 'Do you know about that? – Yes, the Electro-Clarifier. After that was developed, Professor Seldon established this small laboratory and put me in charge of other work in that direction.'

'I'm amazed that such an important advance did not bring you up into the higher echelons of the Project.'

'Oh well,' said Monay, looking a trifle embarrassed. 'I don't want to take all the credit. Actually my work was only that of a technician – a very skilled and creative technician, I like to think – but there you are.'

'And who worked with you?'

'Didn't you know? It was Tamwile Elar. He worked out the theory that made the device possible and I designed and built the actual instrument.'

'Does that mean he took the credit, Dr Monay?'

'No no. You mustn't think that. Dr Elar is not that kind of man. He gave me full credit for my share of the work. In fact, it was his idea to call the device by our names – both our names – but he couldn't.'

'Why not?'

'Well, that's Professor Seldon's rule, you know. All

309

devices and equations are to be given functional names and not personal ones – to avoid resentment. So the device is just the Electro-Clarifier. When we're working together, however, he gives the device our names and, I tell you, Dr Venabili, it sounds grand. Perhaps someday, all of the Project personnel will use the personal name. I hope so.'

'I hope so, too,' said Dors politely. 'You make Elar sound like a very decent individual.'

'He is. He is,' said Monay earnestly. 'He is a delight to work for. Right now, I'm working on a new version of the device, which is more powerful and which I don't quite understand. – I mean, what it's to be used for. However, he's directing me there.'

'And are you making progress?'

'Indeed. In fact, I've given Dr Elar a prototype, which he plans to test. If it works out, we can proceed further.'

'It sounds good,' agreed Dors. 'What do you think would happen if Professor Seldon were to resign as director of the Project? If he were to retire?'

Monay looked surprised. 'Is the professor planning to retire?'

'Not that I know of. I'm presenting you with a hypothetical case. Suppose he retires. Who do you think would be a natural successor? I think from what you have said that you would favor Professor Elar as the new director.'

'Yes, I would,' responded Monay after a trifling hesitation. 'He's far and away the most brilliant of the new people and I think he could run the Project in the best possible way. Still, he's rather young. There are a considerable number of old fossils – well, you know what I mean – who would resent being passed over by a young squirt.'

'Is there any old fossil you're thinking of in particular? Remember, this is confidential.'

'Quite a few of them, but there's Dr Amaryl. He's the heir apparent.'

'Yes, I see what you mean.' Dors rose. 'Well, thank you so much for your help. I'll let you return to your work now.'

She left, thinking about the Electro-Clarifier. And about Amaryl.

Yugo Amaryl said, 'Here you are again, Dors.'

'Sorry, Yugo. I'm bothering you twice this week. Actually you don't see anyone very often, do you?'

Amaryl said, 'I don't encourage people to visit me, no. They tend to interrupt me and break my line of thought. – Not you, Dors. You're altogether special, you and Hari. There's never a day I don't remember what you two have done for me.'

Dors waved her hand. 'Forget it, Yugo. You've worked hard for Hari and any trifling kindness we did for you has long been overpaid. How is the Project going? Hari never talks about it – not to me, anyway.'

Amaryl's face lightened and his whole body seemed to take on an infusion of life. 'Very well. Very well. It's difficult to talk about it without mathematics, but the progress we've made in the last two years is amazing – more than in all the time before that. It's as though, after we've been hammering away and hammering away, things have finally begun to break loose.'

'I've been hearing that the new equations worked out by Dr Elar have helped the situation.'

'The achaotic equations? Yes. Enormously.'

'And the Electro-Clarifier has been helpful, too. I spoke to the woman who designed it.'

'Cinda Monay?'

'Yes. That's the one.'

'A very clever woman. We're fortunate to have her.'

'Tell me, Yugo – You work at the Prime Radiant virtually all the time, don't you?'

'I'm more or less constantly studying it. Yes.'

'And you study it with the Electro-Clarifier.'

'Certainly.'

'Don't you ever think of taking a vacation, Yugo?'

Amaryl looked at her owlishly, blinking slowly. 'A vacation?'

'Yes. Surely you've heard the word. You know what a vacation is.'

'Why should I take a vacation?'

'Because you seem dreadfully tired to me.'

'A little, now and then. But I don't want to leave the work.'

'Do you feel more tired now than you used to?'

'A little. I'm getting older, Dors.'

'You're only forty-nine.'

'That's still older than I've ever been before.'

'Well, let it go. Tell me, Yugo – just to change the subject. How is Hari doing at his work? You've been with him so long that no one could possibly know him better than you do. Not even I. At least, as far as his work is concerned.'

'He's doing very well, Dors. I see no change in him. He still has the quickest and brightest brain in the place. Age is having no effect on him – at least, not so far.'

'That's good to hear. I'm afraid that his own opinion of himself is not as high as yours is. He's not taking his age well. We had a difficult time getting him to celebrate his recent birthday. Were you at the festivities, by the way? I didn't see you.'

'I attended part of the time. But, you know, parties of that kind are not the sort of thing I feel at home with.'

'Do you think Hari is wearing out? I'm not referring to his mental brilliance. I'm referring to his physical capacities. In your opinion, is he growing tired – too tired to bear up under his responsibilities?'

Amaryl looked astonished. 'I never gave it any thought. I can't imagine him growing tired.'

'He may be, just the same. I think he has the impulse, now and then, to give up his post and hand the task over to some younger man.'

Amaryl sat back in his chair and put down the graphic

stylus he had been fiddling with ever since Dors had entered. 'What! That's ridiculous! Impossible!'

'Are you sure?'

'Absolutely. He certainly wouldn't consider such a thing without discussing it with me. And he hasn't.'

'Be reasonable, Yugo. Hari is exhausted. He tries not to show it, but he is. What if he does decide to retire? What would become of the Project? What would become of psychohistory?'

Amaryl's eyes narrowed. 'Are you joking, Dors?'

'No. I'm just trying to look into the future.'

'Surely, if Hari retires, I succeed to the post. He and I ran the Project for years before anyone else joined us. He and I. No one else. Except for him, no one knows the Project as I do. I'm amazed you don't take my succession for granted, Dors.'

Dors said, 'There's no question in my mind or in anyone else's that you are the logical successor, but do you want to be? You may know everything about psychohistory, but do you want to throw yourself into the politics and complexities of a large Project and abandon much of your work in order to do so? Actually it's trying to keep everything moving smoothly that's been wearing Hari down. Can you take on that part of the job?'

'Yes, I can and it's not something I intend to discuss. – Look here, Dors. Did you come here to break the news that Hari intends to ease me out?'

Dors said, 'Certainly not! How could you think that of Hari! Have you ever known him to turn on a friend?'

'Very well, then. Let's drop the subject. Really, Dors, if you don't mind, there are things I must do.' Abruptly he turned away from her and bent over his work once more.

'Of course. I didn't mean to take up this much of your time.'

Dors left, frowning.

23

Raych said, 'Come in, Mom. The coast is clear. I've sent Manella and Wanda off somewhere.'

Dors entered, looked right and left out of sheer habit, and sat down in the nearest chair.

'Thanks,' said Dors. For a while she simply sat there, looking as if the weight of the Empire were on her shoulders.

Raych waited, then said, 'I never got a chance to ask you about your wild trip into the Palace grounds. It isn't every guy who has a mom who can do that.'

'We're not talking about that, Raych.'

'Well then, tell me – You're not one for giving anything away by facial expressions, but you look sorta down. Why is that?'

'Because I feel, as you say, sorta down. In fact, I'm in a bad mood because I have terribly important things on my mind and there's no use talking to your father about it. He's the most wonderful man in the world, but he's very hard to handle. There's no chance that he'd take an interest in the dramatic. He dismisses it all as my irrational fears for his life – and my subsequent attempts to protect him.'

'Come on, Mom, you do seem to have irrational fears where Dad's concerned. If you've got something dramatic in mind, it's probably all wrong.'

'Thank you. You sound just like he does and you leave me frustrated. Absolutely frustrated.'

'Well then, unburden yourself, Mom. Tell me what's on your mind. From the beginning.'

'It starts with Wanda's dream.'

'Wanda's dream! Mom! Maybe you'd better stop right now. I know that Dad won't want to listen if you start

315

that way. I mean, come on. A little kid has a dream and you make a big deal of it. That's ridiculous.'

'I don't think it was a dream, Raych. I think what she *thought* was a dream were two real people, talking about what she thought concerned the death of her grandfather.'

'That's a wild guess on your part. What possible chance does this have of being true?'

'Just suppose it is true. The one phrase that remained with her was "lemonade death." Why should she dream that? It's much more likely that she heard that and distorted the words she heard – in which case, what were the undistorted words?'

'I can't tell you,' said Raych, his voice incredulous.

Dors did not fail to catch that. 'You think this is just my sick invention. Still, if I happen to be right, I might be at the start of unraveling a conspiracy against Hari right here in the Project.'

'Are there conspiracies in the Project? That sounds as impossible to me as finding significance in a dream.'

'Every large project is riddled with angers, frictions, jealousies of all sorts.'

'Sure. Sure. We're talking nasty words and faces and nose thumbing and tale bearing. That's nothing at all like talking conspiracy. It's not like talking about killing Dad.'

'It's just a difference in degree. A small difference – maybe.'

'You'll never make Dad believe that. For that matter, you'll never make *me* believe that.' Raych walked hastily across the room and back again, 'And you've been trying to nose out this so-called conspiracy, have you?'

Dors nodded.

'And you've failed.'

Dors nodded.

'Doesn't it occur to you that you've failed because there is no conspiracy, Mom?'

Dors shook her head. 'I've failed so far, but that doesn't

shake my belief that one exists. I have that feeling.'

Raych laughed. 'You sound very ordinary, Mom. I would expect more from you than "I have that feeling."'

'There is one phrase that I think can be distorted into "lemonade." That's "layman-aided." '

'Laymanayded? What's that?'

'Layman-aided. Two words. A layman is what the mathematicians at the Project call nonmathematicians.'

'Well?'

'Suppose,' interjected Dors firmly, 'someone spoke of "layman-aided death," meaning that some way could be found to kill Hari in which one or more nonmathematicians would play an essential role. Might that not have sounded to Wanda like "lemonade death," considering that she had never heard the phrase "layman-aided" any more than you did, but that she was extraordinarily fond of lemonade?'

'Are you trying to tell me that there were people in Dad's private office, of all places – How many people, by the way?'

'Wanda, in describing her dream, says two. My own feeling is that one of the two was none other than Colonel Hender Linn of the junta and that he was being shown the Prime Radiant and that there must have been a discussion involving the elimination of Hari.'

'You're getting wilder and wilder, Mom. Colonel Linn and another man in Dad's office talking murder and not knowing that there was a little girl hidden in a chair, overhearing them? Is that it?'

'More or less.'

'In that case, if there is mention of laymen, then one of the people, presumably the one that isn't Linn, must be a mathematician.'

'It would seem to be so.'

'That seems utterly impossible. But even if it were true, which mathematician do you suppose might be in question? There are at least fifty in the Project.'

'I haven't questioned them all. I've questioned a few

and some laymen, too, for that matter, but I have uncovered no leads. Of course, I can't be too open in my questions.'

'In short, no one you have interviewed has given you any lead on any dangerous conspiracy.'

'No.'

'I'm not surprised. They haven't done so, because—'

'I know your "because," Raych. Do you suppose people are going to break down and give away conspiracies under mild questioning? I am in no position to try to beat the information out of anyone. Can you imagine what your father would say if I upset one of his precious mathematicians?'

Then, with a sudden change in the intonation of her voice, she said, 'Raych, have you talked to Yugo Amaryl lately?'

'No, not recently. He's not one of your sociable creatures, you know. If you pulled the psychohistory out of him, he'd collapse into a little pile of dry skin.'

Dors made a face at the picture and said, 'I've talked to him twice recently and he seems to me to be a little withdrawn. I don't mean just tired. It is almost as though he's not aware of the world.'

'Yes. That's Yugo.'

'Is he getting worse lately?'

Raych thought awhile. 'He might be. He's getting older, you know. We all are. – Except you, Mom.'

'Would you say that Yugo had crossed the line and become a little unstable, Raych?'

'Who? Yugo? He has nothing to be unstable about. Or with. Just leave him at his psychohistory and he'll mumble quietly to himself for the rest of his life.'

'I don't think so. There is something that interests him – and very strongly, too. That's the succession.'

'What succession?'

'I mentioned that someday your father might want to retire and it turns out that Yugo is determined – absolutely determined – to be his successor.'

318

'I'm not surprised. I imagine that everyone agrees that Yugo is the natural successor. I'm sure Dad thinks so, too.'

'But he seemed to me to be not quite normal about it. He thought I was coming to him to break the news that Hari had shoved him aside in favor of someone else. Can you imagine anyone thinking that of Hari?'

'It is surprising—' Raych interrupted himself and favored his mother with a long look. He said, 'Mom, are you getting ready to tell me that it might be Yugo who's at the heart of this conspiracy you're speaking of? That he wants to get rid of Dad and take over?'

'Is that entirely impossible?'

'Yes, it is, Mom. Entirely. If there's anything wrong with Yugo, it's overwork and nothing else. Staring at all those equations or whatever they are, all day and half the night, would drive anyone crazy.'

Dors rose to her feet with a jerk. 'You're right.'

Raych, startled, said, 'What's the matter?'

'What you've said. It's given me an entirely new idea. A crucial one, I think.' Turning, without another word, she left.

24

Dors Venabili disapproved, as she said to Hari Seldon, 'You've spent four days at the Galactic Library. Completely out of touch and again you managed to go without me.'

Husband and wife stared at each other's image on their holoscreens. Hari had just returned from a research trip to the Galactic Library in Imperial Sector. He was calling Dors from his Project office to let her know he'd returned to Streeling. Even in anger, thought Hari, Dors is beautiful. He wished he could reach out and touch her cheek.

'Dors,' he began, a placating note in his voice, 'I did not go alone. I had a number of people with me, and the Galactic Library, of all places, is safe for scholars, even in these turbulent times. I am going to have to be at the Library more and more often, I think, as time goes on.'

'And you're going to continue to do it without telling me?'

'Dors, I can't live according to these death-filled views of yours. Nor do I want you running after me and upsetting the librarians. They're not the junta. I need them and I don't want to make them angry. But I do think that I – we – should take an apartment nearby.'

Dors looked grim, shook her head, and changed the subject. 'Do you know that I had two talks with Yugo recently?'

'Good. I'm glad you did. He needs contact with the outside world.'

'Yes, he does, because something's wrong with him. He's not the Yugo we've had with us all these years. He's become vague, distant, and – oddly enough – passionate on only one point, as nearly as I can tell – his determination to succeed you on your retirement.'

'That would be natural – if he survives me.'

'Don't you expect him to survive you?'

'Well, he's eleven years younger than I am, but the vicissitudes of circumstance—'

'What you really mean is that you recognize that Yugo is in a bad way. He looks and acts older than you do, for all his younger age, and that seems to be a rather recent development. Is he ill?'

'Physically? I don't think so. He has his periodic examinations. I'll admit, though, that he seems drained. I've tried to persuade him to take a vacation for a few months – a whole year's sabbatical, if he wishes. I've suggested that he leave Trantor altogether, just so that he is as far away from the Project as possible for a while. There would be no problem in financing his stay on Getorin – which is a pleasant resort world not too many light-years away.'

Dors shook her head impatiently. 'And, of course, he won't. I suggested a vacation to him and he acted as though he didn't know the *meaning* of the word. He absolutely refused.'

'So what can we do?' said Seldon.

Dors said, 'We can think a little. Yugo worked for a quarter of a century on the Project and seemed to maintain his strength without any trouble at all and now suddenly he has weakened. It can't be age. He's not yet fifty.'

'Are you suggesting something?'

'Yes. How long have you and Yugo been using this Electro-Clarifier thing on your Prime Radiants?'

'About two years – maybe a little more.'

'I presume that the Electro-Clarifier is used by anyone who uses the Prime Radiant.'

'That's right.

'Which means Yugo and you, mostly?'

'Yes.'

'And Yugo more than you?'

'Yes. Yugo concentrates fiercely on the Prime Radiant

321

and its equations. I, unfortunately, have to spend much of my time on administrative duties.'

'And what effect does the Electro-Clarifier have on the human body?'

Seldon looked surprised. 'Nothing of any significance that I am aware of.'

'In that case, explain something to me, Hari. The Electro-Clarifier has been in operation for over two years and in that time you've grown measurably more tired, crotchety, and a little – out of touch. Why is that?'

'I'm getting older, Dors.'

'Nonsense. Whoever told you that sixty is crystallized senility? You're using your age as a crutch and a defense and I want you to stop it. Yugo, though he's younger, has been exposed to the Electro-Clarifier more than you have and, as a result, he is more tired, more crotchety, and, in my opinion, a great deal less in touch than you are. And he is rather childishly intense about the succession. Don't you see anything significant in this?'

'Age and overwork. That's significant.'

'No, it's the Electro-Clarifier. It's having a long-term effect on the two of you.'

After a pause, Seldon said, 'I can't disprove that, Dors, but I don't see how it's possible. The Electro-Clarifier is a device that produces an unusual electronic field, but it is still only a field of the type to which human beings are constantly exposed. It can't do any unusual harm. – In any case, we can't give up its use. There's no way of continuing the progress of the Project without it.'

'Now, Hari, I must ask something of you and you must cooperate with me on this. Go nowhere outside the Project without telling me and do nothing out of the ordinary without telling me. Do you understand?'

'Dors, how can I agree to this? You're trying to put me into a straitjacket.'

'It's just for a while. A few days. A week.'

'What's going to happen in a few days or a week?'

Dors said, 'Trust me. I will clear up everything.'

25

Hari Seldon knocked gently with an old-fashioned code and Yugo Amaryl looked up. 'Hari, how nice of you to drop around.'

'I should do it more often. In the old days we were together all the time. Now there are hundreds of people to worry about – here, there, and everywhere – and they get between us. Have you heard the news?'

'What news?'

'The junta is going to set up a poll tax – a nice substantial one. It will be announced on TrantorVision tomorrow. It will be just Trantor for now and the Outer Worlds will have to wait. That's a little disappointing. I had hoped it would be Empire-wide all at once, but apparently I didn't give the General enough credit for caution.'

Amaryl said, 'Trantor will be enough. The Outer Worlds will know that their turn will follow in not too long a time.'

'Now we'll have to see what happens.'

'What will happen is that the shouting will start the instant the announcement is out and the riots will begin, even before the new tax goes into effect.'

'Are you sure of it?'

Amaryl put his Prime Radiant into action at once and expanded the appropriate section. 'See for yourself, Hari. I don't see how that can be misinterpreted and that's the prediction under the particular circumstances that now exist. If it doesn't happen, it means that everything we've worked out in psychohistory is wrong and I refuse to believe that.'

'I'll try to have courage,' said Seldon, smiling. Then 'How do you feel lately, Yugo?'

'Well enough. Reasonably well. – And how are you, by the way? I've heard rumors that you're thinking of resigning. Even Dors said something about that.'

'Pay no attention to Dors. These days she's saying all sorts of things. She has a bug in her head about some sort of danger permeating the Project.'

'What kind of danger?'

'It's better not to ask. She's just gone off on one of her tangents and, as always, that makes her uncontrollable.'

Amaryl said, 'See the advantage I have in being single?' Then, in a lower voice, 'If you do resign, Hari, what are your plans for the future?'

Seldon said, 'You'll take over. What other plans can I possibly have?'

And Amaryl smiled.

26

In the small conference room in the main building, Tamwile Elar listened to Dors Venabili with a gathering look of confusion and anger on his face. Finally he burst out, 'Impossible!'

He rubbed his chin, then went on cautiously, 'I don't mean to offend you, Dr Venabili, but your suggestions are ridic— cannot be right. There's no way in which anyone can think that there are, in this Psychohistory Project, any feelings so deadly as to justify your suspicions. I would certainly know if there were and I assure you there are not. Don't think it.'

'I do think it,' said Dors stubbornly, 'and I can find evidence for it.'

Elar said, 'I don't know how to say this without offense, Dr Venabili, but if a person is ingenious enough and intent enough on proving something, he or she can find all the evidence he or she wants – or, at least, something he or she believes is evidence.'

'Do you think I'm paranoid?'

'I think that in your concern for the Maestro – something in which I'm with you all the way – you're, shall we say, overheated.'

Dors paused and considered Elar's statement. 'At least you're right that a person with sufficient ingenuity can find evidence anywhere. I can build a case against you, for instance.'

Elar's eyes widened as he stared at her in total astonishment. 'Against me? I would like to hear what case you can possibly have against me.'

'Very well. You shall. The birthday party was your idea, wasn't it?'

Elar said, 'I thought of it, yes, but I'm sure others did,

325

too. With the Maestro moaning about his advancing years, it seemed a natural way of cheering him up.'

'I'm sure others may have thought of it, but it was you who actually pressed the issue and got my daughter-in-law fired up about it. She took over the details and you persuaded her that it was possible to put together a really large celebration. Isn't that so?'

'I don't know if I had any influence on her, but even if I did, what's wrong with that?'

'In itself, nothing, but in setting up so large and wide-spread and prolonged a celebration, were we not advertising to the rather unstable and suspicious men of the junta that Hari was too popular and might be a danger to them?'

'No one could possibly believe such a thing was in my mind.'

Dors said, 'I am merely pointing out the possibility. – In planning the birthday celebration, you insisted that the central offices be cleared out—'

'Temporarily. For obvious reasons.'

'—and insisted that they remain totally unoccupied for a while. No work was done – except by Yugo Amaryl – during that time.'

'I didn't think it would hurt if the Maestro had some rest in advance of the party. Surely you can't complain about that.'

'But it meant that you could consult with other people in the empty offices and do so in total privacy. The offices are, of course, well shielded.'

'I did consult there – with your daughter-in-law, with caterers, suppliers, and other tradesmen. It was absolutely necessary, wouldn't you say?'

'And if one of those you consulted with was a member of the junta?'

Elar looked as though Dors had hit him. 'I resent that, Dr Venabili. What do you take me for?'

Dors did not answer directly. She said, 'You went on to talk to Dr Seldon about his forthcoming meeting with the General and urged him – rather pressingly – to let you take his place and run the risks that might follow. The result was, of course, that Dr Seldon insisted rather vehemently on seeing the General himself, which one can argue was precisely what you wanted him to do.'

Elar emitted a short nervous laugh. 'With all due respect, this *does* sound like paranoia, Doctor.'

Dors pressed on. 'And then, after the party, it was you, wasn't it, who was the first to suggest that a group of us go to the Dome's Edge Hotel?'

'Yes and I remember you saying it was a good idea.'

'Might it not have been suggested in order to make the junta uneasy, as yet another example of Hari's popularity? And might it not have been arranged to tempt me into invading the Palace grounds?'

'Could I have stopped you?' said Elar, his incredulity giving way to anger. 'You had made up your own mind about that.'

Dors paid no attention. 'And, of course, you hoped that by entering the Palace grounds I might make sufficient trouble to turn the junta even further against Hari.'

'But why, Dr Venabili? Why would I be doing this?'

'One might say it was to get rid of Dr Seldon and to succeed him as director of the Project.'

'How can you possibly think this of me? I can't believe you are serious. You're just doing what you said you would at the start of this exercise – just showing me what can be done by an ingenious mind intent on finding so-called evidence.'

'Let's turn to something else. I said that you were in a position to use the empty rooms for private conversations and that you may have been there with a member of the junta.'

'That is not even worth a denial.'

'But you were overheard. A little girl wandered into the room, curled up in a chair out of sight, and overheard your conversation.'

Elar frowned. 'What did she hear?'

'She reported that two men were talking about death. She was only a child and could not repeat anything in detail, but two words did impress her and they were "lemonade death."'

'Now you seem to be changing from fantasy to – if you'll excuse me – madness. What can "lemonade death" mean and what would it have to do with me?'

'My first thought was to take it literally. The girl in question is very fond of lemonade and there was a good deal of it at the party, but no one had poisoned it.'

'Thanks for granting sanity that much.'

'Then I realized the girl had heard something else, which her imperfect command of the language and her love of the beverage had perverted into "lemonade."'

'And have you invented a distortion?' Elar snorted.

'It did seem to me for a while that what she might have heard was "laymen-aided death."'

'What does that mean?'

'An assassination carried through by laymen – by nonmathematicians.'

Dors stopped and frowned. Her hand clutched her chest.

Elar said with sudden concern, 'Is something wrong, Dr Venabili?'

'No,' said Dors, seeming to shake herself.

For a few moments she said nothing further and Elar cleared his throat. There was no sign of amusement on his face any longer, as he said, 'Your comments, Dr Venabili, are growing steadily more ridiculous and – well, I don't care if I do offend you, but I have grown tired of them. Shall we put an end to this?'

'We are almost at an end, Dr Elar. Layman-aided may indeed be ridiculous, as you say. I had decided that in my own mind, too. – You are, in part, responsible for the development of the Electro-Clarifier, aren't you?'

Elar seemed to stand straighter as he said with a touch of pride, 'Entirely responsible.'

328

'Surely not entirely. I understand it was designed by Cinda Monay.'

'A designer. She followed my instructions.'

'A *layman*. The Electro-Clarifier is a *layman-aided* device.'

With suppressed violence Elar said, 'I don't think I want to hear that phrase again. Once more, shall we put an end to this?'

Dors forged on, as if she hadn't heard his request. 'Though you give her no credit now, you gave Cinda credit to her face – to keep her working eagerly, I suppose. She said you gave her credit and she was very grateful because of it. She said you even called the device by her name and yours, though that's not the official name.'

'Of course not. It's the Electro-Clarifier.'

'And she said she was designing improvements, intensifiers, and so on – and that you had the prototype of an advanced version of the new device for testing.'

'What has all this to do with anything?'

'Since Dr Seldon and Dr Amaryl have been working with the Electro-Clarifier, both have in some ways deteriorated. Yugo, who works with it more, has also suffered more.'

'The Electro-Clarifier can, in no way, do that kind of damage.'

Dors put her hand to her forehead and momentarily winced. She said, 'And now you have a more intense Electro-Clarifier that might do more damage, that might kill quickly, rather than slowly.'

'Absolute nonsense.'

'Now consider the name of the device, a name which, according to the woman who designed it, you are the only one to use. I presume you called it the Elar-Monay Clarifier.'

'I don't ever recall using that phrase,' said Elar uneasily.

'Surely you did. And the new intensified Elar-Monay

329

Clarifier could be used to kill with no blame to be attached to anyone – just a sad accident through a new and untried device. It would be the "Elar-Monay death" and a little girl heard it as "lemonade death."'

Dors's hand groped at her side.

Elar said softly, 'You are not well, Dr Venabili.'

'I am perfectly well. Am I not correct?'

'Look, it doesn't matter what you can twist into lemonade. Who knows what the little girl may have heard? It all boils down to the deadliness of the Electro-Clarifier. Bring me into court or before a scientific investigating board and let experts – as many as you like – check the effect of the Electro-Clarifier, even the new intensified one, on human beings. They will find it has no measurable effect.'

'I don't believe that,' muttered Venabili. Her hands were now at her forehead and her eyes were closed. She swayed slightly.

Elar said, 'It is clear that you are not well, Dr Venabili. Perhaps that means it is my turn to talk. May I?'

Dors's eyes opened and she simply stared.

'I'll take your silence for consent, Doctor. Of what use would it be for me to try to get rid of Dr Seldon and Dr Amaryl in order to take my place as director? You would prevent any attempt I made at assassination, as you now think you are doing. In the unlikely case that I succeeded in such a project and was rid of the two great men, you would tear me to pieces afterward. You're a very unusual woman – strong and fast beyond belief – and while you are alive, the Maestro is safe.'

'Yes,' said Dors, glowering.

'I told this to the men of the junta. – Why should they not consult me on matters involving the Project? They are very interested in psychohistory, as well they ought to be. It was difficult for them to believe what I told them about you – until you made your foray into the Palace grounds. That convinced them, you can be sure, and they agreed with my plan.'

330

'Aha. Now we come to it,' Dors said weakly.

'I told you the Electro-Clarifier cannot harm human beings. It cannot. Amaryl and your precious Hari are just getting *old*, though you refuse to accept it. So what? They are fine – perfectly *human*. The electromagnetic field has no effect of any importance on organic materials. Of course, it may have adverse effects on sensitive electromagnetic machinery and, if we could imagine a human being built of metal and electronics, it might have an effect on it. Legends tell us of such artificial human beings. The Mycogenians have based their religion on them and they call such beings 'robots.' If there were such a thing as a robot, one would imagine it would be stronger and faster by far than an ordinary human being, that it would have properties, in fact, resembling those you have, Dr Venabili. And such a robot could, indeed, be stopped, hurt, even destroyed by an intense Electro-Clarifier, such as the one that I have here, one that has been operating at low energy since we began our conversation. That is why you are feeling ill, Dr Venabili – and for the first time in your existence, I'm sure.'

Dors said nothing, merely stared at the man. Slowly she sank into a chair.

Elar smiled and went on, 'Of course, with you taken care of, there will be no problem with the Maestro and with Amaryl. The Maestro, in fact, without you, may fade out at once and resign in grief, while Amaryl is merely a child in his mind. In all likelihood, neither will have to be killed. How does it feel, Dr Venabili, to be unmasked after all these years? I must admit, you were very good at concealing your true nature. It's almost surprising that no one else discovered the truth before now. But then, I am a brilliant mathematician – an observer, a thinker, a deducer. Even I would not have figured it out were it not for your fanatical devotion to the Maestro and the occasional bursts of superhuman power you seemed to summon at will – when *he* was threatened.

331

'Say good-bye, Dr Venabili. All I have to do now is to turn the device to full power and you will be *history*.'

Dors seemed to collect herself and rose slowly from her seat, mumbling, 'I may be better shielded than you think.' Then, with a grunt, she threw herself at Elar.

Elar, his eyes widening, shrieked and reeled back.

Then Dors was on him, her hand flashing. Its side struck Elar's neck, smashing the vertebrae and shattering the nerve cord. He fell dead on the floor.

Dors straightened with an effort and staggered toward the door. She had to find Hari. He had to know what had happened.

27

Hari Seldon rose from his seat in horror. He had never seen Dors look so, her face twisted, her body canted, staggering as though she were drunk.

'Dors! What happened! What's wrong!'

He ran to her and grasped her around the waist, even as her body gave way and collapsed in his arms. He lifted her (she weighed more than an ordinary woman her size would have, but Seldon was unaware of that at the moment) and placed her on the couch.

'What happened?' he said.

She told him, gasping, her voice breaking now and then, while he cradled her head and tried to force himself to believe what was happening.

'Elar is dead,' she said. 'I finally killed a human being. – First time. – Makes it worse.'

'How badly are you damaged, Dors?'

'Badly. Elar turned on his device – full – when I rushed him.'

'You can be readjusted.'

'How? There's no one – on Trantor – who knows how. I need Daneel.'

Daneel. Demerzel. Somehow, deep inside, Hari had always known. His friend – a robot – had provided him with a protector – a robot – to ensure that psychohistory and the seeds of the Foundations were given a chance to take root. The only problem was, Hari had fallen in love with his protector – a *robot*. It all made sense now. All the nagging doubts and the questions could be answered. And somehow, it didn't matter one bit. All that mattered was Dors.

'We can't let this happen.'

'It must.' Dors's eyes fluttered open and looked at

333

Seldon. 'Must. Tried to save you, but missed – vital point – who will protect you now?'

Seldon couldn't see her clearly. There was something wrong with his eyes. 'Don't worry about me, Dors. It's you – It's you—'

'No. You, Hari. Tell Manella – Manella – I forgive her now. She did better than I. Explain to Wanda. You and Raych – take care of each other.'

'No no no,' said Seldon, rocking back and forth. 'You can't do this. Hang on, Dors. Please. Please, my love.'

Dors's head shook feebly and she smiled even more feebly. 'Good-bye, Hari, my love. Remember always – all you did for me.'

'I did nothing for you.'

'You loved me and your love made me – human.'

Her eyes remained open, but Dors had ceased functioning.

Yugo Amaryl came storming into Seldon's office. 'Hari, the riots are beginning, sooner and harder even than exp—'

And then he stared at Seldon and Dors and whispered, 'What happened?'

Seldon looked up at him in agony. 'Riots! What do I care about riots now? – What do I care about *anything* now?'

334

Part IV

WANDA SELDON

SELDON, WANDA – . . . In the waning years of Hari Seldon's life, he grew most attached to (some say dependent upon) his granddaughter, Wanda. Orphaned in her teens, Wanda Seldon devoted herself to her grandfather's Psychohistory Project, filling the vacancy left by Yugo Amaryl . . .

The content of Wanda Seldon's work remains largely a mystery, for it was conducted in virtually total isolation. The only individuals allowed access to Wanda Seldon's research were Hari himself and a young man named Stettin Palver (whose descendant Preem would four hundred years later contribute to the rebirth of Trantor, as the planet rose from the ashes of the Great Sack [300 F.E.]) . . .

Although the full extent of Wanda Seldon's contribution to the Foundation is unknown, it was undoubtedly of the greatest magnitude . . .

ENCYCLOPEDIA GALACTICA

1

Hari Seldon walked into the Galactic Library (limping a little, as he did more and more often these days) and made for the banks of skitters, the little vehicles that slid their way along the interminable corridors of the building complex.

He was held up, however, by the sight of three men seated at one of the galactography alcoves, with the Galactograph showing the Galaxy in full three-dimensional representation and, of course, its worlds slowly pinwheeling around its core, spinning at right angles to that as well.

From where Seldon stood he could see that the border Province of Anacreon was marked off in glowing red. It skirted the edge of the Galaxy and took up a great volume, but it was sparsely populated with stars. Anacreon was not remarkable for either wealth or culture but was remarkable for its distance from Trantor: ten thousand parsecs away.

Seldon, acting on impulse, took a seat at a computer console near the three and set up a random search he was sure would take an indefinite period. Some instinct told him that such an intense interest in Anacreon must be political in nature – its position in the Galaxy made it one of the least secure holdings of the current Imperial regime. His eyes remained on his screen, but Seldon's ears were open for the discussion near him. One didn't usually hear political discussions in the Library. They were, in point of fact, not supposed to take place.

Seldon did not know any of the three men. That was not entirely surprising. There were habitués of the Library, quite a few, and Seldon knew most of them by sight – and some even to talk to – but the Library was open to all citizens. No qualifications. Anyone could enter and use its facilities. (For a limited period of time, of course. Only a select few, like Seldon, were allowed to 'set up shop' in the Library. Seldon had been granted the use of a locked private office and complete access to Library resources.)

One of the men (Seldon thought of him as Hook Nose, for obvious reasons) spoke in a low urgent voice.

'Let it go,' he said. 'Let it go. It's costing us a mint to try to hold on and, even if we do, it will only be while they're there. They can't stay there forever and, as soon as they leave, the situation will revert to what it was.'

Seldon knew what they were talking about. The news had come over TrantorVision only three days ago that the Imperial government had decided on a show of force to bring the obstreperous Governor of Anacreon into line. Seldon's own psychohistorical analysis had shown him that it was a useless procedure, but the government did not generally listen when its emotions were stirred. Seldon smiled slightly and grimly at hearing Hook Nose say what he himself had said – and the young man said it without the benefit of any knowledge of psychohistory.

Hook Nose went on. 'If we leave Anacreon alone, what do we lose? It's still there, right where it always was, right at the edge of the Empire. It can't pick up and go to Andromeda, can it? So it still has to trade with us and life continues. What's the difference if they salute the Emperor or not? You'll never be able to tell the difference.'

The second man, whom Seldon had labeled Baldy, for even more obvious reasons, said, 'Except this whole business doesn't exist in a vacuum. If Anacreon goes, the other border provinces will go. The Empire will break up.'

'So what?' whispered Hook Nose fiercely. 'The Empire can't run itself effectively anymore, anyway. It's too big. Let the border go and take care of itself – if it can. The Inner Worlds will be all the stronger and better off. The border doesn't have to be ours politically; it will still be ours economically.'

And now the third man (Red Cheeks) said, 'I wish you were right, but that's not the way it's going to work. If the border provinces establish their independence, the first thing each will do will be to try to increase its power at the expense of its neighbors. There'll be war and conflict and every one of the governors will dream of becoming Emperor at last. It will be like the old days before the Kingdom of Trantor – a dark age that will last for thousands of years.'

Baldy said, 'Surely things won't be *that* bad. The Empire may break up, but it will heal itself quickly when people find out that the breakup just means war and impoverishment. They'll look back on the golden days of the intact Empire and all will be well again. We're not barbarians, you know. We'll find a way.'

'Absolutely,' said Hook Nose. 'We've got to remember that the Empire has faced crisis after crisis in its history and has pulled through time and again.'

But Red Cheeks shook his head as he said, 'This is not just another crisis. This is something much worse. The Empire has been deteriorating for generations. Ten years' worth of the junta destroyed the economy and since the fall of the junta and the rise of this new Emperor, the Empire has been so weak that the governors on the Periphery don't have to do anything. It's going to fall of its own weight.'

'And the allegiance to the Emperor—' began Hook Nose.

'What allegiance?' said Red Cheeks. 'We went for years without an Emperor after Cleon was assassinated and no one seemed to mind much. And this new Emperor is just a figurehead. There's nothing he can do. There's nothing anyone can do. This isn't a crisis. This is the *end*.'

The other two stared at Red Cheeks, frowning. Baldy said, 'You really believe it! You think that the Imperial government will just sit there and let it all happen?'

341

'Yes! Like you two, they won't believe it is happening. That is, until it's too late.'

'What would you want them to do if they did believe it?' asked Baldy.

Red Cheeks stared into the Galactograph, as if he might find an answer there. 'I don't know. Look, in due course of time I'll die; things won't be too bad by then. Afterward, as the situation gets worse, other people can worry about it. I'll be gone. And so will the good old days. Maybe forever. I'm not the only one who thinks this, by the way. Ever hear of someone named Hari Seldon?'

'Sure,' said Hook Nose at once. 'Wasn't he First Minister under Cleon?'

'Yes,' said Red Cheeks. 'He's some sort of scientist. I heard him give a talk a few months back. It felt good to know I'm not the *only* one who believes the Empire is failing apart. He said—'

'And he said everything's going to pot and there's going to be a permanent dark age?' Baldy interjected.

'Well no,' said Red Cheeks. 'He's one of these real cautious types. He says it *might* happen, but he's wrong. It *will* happen.'

Seldon had heard enough. He limped toward the table where the three men sat and touched Red Cheeks on the shoulder.

'Sir,' he said, 'may I speak to you for a moment?'

Startled, Red Cheeks looked up and then he said, 'Hey, aren't you Professor Seldon?'

'I always have been,' said Seldon. He handed the man a reference tile bearing his photograph. 'I would like to see you here in my Library office at 4 P.M., day after tomorrow. Can you manage that?'

'I have to work.'

'Call in sick if you have to. It's important.'

'Well, I'm not sure, sir.'

'Do it,' said Seldon. 'If you get into any sort of trouble over it, I'll straighten it out. And meanwhile, gentlemen, do you mind if I study the Galaxy simulation for a moment? It's been a long time since I've looked at one.'

They nodded mutely, apparently abashed at being in the presence of a former First Minister. One by one the men stepped back and allowed Seldon access to the Galactograph controls.

Seldon's finger reached out to the controls and the red that had marked off the Province of Anacreon vanished. The Galaxy was unmarked, a glowing pinwheel of mist brightening into the spherical glow at the center, behind which was the Galactic black hole.

Individual stars could not be made out, of course, unless the view were magnified, but then only one portion or another of the Galaxy would be shown on the screen and Seldon wanted to see the whole thing – to get a look at the Empire that was vanishing.

He pushed a contact and a series of yellow dots appeared on the Galactic image. They represented the habitable planets – twenty-five million of them. They could be distinguished as individual dots in the thin fog that represented the outskirts of the Galaxy, but they were more and more thickly placed as one moved in toward the center. There was a belt of what seemed solid yellow (but which would separate into individual dots under magnification) around the central glow. The central glow itself remained white and unmarked, of course. No habitable planets could exist in the midst of the turbulent energies of the core.

Despite the great density of yellow, not one star in ten thousand, Seldon knew, had a habitable planet circling it. This was true, despite the planet-molding and terraforming capacities of humanity. Not all the molding in the Galaxy could make most of the worlds into anything a human being could walk on in comfort and without the protection of a spacesuit.

Seldon closed another contact. The yellow dots disappeared, but one tiny region glowed blue: Trantor and the various worlds directly dependent on it. As close as it could be to the central core and yet remaining insulated from its deadliness, it was commonly viewed as being located at the 'center of the Galaxy,' which it wasn't – not truly. As usual, one had to be impressed by the smallness of the world of Trantor, a tiny place in the vast realm of the Galaxy, but within it was squeezed the largest concentration of wealth, culture, and governmental authority that humanity had ever seen.

And even that was doomed to destruction.

It was almost as though the men could read his mind or perhaps they interpreted the sad expression on his face.

Baldy asked softly, 'Is the Empire really going to be destroyed?'

Seldon replied, softer still, 'It might. It might. Anything might happen.'

He rose, smiled at the men, and left, but in his thoughts he screamed: It will! It will!

2

Seldon sighed as he climbed into one of the skitters that were ranked side by side in the large alcove. There had been a time, just a few years ago, when he had gloried in walking briskly along the interminable corridors of the Library, telling himself that even though he was past sixty he could manage it.

But now, at seventy, his legs gave way all too quickly and he had to take a skitter. Younger men took them all the time because skitters saved them trouble, but Seldon did it because he had to – and that made all the difference.

After Seldon punched in the destination, he closed a contact and the skitter lifted a fraction of an inch above the floor. Off it went at a rather casual pace, very smoothly, very silently, and Seldon leaned back and watched the corridor walls, the other skitters, the occasional walkers.

He passed a number of Librarians and, even after all these years, he still smiled when he saw them. They were the oldest Guild in the Empire, the one with the most revered traditions, and they clung to ways that were more appropriate centuries before – maybe millennia before.

Their garments were silky and off-white and were loose enough to be almost gownlike, coming together at the neck and billowing out from there.

Trantor, like all the worlds, oscillated, where the males were concerned, between facial hair and smoothness. The people of Trantor itself – or at least most of its sectors – were smooth-shaven and had been smooth-shaven for as far back as he knew – excepting such anomalies as the mustaches worn by Dahlites, such as his own foster son, Raych.

The Librarians, however, clung to the *beards* of long ago. Every Librarian had a rather short neatly cultivated beard running from ear to ear but leaving bare the upper lip. That alone was enough to mark them for what they were and to make the smooth-shaven Seldon feel a little uncomfortable when surrounded by a crowd of them.

Actually the most characteristic thing of all was the cap each wore (perhaps even when asleep, Seldon thought). Square, it was made of a velvety material, in four parts that came together with a button at the top. The caps came in an endless variety of colors and apparently each color had significance. If you were familiar with Librarian lore, you could tell a particular Librarian's length of service, area of expertise, grades of accomplishment, and so on. They helped fix a pecking order. Every Librarian could, by a glance at another's hat, tell whether to be respectful (and to what degree) or overbearing (and to what degree).

The Galactic Library was the largest single structure on Trantor (possibly in the Galaxy), much larger than even the Imperial Palace, and it had once gleamed and glittered, as though boasting of its size and magnificence. However, like the Empire itself, it had faded and withered. It was like an old dowager still wearing the jewels of her youth but upon a body that was wrinkled and wattled.

The skitter stopped in front of the ornate doorway of the Chief Librarian's office and Seldon climbed out.

Las Zenow smiled as he greeted Seldon. 'Welcome, my friend,' he said in his high-pitched voice. (Seldon wondered if he had ever sung tenor in his younger days but had never dared to ask. The Chief Librarian was a compound of dignity always and the question might have seemed offensive.)

'Greetings,' said Seldon. Zenow had a gray beard, rather more than halfway to white, and he wore a pure white hat. Seldon understood *that* without any explanation. It was a case of reverse ostentation. The total

346

absence of color represented the highest peak of position.

Zenow rubbed his hands with what seemed to be an inner glee. 'I've called you in, Hari, because I've got good news for you. – We've found it!'

'By "it," Las, you mean—'

'A suitable world. You wanted one far out. I think we've located the ideal one.' His smile broadened. 'You just leave it to the Library, Hari. We can find anything.'

'I have no doubt, Las. Tell me about this world.'

'Well, let me show you its location first.' A section of the wall slid aside, the lights in the room dimmed, and the Galaxy appeared in three-dimensional form, turning slowly. Again, red lines marked off the Province of Anacreon, so that Seldon could almost swear that the episode with the three men had been a rehearsal for this.

And then a brilliant blue dot appeared at the far end of the province. 'There it is,' said Zenow. 'It's an ideal world. Sizable, well-watered, good oxygen atmosphere, vegetation, of course. A great deal of sea life. It's there just for the taking. No planet-molding or terraforming required – or, at least, none that cannot be done while it is actually occupied.'

Seldon said, 'Is it an unoccupied world, Las?'

'Absolutely unoccupied. No one on it.'

'But why – if it's so suitable? I presume that, if you have all the details about it, it must have been explored. Why wasn't it colonized?'

'It was explored, but only by unmanned probes. And there was no colonization – presumably because it was so far from everything. The planet revolves around a star that is farther from the central black hole than that of any inhabited planet – farther by far. Too far, I suppose, for prospective colonists, but I think not too far for you. You said, "The farther, the better." '

'Yes,' said Seldon, nodding. 'I still say so. Does it have a name or is there just a letter-number combination?'

'Believe it or not, it has a name. Those who sent out the probes named it Terminus, an archaic word meaning "the end of the line." Which it would seem to be.'

Seldon said, 'Is the world part of the territory of the Province of Anacreon?'

'Not really,' said Zenow. 'If you'll study the red line and the red shading, you will see that the blue dot of Terminus lies slightly outside it – fifty light-years outside it, in fact. Terminus belongs to nobody; it's not even part of the Empire, as a matter of fact.'

'You're right, then, Las. It does seem like the ideal world I've been looking for.'

'Of course,' said Zenow thoughtfully, 'once you occupy Terminus, I imagine the Governor of Anacreon will claim it as being under his jurisdiction.'

'That's possible,' said Seldon, 'but we'll have to deal with that when the matter comes up.'

Zenow rubbed his hands again. 'What a glorious conception. Setting up a huge project on a brand-new world, far away and entirely isolated, so that year by year and decade by decade a huge Encyclopedia of all human knowledge can be put together. An epitome of what is present in this Library. If I were only younger, I would love to join the expedition.'

Seldon said sadly, 'You're almost twenty years younger than I am.' (Almost everyone is far younger than I am, he thought, even more sadly.)

Zenow said, 'Ah yes, I heard that you just passed your seventieth birthday. I hope you enjoyed it and celebrated appropriately.'

Seldon stirred. 'I don't celebrate my birthdays.'

'Oh, but you did. I remember the famous story of your sixtieth birthday.'

Seldon felt the pain, as deeply as though the dearest loss in all the world had taken place the day before. 'Please don't talk about it,' he said.

Abashed, Zenow said, 'I'm sorry. We'll talk about something else. – If, indeed, Terminus is the world you want, I imagine that your work on the preliminaries to the Encyclopedia Project will be redoubled. As you know, the Library will be glad to help you in all respects.

'I'm aware of it, Las, and I am endlessly grateful. We will, indeed, keep working.'

He rose, not yet able to smile after the sharp pang induced by the reference to his birthday celebration of ten years back. He said, 'So I must go to continue my labors.'

And as he left, he felt, as always, a pang of conscience over the deceit he was practicing. Las Zenow did not have the slightest idea of Seldon's true intentions.

3

Hari Seldon surveyed the comfortable suite that had been his personal office at the Galactic Library these past few years. It, like the rest of the Library, had a vague air of decay about it, a kind of weariness – something that had been too long in one place. And yet Seldon knew it might remain here, in the same place, for centuries more – with judicious rebuildings – for millennia even.

How did he come to be here?

Over and over again, he felt the past in his mind, ran his mental tendrils along the line of development of his life. It was part of growing older, no doubt. There was so much more in the past, so much less in the future, that the mind turned away from the looming shadow ahead to contemplate the safety of what had gone before.

In his case, though, there was that change. For over thirty years psychohistory had developed in what might almost be considered a straight line – progress creepingly slow but moving straight ahead. Then six years ago there had been a right-angled turn – totally unexpected.

And Seldon knew exactly how it had happened, how a concatenation of events came together to make it possible.

It was Wanda, of course, Seldon's granddaughter. Hari closed his eyes and settled into his chair to review the events of six years before.

Twelve-year-old Wanda was bereft. Her mother, Manella, had had another child, another little girl, Bellis, and for a time the new baby was a total preoccupation.

Her father, Raych, having finished his book on his home sector of Dahl, found it to be a minor success and himself a minor celebrity. He was called upon to talk on the subject, something he accepted with alacrity, for he was fiercely absorbed in the subject and, as he said to Hari with a grin, 'When I talk about Dahl, I don't have to hide my Dahlite accent. In fact, the public expects it of me.'

The net result, though, was that he was away from home a considerable amount of time and when he wasn't, it was the baby he wanted to see.

As for Dors – Dors was gone – and to Hari Seldon that wound was ever-fresh, ever-painful. And he had reacted to it in an unfortunate manner. It had been Wanda's dream that had set in motion the current of events that had ended with the loss of Dors.

Wanda had had nothing to do with it – Seldon knew that very well. And yet he found himself shrinking from her, so that he also failed her in the crisis brought about by the birth of the new baby.

And Wanda wandered disconsolately to the one person who always seemed glad to see her, the one person she could always count on. That was Yugo Amaryl, second only to Hari Seldon in the development of psychohistory and first in his absolute round-the-clock devotion to it. Hari had had Dors and Raych, but psychohistory was Yugo's life; he had no wife and children. Yet whenever Wanda came into his presence, something within him recognized her as a child and he dimly felt – for just that moment – a sense of loss that seemed to be assuaged only by showing the child affection. To be sure, he tended to treat her as a rather undersized adult, but Wanda seemed to like that.

It was six years ago that she had wandered into Yugo's office. Yugo looked up at her with his owlish reconstituted eyes and, as usual, took a moment or two to recognize her.

Then he said, 'Why, it's my dear friend Wanda. – But why do you look so sad? Surely an attractive young woman like you should never feel sad.'

And Wanda, her lower lip trembling, said, 'Nobody loves me.'

351

'Oh come, that's not true.'

'They just love that new baby. They don't care about me anymore.'

'I love you, Wanda.'

'Well, you're the only one then, Uncle Yugo.' And even though she could no longer crawl onto his lap as she had when she was younger, she cradled her head on his shoulder and wept.

Amaryl, totally unaware of what he should do, could only hug the girl and say, 'Don't cry. Don't cry.' And out of sheer sympathy and because he had so little in his own life to weep about, he found that tears were trickling down his own cheeks as well.

And then he said with sudden energy, 'Wanda, would you like to see something pretty?'

'What?' sniffled Wanda.

Amaryl knew only one thing in life and the Universe that was pretty. He said, 'Did you ever see the Prime Radiant?'

'No. What is it?'

'It's what your grandfather and I use to do our work. See? It's right here.'

He pointed to the black cube on his desk and Wanda looked at it woefully. 'That's not pretty,' she said.

'Not now,' agreed Amaryl. 'But watch when I turn it on.'

He did so. The room darkened and filled with dots of light and flashes of different colors. 'See? Now we can magnify it so all the dots become mathematical symbols.'

And so they did. There seemed a rush of material toward them and there, in the air, were signs of all sorts, letters, numbers, arrows, and shapes that Wanda had never seen before.

'Isn't it pretty?' asked Amaryl.

'Yes, it is,' said Wanda, staring carefully at the equations that (she didn't know) represented possible futures. 'I don't like that part, though. I think it's wrong.' She pointed at a colorful equation to her left.

'Wrong. ? Why do you say it's wrong?' said Amaryl, frowning.

'Because it's not . . . pretty. I'd do it a different way.'

Amaryl cleared his throat. 'Well, I'll try to fix it up.' And he moved closer to the equation in question, staring at it in his owlish fashion.

Wanda said, 'Thank you very much, Uncle Yugo, for showing me your pretty lights. Maybe someday I'll understand what they mean.'

'That's all right,' said Amaryl. 'I hope you feel better.'

'A little, thanks,' and, after flashing the briefest of smiles, she left the room.

Amaryl stood there, feeling a trifle hurt. He didn't like having the Prime Radiant's product criticized – not even by a twelve-year-old girl who knew no better.

And as he stood there, he had no idea whatsoever that the psychohistorical revolution had begun.

4

That afternoon Amaryl went to Hari Seldon's office at Streeling University. That in itself was unusual, for Amaryl virtually never left his own office, even to speak with a colleague just down the hall.

'Hari,' said Amaryl, frowning and looking puzzled. 'Something very odd has happened. Very peculiar.'

Seldon looked at Amaryl with deepest sorrow. He was only fifty-three, but he looked much older, bent, worn down to almost transparency. When forced, he had undergone doctors' examinations and the doctors had all recommended that he leave his work for a period of time (some said permanently) and *rest*. Only this, the doctors said, might improve his health. Otherwise – Seldon shook his head. 'Take him away from his work and he'll die all the sooner – and unhappier. We have no choice.'

And then Seldon realized that, lost in such thoughts, he was not hearing Amaryl speak.

He said, 'I'm sorry, Yugo. I'm a little distracted. Begin again.'

Amaryl said, 'I'm telling you that something very odd has happened. Very peculiar.'

'What is it, Yugo?'

'It was Wanda. She came in to see me – very sad, very upset.'

'Why?'

'Apparently it's the new baby.'

'Oh yes,' Hari said with more than a trace of guilt in his voice.

'So she said and cried on my shoulder – I actually cried a bit, too, Hari. And then I thought I'd cheer her up by showing her the Prime Radiant.' Here Amaryl hesitated, as if choosing his next words carefully.

'Go on, Yugo. What happened?'

'Well, she stared at all the lights and I magnified a portion, actually Section 42R254. You're acquainted with that?'

Seldon smiled. 'No, Yugo, I haven't memorized the equations quite as well as you have.'

'Well, you should,' said Amaryl severely. 'How can you do a good job if – But never mind that. What I'm trying to say is that Wanda pointed to a part of it and said it was no good. It wasn't *pretty*.'

'Why not? We all have our personal likes and dislikes.'

'Yes, of course, but I brooded about it and I spent some time going over it and, Hari, there *was* something wrong with it. The programming was inexact and that area, the precise area to which Wanda pointed, was no good. And, really, it wasn't pretty.'

Seldon sat up rather stiffly, frowning. 'Let me get this straight, Yugo. She pointed to something at random, said it was no good, and she was *right*?'

'Yes. She pointed, but it wasn't at random; she was very deliberate.'

'But that's impossible.'

'But it happened. I was there.'

'I'm not saying it didn't happen. I'm saying it was just a wild coincidence.'

'Is it? Do you think, with all your knowledge of psychohistory, you could take one glance at a new set of equations and tell me that one portion is no good?'

Seldon said, 'Well then, Yugo, how did you come to expand that particular portion of the equations? What made you choose *that* piece for magnification?'

Amaryl shrugged. '*That* was coincidence – if you like. I just fiddled with the controls.'

'That couldn't be coincidence,' muttered Seldon. For a few moments he was lost in thought, then he asked the question that pushed forward the psychohistorical revolution that Wanda had begun.

He said, 'Yugo, did you have any suspicions about those equations beforehand? Did you have any reason to believe there was something wrong with them?'

Amaryl fiddled with the sash of his unisuit and seemed embarrassed. 'Yes, I think I did. You see—'

'You *think* you did?'

'I know I did. I seemed to recall when I was setting it up – it's a new section, you know – my fingers seemed to glitch on the programmer. It looked all right then, but I guess I kept worrying about it inside. I remember thinking it looked wrong, but I had other things to do and I just let it go. But then when Wanda happened to point to precisely the area I had been concerned about, I decided to check up on her – otherwise I would just have let it go as a childish statement.'

'And you turned on that very fragment of the equations to show Wanda. As though it were haunting your unconscious mind.'

Amaryl shrugged. 'Who knows?'

'And just before that, you were very close together, hugging, both crying.'

Amaryl shrugged again, looking even more embarrassed.

Seldon said, 'I think I know what happened, Yugo. Wanda read your mind.'

Amaryl jumped, as though he had been bitten. 'That's impossible!'

Slowly Seldon said, 'I once knew someone who had unusual mental powers of that sort' – and he thought sadly of Eto Demerzel or, as Seldon had secretly known him, Daneel – 'only he was somewhat *more* than human. But his ability to read minds, to sense other people's thoughts, to persuade people to act in a certain way – that was a *mental* ability. I think, somehow, that

356

perhaps Wanda has that ability as well.'

'I can't believe it,' said Amaryl stubbornly.

'I can,' said Seldon, 'but I don't know what to do about it.' Dimly he felt the rumblings of a revolution in psycho-historical research – but only dimly.

5

'Dad,' said Raych with some concern, 'you look tired.'

'I dare say,' said Hari Seldon, 'I feel tired. But how are you?'

Raych was forty-four now and his hair was beginning to show a bit of gray, but his mustache remained thick and dark and very Dahlite in appearance. Seldon wondered if he touched it up with dye, but it would have been the wrong thing to ask.

Seldon said, 'Are you through with your lecturing for a while?'

'For a while. Not for long. And I'm glad to be home and see the baby and Manella and Wanda – and you, Dad.'

'Thank you. But I have news for you, Raych. No more lecturing. I'm going to need you here.'

Raych frowned. 'What for?' On two different occasions he had been sent to carry out delicate missions, but those were back during the days of the Joranumite menace. As far as he knew, things were quiet now, especially with the overthrow of the junta and the reestablishment of a pale Emperor.

'It's Wanda,' said Seldon.

'Wanda? What's wrong with Wanda?'

'Nothing's wrong with her, but we're going to have to work out a complete genome for her – and for you and Manella as well – and eventually for the new baby.'

'For Bellis, too? What's going on?'

Seldon hesitated. 'Raych, you know that your mother and I always thought there was something lovable about you, something that inspired affection and trust.'

'I know you thought so. You said so often enough when you were trying to get me to do something difficult. But

358

I'll be honest with you. I never felt it.'

'No, you won over me and . . . and Dors.' (He had such trouble saying the name, even though four years had passed since her destruction.) 'You won over Rashelle of Wye. You won over Jo-Jo Joranum. You won over Manella. How do you account for all that?'

'Intelligence and charm,' said Raych, grinning.

'Have you thought you might have been in touch with their – our – minds?'

'No, I've never thought that. And now that you mention it, I think it's ridiculous. – With all due respect, Dad, of course.'

'What if I told you that Wanda seems to have read Yugo's mind during a moment of crisis?'

'Coincidence or imagination, I should say.'

'Raych, I knew someone once who could handle people's minds as easily as you and I handle conversation.'

'Who was that?'

'I can't speak of him. Take my word for it, though.'

'Well–' said Raych dubiously.

'I've been at the Galactic Library, checking on such matters. There is a curious story, about twenty thousand years old and therefore back to the misty origins of hyperspatial travel. It's about a young woman, not much more than Wanda's age, who could communicate with an entire planet that circled a sun called Nemesis.'

'Surely a fairytale.'

'Surely. And incomplete, at that. But the similarity with Wanda is astonishing.'

Raych said, 'Dad, what are you planning?'

'I'm not sure, Raych. I need to know the genome and I have to find others like Wanda. I have a notion that youngsters are born – not often but occasionally – with such mental abilities, but that, in general, it merely gets them in trouble and they learn to mask it. And as they grow up, their ability, their talent, is buried deep within their minds – sort of an unconscious act of self-preservation. Surely in the Empire or even just among

359

Trantor's forty billion, there must be more of that sort, like Wanda, and if I know the genome I want, I can test those I think may be so.'

'And what would you do with them if you found them, Dad?'

'I have the notion that they are what I need for the further development of psychohistory.'

Raych said, 'And Wanda is the first of the type you know about and you intend to make a psychohistorian out of her?'

'Perhaps.'

'Like Yugo. – Dad, no!'

'Why no?'

'Because I want her to grow up like a normal girl and become a normal woman. I will not have you sitting her before the Prime Radiant and make her into a living monument to psychohistorical mathematics.'

Seldon said, 'It may not come to that, Raych, but we must have her genome. You know that for thousands of years there have been suggestions that every human being have his genome on file. It's only the expense that's kept it from becoming standard practice; no one doubts the usefulness of it. Surely you see the advantages. If nothing else, we will know Wanda's tendencies toward a variety of physiological disorders. If we had ever had Yugo's genome, I am certain he would not now be dying. Surely we can go that far.'

'Well, maybe, Dad, but no further. I'm willing to bet that Manella is going to be a lot firmer on this than I am.'

Seldon said, 'Very well. But remember, no more lecture tours. I need you at home.'

'We'll see,' Raych said and left.

Seldon sat there in a quandary. Eto Demerzel, the one person he knew who could handle minds, would have known what to do. Dors, with her nonhuman knowledge, might have known what to do.

For himself, he had a dim vision of a new psychohistory – but nothing more than that.

6

It was not an easy task to obtain a complete genome of Wanda. To begin with, the number of biophysicists equipped to handle the genome was small and those that existed were always busy.

Nor was it possible for Seldon to discuss his needs openly, in order to interest the biophysicists. It was absolutely essential, Seldon felt, that the true reason for his interest in Wanda's mental powers be kept secret from all the Galaxy.

And if another difficulty was needed, it was the fact that the process was infernally expensive.

Seldon shook his head and said to Mian Endelecki, the biophysicist he was now consulting, 'Why so expensive, Dr Endelecki? I am not an expert in the field, but it is my distinct understanding that the process is completely computerized and that, once you have a scraping of skin cells, the genome can be completely built and analyzed in a matter of days.'

'That's true. But having a deoxyribonucleic acid molecule stretching out for billions of nucleotides, with every puring and pyrimidine in its place, is the least of it; the very least of it, Professor Seldon. There is then the matter of studying each one and comparing it to some standard.

'Now, consider, in the first place, that although we have records of complete genomes, they represent a vanishingly small fraction of the number of genomes that exist, so that we don't really know how standard they are.'

Seldon asked, 'Why so few?'

'A number of reasons. The expense, for one thing. Few people are willing to spend the credits on it unless they have strong reason to think there is something wrong with their genome. And if they have no strong reason, they are reluctant to undergo analysis for fear they *will* find something wrong. Now, then, are you sure you want your granddaughter genomed?'

'Yes, I do. It is terribly important.'

'Why? Does she show signs of a metabolic anomaly?'

'No, she doesn't. Rather the reverse – if I knew the antonym of "anomaly." I consider her a most unusual person and I want to know just what it is that makes her unusual.'

'Unusual in what way?'

'Mentally, but it's impossible for me to go into details, since I don't entirely understand it. Maybe I will, once she is genomed.'

'How old is she?'

'Twelve. She'll soon be thirteen.'

'In that case, I'll need permission from her parents.'

Seldon cleared his throat. 'That may be difficult to get. I'm her grandfather. Wouldn't my permission be enough?'

'For me, certainly. But, you know, we're talking about the law. I don't wish to lose my license to practice.'

It was necessary for Seldon to approach Raych again. This, too, was difficult, as he protested once more that he and his wife, Manella, wanted Wanda to live a normal life of a normal girl. What if her genome did turn out to be abnormal? Would she be whisked away to be prodded and probed like a laboratory specimen? Would Hari, in his fanatical devotion to his Psychohistory Project, press Wanda into a life of all work and no play, shutting her off from other young people her age? But Seldon was insistent.

'Trust me, Raych. I would never do anything to harm Wanda. But this must be done. I need to know Wanda's genome. If it is as I suspect it is, we may be on the verge of altering the course of psychohistory, of the future of the Galaxy itself!'

And so Raych was persuaded and somehow he

obtained Manella's consent, as well. And together, the three adults took Wanda to Dr Endelecki's office.

Mian Endelecki greeted them at the door. Her hair was a shining white, but her face showed no sign of age.

She looked at the girl, who walked in with a look of curiosity on her face but with no signs of apprehension or fear. She then turned her gaze to the three adults who had accompanied Wanda.

Dr Endelecki said with a smile, 'Mother, father, and grandfather – am I right?'

Seldon answered, 'Absolutely right.'

Raych looked hang-dog and Manella, her face a little swollen and her eyes a little red, looked tired.

'Wanda,' began the doctor. 'That is your name, isn't it?'

'Yes, ma'am,' said Wanda in her clear voice.

'I'm going to tell you exactly what I'm going to do with you. You're right-handed, I suppose.'

'Yes, ma'am.'

'Very well, then, I'll spray a little patch on your left forearm with an anesthetic. It will just feel like a cool wind. Nothing else. I'll then scrape a little skin from you – just a tiny bit. There'll be no pain, no blood, no mark afterward. When I'm done, I'll spray a little disinfectant on it. The whole thing will take just a few minutes. Does that sound all right to you?'

'Sure,' said Wanda, as she held out her arm.

When it was over, Dr Endelecki said, 'I'll put the scraping under the microscope, choose a decent cell, and put my computerized gene analyzer to work. It will mark off every last nucleotide, but there are billions of them. It will probably take the better part of a day. It's all automatic, of course, so I won't be sitting here watching it and there's no point in your doing so, either.

'Once the genome is prepared, it will take an even longer time to analyze it. If you want a complete job, it may take a couple of weeks. That is why it's so expensive a procedure. The work is hard and long. I'll call you in

363

when I have it.' She turned away, as if she had dismissed the family, and busied herself with the gleaming apparatus on the table in front of her.

Seldon said, 'If you come across anything unusual, will you get in touch with me instantly? I mean, don't wait for a complete analysis if you find something in the first hour. Don't make me wait.'

'The chances of finding anything in the first hour are very slim, but I promise you, Professor Seldon, that I will be in touch with you at once if it seems necessary.'

Manella snatched Wanda's arm and led her off triumphantly. Raych followed, feet dragging. Seldon lingered and said, 'This is more important than you know, Dr Endelecki.'

Dr Endelecki nodded as she said, 'Whatever the reason, Professor, I'll do my best.'

Seldon left, his lips pressed tightly together. Why he had thought that somehow the genome would be worked out in five minutes and that a glance at it in another five minutes would give him an answer, he did not know. Now he would have to wait for weeks, without knowing what would be found.

He ground his teeth. Would his newest brainchild, the Second Foundation, ever be established or was it an illusion that would remain always just out of reach?

7

Hari Seldon walked into Dr Endelecki's office, a nervous smile on his face.

He said, 'You said a couple of weeks, Doctor. It's been over a month now.'

Dr Endelecki nodded. 'I'm sorry, Professor Seldon, but you wanted everything exact and that is what I have tried to do.'

'Well?' The look of anxiety on Seldon's face did not disappear. 'What did you find?'

'A hundred or so defective genes.'

'What! Defective genes. Are you serious, Doctor?'

'Quite serious. Why not? There are no genomes without at least a hundred defective genes; usually there are considerably more. It's not as bad as it sounds, you know.'

'No, I don't know. You're the expert, Doctor, not I.'

Dr Endelecki sighed and stirred in her chair. 'You don't know anything about genetics, do you, Professor?'

'No, I don't. A man can't know everything.'

'You're perfectly right. I know nothing about this – what do you call it? – this psychohistory of yours.'

Dr Endelecki shrugged, then continued. 'If you wanted to explain anything about it, you would be forced to start from the beginning and I would probably not understand it even so. Now, as to genetics—'

'Well?'

'An imperfect gene usually means nothing. There are imperfect genes – so imperfect and so crucial that they produce terrible disorders. These are very rare, though. Most imperfect genes simply don't work with absolute accuracy. They're like wheels that are slightly out of balance. A vehicle will move along, trembling a bit, but it will move along.'

'Is that what Wanda has?'

'Yes. More or less. After all, if all genes were perfect, we would all look precisely the same, we would all behave precisely the same. It's the difference in genes that makes for different people.'

'But won't it get worse as we grow older?'

'Yes. We all get worse as we grow older. I noticed you limping when you came in. Why is that?'

'A touch of sciatica,' muttered Seldon.

'Did you have it all your life?'

'Of course not.'

'Well, some of your genes have gotten worse with time and now you limp.'

'And what will happen to Wanda with time?'

'I don't know. I can't predict the future, Professor; I believe that is your province. However, if I were to hazard a guess, I would say that nothing unusual will happen to Wanda – at least, genetically – except the gathering of old age.'

Seldon said, 'Are you sure?'

'You have to take my word for it. You wanted to find out about Wanda's genome and you ran the risk of discovering things perhaps it is better not to know. But I tell you that, in my opinion, I can see nothing terrible happening to her.'

'The imperfect genes – should we fix them? Can we fix them?'

'No. In the first place, it would be very expensive. Secondly, the chances are that they would not stay fixed. And finally, people are against it.'

'But why?'

'Because they're against science in general. You should know this as well as anyone, Professor. I'm afraid the situation is such, especially since Cleon's death, that mysticism has been gaining ground. People don't believe in fixing genes scientifically. They would rather cure things by the laying on of hands or by mumbo-jumbo of some sort or other. Frankly it is extremely difficult for me to continue with my job. Very little funding is coming in.'

Seldon nodded. 'Actually I understand this situation all too well. Psychohistory explains it, but I honestly didn't think the situation was growing so bad so rapidly. I've been too involved in my own work to see the difficulties all around me.' He sighed. 'I've been watching the Galactic Empire slowly fall apart for over thirty years now – and now that it's beginning to collapse much more rapidly, I don't see how we can stop it in time.'

'Are you trying to?' Dr Endelecki seemed amused.

'Yes, I am.'

'Lots of luck. – About your sciatica. You know, fifty years ago it could have been cured. Not now, though.'

'Why not?'

'Well, the devices used for it are gone; the people who could have handled them are working on other things. Medicine is declining.'

'Along with everything else,' mused Seldon. '—But let's get back to Wanda. I feel she is a most unusual young woman with a brain that is different from most. What do her genes tell you about her brain?'

Dr Endelecki leaned back in her chair. 'Professor Seldon, do you know just how many genes are involved in brain function?'

'No.'

'I'll remind you that, of all the aspects of the human body, the brain function is the most intricate. In fact, as far as we know, there is nothing in the Universe as intricate as the human brain. So you won't be surprised when I tell you that there are thousands of genes that each play a role in brain function.'

'Thousands?'

'Exactly. And it is impossible to go through those genes and see anything specifically unusual. I will take your word for it, as far as Wanda is concerned. She is an unusual girl with an unusual brain, but I see nothing in her genes that can tell me anything about that brain –

except, of course, that it is normal.'

'Could you find other people whose genes for mental functioning are like Wanda's, that have the same brain pattern?'

'I doubt it very much. Even if another brain were much like hers, there would still be enormous differences in the genes. No use looking for similarities. – Tell me, Professor, just what is it about Wanda that makes you think her brain is so unusual?'

Seldon shook his head. 'I'm sorry. It's not something I can discuss.'

'In that case, I am *certain* that I can find out nothing for you. How did you discover that there was something unusual about her brain – this thing you can't discuss?'

'Accident,' muttered Seldon. 'Sheer accident.'

'In that case, you're going to have to find other brains like hers – also by accident. Nothing else can be done.'

Silence settled over both of them. Finally Seldon said, 'Is there anything else you can tell me?'

'I'm afraid not. Except that I'll send you my bill.'

Seldon rose with an effort. His sciatica hurt him badly. 'Well then, thank you, Doctor. Send the bill and I'll pay it.'

Hari Seldon left the doctor's office, wondering just what he would do next.

8

Like any intellectual, Hari Seldon had made use of the
Galactic Library freely. For the most part, it had been
done long-distance through computer, but occasionally
he had visited it, more to get away from the pressures of
the Psychohistory Project than for any other purpose.
And, for the past couple of years, since he had first for-
mulated his plan to find others like Wanda, he had kept
a private office there, so he could have ready access to
any of the Library's vast collection of data. He had even
rented a small apartment in an adjacent sector under the
dome so that he would be able to walk to the Library
when his ever-increasing research there prevented him
from returning to the Streeling Sector.

Now, however, his plan had taken on new dimensions
and he wanted to meet Las Zenow. It was the first time
he had ever met him face-to-face.

It was not easy to arrange a personal interview with
the Chief Librarian of the Galactic Library. His own
perception of the nature and value of his office was high
and it was frequently said that when the Emperor wished
to consult the Chief Librarian, even he had to visit the
Library himself and wait his turn.

Seldon, however, had no trouble. Zenow knew him
well, though he had never seen Hari Seldon in person.
'An honor, First Minister,' he said in greeting.

Seldon smiled. 'I trust you know that I have not held
that post in sixteen years.'

'The honor of the title is still yours. Besides, sir, you
were also instrumental in ridding us of the brutal rule of
the junta. The junta, on a number of occasions, violated
the sacred rule of the neutrality of the Library.'

(Ah, thought Seldon, *that* accounts for the readiness with which he saw me.)

'Merely rumor,' he said aloud.

'And now, tell me,' said Zenow, who could not resist a quick look at the time band on his wrist, 'what can I do for you?'

'Chief Librarian,' began Seldon, 'I have not come to ask anything easy of you. What I want is more space at the Library. I want permission to bring in a number of my associates. I want permission to undertake a long and elaborate program of the greatest importance.'

Las Zenow's face drew into an expression of distress. 'You ask a great deal. Can you explain the importance of all this?'

'Yes. The Empire is in the process of disintegration.'

There was a long pause. Then Zenow said, 'I have heard of your research into psychohistory. I have been told that your new science bears the promise of predicting the future. Is it psychohistorical predictions of which you are speaking?'

'No. I have not yet reached the point in psychohistory where I can speak of the future with certainty. But you don't need psychohistory to know that the Empire is disintegrating. You can see the evidence yourself.'

Zenow sighed. 'My work here consumes me utterly, Professor Seldon. I am a child when it comes to political and social matters.'

'You may, if you wish, consult the information contained in the Library. Why look around this very office – it is chock-full of every conceivable sort of information from throughout the entire Galactic Empire.'

'I'm the last to keep up with it all, I'm afraid,' Zenow said, smiling sadly. 'You know the old proverb: The shoemaker's child has no shoes. It seems to me, though, that the Empire is restored. We have an Emperor again.'

'In name only, Chief Librarian. In most of the outlying provinces, the Emperor's name is mentioned ritualistically now and then, but he plays no role in what they do. The Outer Worlds control their own programs and, more important, they control the local armed forces, which are outside the grip of the Emperor's authority. If the Emperor were to try to exert his authority anywhere outside the Inner Worlds, he would fail. I doubt that it will take more than twenty years, at the outside, before some of the Outer Worlds declare their independence.'

Zenow sighed again. 'If you are right, we live in worse times than the Empire has ever seen. But what has this to do with your desire for more office space and additional staff here in the Library?'

'If the Empire falls apart, the Galactic Library may not escape the general carnage.'

'Oh, but it must,' said Zenow earnestly. 'There have been bad times before and it has always been understood that the Galactic Library on Trantor, as the repository of all human knowledge, must remain inviolate. And so it will be in the future.'

'It may not be. You said yourself that the junta violated its neutrality.'

'Not seriously.'

'It might be more serious next time and we can't allow this repository of all human knowledge to be damaged.'

'How will your increased presence here prevent that?'

'It won't. But the project I am interested in will. I want to create a great Encyclopedia, containing within it all the knowledge humanity will need to rebuild itself in case the worst happens – an Encyclopedia Galactica, if you will. We don't need everything the Library has. Much of it is trivial. The provincial libraries scattered over the Galaxy may themselves be destroyed and, if not, all but the most local data is obtained by computerized connection with the Galactic Library in any case. What I intend, then, is something that is entirely independent and that contains, in as concise a form as possible, the essential information humanity needs.'

'And if it, too, is destroyed?'

'I hope it will not be. It is my intention to find a world far away on the outskirts of the Galaxy, one where I can transfer my Encyclopedists and where they can work in peace. Until such a place is found, however, I want the nucleus of the group to work here and to use the Library facilities to decide what will be needed for the project.'

Zenow grimaced. 'I see your point, Professor Seldon, but I'm not sure that it can be done.'

'Why not, Chief Librarian?'

'Because being Chief Librarian does not make me an absolute monarch. I have a rather large Board – a kind of legislature – and please don't think that I can just push your Encyclopedia Project through.'

'I'm astonished.'

'Don't be. I am not a popular Chief Librarian. The Board has been fighting, for some years now, for limited access to the Library. I have resisted. It galls them that I have afforded you your small office space.'

'Limited access?'

'Exactly. The idea is that if anyone needs information, he or she must communicate with a Librarian and the Librarian will get the information for the person. The Board does not wish people to enter the Library freely and deal with the computers themselves. They say that the expense required to keep the computers and other Library equipment in shape is becoming prohibitive.'

'But that's impossible. There's a millennial tradition of an open Galactic Library.'

'So there is, but in recent years, appropriations to the Library have been cut several times and we simply don't have the funds we used to have. It is becoming very difficult to keep our equipment up to the mark.'

Seldon rubbed his chin. 'But if your appropriations are

going down, I imagine you have to cut salaries and fire people – or, at least, not hire new ones.'

'You are exactly right.'

'In which case, how will you manage to place new labors on a shrinking work force by asking your people to obtain all the information that the public will request?'

'The idea is that we won't find all the information that the public will request but only those pieces of information that *we* consider important.'

'So that not only will you abandon the open Library but also the complete Library?'

'I'm afraid so.'

'I can't believe that any Librarian would want this.'

'You don't know Gennaro Mummery, Professor Seldon.' At Seldon's blank look, Zenow continued. ' "Who is he?" you wonder. The leader of that portion of the Board that wishes to close off the Library. More and more of the Board are on his side. If I let you and your colleagues into the Library as an independent force, a number of Board members who may not be on Mummery's side but who are dead set against any control of any part of the Library except by Librarians may decide to vote with him. And in that case, I will be forced to resign as Chief Librarian.'

'See here,' said Seldon with sudden energy. 'All this business of possibly closing down the Library, of making it less accessible, of refusing all information – all this business of declining appropriations – all this is itself a sign of Imperial disintegration. Don't you agree?'

'If you put it that way, you may be right.'

'Then let me talk to the Board. Let me explain what the future may hold and what I wish to do. Perhaps I can persuade them, as I hope I've persuaded you.'

Zenow thought for a moment. 'I'm willing to let you try, but you must know in advance that your plan may not work.'

'I've got to take that chance. Please do whatever has to

373

be done and let me know when and where I can meet the Board.'

Seldon left Zenow in a mood of unease. Everything he had told the Chief Librarian was true – and trivial. The real reason he needed the use of the Library remained hidden.

Partly this was because he didn't yet see that use clearly himself.

9

Hari Seldon sat at Yugo Amaryl's bedside – patiently, sadly. Yugo was utterly spent. He was beyond medical help, even if he would have consented to avail himself of such help, which he refused.

He was only fifty-five. Seldon was himself sixty-six and yet he was in fine shape, except for the twinge of sciatica – or whatever it was – that occasionally lamed him.

Amaryl's eyes opened. 'You're still here, Hari?'

Seldon nodded. 'I won't leave you.'

'Till I die?'

'Yes.' Then, in an outburst of grief, he said, 'Why have you done this, Yugo? If you had lived sensibly, you could have had twenty to thirty more years of life.'

Amaryl smiled faintly. 'Live sensibly? You mean, take time off? Go to resorts? Amuse myself with trifles?'

'Yes. Yes.'

'And I would either have longed to return to my work or I would have learned to like wasting my time and, in the additional twenty to thirty years you speak of, I would have accomplished no more. Look at you.'

'What about me?'

'For ten years you were First Minister under Cleon. How much science did you do then?'

'I spent about a quarter of my time on psychohistory,' said Seldon gently.

'You exaggerate. If it hadn't been for me, plugging away, psychohistorical advance would have screeched to a halt.'

Seldon nodded. 'You are right, Yugo. For that I am grateful.'

'And before and since, when you spend at least half

375

your time on administrative duties, who does – did – the real work? Eh?'

'You, Yugo.'

'Absolutely.' His eyes closed again.

Seldon said, 'Yet you always wanted to take over those administrative duties if you survived me.'

'No! I wanted to head the Project to keep it moving in the direction it had to move in, but I would have delegated all administration.'

Amaryl's breathing was growing stertorous, but then he stirred and his eyes opened, staring directly at Hari. He said, 'What will happen to psychohistory when I'm gone? Have you thought of that?'

'Yes, I have. And I want to speak to you about it. It may please you. Yugo, I believe that psychohistory is being revolutionized.'

Amaryl frowned slightly. 'In what way? I don't like the sound of that.'

'Listen. It was your idea. Years ago, you told me that two Foundations should be established. Separate – isolated and safe – and arranged so that they would serve as nuclei for an eventual Second Galactic Empire. Do you remember? That was your idea.'

'The psychohistoric equations—'

'I know. They suggested it. I'm busy working on it now, Yugo. I've managed to wangle an office in the Galactic Library—'

'The Galactic Library.' Amaryl's frown deepened. 'I don't like them. A bunch of self-satisfied idiots.'

'The Chief Librarian, Las Zenow, is not so bad, Yugo.'

'Did you ever meet a Librarian named Mummery, Gennaro Mummery?'

'No, but I've heard of him.'

'A miserable human being. We had an argument once when he claimed I had misplaced something or other. I had done no such thing and I grew very annoyed, Hari. All of a sudden I was back in Dahl. – One thing about the Dahlite culture, Hari, it is a cesspool of invective. I

376

used some of it on him and I told him he was interfering with psychohistory and he would go down in history as a villain. I didn't just say "villain," either.' Amaryl chuckled faintly. 'I left him speechless.'

Suddenly Seldon could see where Mummery's animosity toward outsiders and, most probably, psychohistory must come from – at least, in part – but he said nothing.

'The point is, Yugo, you wanted two Foundations, so that if one failed, the other would continue. But we've gone beyond that.'

'In what way?'

'Do you remember that Wanda was able to read your mind two years ago and see that something was wrong with a portion of the equations in the Prime Radiant?'

'Yes, of course.'

'Well, we will find others like Wanda. We will have one Foundation that will consist largely of physical scientists, who will preserve the knowledge of humanity and serve as the nucleus for the Second Empire. And there will be a Second Foundation of psychohistorians only – mentalists, mind-touching psychohistorians – who will be able to work on psychohistory in a multiminded way, advancing it far more quickly than individual thinkers ever could. They will serve as a group who will introduce fine adjustments as time goes on, you see. Ever in the background, watching. They will be the Empire's guardians.'

'Wonderful!' said Amaryl weakly. 'Wonderful! You see how I've chosen the right time to die? There's nothing left for me to do.'

'Don't say that, Yugo.'

'Don't make such a fuss over it, Hari. I'm too tired to do anything. Thank you – thank you – for telling me' – his voice was weakening – 'about the revolution. It makes me – happy – happy – hap—'

And those were Yugo Amaryl's last words.

Seldon bent over the bed. Tears stung his eyes and rolled down his cheeks.

Another old friend gone. Demerzel, Cleon, Dors, now Yugo . . . leaving him emptier and lonelier as he grew old.

And the revolution that had allowed Amaryl to die happy might never come to pass. Could he manage to make use of the Galactic Library? Could he find more people like Wanda? Most of all, how long would it take?

Seldon was sixty-six. If only he could have started this revolution at thirty-two when he first came to Trantor . . .

Now it might be too late.

10

Gennaro Mummery was making him wait. It was a studied discourtesy, even insolence, but Hari Seldon remained calm.

After all, Seldon needed Mummery badly and for him to become angry with the Librarian would only hurt himself. Mummery would, in fact, be delighted with an angry Seldon.

So Seldon kept his temper and waited and eventually Mummery did walk in. Seldon had seen him before – but only at a distance. This was the first time they would be together alone.

Mummery was short and plump, with a round face and a dark little beard. He wore a smile on his face, but Seldon suspected that smile of being a meaningless fixture. It revealed yellowish teeth and Mummery's inevitable hat was of a similar shade of yellow with a brown line snaking around it.

Seldon felt a touch of nausea. It seemed to him that he would dislike Mummery, even if he had no reason to do so.

Mummery said, without any preliminaries, 'Well, Professor, what can I do for you?' He looked at the time-strip on the wall but made no apology for being late.

Seldon said, 'I would like to ask you, sir, to put an end to your opposition to my remaining here at the Library.'

Mummery spread his hands. 'You've been here for two years. What opposition are you speaking of?'

'So far, that portion of the Board represented by you and those who believe as you do have been unable to out-vote the Chief Librarian, but there will be another meeting next month and Las Zenow tells me he is uncertain of the result.'

Mummery shrugged. 'So am I uncertain. Your lease – if we can call it that – may well be renewed.'

'But I need more than that, Librarian Mummery. I wish to bring in some colleagues. The project in which I am engaged – the establishment of what is needed in the way of the eventual preparation of a very special Encyclopedia – is not one I can do alone.'

'Surely your colleagues can work wherever they please. Trantor is a large world.'

'We must work in the Library. I am an old man, sir, and I am in a hurry.'

'Who can stay the advance of time? I don't think the Board will allow you to bring in colleagues. The thin edge of the wedge, Professor?'

(Yes, indeed, thought Seldon, but he said nothing.)

Mummery said, 'I have not been able to keep you out, Professor. Not so far. But I think I can continue to keep out your colleagues.'

Seldon realized that he was getting nowhere. He opened the touch of frankness a notch. He said, 'Librarian Mummery, surely your animosity toward me is not personal. Surely you understand the importance of the work I am doing.'

'You mean, your psychohistory. Come, you have been working on it for over thirty years. What has come of it?'

'That's the point. Something may come of it now.'

'Then let something come of it at Streeling University. Why must it be at the Galactic Library?'

'Librarian Mummery. Listen to me. What you want is to close the Library to the public. You wish to smash a long tradition. Have you the heart to do that?'

'It's not heart we need. It's funding. Surely the Chief Librarian has wept on your shoulder in telling you our woes. Appropriations are down, salaries are cut, needed maintenance is absent. What are we to do? We've got to cut services and we certainly can't afford to support you and your colleagues with offices and equipment.'

'Has this situation been put to the Emperor?'

'Come, Professor, you're dreaming. Isn't it true that your psychohistory tells you that the Empire is deteriorating? I've heard you referred to as Raven Seldon, something that, I believe, refers to a fabled bird of ill omen.'

'It's true that we are entering bad times.'

'And do you believe the Library is immune to those bad times? Professor, the Library is my life and I want it to continue, but it won't continue unless we can find ways of making our dwindling appropriations do. – And you come here expecting an open Library, with yourself as beneficiary. It won't do, Professor. It just won't do.'

Seldon said desperately, 'What if I find the credits for you?'

'Indeed. How?'

'What if I talk to the Emperor? I was once First Minister. He'll see me and he'll listen to me.'

'And you'll get funding from him?' Mummery laughed.

'If I do, if I increase your appropriations, may I bring in my colleagues?'

'Bring in the credits first,' said Mummery, 'and we'll see. But I don't think you will succeed.'

He seemed very sure of himself and Seldon wondered how often and how uselessly the Galactic Library had already appealed to the Emperor.

And whether his own appeal would get anywhere at all.

11

The Emperor Agis XIV had no real right to the name. He had adopted it upon succeeding to the throne with the deliberate purpose of connecting himself with the Agises who had ruled two thousand years ago, most of them quite ably – particularly Agis VI, who had ruled for forty-two years and who had kept order in a prosperous Empire with a firm but nontyrannical hand.

Agis XIV did not look like any of the old Agises – if the holographic records had any value. But, then again, truth be told, Agis XIV did not look much like the official holograph that was distributed to the public.

As a matter of fact, Hari Seldon thought, with a twinge of nostalgia, that Emperor Cleon, for all his flaws and weaknesses, had certainly looked Imperial.

Agis XIV did not. Seldon had never seen him at close quarters and the few holographs he had seen were outrageously inaccurate. The Imperial holographer knew his job and did it well, thought Seldon wryly.

Agis XIV was short, with an unattractive face and slightly bulging eyes that did not seem alight with intelligence. His only qualification for the throne was that he was a collateral relative of Cleon.

To do him credit, however, he did not try to play the role of the mighty Emperor. It was understood that he rather liked to be called the 'Citizen Emperor' and that only Imperial protocol and the outraged outcry of the Imperial Guard prevented him from exiting the dome and wandering the walkways of Trantor. Apparently, the story went, he wished to shake hands with the citizens and hear their complaints in person.

(Score one for him, thought Seldon, even if it could never come to pass.)

With a murmur and a bow, Seldon said, 'I thank you, Sire, for consenting to see me.'

Agis XIV had a clear and rather attractive voice, quite out of keeping with his appearance. He said, 'An ex-First Minister must surely have his privileges, although I must give myself credit for amazing courage in agreeing to see you.'

There was humor in his words and Seldon found himself suddenly realizing that a man might not look intelligent and yet might be intelligent just the same.

'Courage, Sire?'

'Why, of course. Don't they call you Raven Seldon?'

'I heard the expression, Sire, the other day for the first time.'

'Apparently the reference is to your psychohistory, which seems to predict the Fall of the Empire.'

'It points out the possibility only, Sire—'

'So that you are coupled with a mythic bird of ill omen. Except that I think you yourself are the bird of ill omen.'

'I hope not, Sire.'

'Come, come. The record is clear. Eto Demerzel, Cleon's old First Minister, was impressed with your work and look what happened – he was forced out of his position and into exile. The Emperor Cleon himself was impressed with your work and look what happened – he was assassinated. The military junta was impressed with your work and look what happened – they were swept away. Even the Joranumites, it is said, were impressed with your work and, behold, they were destroyed. And now, O Raven Seldon, you come to see me. What may I expect?'

'Why, nothing evil, Sire.'

'I imagine not, because unlike all these others I have mentioned, I am not impressed with your work. Now tell me why you are here.'

He listened carefully and without interruption while Seldon explained the importance of setting up a Project designed to prepare an encyclopedia that would preserve human learning if the worst happened.

'Yes yes,' said Agis XIV finally, 'so you are, indeed, convinced the Empire will fall.'

'It is a strong possibility, Sire, and it would not be prudent to refuse to take that possibility into account. In a way, I wish to prevent it if I can – or ameliorate the effects if I can't.'

'Raven Seldon, if you continue to poke your nose into matters, I am convinced that the Empire *will* fall and that nothing can help it.'

'Not so, Sire. I ask only permission to work.'

'Oh, you have that, but I fail to see what it is you wish of me. Why have you told me all this about an encyclopedia?'

'Because I wish to work in the Galactic Library, Sire, or, more accurately, I wish others to work there with me.'

'I assure you that I won't stand in your way.'

'That is not enough, Sire. I want you to help.'

'In what way, ex-First Minister?'

'With funding. The Library must have appropriations or it will close its doors to the public and evict me.'

'Credits!' A note of astonishment came into the Emperor's voice. 'You came to me for credits?'

'Yes, Sire.'

Agis XIV stood up in some agitation. Seldon stood up at once also, but Agis waved him down.

'Sit down. Don't treat me as an Emperor. I'm not an Emperor. I didn't want this job, but they made me take it. I was the nearest thing to the Imperial family and they jabbered at me that the Empire needed an Emperor. So they have me and a lot of good I am to them.

'Credits! You expect me to have credits! You talk about the Empire disintegrating. How do you suppose it disintegrates? Are you thinking of rebellion? Of civil war? Of disorders here and there?

'No. Think of *credits*. Do you realize that I cannot collect any taxes at all from half the provinces in the

Empire? They're still part of the Empire – "Hail the Imperium!" – "All honor to the Emperor!" – but they don't pay anything and I don't have the necessary force to collect it. And if I can't get the credits out of them, they are not really part of the Empire, are they?

'Credits! The Empire runs a chronic deficit of appalling proportions. There's nothing I can pay for. Do you think there is enough funding to maintain the Imperial Palace grounds? Just barely. I must cut corners. I must let the Palace decay. I must let the number of retainers die down by attrition.

'Professor Seldon. If you want credits, I have nothing. Where will I find appropriations for the Library? They should be grateful I manage to squeeze out something for them each year at all.' As he finished, the Emperor held out his hands, palms up, as if to signify the emptiness of the Imperial coffers.

Hari Seldon was stunned. He said, 'Nevertheless, Sire, even if you lack the credits, you still have the Imperial prestige. Can you not order the Library to allow me to keep my office and let my colleagues in to help me with our vital work?'

And now Agis XIV sat down again as though, once the subject was not credits, he was no longer in a state of agitation.

He said, 'You realize that, by long tradition, the Galactic Library is independent of the Imperium, as far as its self-government is concerned. It sets up its rules and has done so since Agis VI, my namesake' – he smiled – 'attempted to control the news functions of the Library. He failed and, if the great Agis VI failed, do you think I can succeed?'

'I'm not asking you to use force, Sire. Merely expressing a polite wish. Surely, when no vital function of the Library is involved, they will be pleased to honor the Emperor and oblige his wishes.'

'Professor Seldon, how little you know of the Library. I have but to express a wish, however gently and

385

tentatively, to make it certain that they will proceed, in dudgeon, to do the opposite. They are very sensitive to the slightest sign of Imperial control.'

Seldon said, 'Then what do I do?'

'Why, I'll tell you what. A thought occurs to me. I am a member of the public and I can visit the Galactic Library if I wish. It is located on the Palace grounds, so I won't be violating protocol if I visit it. Well, you come with me and we shall be ostentatiously friendly. I will not ask them for anything, but if they note us walking arm-in-arm, then perhaps some of the precious Board of theirs may feel more kindly toward you than otherwise. – But that's all I can do.'

And the deeply disappointed Seldon wondered if that could possibly be enough.

12

Las Zenow said with a certain trace of awe in his voice, 'I didn't know you were so friendly with the Emperor, Professor Seldon.'

'Why not? He's a very democratic fellow for an Emperor and he was interested in my experiences as a First Minister in Cleon's time.'

'It made a deep impression on us all. We haven't had an Emperor in our halls for many years. Generally, when the Emperor needs something from the Library—'

'I can imagine. He calls for it and it is brought to him as a matter of courtesy.'

'There was once a suggestion,' said Zenow chattily, 'that the Emperor be outfitted with a complete set of computerized equipment in his palace, hooked directly into the Library system, so that he would not need to wait for service. This was in the old days when credits were plentiful, but, you know, it was voted down.'

'Was it?'

'Oh yes, almost the entire Board agreed that it would make the Emperor too much a part of the Library and that this would threaten our independence from the government.'

'And does this Board, which will not bend to honor an Emperor, consent to let me remain at the Library?'

'At the present moment, yes. There is a feeling – and I've done my best to encourage it – that if we are not polite to a personal friend of the Emperor, the chance of a rise in appropriations will be gone altogether, so—'

'So credits – or even the dim prospect of credits – talk.'

'I'm afraid so.'

'And can I bring in my colleagues?'

Zenow looked embarrassed. 'I'm afraid not. The

Emperor was seen walking only with you – not with your colleagues. I'm sorry, Professor.'

Seldon shrugged and a mood of deep melancholy swept over him. He had no colleague to bring in, anyhow. For some time he had hoped to locate others like Wanda and he had failed. He, too, would need funding to mount an adequate search. And he, too, had nothing.

13

Trantor, the capital world-city of the Galactic Empire, had changed considerably since the day Hari first stepped off the hypership from his native Helicon thirty-eight years ago. Was it the pearly haze of an old man's memory that made the Trantor of old shine so brightly in his mind's eye, Hari wondered. Or perhaps it had been the exuberance of youth – how could a young man from a provincial Outer World such as Helicon not be impressed by the gleaming towers, sparkling domes, the colorful, rushing masses of people that had seemed to swirl through Trantor, day and night.

Now, Hari thought sadly, the walkways are nearly deserted, even in the full light of day. Roving gangs of thugs controlled various areas of the city, competing among themselves for territory. The security establishment had dwindled; those who were left had their hands full processing complaints at the central office. Of course, security officers were dispatched as emergency calls came through, but they made it to the scene only *after* a crime was committed – they no longer made even a pretense of protecting the citizens of Trantor. A person went out at his own risk – and a great risk it was. And yet Hari Seldon still took that risk, in the form of a daily walk, as if defying the forces that were destroying his beloved Empire to destroy him as well.

And so Hari Seldon walked along, limping – and thoughtful.

Nothing worked. Nothing. He had been unable to isolate the genetic pattern that set Wanda apart – and without that, he was unable to locate others like her.

Wanda's ability to read minds had sharpened considerably in the six years since she had identified the flaw in Yugo Amaryl's Prime Radiant. Wanda was special in more ways than one. It was as if, once she realized that her mental ability set her apart from other people, she was determined to understand it, to harness its energy, to direct it. As she had progressed through her teen years, she had matured, throwing off the girlish giggles that had so endeared her to Hari, at the same time becoming even dearer to him in her determination to help him in his work with the powers of her 'gift.' For Hari Seldon had told Wanda about his plan for a Second Foundation and she had committed herself to realizing that goal with him.

Today, though, Seldon was in a dark mood. He was coming to the conclusion that Wanda's mentalic ability would get him nowhere. He had no credits to continue his work – no credits to locate others like Wanda, no credits to pay his workers on the Psychohistory Project at Streeling, no credits to set up his all-important Encyclopedia Project at the Galactic Library.

Now what?

He continued to walk toward the Galactic Library. He would have been better off taking a gravicab, but he wanted to walk – limp or not. He needed time to think.

He heard a cry – 'There he is!' – but paid no attention.

It came again. 'There he is! Psychohistory!'

The word forced him to look up. – Psychohistory.

A group of young men was closing in around him.

Automatically Seldon placed his back against the wall and raised his cane. 'What is it you want?'

They laughed. 'Credits, old man. Do you have any credits?'

'Maybe, but why do you want them from me? You said, "Psychohistory!" Do you know who I am?'

'Sure, you're Raven Seldon,' said the young man in the lead. He seemed both comfortable and pleased.

'You're a creep,' shouted another.

'What are you going to do if I don't give you any credits?'

'We'll beat you up,' said the leader, 'and we'll take them.'

'And if I give you my credits?'

'We'll beat you up anyway!' They all laughed.

Hari Seldon raised his cane higher. 'Stay away. All of you.'

By now he had managed to count them. There were eight.

He felt himself choking slightly. Once he and Dors and Raych had been attacked by ten and they had had no trouble. He had been only thirty-two at the time and Dors – was Dors.

Now it was different. He waved his cane.

The leader of the hoodlums said, 'Hey, the old man is going to attack us. What are we going to do?'

Seldon looked around swiftly. There were no security officers around. Another indication of the deterioration of society. An occasional person or two passed by, but there was no use calling for help. Their footsteps increased in speed and made a wide detour. No one was going to run any risks of getting involved in an imbroglio.

Seldon said, 'The first one of you who approaches gets a cracked head.'

'Yeah?' And the leader stepped forward rapidly and seized the cane. There was a short sharp struggle and the cane was wrested from Seldon's grip. The leader tossed it to one side.

'Now what, old man?'

Seldon shrunk back. He could only wait for the blows. They crowded around him, each eager to land a blow or two. Seldon lifted his arms to try to ward them off. He could still Twist – after a fashion. If he were facing only one or two, he might be able to Twist his body, avoid their blows, strike back. But not against eight – surely not against eight.

He tried, at any rate, moving quickly to one side to avoid the blows and his right leg, with its sciatica, doubled under him. He fell and knew himself to be utterly helpless.

Then he heard a stentorian voice shouting, 'What's going on here? Get back, you thugs! Back or I'll kill you all!'

The leader said, 'Well, another old man.'

'Not that old,' said the newcomer. With the back of one hand, he struck the leader's face, turning it an ugly red.

Seldon said in surprise, 'Raych, it's you.'

Raych's hand swept back. 'Stay out of this, Dad. Just get up and move away.'

The leader, rubbing his cheek, said, 'We'll get you for that.'

'No, you won't,' said Raych, drawing out a knife of Dahlite manufacture, long and gleaming. A second knife was withdrawn and he now held one in each hand.

Seldon said weakly, 'Still carrying knives, Raych?'

'Always,' said Raych. 'Nothing will ever make me stop.'

'I'll stop you,' said the leader, drawing out a blaster.

Faster than the eye could follow, one of Raych's knives went sailing through the air and struck the leader's throat. He made a loud gasp, then a gurgling sound, and fell, while the other seven stared.

Raych approached and said, 'I want my knife back.' He drew it out of the hoodlum's throat and wiped it on the man's shirtfront. In doing so, he stepped on the man's hand, bent down, and picked up his blaster.

Raych dropped the blaster into one of his capacious pockets. He said, 'I don't like to use a blaster, you bunch of good-for-nothings, because sometimes I miss. I never miss with a knife, however. Never! That man is dead. There are seven of you standing. Do you intend to stay standing or will you leave?'

'Get him!' shouted one of the hoodlums and the seven made a concerted rush.

Raych took a backward step. One knife flashed and then the other and two of the hoodlums stopped with, in each case, a knife buried in his abdomen.

'Give me back my knives,' said Raych, pulling each out with a cutting motion and wiping them.

'These two are still alive, but not for long. That leaves five of you on your feet. Are you going to attack again or are you going to leave?'

They turned and Raych called out, 'Pick up your dead and dying. I don't want them.'

Hastily they flung the three bodies over their shoulders, then they turned tail and ran.

Raych bent to pick up Seldon's cane. 'Can you walk, Dad?'

'Not very well,' said Seldon. 'I twisted my leg.'

'Well then, get into my car. What were you doing walking, anyway?'

'Why not? Nothing's ever happened to me.'

'So you waited till something did. Get into my car and I'll give you a lift back to Streeling.'

He programmed the ground-car quietly, then said, 'What a shame we didn't have Dors with us. Mom would have attacked them with her bare hands and left all eight dead in five minutes.'

Seldon felt tears stinging his eyelids. 'I know, Raych, I know. Do you think I don't miss her every day?'

'I'm sorry,' said Raych in a low voice.

Seldon asked, 'How did you know I was in trouble?'

'Wanda told me. She said there were evil people lying in wait for you and told me where they were and I took right off.'

'Didn't you doubt that she knew what she was talking about?'

'Not at all. We know enough about her now to know that she has some sort of contact with your mind and with the things around you.'

'Did she tell you how many people were attacking me?'

'No. She just said, "Quite a few."'

'So you came out all by yourself, did you, Raych?'

'I had no time to put together a posse, Dad. Besides, one of me was enough.'

'Yes, it was. Thank you, Raych.'

14

They were back at Streeling now and Seldon's leg was stretched out on a hassock.

Raych looked at him somberly. 'Dad,' he began, 'you're not to go walking around Trantor on your own from now on.'

Seldon frowned. 'Why, because of one incident?'

'It was enough of an incident. You can't take care of yourself any longer. You're seventy years old and your right leg will not support you in an emergency. And you have enemies—'

'Enemies!'

'Yes, indeed. And you know it. Those sewer rats were not after simply anyone. They were not looking for just any unwary person to rip off. They identified *you* by calling out, "Psychohistory!" And they called you a creep. Why do you suppose that was?'

'I don't know why.'

'That's because you live in a world all your own, Dad, and you don't know what's going on on Trantor. Don't you suppose the Trantorians know that their world is going downhill at a rapid rate? Don't you suppose they know that your psychohistory has been predicting this for years? Doesn't it occur to you that they may blame the messenger for the message? If things go bad – and they *are* going bad – there are many who think that you are responsible for it.'

'I can't believe that.'

'Why do you suppose there's a faction at the Galactic Library that wants you out of there? They don't want to be in the way when you are mobbed. So – you've got to take care of yourself. You can't go out alone. I'll have to be with you or you will have to have bodyguards.

That's the way it's going to be, Dad.'

Seldon looked dreadfully unhappy.

Raych softened and said, 'But not for long, Dad. I've got a new job.'

Seldon looked up. 'A new job. What kind?'

'Teaching. At a University.'

'Which University?'

'Santanni.'

Seldon's lips trembled. 'Santanni! That's nine thousand parsecs away from Trantor. It's a provincial world on the other side of the Galaxy.'

'Exactly. That's why I want to go there. I've been on Trantor all my life, Dad, and I'm tired of it. There's no world in all the Empire that's deteriorating the way Trantor is. It's become a haunt of crime with no one to protect us. The economy is limping, the technology is failing. Santanni, on the other hand, is a decent world, still humming along, and I want to be there to build a new life, along with Manella and Wanda and Bellis. We're all going there in two months.'

'All of you!'

'And you, Dad. And you. We wouldn't leave you behind on Trantor. You're coming with us to Santanni.'

Seldon shook his head. 'Impossible, Raych. You know that.'

'Why impossible?'

'You know why. The Project. My psychohistory. Are you asking me to abandon my life's work?'

'Why not? It's abandoned you.'

'You're mad.'

'No, I'm not. Where are you going with it? You have no credits. You can't get any. There's no one left on Trantor who's willing to support you.'

'For nearly forty years—'

'Yes, I admit that. But after all that time, you've *failed*, Dad. There's no crime in failing. You've tried so hard and you've gone so far, but you've run into a deteriorating economy, a failing Empire. It's the very thing you've been predicting for so long that's stopping you at last. So—'

'No. I will not stop. Somehow or other, I will keep going.'

'I tell you what, Dad. If you're really going to be so stubborn, then take psychohistory with you. Start it again on Santanni. There may be enough credits – and enthusiasm – to support it there.'

'And the men and women who have been working for me so faithfully?'

'Oh bull, Dad. They've been *leaving* you because you can't pay them. You hang around here for the rest of your life and you'll be alone. – Oh, come on, Dad. Do you think I like to talk to you this way? It's because no one has wanted to – because no one has had the *heart* to – that you're in your present predicament. Let's be honest with each other now. When you walk the streets of Trantor and you're attacked for no reason other than that you're Hari Seldon, don't you think it's time for a little bit of truth?'

'Never mind the truth. I have no intention of leaving Trantor.'

Raych shook his head. 'I was sure you'd be stubborn, Dad. You've got two months to change your mind. Think about it, will you?'

15

It had been a long time since Hari Seldon had smiled. He had conducted the Project in the same fashion that he always did: pushing always forward in the development of psychohistory, making plans for the Foundation, studying the Prime Radiant.

But he did not smile. All he did was to force himself through his work without any feeling of impending success. Rather, there was a feeling of impending failure about everything.

And now, as he sat in his office at Streeling University, Wanda entered. He looked up at her and his heart lifted. Wanda had always been special. Seldon couldn't put his finger on just when he and the others had started accepting her pronouncements with more than the usual enthusiasm; it just seemed always to have been that way. As a little girl, she had saved his life with her uncanny knowledge of 'lemonade death' and all through her childhood she had somehow just *known* things.

Although Dr Endelecki had asserted that Wanda's genome was perfectly normal in every way, Seldon was still positive that his granddaughter possessed mental abilities far beyond those of average humans. And he was just as sure that there were others like her in the Galaxy – on Trantor, even. If only he could find them, these mentalics, what a great contribution they could make to the Foundation. The potential for such greatness all centered in his beautiful granddaughter. Seldon gazed at her, framed in his office doorway, and he felt as if his heart would break. In a few days, she would be gone.

How could he bear it? She was such a beautiful girl – eighteen. Long blond hair, face a little broad but with a tendency to smile. She was even smiling now and Seldon thought, Why not? She's heading for Santanni and for a new life.

He said, 'Well, Wanda, just a few more days.'

'No. I don't think so, Grandpa.'

He stared at her. 'What?'

Wanda approached him and put her arms around him. 'I'm not going to Santanni.'

'Have your father and mother changed their minds?'

'No, they're going.'

'And you're not? Why? Where are you going?'

'I'm going to stay here, Grandpa. With you.' She hugged him. 'Poor Grandpa!'

'But I don't understand. Why? Are they allowing this?'

'You mean Mom and Dad. Not really. We've been arguing over this for weeks, but I've won out. Why not, Grandpa? They'll go to Santanni and they'll have each other – and they'll have little Bellis, too. But if I go with them and leave you here, you'll have no one. I don't think I could stand that.'

'But how did you get them to agree?'

'Well, you know – I pushed.'

'What does that mean?'

'It's my mind. I can see what you have in yours and in theirs and, as time goes on, I can see more clearly. And I can push them to do what I want.'

'How do you do that?'

'I don't know. But after a while, they get tired of being pushed and they're willing to let me have my way. So I'm going to stay with you.'

Seldon looked up at her with helpless love. 'This is wonderful, Wanda. But Bellis—'

'Don't worry about Bellis. She doesn't have a mind like mine.'

'Are you certain?' Seldon chewed at his lower lip.

'Quite certain. Besides, Mom and Dad have to have someone, too.'

Seldon wanted to rejoice, but he couldn't do so openly. There were Raych and Manella. What of them?

He said, 'Wanda, what about your parents? Can you be so cold-blooded about them?'

'I'm not cold-blooded. They understand. They realize I must be with you.'

'How did you manage that?'

'I pushed,' said Wanda simply, 'and eventually they came to see it my way.'

'You can do that?'

'It wasn't easy.'

'And you did it because—' Seldon paused.

Wanda said, 'Because I love you. Of course. And because—'

'Yes?'

'I must learn psychohistory. I know quite a bit of it already.'

'How?'

'From your mind. From the minds of others at the Project, especially from Uncle Yugo before he died. But it's in rags and tatters, so far. I want the real thing. Grandpa, I want a Prime Radiant of my own.' Her face lit up and her words came quickly, with passion. 'I want to study psychohistory in great detail. Grandpa, you're quite old and quite tired. I'm young and eager. I want to learn all I can, so I can carry on when—'

Seldon said, 'Well, that would be wonderful – if you could do it – but there is no funding anymore. I'll teach you all I can, but – we can't *do* anything.'

'We'll see, Grandpa. We'll see.'

16

Raych, Manella, and little Bellis were waiting at the spaceport.

The hypership was preparing for liftoff and the three had already checked their baggage.

Raych said, 'Dad, come along with us.'

Seldon shook his head. 'I cannot.'

'If you change your mind, we will always have a place for you.'

'I know it, Raych. We've been together for almost forty years – and they've been good years. Dors and I were lucky to find you.'

'I'm the lucky one.' His eyes filled with tears. 'Don't think I don't think of Mother every day.'

'Yes.' Seldon looked away miserably. Wanda was playing with Bellis when the call rang out for everyone to board the hypership. They did, after a tearful last embrace of Wanda by her parents. Raych looked back to wave at Seldon and to try to plant a crooked smile on his face.

Seldon waved and one hand moved out blindly to embrace Wanda's shoulders.

She was the only one left. One by one through his long life, he had lost his friends and those he had loved. Demerzel had left, never to return; Emperor Cleon was gone; his beloved Dors was gone; his faithful friend Yugo Amaryl was gone; and now Raych, his only son, was gone as well.

He was left only with Wanda.

17

Hari Seldon said, 'It is beautiful outside – a marvelous evening. Considering that we live under a dome, you would think we would have beautiful weather like this every evening.'

Wanda said indifferently, 'We would grow tired of it, Grandpa, if it were beautiful all the time. A little change from night to night is good for us.'

'For you, because you're young, Wanda. You have many, many evenings ahead of you. I don't. I want more good ones.'

'Now, Grandpa, you're not old. Your leg is doing well and your mind is as sharp as ever. I *know*.'

'Sure. Go ahead. Make me feel better.' He then said with an air of discomfort, 'I want to walk. I want to get out of this tiny apartment and take a walk to the Library and enjoy this beautiful evening.'

'What do you want at the Library?'

'At the moment, nothing. I want the walk. – But . . .'

'Yes. But?'

'I promised Raych I wouldn't go walking around Trantor without a bodyguard.'

'Raych isn't here.'

'I know,' mumbled Seldon, 'but a promise is a promise.'

'He didn't say who the bodyguard should be, did he? Let's go for a walk and I'll be your bodyguard.'

'You?' Seldon grinned.

'Yes, me. I hereby volunteer my services. Get yourself ready and we'll go for a walk.'

Seldon was amused. He had half a mind to go without his cane, since his leg was scarcely painful of late, but, on the other hand, he had a new cane, one in which the head had been filled with lead. It was both heavier and stronger than his old cane and, if he was going to have none other than Wanda as a bodyguard, he thought he had better bring his new cane.

The walk was delightful and Seldon was terribly glad he had given in to the temptation – until they reached a certain spot.

Seldon lifted his cane in a mixture of anger and resignation and said, 'Look at that!'

Wanda lifted her eyes. The dome was glowing, as it always did in the evening, in order to lend an air of first twilight. It grew darker as night went on, of course.

What Seldon was pointing at, however, was a strip of darkness along the dome. A section of lights had gone out.

Seldon said, 'When I first came to Trantor, anything like that was unthinkable. There were people tending the lights at all times. The city *worked*, but now it is falling apart in all these little ways and what bothers me most is that no one cares. Why aren't there petitions to the Imperial Palace? Why aren't there meetings of indignation? It is as though the people of Trantor expect the city to be falling apart and then they find themselves annoyed with me because I am pointing out that this is exactly what is happening.'

Wanda said softly, 'Grandpa, there are two men behind us.'

They had walked into the shadows beneath the broken dome lights and Seldon asked, 'Are they just walking?'

'No.' Wanda did not look at them. She did not have to. 'They're after you.'

'Can you stop them – push them?'

'I'm trying, but there are two and they are determined. It's – it's like pushing a wall.'

'How far behind me are they?'

'About three meters.'

'Closing in?'

'Yes, Grandpa.'

'Tell me when they're a meter behind me.' He slid his hand down his cane till he was holding the thin end, leaving the leaded head swinging free.

'*Now*, Grandpa!' hissed Wanda.

And Seldon turned, swinging his cane. It came down hard upon the shoulder of one of the men behind him, who went down with a scream, writhing on the pavement.

Seldon said, 'Where's the other guy?'

'He took off.'

Seldon looked down on the man on the ground and put his foot on his chest. He said, 'Go through his pockets, Wanda. Someone must have paid him and I'd like to find his credit file – perhaps I can identify where they came from.' He added thoughtfully, 'I meant to hit him on the head.'

'You'd have killed him, Grandpa.'

Seldon nodded. 'It's what I wanted to do. Rather shameful. I'm lucky I missed.'

A harsh voice said, 'What is all this?' A figure in uniform came running up, perspiring. 'Give me that cane, you!'

'Officer,' said Seldon mildly.

'You can give me your story later. We've got to call an ambulance for this poor man.'

'*Poor man*,' said Seldon angrily. 'He was going to assault me. I acted in self-defense.'

'I saw it happen,' said the security officer. 'This guy never laid a finger on you. You turned on him and struck him without provocation. That's not self-defense. That's assault and battery.'

'Officer, I'm telling you that—'

'Don't tell me anything. You can tell it in court.'

Wanda said in a sweet small voice, 'Officer, if you will just listen to us—'

The officer said, 'You go along home, young lady.'

Wanda drew herself up. 'I most certainly won't, Officer. Where my grandfather goes, there go I.' Her eyes flashed and the security officer muttered, 'Well, come along, then.'

18

Seldon was enraged. 'I've never been in custody before in
my entire life. A couple of months ago eight men
assaulted me. I was able to fight them off with the help
of my son, but while that was going on was there a
security officer in sight? Did people stop to help me? No.
This time, I'm better prepared and I knocked a man flat
who had been about to assault me. Was there a security
officer in sight? Absolutely. She put the collar on me.
There were people watching, too, and they were amused
at seeing an old man being taken in for assault and battery. What kind of world do we live on?'

Civ Novker, Seldon's lawyer, sighed and said calmly,
'A corrupt world, but don't worry. Nothing will happen
to you. I'll get you out on bail and then, eventually, you'll
come back for trial before a jury of your peers and the
most you'll get – the very most – are some hard words
from the bench. Your age and your reputation—'

'Forget my reputation,' said Seldon, still angry. 'I'm a
psychohistorian and, at the present time, *that* is a dirty
word. They'll be glad to see me in jail.'

'No, they won't,' said Novker. 'There may be some
screwballs who have it in for you, but I'll see to it that
none of them gets on the jury.'

Wanda said, 'Do we really have to subject my grandfather to all this? He's not a young man anymore. Can't
we just appear before the magistrate and not bother with
a jury trial?'

The lawyer turned to her. 'It can be done. If you're
insane, maybe. Magistrates are impatient power-mad
people who would just as soon put a person into jail for
a year as listen to him. No one goes up before a
magistrate.'

'I think we should,' said Wanda.

Seldon said, 'Well now, Wanda, I think we ought to listen to Civ—' But as he said that, he felt a strong churning in his abdomen. It was Wanda's 'push.' Seldon said, 'Well – if you insist.'

'She can't insist,' said the lawyer. 'I won't allow it.'

Wanda said, 'My grandfather is your client. If he wants something done his way, you've got to do it.'

'I can refuse to represent him.'

'Well then, leave,' said Wanda sharply, 'and we'll face the magistrate alone.'

Novker thought and said, 'Very well, then – if you're going to be so adamant. I've represented Hari for years and I suppose I won't abandon him now. But I warn you, the chances are he'll get a jail sentence and I'll have to work like the devil to get it lifted – if I can do it at all.'

'I'm not afraid,' said Wanda.

Seldon bit his lip and the lawyer turned to him. 'What about you? Are you willing to let your granddaughter call the shots?'

Seldon thought a bit, then admitted, much to the old lawyer's surprise, 'Yes. Yes, I am.'

19

The magistrate looked sourly at Seldon as he gave his story.

The magistrate said, 'What makes you think it was the intention of this man you struck to attack you? Did he strike you? Did he threaten you? Did he in any way place you under bodily fear?'

'My granddaughter was aware of his approach and was quite certain that he was planning to attack me.'

'Surely, sir, that cannot be enough. Is there anything else you can tell me before I pass judgment?'

'Well now, wait a while,' said Seldon indignantly. 'Don't pass judgment so quickly. I was assaulted a few weeks ago by eight men whom I held off with the help of my son. So, you see, I have reason to think that I might be assaulted again.'

The magistrate shuffled his papers. 'Assaulted by eight men. Did you report that?'

'There were no security officers around. Not one.'

'Aside from the point. Did you report it?'

'No, sir.'

'Why not?'

'For one thing, I was afraid of getting into long drawn-out legal proceedings. Since we had driven off eight men and were safe, it seemed useless to ask for more trouble.'

'How did you manage to ward off *eight* men – just you and your son?'

Seldon hesitated. 'My son is now on Santanni and outside Trantorian control. Thus, I can tell you that he had Dahlite knives and was expert in their use. He killed one man and badly hurt two others. The rest ran, carrying off the dead and wounded.'

'But did you not report the death of a man and the wounding of two others?'

'No, sir. Same reason as before. And we fought in self-defense. However, if you can track down the three dead and wounded, you will have evidence that we were attacked.'

The magistrate said, 'Track down one dead and two wounded nameless faceless Trantorians? Are you aware that on Trantor over two thousand people are found dead every day – by knife wounds *alone*. Unless these things are reported to us at once, we are helpless. Your story of being assaulted once before will not hold water. What we must do is deal with the events of today, which *were* reported and which had a security officer as a witness.

'So, let's consider the situation as of now. Why do you think the fellow was going to attack? Simply because you happened to be passing by? Because you seemed old and defenseless? Because you looked like you might be carrying a great deal of credits? What do you think?'

'I think, Magistrate, it was because of who I am.'

The magistrate looked at his papers. 'You are Hari Seldon, a professor and a scholar. Why should that make you subject to assault, particularly?'

'Because of my views.'

'Your views. Well—' The magistrate shuffled some papers perfunctorily. Suddenly he stopped and looked up, peering at Seldon. 'Wait – Hari Seldon.' A look of recognition spread across his face. 'You're the psycho-history buff, aren't you?'

'Yes, Magistrate.'

'I'm sorry. I don't know anything about it except the name and the fact that you go around predicting the end of the Empire or something like that.'

'Not quite, Magistrate. But my views have become unpopular because they are proving to be true. I believe it is for that reason that there are those who want to assault me or, even more likely, are being paid to assault me.'

The magistrate stared at Seldon and then called over the arresting security officer. 'Did you check up on the man who was hurt? Does he have a record?'

The security officer cleared her throat. 'Yes, sir. He's been arrested several times. Assault, mugging.'

'Oh, he's a repeat offender, is he? And does the professor have a record?'

'No, sir.'

'So we have an old and innocent man fighting off a known mugger – and you arrest the old and innocent man. Is that it?'

The security officer was silent.

The magistrate said, 'You may go, Professor.'

'Thank you, sir. May I have my cane?'

The magistrate snapped his fingers at the officer, who handed over the cane.

'But one thing, Professor,' said the magistrate. 'If you use that cane again, you had better be absolutely certain you can prove it was in self-defense. Otherwise—'

'Yes, sir.' And Hari Seldon left the magistrate's chambers, leaning heavily on his cane but with his head held high.

20

Wanda was crying bitterly, her face wet with tears, her eyes red, her cheeks swollen.

Hari Seldon hovered over her, patting her on the back, not knowing quite how to comfort her.

'Grandpa, I'm a miserable failure. I thought I could push people – and I could when they didn't mind being pushed too much, like Mom and Dad – and even then it took a long time. I even worked out a rating system of sorts, based on a ten-point scale – sort of a mental pushing power gauge. Only I assumed too much. I assumed that I was a ten, or at least a nine. But now I realize that, at most, I rate a seven.'

Wanda's crying had stopped and she sniffed occasionally as Hari stroked her hand. 'Usually – usually – I have no trouble. If I concentrate, I can hear people's thoughts and when I want, I push them. But those muggers! I could hear them all right, but there was nothing I could do to push them away.'

'I thought you did very well, Wanda.'

'I *didn't*. I had a fan – fantasy. I thought people would come up behind you and in one mightly push I'd send them flying. That way I was going to be your bodyguard. That's why I offered to be your bod – bodyguard. Only I wasn't. Those two guys came up and I couldn't do a thing.'

'But you could. You made the first man hesitate. That gave me a chance to turn and clobber him.'

'No no. I had nothing to do with it. All I could do was warn you he was there and you did the rest.'

'The second man ran away.'

'Because you clobbered the first guy. I had nothing to do with it.' She broke out again in tears of frustration.

411

'And then the magistrate. I insisted on the magistrate. I thought I would push and he would let you go at once.'

'He did let me go and it was practically at once.'

'No. He put you through a miserable routine and saw the light only when he realized who you were. I had nothing to do with it. I flopped everywhere. I could have gotten you into so much trouble.'

'No, I refuse to accept that, Wanda. If your pushing didn't work quite as well as you had hoped it would, it was only because you were working under emergency conditions. You couldn't have helped it. But, Wanda, look – I have an idea.'

Catching the excitement in his voice, she looked up. 'What kind of idea, Grandpa?'

'Well, it's like this, Wanda. You probably realize that I've got to have credits. Psychohistory simply can't continue without it and I cannot bear the thought of having it all come to nothing after so many years of hard work.'

'I can't bear it, either. But how can we get the credits?'

'Well, I'm going to request an audience with the Emperor again. I've seen him once already and he's a good man and I like him. But he's not exactly drowning in wealth. However, if I take you with me and if you push him – gently – it may be that he will find a source of credits, some source somewhere, and keep me going for a while, till I can think of something else.'

'Do you really think it will work, Grandpa?'

'Not without you. But with you – maybe. Come, isn't it worth trying?'

Wanda smiled. 'You know I'll do anything you ask, Grandpa. Besides, it's our only hope.'

21

It was not difficult to see the Emperor. Agis's eyes sparkled as he greeted Hari Seldon. 'Hello, old friend,' he said. 'Have you come to bring me bad luck?'

'I hope not,' said Seldon.

Agis unhooked the elaborate cloak he was wearing and, with a weary grunt, threw it into the corner of the room, saying, 'And *you* lie there.'

He looked at Seldon and shook his head. 'I hate that thing. It's as heavy as sin and as hot as blazes. I always have to wear it when I'm being smothered under meaningless words, standing there upright like a carved image. It's just plain horrible. Cleon was born to it and he had the appearance for it. I was not and I don't. It's just my misery that I'm a third cousin of his on my mother's side so that I qualified as Emperor. I'd be glad to sell it for a very small sum. Would you like to be Emperor, Hari?'

'No no, I wouldn't dream of it, so don't get your hopes up,' said Seldon, laughing.

'But tell me, who is this extraordinarily beautiful young woman you have brought with you today?'

Wanda flushed and the Emperor said genially, 'You mustn't let me embarrass you, my dear. One of the few perquisites an Emperor possesses is the right to say anything he chooses. No one can object or argue about it. They can only say, "Sire." However, I don't want any "Sires" from you. I hate that word. Call me Agis. That is not my birth name, either. It's my Imperial name and I've got to get used to it. So . . . tell me what's doing, Hari. What's been happening to you since the last time we met?'

Seldon said briefly, 'I've been attacked twice.'

The Emperor didn't seem to be sure whether this was a joke or not. He said, 'Twice? Really?'

The Emperor's face darkened as Seldon told the story of the assaults. 'I suppose there wasn't a security officer around when those eight men threatened you.'

'Not one.'

The Emperor rose from his chair and gestured at the other two to keep theirs. He walked back and forth, as though he were trying to work off some anger. Then he turned and faced Seldon.

'For thousands of years,' he began, 'whenever something like this happened, people would say, "Why don't we appeal to the Emperor?" or "Why doesn't the Emperor do something?" And, in the end, the Emperor *can* do something and *does* do something, even if it isn't always the intelligent thing to do. But I . . . Hari, I'm powerless. Absolutely powerless.

'Oh yes, there is the so-called Commission of Public Safety, but they seem more concerned with *my* safety than that of the public. It's a wonder we're having this audience at all, for you are not at all popular with the Commission.

'There's *nothing* I can do about anything. Do you know what's happened to the status of the Emperor since the fall of the junta and the restoration of – hah! – Imperial power?'

'I think I do.'

'I'll bet you don't – fully. We've got democracy now. Do you know what democracy is?'

'Certainly.'

Agis frowned. He said, 'I'll bet you think it's a good thing.'

'I think it *can* be a good thing.'

'Well, there you are. It isn't. It's completely upset the Empire.

'Suppose I want to order more officers onto the streets of Trantor. In the old days, I would pull over a piece of paper prepared for me by the Imperial Secretary and

414

would sign it with a flourish – and there would be more security officers.

'Now I can't do anything of the sort. I have to put it before the Legislature. There are seventy-five hundred men and women who instantly turn into uncounted gaggles of geese the instant a suggestion is made. In the first place, where is the funding to come from? You can't have, say, ten thousand more officers without having to pay ten thousand more salaries. Then, even if you agreed to something of the sort, who selects the new security officers? Who controls them?

'The Legislature shouts at each other, argues, thunders, and lightens, and in the end – nothing is done. Hari, I couldn't even do as small a thing as fix the broken dome lights you noticed. How much will it cost? Who's in charge? Oh, the lights will be fixed, but it can easily take a few months to do it. *That's* democracy.'

Hari Seldon said, 'As I recall, the Emperor Cleon was forever complaining that he could not do what he wished to do.'

'The Emperor Cleon,' said Agis impatiently, 'had two first-class First Ministers – Demerzel and yourself – and you each labored to keep Cleon from doing anything foolish. I have seventy-five hundred First Ministers, all of whom are foolish from start to finish. But surely, Hari, you haven't come to complain to me about the attacks.'

'No, I haven't. Something much worse. Sire – Agis – I need credits.'

The Emperor stared at him. 'After what I've been telling you, Hari? I have no credits. – Oh yes, there're credits to run this establishment, of course, but in order to get them I have to face my seventy-five hundred legislators. If you think I can go to them and say, "I want credits for my friend, Hari Seldon," and if you think I'll get one quarter of what I ask for in anything less than two years, you're crazy. It won't happen.'

He shrugged and said, more gently, 'Don't get me wrong, Hari. I would like to help you if I could. I would particularly like to help you for the sake of your grand-daughter. Looking at her makes me feel as though I should give you all the credits you would like – but it can't be done.'

Seldon said, 'Agis, if I don't get funding, psychohistory will go down the drain – after nearly forty years.'

'It's come to nothing in nearly forty years, so why worry?'

'Agis,' said Seldon, 'there's nothing more I can do now. The assaults on me were precisely because I'm a psycho-historian. People consider me a predictor of destruction.'

The Emperor nodded. 'You're bad luck, Raven Seldon. I told you this earlier.'

Seldon stood up wretchedly. 'I'm through, then.'

Wanda stood, too, next to Seldon, the top of her head reaching her grandfather's shoulder. She gazed fixedly at the Emperor.

As Hari turned to go, the Emperor said, 'Wait. Wait. There's a little verse I once memorized:

> *"Ill fares the land*
> *To hastening ills a prey*
> *Where wealth accumulates*
> *And men decay."'*

'What does it mean?' asked a dispirited Seldon.

'It means that the Empire is steadily deteriorating and falling apart, but that doesn't keep some individuals from growing rich. Why not turn to some of our wealthy entrepreneurs? They don't have legislators and can, if they wish, simply sign a credit voucher.'

Seldon stared. 'I'll try that.'

22

'Mr Bindris,' said Hari Seldon, reaching out his hand to shake the other's. 'I am so glad to be able to see you. It was good of you to agree to see me.'

'Why not?' said Terep Bindris jovially. 'I know you well. Or, rather, I know *of* you well.'

'That's pleasant. I take it you've heard of psycho-history, then.'

'Oh yes, what intelligent person hasn't? Not that I *understand* anything about it, of course. And who is this young lady you have with you?'

'My granddaughter, Wanda.'

'A very pretty young woman.' He beamed. 'Somehow I feel I'd be putty in her hands.'

Wanda said, 'I think you exaggerate, sir.'

'No, really. Now, please, sit down and tell me what it is I can do for you.' He gestured expansively with his arm, indicating that they be seated on two overstuffed, richly brocaded chairs in front of the desk at which he sat. The chairs, like the ornate desk, the imposing carved doors which had slid back noiselessly at their arrival signal, and the gleaming obsidian floor of Bindris's vast office, were of the finest quality. And, although his surroundings were impressive – and imposing – Bindris himself was not. The slight cordial man would not be taken, at first glance, for one of Trantor's leading financial powerbrokers.

'We're here, sir, at the Emperor's suggestion.'

'The Emperor?'

'Yes, he could not help us, but he thought a man like you might be able to do so. The question, of course, is credits.'

Bindris's face fell. 'Credits?' he said. 'I don't understand.'

'Well,' said Seldon, 'for nearly forty years, psycho-history has been supported by the government. However, times change and the Empire is no longer what it was.'

'Yes, I know that.'

'The Emperor lacks the credits to support us or, even if he did have the credits, he couldn't get the request for funding past the Legislature. He recommends, therefore, that I see businesspeople who, in the first place, still have credits and, in the second place, can simply write out a credit voucher.'

There was a longish pause and Bindris finally said, 'The Emperor, I'm afraid, knows nothing about business. – How many credits do you want?'

'Mr Bindris, we're talking about an enormous task. I'm going to need several million.'

'Several *million*!'

'Yes, sir.'

Bindris frowned. 'Are we talking about a loan here? When do you expect to be able to pay it back?'

'Well, Mr. Bindris, I can't honestly say I ever expect to be able to pay it back. I'm looking for a gift.'

'Even if I wanted to give you the credits – and let me tell you, for some strange reason I very much want to do so – I couldn't. The Emperor may have his Legislature, but I have my Board members. I can't make a gift of that sort without the Board's permission and they'll never grant it.'

'Why not? Your firm is enormously wealthy. A few million would mean nothing to you.'

'That sounds good,' said Bindris, 'but I'm afraid that the firm is in a state of decline right now. Not sufficiently to bring us into serious trouble, but enough to make us unhappy. If the Empire is in a state of decay, different individual parts of it are decaying, too. We are in no position to hand out a few million. – I'm truly sorry.'

Seldon sat there silently and Bindris seemed unhappy. He shook his head at last and said, 'Look, Professor Seldon, I would really like to help you out, particularly for the sake of the young lady you have with you. It just can't be done. – However, we're not the only firm in Trantor. Try others, Professor. You may have better luck elsewhere.'

'Well,' said Seldon, raising himself to his feet with an effort, 'we shall try.'

23

Wanda's eyes were filled with tears, but the emotion they represented was not sorrow but fury.

'Grandpa,' she said, 'I don't understand it. I simply don't understand it. We've been to four different firms. Each one was ruder and nastier to us than the one before. The fourth one just kicked us out. And since then, no one will let us in.'

'It's no mystery, Wanda,' said Seldon gently. 'When we saw Bindris, he didn't know what we were there for and he was perfectly friendly until I asked for a gift of a few million credits. Then he was a great deal less friendly. I imagine the word went out as to what we wanted and each additional time there was less friend-liness until now, when people won't receive us at all. Why should they? They're not going to give us the credits we need, so why waste time with us?'

Wanda's anger turned on herself. 'And what did I do? I just sat there. Nothing.'

'I wouldn't say that,' said Seldon. 'Bindris was affected by you. It seems to me that he really wanted to give me the credits, largely because of you. You were pushing him and accomplishing something.'

'Not nearly enough. Besides, all he cared about was that I was pretty.'

'Not pretty,' muttered Seldon. 'Beautiful. Very beautiful.'

'So what do we do now, Grandpa?' asked Wanda. 'After all these years, psychohistory will collapse.'

'I suppose that,' said Seldon, 'in a way, it's something that can't be helped. I've been predicting the breakdown of the Empire for nearly forty years and now that it's come, psychohistory breaks down with it.'

'But psychohistory will save the Empire, at least partly.'

'I know it will, but I can't force it to.'

'Are you just going to let it collapse?'

Seldon shook his head. 'I'll try to keep it from doing so, but I must admit that I don't know how I'm going to do it.'

Wanda said, 'I'm going to practice. There must be some way I can strengthen my push, make it easier for me to force people to do what I want them to do.'

'I wish you could manage.'

'What are you going to do, Grandpa?'

'Well, nothing much. Two days ago, when I was on my way to see the Chief Librarian, I encountered three men in the Library who were arguing about psychohistory. For some reason, one of them impressed me very much. I urged him to come see me and he agreed. The appointment is for this afternoon at my office.'

'Are you going to have him work for you?'

'I would like to – if I have enough credits to pay him with. But it can't hurt to talk with him. After all, what can I lose?'

24

The young man arrived at precisely 4 T.S.T. (Trantorian Standard Time) and Seldon smiled. He loved punctual people. He placed his hands on his desk and made ready to heave to his feet, but the young man said, 'Please, Professor, I know you have a bad leg. You needn't stand up.'

Seldon said, 'Thank you, young man. However, that does not mean that you cannot sit down. Please do.'

The young man removed his jacket and sat down.

Seldon said, 'You must forgive me . . . when we met and set up this appointment, I neglected to learn your name – which is . . . ?'

'Stettin Palver,' said the young man.

'Ah. Palver! Palver! The name sounds familiar.'

'It should, Professor. My grandfather boasted frequently of having known you.'

'Your grandfather. Of course. Joramis Palver. He was two years younger than I was, as I recall. I tried to get him to join me in psychohistory, but he refused. He said there was no chance of his ever learning enough mathematics to make it possible. Too bad! How is Joramis, by the way?'

Palver said solemnly, 'I'm afraid that Joramis has gone the way of old men generally. He's dead.'

Seldon winced. Two years younger than he himself was – and dead. An old friend and they had lost touch to such a degree that, when death came, it did so unknowingly.

Seldon sat there for a while and finally muttered, 'I'm sorry.'

The young man shrugged. 'He had a good life.'

'And you, young man, where did you have your schooling?'

'Langano University.'

Seldon frowned. 'Langano? Stop me if I'm wrong, but that's not on Trantor, is it?'

'No. I wanted to try a different world. The Universities on Trantor, as you undoubtedly know very well, are all overcrowded. I wanted to find a place where I could study in peace.'

'And what did you study?'

'Nothing much. History. Not the sort of thing that would lead one to a good job.'

(Another wince, even worse than the first. Dors Venabili had been a historian.)

Seldon said, 'But you're back here on Trantor. Why is that?'

'Credits. Jobs.'

'As an historian?'

Palver laughed. 'Not a chance. I run a device that pulls and hauls. Not exactly a professional occupation.'

Seldon looked at Palver with a twinge of envy. The contours of Palver's arms and chest were highlighted by the thin fabric of his shirt. He was well muscled. Seldon had never himself been quite that muscular.

Seldon said, 'I presume that when you were at the University, you were on the boxing team.'

'Who, me? Never. I'm a Twister.'

'A Twister!' Seldon's spirits jumped. 'Are you from Helicon?'

Palver said with a certain contempt, 'You don't have to come from Helicon to be a good Twister.'

No, thought Seldon, but that's where the best ones come from.

However, he said nothing.

He did say, though, 'Well, your grandfather would not join me. How about you?'

'Psychohistory?'

'I heard you talking to the others when I first encountered you and it seemed to me that you were talking quite intelligently about psychohistory. Would you like to join me, then?'

'As I said, Professor, I have a job.'

'Pushing and hauling. Come, come.'

'It pays well.'

'Credits aren't everything.'

'They're quite a bit. Now you, on the other hand, can't pay me much. I'm quite certain that you're short of credits.'

'Why do you say that?'

'I'm guessing, in a way, I suppose. – But am I wrong?'

Seldon's lips pressed together hard, then he said, 'No, you're not wrong and I can't pay you much. I'm sorry. I suppose that ends our little interview.'

'Wait, wait, wait.' Palver held up his hands. 'Not quite so fast, please. We're still talking about psychohistory. If I work for you, I will be taught psychohistory, right?'

'Of course.'

'In that case, credits aren't everything, after all. I'll make you a deal. You teach me all the psychohistory you can and you pay me whatever you can and I'll get by somehow. How about it?'

'Wonderful,' said Seldon joyously. 'That sounds great. Now, one more thing.'

'Oh?'

'Yes. I've been attacked twice in recent weeks. The first time my son came to my defense, but he has since gone to Santanni. The second time I made use of my lead-filled walking stick. It worked, but I was dragged before a magistrate and accused of assault and battery—'

'Why the attacks?' interjected Palver.

'I am not popular. I have been preaching the Fall of the Empire for so long that, now that it is coming, I am blamed for it.'

'I see. Now then, what does all that have to do with the

one more thing you mentioned?'

'I want you to be my bodyguard. You're young, you're strong, and, most of all, you're a Twister. You're exactly what I need.'

'I suppose it can be managed,' Palver said with a smile.

'See there, Stettin,' Seldon said as the two were taking an early evening stroll in one of Trantor's residential sectors near Streeling. The older man pointed to debris – assorted refuse jettisoned from passing ground-cars or dropped by careless pedestrians – strewn along the walkway. 'In the old days,' Seldon continued, 'you would never see litter like this. The security officers were vigilant and municipal maintenance crews provided round-the-clock upkeep of all public areas. But, most important, no one would even *think* of dumping his trash in such a manner. Trantor was our home; we took pride in it. Now' – Seldon shook his head sadly, resignedly, and sighed – 'it's—' He broke off abruptly.

'You there, young man!' Seldon shouted at an ill-kempt fellow who had moments before passed them, going in the opposite direction. He was munching a treat just popped into his mouth; the wrapper had been tossed to the ground without so much as a downward glance. 'Pick that up and dispose of it properly,' Seldon admonished as the young man eyed him sullenly.

'Pick it up yourself,' the boy snarled and then he turned and walked away.

'It's another sign of society's breakdown, as predicted by your psychohistory, Professor Seldon,' Palver said.

'Yes, Stettin. All around us the Empire is falling apart, piece by piece. In fact, it's already smashed – there's no turning back now. Apathy, decay, and greed have all played their parts in destroying the once-glorious Empire. And what will take its place? Why—'

Here Seldon broke off at the sight of Palver's face. The younger man seemed to be listening intently – but not to Seldon's voice. His head was cocked to one side and his face had a far-off look. It was as if Palver were straining to hear some sound inaudible to everyone but himself.

Suddenly he snapped back to the here and now. With an urgent glance around them, Palver took hold of Seldon's arm. 'Hari, quick, we must get away. They're coming . . .' And then the still evening was broken by the harsh sound of rapidly approaching footsteps. Seldon and Palver spun around, but it was too late; a band of attackers was upon them. This time, however, Hari Seldon was prepared. He immediately swung his cane in a wide arc around Palver and himself. At this, the three attackers – two boys and a girl, all teenage ruffians – laughed.

'So, you're not goin' to make it easy, are you, old man?' snorted the boy who appeared to be the group's ringleader. 'Why, me and my buddies, we'll take you out in two seconds flat. We'll—' All of a sudden, the ringleader was down, the victim of a perfectly placed Twist-kick to his abdomen. The two ruffians who were still standing quickly dropped to a crouch in preparation for attack. But Palver was quicker. They, too, were felled almost before they knew what hit them.

And then it was over – almost as soon as it started. Seldon stood off to the side, leaning heavily on his cane, shaking at the thought of his narrow escape. Palver, panting slightly from exertion, surveyed the scene. The three attackers were out cold on the deserted walkway under the darkening dome.

'Come on, let's get out of here quickly!' Palver urged again, only this time it was not the attackers they would be fleeing.

'Stettin, we can't leave,' protested Seldon. He gestured toward the unconscious would-be muggers. 'They're really nothing more than children. They may be dying. How can we just walk away? It's inhumane – that's what it is – and humanity is exactly what I've been working all these years to protect.' Seldon struck the ground with his cane for emphasis and his eyes gleamed with conviction.

427

'Nonsense,' retorted Palver. 'What's inhumane is the way muggers like that prey on innocent citizens like you. Do you think they'd have given *you* a second thought? They'd just as soon stick a knife in your gut to steal your last credit – and then kick you as they ran! They'll come to soon enough and slink away to lick their wounds. Or someone will find them and call the central office.

'But, Hari, you must *think*. After what happened last time, you stand to lose everything if you're linked to another beating. Please, Hari, we must run!' With this, Palver grabbed Seldon's arm and Seldon, after a last backward glance, allowed himself to be led away.

As the footsteps of the rapidly departing Seldon and Palver diminished in the distance, another figure emerged from his hiding place behind some trees. Chuckling to himself, the sullen-eyed youth muttered, 'You're a fine one to tell me what's right and what's wrong, Professor.' With that, he spun on his heel and headed off to summon the security officers.

26

'Order! I will have order!' bellowed Judge Tejan Popjens Lih. The public hearing of Professor Raven Seldon and his young associate, Stettin Palver, had generated a hue and cry among the populace of Trantor. Here was the man who had predicted the Fall of the Empire, the decay of civilization, who exhorted others to harken back to the golden age of civility and order – here was he who, according to an *eyewitness*, had ordered the brutal beating of three young Trantorians for no apparent provocation. Ah yes, it promised to be a spectacular hearing, one which would lead, no doubt, to an even more spectacular trial.

The judge pressed a contact set into a recessed panel on her bench and a sonorous gong resounded through the packed courtroom. 'I *will* have order,' she repeated to the now-hushed throng. 'If need be, the courtroom will be cleared. That is a warning. It will not be repeated.'

The judge cut an imposing figure in her scarlet robe. Originally from the Outer World of Lystena, Lih's complexion had a slight bluish cast, which turned darker when she became exercised, practically purple when she was really angry. It was rumored that, for all her years on the bench, in spite of her reputation as a top judicial mind, notwithstanding her position as one of the most revered interpreters of Imperial law, Lih was ever so slightly *vain* about the colorful appearance she gave, the way in which the bright red robes set off her soft turquoise skin.

Nevertheless, Lih had a reputation for coming down hard on those who brooked Imperial law; she was one of the few judges left who upheld the civil code without wavering.

'I have heard of you, Professor Seldon, and your theories about our imminent destruction. And I have spoken with the magistrate who recently heard another case in which you were involved, one in which you struck a man with your lead-filled cane. In that instance, too, you claimed to be the victim of assault. Your reasoning stemmed, I believe, from a previous unreported incident in which you and your son allegedly were assaulted by *eight* hoodlums. You were able to convince my esteemed colleague, Professor Seldon, of your plea of self-defense, even though an eyewitness testified otherwise. This time, Professor, you will have to be much more convincing.'

The three hoodlums who were bringing charges against Seldon and Palver snickered in their seats at the plaintiff's table. They presented a much different appearance today than they had the evening of the attack. The young men were sporting clean loose-fitting unisuits; the young lady was wearing a crisply pleated tunic. All in all, if one didn't look (or listen) too closely, the three presented a reassuring picture of Trantorian youth.

Seldon's lawyer, Civ Novker (who was representing Palver as well), approached the bench. 'Your Honor, my client is an upstanding member of the Trantorian community. He is a former First Minister of stellar repute. He is a personal acquaintance of our Emperor Agis XIV. What possible benefit could Professor Seldon derive from attacking innocent young people? He is one of the most vocal proponents of stimulating the intellectual creativity of Trantorian youth – his Psychohistory Project employs numerous student volunteers; he is a beloved member of the Streeling University faculty.

'*Further*—' Here Novker paused, sweeping his gaze around the packed courtroom, as if to say, Wait till you hear this – you'll be *ashamed* that you ever for a second doubted the veracity of my client's claims, 'Professor Seldon is one of the very few private individuals officially allied with the prestigious Galactic Library. He has been granted unlimited use of Library facilities for work on what he calls the Encyclopedia Galactica, a veritable paean to Imperial civilization.

'I ask you, how can this man even be questioned in such a matter?'

With a flourish of his arm, Novker gestured toward Seldon, who was sitting at the defendant's table with Stettin Palver, looking decidedly uncomfortable. Hari's cheeks were flushed from the unaccustomed praise (after all, lately his name was the subject of derisive snickers rather than flowery plaudits) and his hand shook slightly on the carved handle of his trusty cane.

Judge Lih gazed down at Seldon, clearly unimpressed. 'What benefit, indeed, Counselor. I have been asking myself that very question. I've lain awake these past nights, racking my brains for a plausible reason. Why would a man of Professor Seldon's stature commit unprovoked assault and battery when he himself is one of our most outspoken critics of the so-called "breakdown" of civil order?

'And then it dawned on me. Perhaps, in his frustration at *not* being believed, Professor Seldon feels he must *prove* to the worlds that his predictions of doom and gloom really are coming to pass. After all, here is a man who has spent his entire career foretelling the Fall of the Empire and all he can really point to are a few burned-out bulbs in the dome, an occasional glitch in public transport, a budget cut here or there – nothing very dramatic. But an attack – or two or three – now, *that* would be something.'

Lih sat back and folded her hands in front of her, a satisfied expression on her face. Seldon stood, leaning heavily on the table for support. With great effort, he approached the bench, waving off his lawyer, walking headlong into the steely gaze of the judge.

'Your Honor, please permit me to say a few words in my defense.'

'Of course, Professor Seldon. After all, this is not a

trial, only a hearing to air all allegations, facts, and theories pertinent to the case before deciding whether or not to go ahead with a trial. I have merely expressed a theory; I am most interested to hear what you have to say.'

Seldon cleared his throat before beginning. 'I have devoted my life to the Empire. I have faithfully served the Emperors. My science of psychohistory, rather than being a harbinger of destruction, is intended to be used as an agent for rejuvenation. With it we can be *prepared* for whatever course civilization takes. If, as I believe, the Empire continues to break down, psychohistory will help us put into place building blocks for a new and better civilization founded on all that is good from the old. I love our worlds, our peoples, our *Empire* – what would it behoove me to contribute to the lawlessness that saps its strength daily?

'I can say no more. You must believe me. I, a man of intellect, of equations, of science – I am speaking from my heart.' Seldon turned and made his way slowly back to his chair beside Palver. Before sitting, his eyes sought Wanda, sitting in the spectators' gallery. She smiled wanly and winked at him.

'From the heart or not, Professor Seldon, this decision will require much thought on my part. We have heard from your accusers; we have heard from you and Mr Palver. There is one more party whose testimony I need. I'd like to hear from Rial Nevas, who has come forward as an eyewitness to this incident.'

As Nevas approached the bench, Seldon and Palver looked at each other in alarm. It was the boy whom Hari had admonished just before the attack.

Lih was asking the youth a question. 'Would you describe, Mr Nevas, exactly what you witnessed on the night in question?'

'Well,' started Nevas, fixing Seldon with his sullen stare, 'I was walkin' along, mindin' my own business, when I saw those two,' – he turned and pointed at

Seldon and Palver – 'on the other side of the walkway, comin' toward me. And then I saw those three kids.' (Another point of the finger, this time toward the three sitting at the plaintiff's table.) 'The two older guys were walkin' behind the kids. They didn't see me, though, on account of I was on the other side of the walkway and besides, they were concentratin' on their victims. Then *wham*! Just like that, that old guy swings at 'em with his stick, then the younger guy jumps 'em and kicks 'em and before you know it, they're all down on the ground. Then the old guy and his pal, they just took off, just like that. I couldn't believe it.'

'That's a lie!' Seldon exploded. 'Young man, you're playing with our lives here!' Nevas only stared back at Seldon impassively.

'Judge,' Seldon implored, 'can't you see that he is lying? I remember this fellow. I scolded him for littering just minutes before we were attacked. I pointed it out to Stettin as another instance of the breakdown of our society, the apathy of the citizenry, the—'

'Enough, Professor Seldon,' commanded the judge. 'Another outburst like that and I will have you ejected from this courtroom. Now, Mr Nevas,' she said, turning back to the witness. 'What did you do throughout the sequence of events you just described?'

'I, uh, I hid. Behind some trees. I hid. I was afraid they'd come after me if they saw me, so I hid. And when they were gone, well, I ran and called the security officers.'

Nevas had started to sweat and he inserted a finger into the constricting collar of his unisuit. He fidgeted, shifting his weight from one foot to the other as he stood on the raised speaker's platform. He was uncomfortably aware of the crowd's eyes upon him; he tried to avoid looking into the audience, but each time he did, he found himself drawn to the steady gaze of a pretty blond girl sitting in the first row. It was as if she was asking him a question, pressing him for an answer, willing him to speak.

433

'Mr Nevas, what do you have to say about Professor Seldon's allegation that he and Mr Palver did see you prior to the attack, that the professor actually exchanged words with you?'

'Well, uh, no, you see, it was just like I said . . . I was walkin' along and—' And now Nevas looked over at Seldon's table. Seldon looked at the young man sadly, as if he realized all was lost. But Seldon's companion, Stettin Palver, turned a fierce gaze on Nevas and Nevas jumped, startled, at the words he heard: *Tell the truth!* It was as if Palver had spoken, but Palver's lips hadn't moved. And then, confused, Nevas snapped his head in the direction of the blond girl; he thought he heard her speak – *Tell the truth!* – but her lips were still as well.

'Mr Nevas, Mr Nevas,' the judge's voice broke in on the youth's jumbled thoughts. 'Mr Nevas, if Professor Seldon and Mr Palver were walking *toward* you, *behind* the three plaintiffs, how is it that you noticed Seldon and Palver *first*? That is how you put it in your statement, is it not?'

Nevas glanced around the courtroom wildly. He couldn't seem to escape the eyes, all the eyes screaming at him to *Tell the truth!* Looking over at Hari Seldon, Rial Nevas said simply, 'I'm sorry' and, to the amazement of the entire courtroom assemblage, the fourteen-year-old boy started to cry.

27

It was a lovely day, neither too warm nor too cold, not too bright nor too gray. Even though the groundskeeping budget had given out years ago, the few straggly perennials lining the steps leading up to the Galactic Library managed to add a cheerful note to the morning. (The Library, having been built in the classical style of antiquity, was fronted with one of the grandest stairways to be found in the entire Empire, second only to the steps at the Imperial Palace itself. Most Library visitors, however, preferred to enter via the gliderail) Seldon had high hopes for the day.

Since he and Stettin Palver had been cleared of all charges in their recent assault and battery case, Hari Seldon felt like a new man. Although the experience had been painful, its very public nature had advanced Seldon's cause. Judge Tejan Popjens Lih, who was considered one of, if not *the* most influential judge on Trantor, had been quite vociferous in her opinion, delivered the day following Rial Nevas's emotional testimony.

'When we come to such a crossroads in our "civilized" society,' the judge intoned from her bench, 'that a man of Professor Hari Seldon's standing is made to bear the humiliation, abuse, and lies of his peers simply because of who he is and what he stands for, it is truly a dark day for the Empire. I admit that I, too, was taken in – at first. "Why *wouldn't* Professor Seldon," I reasoned, "resort to such trickery in an attempt to prove his predictions?" But, as I came to see, I was most grievously wrong.' Here the judge's brow furrowed, a dark blue flush began creeping up her neck and into her cheeks. 'For I was ascribing to Professor Seldon motives born of our new society, a society in which honesty, decency, and goodwill are likely to get one killed, a society in which it appears one must resort to dishonesty and trickery merely to survive.

'How far we have strayed from our founding principles. We were lucky this time, fellow citizens of Trantor. We owe a debt of thanks to Professor Hari Seldon for showing us our true selves; let us take his example to heart and resolve to be vigilant against the baser forces of our human nature.'

Following the hearing, the Emperor had sent Seldon a congratulatory holo-disc. On it he expressed the hope that perhaps now Seldon would find renewed funding for his Project.

As Seldon slid up the entrance gliderail, he reflected on the current status of his Psychohistory Project. His good friend – the former Chief Librarian Las Zenow – had retired. During his tenure, Zenow had been a strong proponent of Seldon and his work. More often than not, however, Zenow's hands had been tied by the Library Board. But, he had assured Seldon, the affable new Chief Librarian, Tryma Acarnio, was as progressive as he himself, and was popular with many factions among the Board membership.

'Hari, my friend,' Zenow had said before leaving Trantor for his home world of Wencory, 'Acarnio is a good man, a person of deep intellect and an open mind. I'm sure he'll do all that he can to help you and the Project. I've left him the entire data file on you and your Encyclopedia; I know he'll be as excited as I about the contribution to humanity it represents. Take care, my friend – I'll remember you fondly.'

And so today Hari Seldon was to have his first official meeting with the new Chief Librarian. He was cheered by the reassurances Las Zenow had left with him and he was looking forward to sharing his plans for the future of the Project and the Encyclopedia.

Tryma Acarnio stood as Hari entered the Chief Librarian's office. Already he had made his mark on the place; whereas Zenow had stuffed every nook and cranny of the room with holo-discs and tridijournals from the different sectors of Trantor, and a dizzying array of visiglobes representing various worlds of the Empire had spun in midair, Acarnio had swept clear the mounds of data and images that Zenow had liked to keep at his fingertips. A large holoscreen now dominated one wall on which, Seldon presumed, Acarnio could view any publication or broadcast that he desired.

Acarnio was short and stocky, with a slightly distracted look – from a childhood corneal correction that had gone awry – that belied a fearsome intelligence and constant awareness of everything going on around him at all times.

'Well, well. Professor Seldon. Come in. Sit down.' Acarnio gestured to a straight-backed chair facing the desk at which he sat. 'It was, I felt, quite fortuitous that you requested this meeting. You see, I had intended to get in touch with you as soon as I settled in.'

Seldon nodded, pleased that the new Chief Librarian had considered him enough of a priority to plan to seek him out in the hectic early days of his tenure.

'But, first, Professor, please let me know why you wanted to see me before we move on to my, most likely, more prosaic concerns.'

Seldon cleared his throat and leaned forward. 'Chief Librarian, Las Zenow has no doubt told you of my work here and of my idea for an Encyclopedia Galactica. Las was quite enthusiastic, and a great help, providing a private office for me here and unlimited access to the Library's vast resources. In fact, it was he who located the eventual home of the Encyclopedia Project, a remote Outer World called Terminus.

'There was one thing, however, that Las could not provide. In order to keep the Project on schedule, I must have office space and unlimited access granted to a number of my colleagues, as well. It is an enormous undertaking, just gathering the information to be copied and transferred to Terminus before we can begin the actual work of compiling the Encyclopedia.

'Las was not popular with the Library Board, as you undoubtedly are aware. You, however, are. And so I ask you, Chief Librarian: Will you see to it that my colleagues are granted insiders' privileges so that we may continue our most vital work?'

Here Hari stopped, almost out of breath. He was sure that his speech, which he had gone over and over in his mind the night before, would have the desired effect. He waited, confident in Acarnio's response.

'Professor Seldon,' Acarnio began. Seldon's expectant smile faded. There was an edge to the Chief Librarian's voice that Seldon had not expected. 'My esteemed predecessor provided me – in exhaustive detail – an explication of your work here at the Library. He was quite enthusiastic about your research and committed to the idea of your colleagues joining you here. As was I, Professor Seldon' – at Acarnio's pause, Seldon looked up sharply – 'at first. I was prepared to call a special meeting of the Board to propose that a larger suite of offices be prepared for you and your Encyclopedists. But, Professor Seldon, all that has now changed.'

'Changed! But why?'

'Professor Seldon, you have just finished serving as principal defendant in a most sensational assault and battery case.'

'But I was acquitted,' Seldon broke in. 'The case never even made it to trial.'

'Nonetheless, Professor, your latest foray into the public eye has given you an undeniable – how shall I say it? – *tinge* of ill repute. Oh yes, you were acquitted of all charges. But in order to get to that acquittal, your name, your past, your beliefs, and your work were paraded before the eyes of all the worlds. And even if one progressive right-thinking judge has proclaimed you faultless, what of the millions – perhaps billions – of other average citizens who see not a pioneering psychohistorian striving to preserve his civilization's glory but a raving lunatic shouting doom and gloom for the great and mighty Empire?

'You, by the very nature of your work, are threatening the essential fabric of the Empire. I don't mean the huge, nameless, faceless, monolithic Empire. No, I am referring to the heart and soul of the Empire – its people. When you tell them the Empire is failing, you are saying that *they* are failing. And this, my dear Professor, the average citizen cannot face.

'Seldon, like it or not, you have become an object of derision, a subject of ridicule, a laughingstock.'

'Pardon me, Chief Librarian, but for years now I have been, to some circles, a laughingstock.'

'Yes, but only to some circles. But this latest incident – and the very public forum in which it was played out – has opened you up to ridicule not only here on Trantor but throughout the worlds. And, Professor, if, by providing you an office, we, the Galactic Library, give tacit approval to your work, then, by inference, we, the Library, also become a laughingstock throughout the worlds. And no matter how strongly I may *personally* believe in your theory and your Encyclopedia, as Chief Librarian of the Galactic Library on Trantor, I must think of the Library first.

'And so, Professor Seldon, your request to bring in your colleagues is denied.'

Hari Seldon jerked back in his chair as if struck.

'Further,' Acarnio continued, 'I must advise you of a two-week temporary suspension of all Library privileges – effective immediately. The Board has called that special meeting, Professor Seldon. In two weeks' time we will notify you whether or not we've decided that our association with you must be terminated.'

Here, Acarnio stopped speaking and, placing his palms on the glossy, spotless surface of his desk, stood up. 'That is all, Professor Seldon – for now.'

Hari Seldon stood as well, although his upward

movement was not as smooth, nor as quick, as Tryma Acarnio's.

'May I be permitted to address the Board?' asked Seldon. 'Perhaps if I were able to explain to them the vital importance of psychohistory and the Encyclopedia—'

'I'm afraid not, Professor,' said Acarnio softly and Seldon caught a brief glimmer of the man Las Zenow had told him about. But, just as quickly, the icy bureaucrat was back as Acarnio guided Seldon to the door.

As the portals slid open, Acarnio said, 'Two weeks, Professor Seldon. Till then.' Hari stepped through to his waiting skitter and the doors slid shut.

What am I going to do now? wondered Seldon disconsolately. Is this the end of my work?

28

'Wanda dear, what is it that has you so engrossed?' asked Hari Seldon as he entered his granddaughter's office at Streeling University. The room had been the office of the brilliant mathematician Yugo Amaryl, whose death had impoverished the Psychohistory Project. Fortunately, Wanda had gradually taken over Yugo's role in recent years, further refining and adjusting the Prime Radiant.

'Why, I'm working on an equation in Section 33A2Dl7. See, I've recalibrated this section' – she gestured to a glowing violet patch suspended in midair in front of her face – 'taking into consideration the standard quotient and – There! Just what I thought – I think.' She stepped back and rubbed her eyes.

'What is it, Wanda?' Hari moved in closer to study the equation. 'Why, this looks like the Terminus equation and yet . . . Wanda, this is an *inverse* of the Terminus equation, isn't it?'

'Yes, Grandpa. See, the numbers weren't working quite right in the Terminus equation – look.' Wanda touched a contact in a recessed wallstrip and another patch sprang to life in vivid red on the other side of the room. Seldon and Wanda walked over to inspect it. 'You see how it's all hanging together fine now, Grandpa? It's taken me weeks to get it this way.'

'How did you do it?' asked Hari, admiring the equation's lines, its logic, its elegance.

'At first, I concentrated on it from over here only. I blocked out all else. In order to get Terminus to work, work on Terminus – stands to reason, doesn't it? But then I realized that I couldn't just introduce this equation into the Prime Radiant system and expect it to blend right in smoothly, as if nothing happened. A placement means a displacement somewhere else. A weight needs a counter-weight.'

'I think the concept to which you are referring is what the ancients called "*yin* and *yang*."'

'Yes, more or less. *Yin* and *yang*. So, you see, I realized that to perfect the *yin* of Terminus, I had to locate its *yang*. Which I did, over there.' She moved back to the violet patch, tucked away at the other edge of the Prime Radiant sphere. 'And once I adjusted the figures here, the Terminus equation fell into place as well. Harmony!' Wanda looked pleased with herself, as if she'd solved all the problems of the Empire.

'Fascinating, Wanda, and later on you must tell me what you think it all means for the Project. – But right now you must come with me to the holoscreen. I received an urgent message from Santanni a few minutes ago. Your father wants us to call him immediately.'

Wanda's smile faded. She had been alarmed at the recent reports of fighting on Santanni. As Imperial budget cutbacks went into effect, the citizens of the Outer Worlds suffered most. They had limited access to the richer, more populous Inner Worlds and it became more and more difficult to trade their worlds' products for much needed imports. Imperial hyperships going in and out of Santanni were few and the distant world felt isolated from the rest of the Empire. Pockets of rebellion had erupted throughout the planet.

'Grandfather, I hope everything's all right,' said Wanda, her fear revealed by her voice.

'Don't worry, dear. After all, they must be safe if Raych was able to send us a message.'

In Seldon's office, he and Wanda stood before the holoscreen as it activated. Seldon punched a code on the keypad alongside the screen and they waited a few seconds for the intragalactic connection to be established. Slowly the screen seemed to stretch back into the wall, as if it were the entrance to a tunnel – and out of the tunnel, dimly at first, came the familiar figure of a stocky powerfully built man. As the connection sharpened, the man's features became clearer. When Seldon and Wanda were able to make out Raych's bushy Dahlite mustache, the figure sprang to life.

'Dad! Wanda!' said Raych's three-dimensional hologram, projected to Trantor from Santanni. 'Listen, I don't have much time.' He flinched, as if startled by a loud noise. 'Things have gotten pretty bad here. The government has fallen and a provisional party has taken over. Things are a mess, as you can imagine. I just put Manella and Bellis on a hypership to Anacreon. I told them to get in touch with you from there. The name of the ship is the *Arcadia VII*.

'You should have seen Manella, Dad. Mad as anything that she had to go. The only way I was able to convince her to leave was to point out that it was for Bellis's sake.

'I know what you're thinking, Dad and Wanda. Of course I would have gone with them – if I could have. But there wasn't enough room. You should've seen what I had to go through just to get *them* onto the ship.' Raych flashed one of his lopsided grins that Seldon and Wanda loved so much, then continued. 'Besides, since I'm here, I have to help guard the University – we may be part of the *Imperial* University system, but we're a place of learning and building, not of destruction. I tell you, if one of those hot-headed Santanni rebels comes near our stuff—'

'Raych,' Hari broke in, 'How bad is it? Are you close to the fighting?'

'Dad, are you in danger?' asked Wanda.

They waited a few seconds for their message to travel the nine thousand parsecs across the Galaxy to Raych.

'I – I – I couldn't quite make out what you said,' the hologram replied. 'There's a bit of fighting going on. It's sort of exciting, actually,' Raych said, breaking into that grin again. 'So I'm going to sign off now. Remember, find out what happened to the *Arcadia VII* going to Anacreon. I'll be back in touch as soon as I'm able. Remember, I—' The transmission broke off and the

443

hologram faded. The holoscreen tunnel collapsed in on itself so that Seldon and Wanda were left staring at a blank wall.

'Grandpa,' said Wanda, 'what do you think he was going to say?'

'I have no idea, dear. But there is one thing I do know and that is that your father can take care of himself. I pity any rebel who gets near enough for a well-placed Twist-kick from your dad! – Come, let's get back to that equation and in a few hours we'll check on the *Arcadia VII*.'

'Commander, have you no idea what happened to the ship?' Hari Seldon was again engaged in intragalactic conversation, but this time it was with an Imperial navy commander stationed at Anacreon. For this communication, Seldon was making use of the visiscreen – much less realistic than the holoscreen but also much simpler.

'I'm telling you, Professor, that we have no record of that hypership requesting permission to enter the Anacreonic atmosphere. Of course, communications with Santanni have been broken for several hours and sporadic at best for the last week. It is possible that the ship tried to reach us on a Santanni-based channel and could not get through, but I doubt it.

'No, it's more likely that the *Arcadia VII* changed destination. Voreg, perhaps, or Sarip. Have you tried either of those worlds, Professor?'

'No,' said Seldon wearily, 'but I see no reason if the ship was bound for Anacreon that it would not go to Anacreon. Commander, it is vital that I locate that ship.'

'Of course,' the commander ventured, 'the *Arcadia VII* might not have made it. Out safely, I mean. There's a lot of fighting going on. Those rebels don't care who they blow up. They just train their lasers and pretend it's the Emperor Agis they're blasting. I tell you, it's a whole different game out here on the fringe, Professor.'

'My daughter-in-law and granddaughter are on that ship, Commander,' Seldon said in a tight voice.

'Oh, I'm sorry, Professor,' said an abashed commander. 'I'll be in touch with you as soon as I hear anything.'

Dispiritedly Hari closed the visiscreen contact. How tired I am, he thought. And, he mused, I'm not surprised – I've known that this would come for nearly forty years.

Seldon chuckled bitterly to himself. Perhaps that commander had thought he was shocking Seldon, impressing him with the vivid detail of life 'on the fringe.' But Seldon knew all about the fringe. And as the fringe came apart, like a piece of knitting with one loose thread, the whole piece would unravel to the core: Trantor.

Seldon became aware of a soft buzzing sound. It was the door signal. 'Yes?'

'Grandpa,' said Wanda, entering the office, 'I'm scared.'

'Why, dear?' asked Seldon with concern. He didn't want to tell her yet what he had learned – or *hadn't* learned – from the commander on Anacreon.

'Usually, although they're so far away, I *feel* Dad and Mom and Bellis – feel them in here' – she pointed to her head – 'and in here' – she placed her hand over her heart. 'But now, today, I don't feel them – it feels less, as if they're fading, like one of the dome bulbs. And I want to stop it. I want to pull them back, but I can't.'

'Wanda, I really think this is merely a product of your concern for your family in light of the rebellion. You know that uprisings occur all over the Empire all the time – little eruptions to let off steam. Come now, you know that chances of anything happening to Raych, Manella, or Bellis are vanishingly small. Your dad will call any day to say all is well; your mom and Bellis will land on Anacreon at any moment and enjoy a little vacation. We are the ones to be pitied – we're stuck here up to our ears in work! So, sweetheart, go to bed and think only good thoughts. I promise you, tomorrow, under the sunny dome, things will look much better.'

'All right, Grandpa,' said Wanda, not sounding

entirely convinced. 'But tomorrow – if we haven't heard by tomorrow – we'll have to – to—'

'Wanda, what can we do, except wait?' asked Hari, his voice gentle.

Wanda turned and left, the weight of her worries showing in the slope of her shoulders. Hari watched her go, finally allowing his own worries to come to the surface.

It had been three days since the hologram transmission from Raych. Since then – nothing. And today the naval commander at Anacreon denied ever having heard of a ship called *Arcadia VII*.

Hari had tried earlier to get through to Raych on Santanni, but all communication beams were down. It was as if Santanni – and the *Arcadia VII* – had simply broken off from the Empire, like a petal from a flower.

Seldon knew what he had to do now. The Empire might be down, but it was not out. Its power, when properly wielded, was still awesome. Seldon placed an emergency transmission to Emperor Agis XIV.

29

'What a surprise – my friend Hari!' Agis's visage beamed at Seldon through the holoscreen. 'I am glad to hear from you, although you usually request the more formal personal audience. Come, you've piqued my interest. Why the urgency?'

'Sire,' began Seldon, 'my son, Raych, and his wife and daughter live on Santanni.'

'Ah, Santanni,' the Emperor said as his smile faded. 'A bunch of misguided wretches if I ever—'

'Sire, please,' broke in Seldon, surprising both the Emperor and himself with this flagrant breach of Imperial protocol. 'My son was able to get Manella and Bellis onto a hypership, the *Arcadia VII*, bound for Anacreon. He, however, had to remain. That was three days ago. The ship has not landed at Anacreon. And my son seems to have disappeared. My calls to Santanni have gone unanswered and now the communication beams are broken.

'Please, Sire, can you help me?'

'Hari, as you know, officially all ties between Santanni and Trantor have been severed. However, I still hold some influence in selected areas of Santanni. That is, there are still a few loyal to me who have not yet been found out. Although I cannot make direct contact with any of my operatives on that world, I can share with you any reports I receive from there. These are, of course, highly confidential, but considering your situation and our relationship, I will allow you access to those pieces that might interest you.

'I am expecting another dispatch within the hour. If you like, I'll recontact you when it arrives. In the meantime, I'll have one of my aides go over all transmissions from Santanni for the past three days to look for anything pertaining to Raych, Manella, or Bellis Seldon.'

'Thank you, Sire. I thank you most humbly.' And Hari Seldon dipped his head as the Emperor's image faded from the holoscreen.

Sixty minutes later Hari Seldon was still sitting at his desk, waiting to hear from the Emperor. The past hour had been one of the most difficult he had ever spent, second only to the hours after Dors's destruction.

It was the not knowing that did Hari in. He had made a career of *knowing* – the future as well as the present. And now he had no idea at all about three of the people most precious to him.

The holoscreen buzzed softly and Hari pressed a contact in response. Agis appeared.

'Hari,' began the Emperor. From the soft slow sadness in his voice, Hari knew this call brought bad news.

'My son,' said Hari.

'Yes,' replied the Emperor. 'Raych was killed, earlier today, in a bombardment on Santanni University. I've learned from my sources that Raych knew the attack was coming but refused to desert his post. You see, a good number of the rebels are students and Raych felt that, if they knew that he was still there, they would never . . . But hate overcame all reason.

'The University is, you see, an *Imperial* University. The rebels feel they must destroy all things Imperial before rebuilding anew. The fools! Why—' And here Agis stopped, as if suddenly realizing that Seldon did not care about Santanni University or the plans of the rebels – not right now, at least.

'Hari, if it makes you feel any better, remember that your son died in defense of knowledge. It was not the Empire Raych fought and died for but humanity itself.'

Seldon looked up out of tear-filled eyes. Weakly he asked, 'And Manella and little Bellis? What of them? Have you found the *Arcadia VII?*'

'That search has proved fruitless, Hari. The *Arcadia*

VII left Santanni, as you were told. But it seems to have disappeared. It may have been hijacked by rebels or it may have made an emergency detour – at this point, we just don't know.'

Seldon nodded. 'Thank you, Agis. Although you have brought me tragic news, at least you have brought it. Not knowing was worse. You are a true friend.'

'And so, my friend,' said the Emperor, 'I'll leave you to yourself now – and your memories.' The Emperor's image faded from the screen as Hari Seldon folded his arms in front of him on his desk, put his head down, and wept.

30

Wanda Seldon adjusted the waistband of her unisuit, pulling it a little tighter around her middle. Taking up a hand hoe, she attacked some weeds that had sprung up in her small flower garden outside the Psychohistory Building at Streeling. Generally Wanda spent the bulk of her time in her office, working with her Prime Radiant. She found solace in its precise statistical elegance; the unvarying equations were somehow reassuring in this Empire gone so crazy. But when thoughts of her beloved father, mother, and baby sister became too much to bear, when even her research could not keep her mind off the horrible losses she'd so recently undergone, Wanda invariably found herself out here, scratching at the terraformed ground, as if coaxing a few plants to life might somehow, in some tiny measure, ameliorate her pain.

Since her father's death a month ago and the disappearance of Manella and Bellis, Wanda, who had always been slim, had been losing weight. Whereas a few months ago Hari Seldon would have been concerned over his darling granddaughter's loss of appetite, now he, stuck in his own grief, seemed not to notice.

A profound change had come over Hari and Wanda Seldon – and the few remaining members of the Psychohistory Project. Hari seemed to have given up. He now spent most of his days sitting in an armchair in the Streeling solarium, staring out at the University grounds, warmed by the bright bulbs overhead. Occasionally Project members told Wanda that his bodyguard, a man named Stettin Palver, would badger Seldon into a walk out under the dome or try to engage him in a discussion of the future direction of the Project.

Wanda retreated deeper into her study of the Prime Radiant's fascinating equations. She could feel the future her grandfather had worked so hard to achieve finally taking shape, and he was right: The Encyclopedists must be established on Terminus; they would be the Foundation.

And Section 33A2D17 – in it Wanda could see what Seldon referred to as the Second, or secret, Foundation. But how? Without Seldon's active interest, Wanda was at a loss as to how to proceed. And her sorrow over the destruction of her family cut so deep that she didn't seem to have the strength to figure it out.

The members of the Project itself, those fifty or so hardy souls who remained, continued their work as well as possible. The majority were Encyclopedists, research-ing the source materials they would need to copy and catalogue for their eventual move to Terminus – when and if they gained full access to the Galactic Library. At this point, they were working on faith alone. Professor Seldon had lost his private office at the Library, so the prospects of any other Project member gaining special access were slim.

The remaining Project members (other than the Encyclopedists) were historical analysts and mathema-ticians. The historians interpreted past and current human actions and events, turning their findings over to the mathematicians, who in turn fit those pieces into the great Psychohistorical Equation. It was long painstaking work.

Many Project members had left because the rewards were so few – psychohistorians were the butt of many jokes on Trantor and limited funds had forced Seldon to enact drastic pay cuts. But the constant reassuring presence of Hari Seldon had – till now – overcome the dif-ficult working conditions of the Project. Indeed, the Project members who had stayed on had, to a person, done so out of respect and devotion to Professor Seldon.

Now, thought Wanda Seldon bitterly, what reason is

left for them to stay? A light breeze blew a piece of her blond hair across her eyes; she pushed it back absent-mindedly and continued her weeding.

'Miss Seldon, may I have a moment of your time?' Wanda turned and looked up. A young man – she judged him to be in his early twenties – stood on the gravel path next to her. She immediately sensed him to be strong and fearsomely intelligent. Her grandfather had chosen wisely. Wanda rose to speak with him.

'I recognize you. You are my grandfather's bodyguard, are you not? Stettin Palver, I believe?'

'Yes, that's correct, Miss Seldon,' Palver said and his cheeks reddened slightly, as if he were pleased that so pretty a girl should have given him any notice. 'Miss Seldon, it is your grandfather I'd like to talk to you about. I'm very worried about him. We must do something.'

'Do what, Mr Palver? I am at a loss. Since my father' – she swallowed hard, as if she were having difficulty speaking – 'died and my mother and sister disappeared, it is all I can do to get him out of bed in the morning. And to tell you the truth, it has affected me very deeply as well. You understand, don't you?' She looked into his eyes and knew that he did.

'Miss Seldon,' Palver said softly, 'I am terribly sorry about your losses. But you and Professor Seldon are *alive* and you must keep working at psychohistory. The professor seems to have given up. I was hoping that maybe you – we – could come up with something to give him hope again. You know, a reason to go on.'

Ah, Mr Palver, thought Wanda, *maybe Grandpa has it right. I wonder if there truly is any reason to go on.* But she said, 'I'm sorry, Mr Palver, I can think of nothing.' She gestured toward the ground with her hoe. 'And now, as you can see, I must get back to these pesky weeds.'

'I don't think your grandfather has got it right. I think there truly is a reason to go on. We just have to find it.'

The words struck her with full force. How had he known what she had been thinking? Unless – 'You can

452

handle minds, can't you?' Wanda asked, holding her breath, as if afraid to hear Palver's response.

'Yes, I can,' the young man replied. 'I always have, I think. At least, I can't remember *not* doing it. Half the time I'm not even consciously aware of it – I just know what people are thinking – or have thought.

'Sometimes,' he continued, encouraged by the understanding he felt emanating from Wanda, 'I get *flashes* of it coming from someone else. It's always in a crowd, though, and I can't locate whoever it is. But I know there are others like me – us – around.'

Wanda grabbed Palver's hand excitedly, her gardening tool tossed to the ground, forgotten. 'Have you any idea what this might mean? For Grandpa, for psychohistory? One of us alone can do only so much, but both of us together—' Wanda started walking into the Psychohistory Building, leaving Palver standing on the gravel path. Almost to the entrance she stopped and turned. *Come, Mr Palver, we must tell my grandfather*, Wanda said without opening her mouth. *Yes, I suppose we should*, answered Palver as he joined her.

31

'Do you mean to say I have been searching Trantor-wide for someone with your powers, Wanda, and he's been here with us for the past few months, and we never knew it?' Hari Seldon was incredulous. He had been dozing in the solarium when Wanda and Palver shook him awake to give him their amazing news.

'Yes, Grandpa. Think about it. I've never had occasion to meet Stettin. Your time with him has primarily been away from the Project and I spend the majority of my time closeted in my office, working with the Prime Radiant. When *would* we have met? In fact, the one time our paths did cross, the results were most significant.'

'When was that?' asked Seldon, searching his memory.

'Your last hearing – before Judge Lih,' Wanda replied immediately. 'Remember the eyewitness who swore that you and Stettin had attacked those three muggers? Remember how he broke down and told the truth – and even he didn't seem to know why. But Stettin and I have pieced it together. We were both pushing Rial Nevas to come clean. He had been very steadfast in his original claim; I doubt that either one of us would have been able to push him alone. But *together*' – she stole a shy glance at Palver, who was standing off to the side – 'our power is awesome!'

Hari Seldon took all this in and then made as if to speak. But Wanda continued. 'In fact, we plan to spend the afternoon testing our mentalic abilities, separately and together. From the little we've discovered so far, it seems as if Stettin's power is slightly lower than mine – perhaps a five on my rating scale. But his five, combined with my seven, gives us a twelve! Think of it, Grandpa. Awesome!'

'Don't you see, Professor?' Palver spoke up. 'Wanda and I are that breakthrough you're looking for. We can help you convince the worlds of the validity of psychohistory, we can help find others like us, we can help put psychohistory back on track.'

Hari Seldon gazed up at the two young people standing in front of him. Their faces were aglow with youth and vigor and enthusiasm and he realized it did his old heart good. Perhaps all was not lost, after all. He had not thought he would survive this latest tragedy, the death of his son and the disappearance of his son's wife and child, but now he could see that Raych lived on in Wanda. And in Wanda and Stettin, he now knew, lived the future of the Foundation.

'Yes, yes,' agreed Seldon, nodding forcefully. 'Come you two, help me up. I must get back to my office to plan our next step.'

32

'Professor Seldon, come in,' said Chief Librarian Tryma Acarnio in an icy tone of voice. Hari Seldon, accompanied by Wanda and Palver, entered the Chief Librarian's imposing office.

'Thank you, Chief Librarian,' said Seldon as he settled into a chair and faced Acarnio across the vast desk. 'May I introduce my granddaughter Wanda and my friend Stettin Palver. Wanda is a most valuable member of the Psychohistory Project, her specialty being in the field of mathematics. And Stettin, well, Stettin is turning into a first-rate general psychohistorian – when he's not performing his duties as my bodyguard, that is.' Seldon chuckled amiably.

'Yes, well, that's all well and good, Professor,' said Acarnio, baffled by Seldon's good humor. He had expected the professor to come in groveling, begging for another chance at special Library privileges.

'But I don't understand what it is you wanted to see me about. I assume you realize that our position is firm: We cannot allow a Library association with someone so extremely unpopular with the general population. We are, after all, a *public* library and we must keep the public's sentiments in mind.' Acarnio settled back – perhaps *now* the groveling would begin.

'I realize that I have not been able to sway you. However, I thought that if you heard from a couple of the Project's younger members – the psychohistorians of tomorrow, as it were – that perhaps you'd get a better feel about what a vital role the Project – and the Encyclopedia, in particular – will play in our future. Please hear Wanda and Stettin out.'

Acarnio cast a cold eye toward the two young people

flanking Seldon. 'Very well, then,' he said, pointedly eyeing the timestrip on the wall. 'Five minutes and no more. I have a Library to run.'

'Chief Librarian,' began Wanda, 'as my grandfather has undoubtedly explained to you, psychohistory is a most valuable tool to be used for the preservation of our culture. Yes, *preservation*,' she repeated, upon seeing Acarnio's eyes widen at the word. 'Undue emphasis has been placed on the destruction of the Empire. By doing so, the true value of psychohistory has been overlooked. For, with psychohistory, as we are able to predict the inevitable decline of our civilization, so are we able to take steps toward its preservation. That is what the Encyclopedia Galactica is all about. And that is why we need your help, and the help of your great Library.'

Acarnio could not resist smiling. The young lady had an undeniable charm. She was so earnest, so well spoken. He gazed at her sitting in front of him, her blond hair pulled back in a rather severe scholarly style, one which could not hide her attractive features but, rather, showed them off. What she was saying was starting to make sense. Maybe Wanda Seldon was right – maybe he had been looking at this problem from the wrong angle. If it were actually a matter of *preservation*, rather than *destruction* . . .

'Chief Librarian,' began Stettin Palver, 'this great Library has stood for millennia. It, perhaps even more than the Imperial Palace, represents the vast power of the Empire. For, the Palace houses only the Empire's leader, while the Library is home to the sum total of Imperial knowledge, culture, and history. Its value is incalculable.

'Does it not make sense to prepare a tribute to this great repository? The Encyclopedia Galactica will be just that – a giant summary of all the knowledge contained within these very walls. Think of it!'

All of a sudden it seemed so very clear to Acarnio. How could he have let the Board (especially that sourpuss

Gennaro Mummery) convince him to rescind Seldon's privileges? Las Zenow, a person whose judgment he greatly esteemed, had been a whole-hearted supporter of Seldon's Encyclopedia.

He glanced again at the three in front of him, waiting for his decision. The Board would be hard-pressed to find anything to complain about with the Project members – if the young people now in his office were a representative sample of the kind of persons involved with Seldon.

Acarnio rose and walked across his office, his brow furrowed, as if framing his thoughts. He picked up a milky crystal sphere from a table and hefted it in his palm.

'Trantor,' Acarnio began thoughtfully, 'seat of the Empire, center of all the Galaxy. Quite amazing, when you think of it. – We have, perhaps, been too quick to judge Professor Seldon. Now that your Project, this Encyclopedia Galactica, has been presented to me in such a light' – he gave a brief nod to Wanda and Palver – 'I realize how important it would be to allow you to continue your work here. And, of course, to grant access to a number of your colleagues.'

Seldon smiled gratefully and squeezed Wanda's hand.

'It is not only for the greater glory of the Empire that I am recommending this,' continued Acarnio, apparently warming to the idea (and the sound of his own voice). 'You are famous, Professor Seldon. Whether people think of you as a crackpot or a genius, *everyone* seems to have an opinion. If an academic of your stature is allied with the Galactic Library, it can only increase our prestige as a bastion of intellectual pursuit of the highest order. Why, the luster of your presence can be used to raise much-needed funds to update our collections, increase our staff, keep our doors open to the public longer . . .

'And the prospect of the Encyclopedia Galactica itself – what a monumental project! Imagine the reaction when the public learns that the Galactic Library is involved with such an undertaking designed to highlight the splendor of our civilization – our glorious history, our brilliant achievements, our magnificent cultures. And to think that I, Chief Librarian Tryma Acarnio, is responsible for making sure that this great Project gets its start—'

Acarnio gazed intently into the crystal sphere, lost in reverie.

'Yes, Professor Seldon,' Acarnio pulled himself back to the here and now. 'You and your colleagues will be granted full insiders' privileges – and a suite of offices in which to work.' He placed the crystal sphere back on its table and, with a swish of robes, moved back to his desk.

'It might take a little doing, of course, to persuade the Board – but I am confident that I can handle them. Just leave it to me.'

Seldon, Wanda, and Palver looked at each other in triumph, with small smiles playing at the corner of their mouths. Tryma Acarnio gestured that they could go and so they did, leaving the Chief Librarian settled in his chair, dreaming of the glory and honor that would come to the Library under his aegis.

'Amazing,' said Seldon when the three were safely ensconced in their ground-car. 'If you could have seen him at our last meeting. He said I was "threatening the essential fabric of our Empire" or some such rot. And today, after just a few minutes with you two—'

'It wasn't too hard, Grandpa,' Wanda said as she pressed a contact, moving the ground-car out into traffic. She sat back as the auto-propel took over; Wanda had punched their destination coordinates into the control panel. 'He is a man with a strong sense of self-importance. All we had to do was play up the positive aspects of the Encyclopedia and his ego took over from there.'

'He was a goner the minute Wanda and I walked in,' Palver said from the back. 'With both of us pushing him, it was a piece of cake.' Palver reached forward and squeezed Wanda's shoulder affectionately. She smiled, reached up, and patted his hand.

'I must alert the Encyclopedists as soon as possible,' Seldon said. 'Although there are only thirty-two left, they

459

are good and dedicated workers. I'll get them installed at the Library and then I'll tackle the next hurdle – credits. Perhaps this alliance with the Library is what I need to convince people to give us funding. Let's see – I'll call upon Terep Bindris again and I'll take you two with me. He was kindly disposed toward me, at least at first. But how will he be able to resist us now?'

The ground-car eventually came to a halt outside the Psychohistory Building at Streeling. The side panels slid open, but Seldon did not immediately move to disembark. He turned to face Wanda.

'Wanda, you know what you and Stettin were able to accomplish with Acarnio; I'm sure you both can push some credits out of a few financial benefactors as well.

'I know how you hate to leave your beloved Prime Radiant, but these visits will give you two a chance to practice, to hone your skills, to get an idea of just what you can do.'

'All right, Grandpa, although I'm sure that, now that you have the Library's imprimatur, you will find that resistance to your requests has lessened.'

'There's another reason I think it's important for the two of you to get out and around together. – Stettin, I believe you said that on certain occasions you've "felt" another mind like yours but haven't been able to identify it.'

'Yes,' answered Palver, 'I've had flashes, but each time I was in a crowd. And, in my twenty-four years, I can remember feeling such a flash just four or five times.'

'But, Stettin,' said Seldon, his voice low with intensity, 'each flash was, potentially, the mind of another person like you and Wanda – another mentalic. Wanda's never felt these flashes because, frankly, she's been sheltered all her life. The few times she's been out in a crowd there must not have been any other mentalics around.

'That's one reason – perhaps the most important reason – for you two to get out – with me or without me. We must find other mentalics. The two of you alone are

460

strong enough to push a single person. A large group of you, all pushing together, will have the power to move an Empire!'

With that, Hari Seldon swung his legs around and hoisted himself out of the ground-car. As Wanda and Palver watched him limp up the pathway to the Psychohistory Building, they were only dimly aware of the enormous responsibility Seldon had just placed on their young shoulders.

33

It was midafternoon and the Trantorian sun glinted on the metal skin covering the great planet. Hari Seldon stood at the edge of the Streeling University observation deck, attempting to shield his eyes from the harsh glare with his hand. It had been years since he'd been out from under the dome, save for his few visits to the Palace, and somehow those didn't count; one was still very much *enclosed* on the Imperial grounds.

Seldon no longer traveled around only if accompanied. In the first place, Palver spent the majority of his time with Wanda, either working on the Prime Radiant, absorbed in mentalic research, or searching for others like them. But if he had wanted, Seldon could have found another young man – a University student or a Project member – to act as his bodyguard.

However, Seldon knew that a bodyguard was no longer necessary. Since the much publicized hearing and the reestablishment of ties with the Galactic Library, the Commission for Public Safety had taken a keen interest in Seldon. Seldon knew that he was being followed; he had caught sight of his 'shadow' on a number of occasions in the past few months. He also had no doubt that his home and office had been infiltrated by listening devices, but he himself activated a static shield whenever he engaged in sensitive communications.

Seldon was not sure what the Commission thought of him – perhaps they were not yet sure themselves. Regardless of whether they believed him to be a prophet or a crackpot, they made it their business to know where he was at all times – and that meant that, until the Commission deemed otherwise, at all times Seldon was safe.

A light breeze billowed the deep blue cloak Seldon had

draped over his unisuit and ruffled the few wispy white hairs remaining on his head. He glanced down over the railing, taking in the seamless steel blanket below. Beneath that blanket, Seldon knew, rumbled the machinery of a vastly complicated world. If the dome were transparent, one would see ground-cars racing, gravicabs swooshing through an intricate network of interconnecting tunnels, space hyperships being loaded and unloaded with grain and chemicals and jewels bound for and from practically every world of the Empire.

Below the gleaming metal cover, the lives of forty billion people were being conducted, with all the attendant pain, joy, and drama of human life. It was an image he loved dearly – this panorama of human achievement – and it pierced his heart to know that, in just a few centuries, all that now lay before him would be in ruins. The great dome would be ripped and scarred, torn away to reveal the desolate wasteland of what was once the seat of a thriving civilization. He shook his head in sadness, for he knew there was nothing he could do to prevent that tragedy. But, as Seldon foresaw the ruined dome, he also knew that from the ground laid bare by the last battles of the Empire living shoots would spring and somehow Trantor would reemerge as a vital member of the new Empire. The Plan saw to that.

Seldon lowered himself onto one of the benches ringing the deck's perimeter. His leg was throbbing painfully; the exertion of the trip had been a bit much. But it had been worth it to gaze once again at Trantor, to feel the open air around him and see the vast sky above.

Seldon thought wistfully of Wanda. He rarely saw his granddaughter at all anymore and invariably Stettin Palver was present when he did. In the three months since Wanda and Palver had met, they seemed to be inseparable. Wanda assured Seldon that the constant involvement was necessary for the Project, but Seldon suspected it went deeper than mere devotion to one's job.

He remembered the telltale signs from his early days with Dors. It was there in the way the two young people looked at each other, with an intensity born not only of intellectual stimulation but emotional motivation as well.

Further, by their very natures, Wanda and Palver seemed to be more comfortable with each other than with other people. In fact, Seldon had discovered that when no one else was around, Wanda and Palver didn't even *talk* to each other; their mentalic abilities were sufficiently advanced that they had no need of *words* to communicate.

The other Project members were not aware of Wanda's and Palver's unique talents. Seldon had felt it best to keep the mentalics' work quiet, at least until their role in the Plan was firmly defined. Actually the Plan itself was firmly defined – but solely in Seldon's mind. As a few more pieces fell into place, he would reveal his Plan to Wanda and Palver and someday, of necessity, to one or two others.

Seldon stood slowly, stiffly. He was due back at Streeling in an hour to meet Wanda and Palver. They had left word for him that they were bringing a great surprise. Another piece for the puzzle, Seldon hoped. He looked out one last time over Trantor and, before turning to make his way back to the gravitic repulsion elevator, smiled and softly said, 'Foundation.'

34

Hari Seldon entered his office to find that Wanda and Palver had already arrived and were seated around the conference table at the far end of the room. As was usual with those two, the room was completely silent.

Then Seldon stopped short, noticing that a new fellow was sitting with them. How strange – out of politeness, Wanda and Palver usually reverted to standard speech when in the company of other people, yet none of the three was speaking.

Seldon studied the stranger – an odd-looking man, about thirty-five years old, with the myopic look of one caught up for too long in his studies. If it weren't for a certain determined set to the stranger's jaw, Seldon thought he might be dismissed as ineffectual, but that would obviously be a mistake. There was both strength and kindness in the man's face. A trustworthy face, Seldon decided.

'Grandfather,' Wanda said, rising gracefully from her chair. Seldon's heart ached as he looked at his granddaughter. She'd changed so much in the past few months, since the loss of her family. Whereas before she had always called him Grandpa, now it was the more formal Grandfather. In the past it seemed she could barely refrain from grins and giggles; lately her serene gaze was lightened only occasionally by a beatific smile. But – now as always – she was beautiful and that beauty was surpassed only by her stunning intellect.

'Wanda, Palver,' Seldon said, kissing the former on the cheek and slapping the latter on the shoulder.

'Hello,' Seldon said, turning to the stranger, who had also stood. 'I am Hari Seldon.'

'I am most honored to meet you, Professor,' the man

465

replied. 'I am Bor Alurin.' Alurin offered a hand to Seldon in the archaic and, hence, most formal mode of greeting.

'Bor is a psychologist, Hari,' said Palver, 'and a great fan of your work.'

'More important, Grandfather,' said Wanda, 'Bor is one of us.'

'One of you?' Seldon looked searchingly from one to the other. 'Do you mean . . . ?' Seldon's eyes sparkled.

'Yes, Grandfather. Yesterday Stettin and I were walking through Ery Sector, getting out and around, as you'd suggested, probing for others. All of a sudden – *wham!* – there it was.'

'We recognized the thought patterns immediately and began to look around, trying to establish a link,' Palver said, taking up the story. 'We were in a commercial area, near the spaceport, so the walkways were clogged with shoppers and tourists and Outworld traders. It seemed hopeless, but then Wanda simply stopped and signaled *Come here* and out of the crowd Bor appeared. He just walked up to us and signaled *Yes?'*

'Amazing,' Seldon said, beaming at his grand-daughter. 'And Dr – it is Doctor, isn't it? – Alurin, what do you make of all this?'

'Well,' began the psychologist thoughtfully, 'I am pleased. I've always felt different somehow and now I know why. And if I can be of any help to you, why—' The psychologist looked down at his feet, as if all of a sudden he realized he was being presumptuous. 'What I mean is, Wanda and Stettin said I may be able to contribute in some way to your Psychohistory Project. Professor, nothing would please me more.'

'Yes yes. That's quite true, Dr Alurin. In fact, I think you may make a great contribution to the Project – if you'll join me. Of course, you'll have to give up whatever it is you do now, whether it is teaching or private practice. Can you manage that?'

'Why, yes, Professor, of course. I may need a little help

convincing my wife—' At this he chuckled slightly, glancing shyly at each of his three companions in turn. 'But I seem to have a way with *that*.'

'So it's set, then,' said Seldon briskly. 'You will join the Psychohistory Project. I promise you, Dr Alurin, this is a decision you will not regret.'

'Wanda, Stettin,' Seldon said later, after Bor Alurin had left. 'This is a most welcome breakthrough. How quickly do you think you can find more mentalics?'

'Grandfather, it took us over a month to locate Bor – we cannot predict with what frequency others will be found.

'To tell you the truth, all this "out and around" takes us away from our work on the Prime Radiant and it is distracting as well. Now that I have Stettin to "talk" to, verbal communication is somewhat too harsh, too *loud*.'

Seldon's smile faded. He had been afraid of this. As Wanda and Palver had been honing their mentalic skills, so their tolerance for 'ordinary' life had diminished. It only made sense; their mentalic manipulations set them apart.

'Wanda, Stettin, I think it may be time for me to tell you more about the idea Yugo Amaryl had years ago and about the Plan I've devised as a result of that idea. I haven't been ready to elaborate upon it until now, because until this moment, all the pieces have not been in place.

'As you know, Yugo felt we must establish two Foundations – each as a fail-safe measure for the other. It was a brilliant idea, one which I wish Yugo could have lived long enough to see realized.' Here Seldon paused, heaving a regretful sigh.

'But I digress. – Six years ago, when I was certain that Wanda had mentalic, or mind-touching, capabilities, it came to me that not only should there be two Foundations but that they should be distinct in nature, as well. One would be made up of physical scientists – the

Encyclopedists will be their pioneer group on Terminus. The second would be made up of true psychohistorians; mentalists – *you*. That is why I've been so eager for you to find others like you.

'Finally, though, is this: The Second Foundation must be secret. Its strength will lie in its seclusion, in its telepathic omnipresence and omnipotence.

'You see, a few years ago, when it became apparent that I would require the services of a bodyguard, I realized that the Second Foundation must be the strong, silent, secret bodyguard of the primary Foundation.

'Psychohistory is not infallible – its predictions are, however, highly probable. The Foundation, especially in its infancy, will have many enemies, as do I today.

'Wanda, you and Palver are the pioneers of the Second Foundation, the guardians of the Terminus Foundation.'

'But *how*, Grandfather?' demanded Wanda. 'We are just two – well, three, if you count Bor. To guard the entire Foundation, we would need—'

'Hundreds? Thousands? Find however many it takes, Granddaughter. You can do it. And you know how.

'Earlier, when relating the story of finding Dr Alurin, Stettin said you simply stopped and communicated *out* to the mentalic presence you felt and he came to you. Don't you see? All along I've been urging you to go out and find others like you. But this is difficult, almost painful for you. I realize now that you and Stettin must seclude yourselves, in order to form the nucleus of the Second Foundation. From there you will cast your nets into the ocean of humanity.'

'Grandfather, what are you saying?' Wanda asked in a whisper. She had left her seat and was kneeling next to Seldon's chair. 'Do you want me to leave?'

'No, Wanda,' Seldon replied, his voice choked with emotion. 'I don't want you to leave, but it is the only way. You and Stettin must isolate yourselves from the crude physicality of Trantor. As your mentalic abilities grow stronger, you will attract others to you – the silent and secret Foundation will grow.

'We will be in touch – occasionally, of course. And each of us has a Prime Radiant. You see, don't you, the truth – and the absolute necessity – of what I am saying, don't you?'

'Yes, I do, Grandfather,' said Wanda. 'More important, I *feel* the brilliance of it as well. Rest assured; we won't let you down.'

'I know you won't, dear,' Seldon said wearily.

How could he do this – how could he send his darling granddaughter away? She was his last link to his happiest days, to Dors, Yugo, and Raych. She was the only other Seldon in the Galaxy.

'I shall miss you terribly, Wanda,' Seldon said as a tear worked its way down his finely creased cheek.

'But, Grandfather,' Wanda said as she stood with Palver, preparing to leave. 'Where shall we go? Where *is* the Second Foundation?'

Seldon looked up and said, 'The Prime Radiant has already told you, Wanda.'

Wanda looked at Seldon blankly, searching her memory.

Seldon reached out and clutched at his granddaughter's hand.

'Touch my mind, Wanda. It is there.'

Wanda's eyes widened as she reached into Seldon's mind.

'I see,' Wanda whispered to Seldon.

Section 33A2D17: Star's End.

Part V

EPILOGUE

I am Hari Seldon. Former First Minister to Emperor Cleon I. Professor Emeritus of Psychohistory at Streeling University on Trantor. Director of the Psychohistory Research Project. Executive Editor of the Encyclopedia Galactica. Creator of the Foundation.

It all sounds quite impressive, I know. I have done a great deal in my eighty-one years and I am tired. Looking back over my life, I wonder if I could have – should have – done certain things differently. For instance: Was I so concerned with the grand sweep of psychohistory that the people and events that intersected my life sometimes seemed inconsequential by comparison?

Perhaps I neglected to make some small incidental adjustments here or there that would have in no way compromised the future of humanity but might have dramatically improved the life of an individual dear to me. – Yugo, Raych . . . I can't help but wonder . . . Was there something I could have done to save my beloved Dors?

Last month I finished recording the Crisis holograms. My assistant, Gaal Dornick, has taken them to Terminus to oversee their installation in the Seldon Vault. He will make sure that the Vault is sealed and that the proper instructions are left for the eventual openings of the Vault, during the Crises.

I'll be dead by then, of course.

What will they think, those future Foundationers, when they see me (or, more accurately, my hologram) during the First Crisis, almost fifty years from now? Will they comment on how old I look or how weak my voice is or how small I seem, bundled in this wheelchair? Will they understand – appreciate – the message I've left for

473

them? – Ah well, there's really no point in speculating. As the ancients would say: The die is cast.

I heard from Gaal yesterday. All is going well on Terminus. Bor Alurin and the Project members are flourishing in 'exile.' I shouldn't gloat, but I can't help but chuckle when I recall the self-satisfied look on the face of that pompous idiot Linge Chen when he banished the Project to Terminus two years ago. Although ultimately the exile was couched in terms of an Imperial Charter ('A state-supported scientific institution and part of the personal domain of His August Majesty, the Emperor' – the Chief Commissioner wanted us off Trantor and out of his hair, but he could not bear the thought of giving up complete control), it is still a source of secret delight to know that it was Las Zenow and I who chose Terminus as Foundation's home.

My one regret where Linge Chen is concerned is that we were not able to save Agis. That Emperor was a good man and a noble leader, even if he was Imperial in name only. His mistake was to believe in his title and the Commission of Public Safety would not tolerate the burgeoning Imperial independence.

I often wonder what they did to Agis – was he exiled to some remote Outer World or assassinated like Cleon?

The boy-child who sits on the throne today is the perfect puppet Emperor. He obeys every word Linge Chen whispers in his ear and fancies himself a budding statesman. The Palace and trappings of Imperial life are but toys to him in some vast fantastical game.

What will I do now? With Gaal finally gone to join the Terminus group, I am utterly alone. I hear from Wanda occasionally. The work at Star's End continues on course; in the past decade she and Stettin have added dozens of mentalics to their number. They increasingly grow in power. It was the Star's End contingent – my secret Foundation – who pushed Linge Chen into sending the Encyclopedists to Terminus.

I miss Wanda. It has been many years since I've seen

her, sat with her quietly, holding her hand. When Wanda left, even though I had asked her to go, I thought I would die of heartbreak. That was, perhaps, the most difficult decision I ever had to make and, although I never told her, I almost decided against it. But for the Foundation to succeed, it was necessary for Wanda and Stettin to go to Star's End. Psychohistory decreed it, — so perhaps it wasn't really my decision, after all.

I still come here every day, to my office in the Psychohistory Building. I remember when this structure was filled with people, day and night. Sometimes I feel as if it's filled with voices, those of my long-departed family, students, colleagues – but the offices are empty and silent. The hallways echo with the whirr of my wheelchair motor.

I suppose I should vacate the building, return it to the University to allocate to another department. But somehow it's hard to let go of this place. There are so many memories . . .

All I have now is this, my Prime Radiant. This is the means by which psychohistory can be computed, through which every equation in my Plan may be analyzed, all here in this amazing, small black cube. As I sit here, this deceptively simple-looking tool in the palm of my hand, I wish I could show it to R. Daneel Olivaw . . .

But I am alone, and need only to close a contact for the office lights to dim. As I settle back in my wheelchair, the Prime Radiant activates, its equations spreading around me in three-dimensional splendor. To the untrained eye, this multicolored swirl would be merely a jumble of shapes and numbers, but for me – and Yugo, Wanda, Gaal – this is psychohistory, come to life.

What I see before me, around me, is the future of humanity. Thirty thousand years of potential chaos, compressed into a single millennium . . .

That patch, glowing more strongly day by day, is the Terminus equation. And there – skewed beyond repair –

are the Trantor figures. But I can see . . . yes, softly beaming, a steady light of hope . . . Star's End!

This – *this* – was my life's work. My past – humanity's future. Foundation. So beautiful, so alive. And nothing can . . .

Dors!

SELDON, HARI – . . . found dead, slumped over his desk in his office at Streeling University in 12,069 G.E. (1 F.E.). Apparently Seldon had been working up to his last moments on psychohistorical equations; his activated Prime Radiant was discovered clutched in his hand . . .

According to Seldon's instructions, the instrument was shipped to his colleague Gaal Dornick who had recently emigrated to Terminus . . .

Seldon's body was jettisoned into space, also in accordance with instructions he'd left. The official memorial service on Trantor was simple, though well attended. It is worth noting that Seldon's old friend former First Minister Eto Demerzel attended the event. Demerzel had not been seen since his mysterious disappearance immediately following the Joranumite Conspiracy during the reign of Emperor Cleon I. Attempts by the Commission of Public Safety to locate Demerzel in the days following the Seldon memorial proved to be unsuccessful . . .

Wanda Seldon, Hari Seldon's granddaughter, did not attend the ceremony. It was rumored that she was grief-stricken and had refused all public appearances. To this day, her whereabouts from then on remain unknown . . .

It has been said that Hari Seldon left this life as he lived it, for he died with the future he created unfolding all around him . . .

ENCYCLOPEDIA GALACTICA

THE END

NEMESIS
by Isaac Asimov

Tearing its way through space on a collision course for Earth is NEMESIS, a fiery ball of destruction, a dwarf star as red as the colour of blood.

Circling NEMESIS is ROTOR, an Earth colony whose occupants have cut themselves off from the anarchy and degeneration of an old and wasted world.

For them ROTOR is a kind of Ark

And NEMESIS is the Flood . . .

'A compelling read'
Sunday Telegraph

'A cracker . . . a yarn bristling with ideas'
Manchester Evening News

'His best book for ages'
The Times

A Bantam Paperback
0 553 40069 X

Enter the magical worlds of *New York Times*
bestselling authors

MARGARET WEIS and TRACY HICKMAN

THE DARKSWORD TRILOGY
Forging the Darksword
Doom of the Darksword
Triumph of the Darksword

ROSE OF THE PROPHET
The Will of the Wanderer
The Paladin of the Night
The Prophet of Akhran

THE DEATH GATE CYCLE
Dragon Wing
Elven Star
Fire Sea

and by Margaret Weis

STAR OF THE GUARDIANS
The Lost King
King's Test
King's Sacrifice

All available in Bantam Paperback

A SELECTION OF SCIENCE FICTION AND FANTASY TITLES FROM BANTAM BOOKS

THE PRICES SHOWN BELOW WERE CORRECT AT THE TIME OF GOING TO PRESS. HOWEVER TRANSWORLD PUBLISHERS RESERVE THE RIGHT TO SHOW NEW RETAIL PRICES ON COVERS WHICH MAY DIFFER FROM THOSE PREVIOUSLY ADVERTISED IN THE TEXT OR ELSEWHERE.

☐	40068 1	AZAZEL	Isaac Asimov	£3.99
☐	40069 X	NEMESIS	Isaac Asimov	£4.99
☐	29138 6	STAR TREK 1	James Blish	£3.99
☐	29139 4	STAR TREK 2	James Blish	£3.99
☐	29140 8	STAR TREK 3	James Blish	£3.99
☐	17162 3	SUNDIVER	David Brin	£3.99
☐	17452 5	STARTIDE RISING	David Brin	£4.99
☐	17184 4	THE PRACTICE EFFECT	David Brin	£3.99
☐	40317 6	ÆSTIVAL TIDE	Elizabeth Hand	£4.99
☐	17351 0	STAINLESS STEEL RAT GETS DRAFTED	Harry Harrison	£2.99
☐	17396 0	STAINLESS STEEL RAT SAVES THE WORLD	Harry Harrison	£2.50
☐	40371 0	KING OF MORNING, QUEEN OF DAY	Ian McDonald	£4.99
☐	40274 9	STAR OF THE GUARDIANS Book 1: The Lost King	Margaret Weis	£3.99
☐	40275 7	STAR OF THE GUARDIANS Book 2: The King's Test	Margaret Weis	£4.99
☐	40276 5	STAR OF THE GUARDIANS Book 3: King's Sacrifice	Margaret Weis	£4.99
☐	17586 6	FORGING THE DARKSWORD	Margaret Weis & Tracy Hickman	£3.99
☐	17535 1	DOOM OF THE DARKSWORD	Margaret Weis & Tracy Hickman	£3.50
☐	17536 X	TRIUMPH OF THE DARKSWORD	Margaret Weis & Tracy Hickman	£4.99
☐	40265 X	DEATH GATE CYCLE 1: Dragon Wing	Margaret Weis & Tracy Hickman	£4.99
☐	40266 8	DEATH GATE CYCLE 2: Elven Star	Margaret Weis & Tracy Hickman	£4.99
☐	40375 3	DEATH GATE CYCLE 3: Fire Sea	Margaret Weis & Tracy Hickman	£4.99
☐	17684 6	ROSE OF THE PROPHET 1: The Will of the Wanderer	Margaret Weis & Tracy Hickman	£3.99
☐	40045 2	ROSE OF THE PROPHET 2: Paladin of the Night	Margaret Weis & Tracy Hickman	£3.99
☐	40177 7	ROSE OF THE PROPHET 3: The Prophet of Akhran	Margaret Weis & Tracy Hickman	£4.50
☐	40471 7	STAR WARS 1: Heir to the Empire	Timothy Zahn	£3.99
☐	40442 5	STAR WARS 2: Dark Forces Rising	Timothy Zahn	£3.99

All Corgi/Bantam Books are available at your bookshop or newsagent, or can be ordered from the following address:
Corgi/Bantam Books,
Cash Sales Department,
P.O. Box 11, Falmouth, Cornwall TR10 9EN

UK and B.F.P.O. customers please send a cheque or postal order (no currency) and allow £1.00 for postage and packing for the first book plus 50p for the second book and 30p for each additional book to a maximum charge of £3.00 (7 books plus).

Overseas customers, including Eire, please allow £2.00 for postage and packing for the first book plus £1.00 for the second book and 50p for each subsequent title ordered.

NAME (Block Letters) ....

ADDRESS ....

....